# Also by A.C. Arthur

Temptation Rising

Seduction's Shift

Passion's Prey

# SHIFTER'S CLAIM

## A.C. ARTHUR

St. Martin's Paperbacks

This is a work of fiction. All of the characters, organizations, and events portrayed in this novel are either products of the author's imagination or are used fictitiously.

SHIFTER'S CLAIM

For information address St. Martin's Press, 175 Fifth Avenue, New York, NY 10010.

ISBN: 978-1-250-04291-0

Printed in the United States of America

St. Martin's Paperbacks edition / August 2014

St. Martin's Paperbacks are published by St. Martin's Press, 175 Fifth Avenue, New York, NY 10010.

10  9  8  7  6  5  4  3  2  1

# Glossary of Terms

**Shadow Shifter Tribes**

**Topètenia**—the jaguars

**Croesteriia**—the cheetahs

**Lormenia**—the white Bengal tigers

**Bosinia**—the cougars

**Serfins**—the white lions

**Acordado**—the awakening, the Shadow Shifter's first shift

**Alma**—the name of the spa at Perryville Resorts Sedona. Means "soul" in Portuguese

**Amizade**—annex to the Elders' Grounds used as a fellowship hall

**Companheiro**—mate

**Companheiro calor**—the scent shared between mates

**Curandero**—the medicinal and spiritual healer of the tribes

**Elders**—senior members of the tribe

**Ètica**—the Shadow Shifter Code of Ethics

**Joining**—the union of mated shifters

**La Selva**—the name of the restaurant at Perryville Resorts. Means "the jungle" in Portuguese

**Pessoal**—secondary building of the Elders' Grounds which houses the personal rooms of each Elder

**Rogue**—a Shadow Shifter who has turned from the tribes, refusing to follow the *Ètica*, in an effort to become their own distinct species

**Santa Casa**—main building of the Elders' Grounds that is the holy house of the Elders

**The Assembly**—three Elders from each tribe that make up the governing council of shifters in the Gungi

# Prologue

**The Gungi Rainforest, South America**
**Fourteen years ago**

He saw red.

Everything was red.

Blood red.

The rain, the leaves, even the muddy dirt puddles at his feet. The acidic stench burned his nostrils and had his stomach churning until he fought to keep from vomiting. Beneath his feet branches cracked and rustled. Rain, cold like slivers of ice, pelted his naked body, as a form of punishment, maybe. Because he'd been too late.

Her body lay on the ground, mutilated, floating in the pool of blood. His fingers shook as an arm reached out. Her eyes had been blue, like a summer's sky. He remembered them clearly, remembered how they'd stared at him brimming with tears as he'd explained their time together had run its course. Pressing against the lids he closed them, not wanting to see them any longer. Not wanting her to be disappointed by him yet again.

Bas cursed. The words rolling from his lips in a long fluid succession that sounded more like a drunk in a gangster movie than a man heading for his senior year in college. Then again he wasn't in New York anymore. He was in the forest where he'd been born. After his parents' divorce it just made more sense to come here than go back to the house in the Hamptons where there were expensive things like rugs and lamps, statues and paintings and memories. But no people, not anymore. In the midst of the two-year-long his versus hers tug-of-war they'd left the house to Bas. Then, after too many failed attempts to get them back together, Bas had simply left the damned house.

He'd also left Mariah. After dating the sophomore whom he'd met at a party for almost a month, Bas had told her it was over. Whatever faith he'd had in lasting relationships had been dashed with his parents' actions. In his mind it hadn't mattered anyway because he hadn't been in love with Mariah—he'd known she wasn't his mate—and because she was a human. And he was not. Their laws were very clear in that regard—no exposure to humans. Ever.

And now look where he was and what adhering to that law had done.

No, what they'd done. He was very clear on the fact that those bastard rogues had killed Mariah without any remorse and so he'd done the only thing he could do. He'd ripped their fucking throats out, without remorse, of course.

Mariah was dead and there was nothing he could do about that. She'd died right in front of him, screaming and writhing until she could do neither anymore. If he'd just been a second faster, a minute more alert instead of basking in his own problems. He could have what? Saved her from being killed by shifting into a jaguar and ripping the heads off the four other men who changed into jaguars right in front of her.

That would have gone over real well.

Exposure was the biggest warning in the *Ètica*. In other words it was a huge no-no that all the Shadow Shifters lived with every day of their lives. Don't tell humans who and what you are. Keep the secret, blend in, but do not become one of them. All his life he'd been taught this, the philosophy had been practically beaten into his head.

And he believed in that philosophy just as he believed in the Ètica and the upward movement of the Shadow Shifters who now took residence in the United States and who were working together toward a democracy for their kind, also known as the Stateside Shadow Shifters.

What he did not believe in was senseless death. And as he lifted what was left of Mariah into his arms, carrying her through the rain deeper into the Gungi, inhaling the stench of her blood that dripped continuously from her body, Bas cursed the rogues. He cursed their very existence even as he took pride in his own.

He also cursed himself for being so foolish as to become involved with a female, especially a human. How she'd come to be in the Gungi at all had been a mystery to him since the last time he'd seen her had been over a week ago. She hadn't taken the break-up well, which was also something Bas had downplayed. He'd seen the look of hurt in her eyes when he'd so callously spoken those words and hadn't bothered to look back after he'd left her standing in the hallway of her dorm. Had she come here looking for him? Had she thought following him would get them back together? His temples throbbed with what might be the worst headache ever.

Bas cursed not only the thoughts of how she'd come to be here but the fact that she'd made him feel weak and insignificant, a failure and a disgrace. Sort of like he'd felt when all his talking hadn't kept the two people he'd loved most in this world together.

Beneath the heavy canopy of the forest and the dense rain that fell on a daily basis, Bas had buried Mariah, closing his eyes to pray over the mound of mud he'd padded tightly over her body. There would be no human funeral for her, the remains of her body could not be found. Too many questions would be asked. In time her parents would have her declared dead, they would grieve and then eventually move on. As for Bas, he would keep this secret with him for the rest of his days. But he vowed to never make this mistake again. "Never." His voice was low but deep, traveling on the wind throughout the forest where he'd once taken solace.

**Comastaz Laboratories**
**Sedona, Arizona**
**One year ago**

"So we're kidnappers now?"

"We're not kidnappers. You are a scientist and I am a decorated officer of the United States Marine Corps. We're both employed by the United States government and we have a responsibility to develop new and improved ways for our country's defense."

Dr. Mario DiLaurent scratched the back of his head, looking skeptically at the body lying still as a corpse on the examining table. It was encased half in and half out of a body bag, adding credence to the "dead" theory. But there was a pulse. He'd touched the wrist of what looked to be a Hispanic male, between the ages of twenty-five and thirty. His physique was huge, built like a battering ram, perfectly sculpted like a model. And he was in Mario's lab, where the only humans allowed wore white coats and valid ID badges.

"We specialize in chemical warfare," he reminded Captain Lawrence Crowe, the director of the lab's defense program.

"No," Captain Crowe replied, walking to stand on the other side of the table where the man lay. "We specialize in warfare."

"This is a man," Mario pointed out, about three seconds too soon.

In the next instant the naked man had jumped off the table, hitting the tile floor on his hands and knees. Mario jumped back, barely holding on to a scream he knew would sound more feminine than Captain Crowe and his macho persona would appreciate. Crowe, true to his Marine Corps training, reached for his weapon, bringing both hands together and pointing it directly at the man.

A noise echoed through the room. No, it wasn't just a noise but a growl, fierce, loud, and lethal. Mario wanted to run but the man blocked the door. He was about to look to Crowe to ask him what the hell was going on when the man opened his mouth and growled again.

"Oh. My. God," Mario mumbled.

The man had incisors more than an inch long, and the cheeks that had looked normal just a few minutes ago had now morphed into a broad muzzle, and his eyes were an eerie yellow color that sent a shiver of fear straight down Mario's spine. When the man or beast or whatever it was growled again it came up on its hind legs, standing taller than the door frame, looking more fierce than anything Mario had ever seen.

Three shots were fired from behind him, the sound causing him to jump each time, a hand going to his chest as if he thought that would still his pounding heartbeat.

"What the hell?" he managed after watching the big form slide to the floor, now unconscious.

He took a step forward when the captain had yet to answer him and stared down at what he wanted to call a big man cat. Right before his eyes, the muzzled face deflated and looked once more like a man. The large chest heaved up, down, up, down, until it slowed to a steady, slow rhythm.

"That's what I want you to find out," Crowe said, coming up behind him.

Now they both stood looking down at what . . . they had absolutely no idea. Crowe was anxious; Mario could almost feel the adrenaline pouring off the man in waves. He was planning something and it was going to be big. It was also going to include Mario and he wasn't 100 percent positive he was happy about that.

# Chapter 1

**The Willard InterContinental Hotel**
**Washington, D.C.**
**Present day**

"What do you want?" he asked even though he had one arm wrapped firmly around her waist, the other clapped tightly over her mouth.

She'd been following him all night, her gaze fixated on him like a beacon in the dark of night. Bas had tried to ignore it, no, actually he hadn't. He'd seen her about two minutes after she'd taken her seat at the table just ten feet away from his. She'd smiled and conversed with the others around her, all the while casing the room for something, until landing on him. Females did not normally affect him this way, they didn't look at him and cause all the blood in his body to run hotter and faster throughout his veins. They didn't call to him throughout the night in a room full of about six hundred people and they definitely did not wander around hotel hallways attempting to break into private suites—the private suites of Roman Reynolds, Leader of the Stateside Assembly.

She mumbled something against his hand, her lips brushing over his skin with the effort. His teeth gritted so hard he thought his jaw might break, warmth flooding him so fast and so potently he felt like he might melt with the intensity. In seconds his defensive stance shifted to something more powerful, more lethal to anyone on its receiving end. He pressed his body closer, let the curves of hers fit perfectly against him. Her ass was cradled by his now-jutting hips, and felt so sweet he almost gasped. Moving his arm upward just a few inches had the curve of her breasts resting against his arms. But both those actions and reactions were basic—male body parts plus female body parts equaled sexual desire, plain and simple, the circle of life so to speak.

Then he inhaled and that circle broke, it bent and reshaped until Bas felt like it was a lasso instead, tightening slowly, keeping them together regardless. Her scent consumed him, filtering through his body like an infusion of pleasure, a drug so pure and so powerful he automatically wanted more. Leaning forward, his lips only inches from her earlobe he whispered, "If you scream I'll break your neck."

Slowly, he moved his hand away from her mouth, keeping her body pressed tightly against the wall, firmly covered by his own.

"You really need to work on your greeting," came her cool response, delivered in a sultry voice that wasn't so deep as to be off-putting and wasn't too high as to work his nerves. It was, he thought, inhaling another dangerous whiff of her scent, alluring.

"Do I now?" Bas asked with a slight chuckle to his tone. "And what do you need to work on? Your surveillance skills maybe? You picked the wrong room and the wrong person to follow tonight."

Her next move was totally surprising, especially to Sebastian Perry, multimillionaire resort owner and playboy extraordinaire. She wiggled her ass against his now-throbbing erection, turned, and tilted her head so that when she spoke her next words he could actually see her lips move and feel her warm breath fan over his face.

"Maybe I need to work on you," she whispered about two seconds before her elbow smashed into the right side of his ribs.

Another man, a human, may have buckled at the assault but Bas, a Faction Leader in the Stateside Assembly, barely blinked. He did, however, take about a five-inch step back, which gave her enough time to spin around and face him, but not get away.

"Oh, that can definitely be arranged," he replied, moving into her once more.

While he'd loved the enticing cushion of her ass against his dick, he was now enjoying the heavy swells of her breasts pressed against his chest, threatening to overflow from the tight bodice of her dress. Her hair was short, shorter than he usually preferred on his females but cut in a chic style that he now realized echoed her snappy and courageous personality. She had a small face, plump lips, wide eyes, and high cheekbones. Everything about her seemed to scream blatant desire, and yet, there was something else.

"This may be some form of harassment," she told him, her hands pushing futilely against his chest.

Bas, the smooth, cocky sonofabitch he was sometimes known as, only smiled. "No, this would be harassment," he told her a second before cupping her ass cheeks in his palms and leaning forward to lick the seam of her lips.

He pressed her into him so hard and so fast his dick just about burst through the zipper of his tuxedo pants. Against his spine his cat pressed for more, teeth bared with the idea of conquest. He should have moved away at the quick inhale of her breath, the renewed effort to break free, but that only spurred Bas on, flicking on a switch inside him that had almost been permanently off.

Moving slightly to the right, his tongue ran a line along

her jaw, down the length of her neck to her collarbone, which was left open for his perusal by the extremely low cut of her come-fuck-me red dress. Her breath had hitched, her heart pounding against her chest, her fingers clenching in the lapels of his jacket just as his teeth nipped along her soft skin.

Then she moved and Bas knew what would come next. His hand followed her motion, slipping down the back of her thigh to grab her calf just as her knee planned to slam into his groin. When she pushed at him he let her, but still held on to her leg, leaving her to flail against falling flat on the floor. After a split second of her looking helpless and extremely pissed off, he circled her waist with his free arm, holding her once more against him.

"We just keep ending up in this position," he said as this time she stood with only one foot on the ground, her other leg—the one that had been meant to assault him—hiked up against his side.

"Is this how you like it? Standing up against the wall, your legs wrapped around me while I pump you until you come?" She opened her mouth to speak, clapped those medium-thick lips shut, and glared up at him instead.

"Let me go," she said. "Or I'll scream so loud every security officer in this building will come running."

"You mean the security officers that allowed you to come onto this private floor and skulk around this private suite?" Bas shook his head. "Apparently, they're on a smoke break." He let her leg fall to the ground and moved so that now his fingers traced the line of her neck. "Now, I'll ask you one more time what you were doing here and you can either answer me"—he lowered his voice purposely, letting his finger glide over the spot on her collarbone he'd just licked seconds before—"or you can fuck mc. I'll lct you make the choice."

\* \* \*

Curiosity killed the cat.

That old saying ran back and forth through Priya's head, bringing forth the memory of sneaking into the boxes underneath her mother's bed in search of whatever her mother reached for at night that left her so out of it, she couldn't even get up in the morning to get her kids ready for school.

Now, true to its meaning, it seemed her curious nature had gotten her into another mess she wished she'd never laid eyes on. Only, this six-foot-plus, built like a quarterback, smooth as the buttery tone of his skin, and sexy as . . . well, sexy as in had her nipples so hard they now hurt, man wasn't precisely the same as finding her mother's stash of crack cocaine.

She'd seen him before, earlier tonight at the reception for President Wilson Reed, in the ballroom. Up close and personal he was even more handsome than he had been from two tables away. His skin tone was light, hair wavy and dark, his face was clean-shaven with a strong nose and jawline. And his eyes, they weren't the smoky-gray color she'd originally surmised. Stormy would be the better word as he glared at her with what she thought could pass as either barely masked contempt or intense sexual desire—she wasn't really in the mood for either at the moment.

"Look, there's been some type of misunderstanding," she tried to tell him, the final word coming as a partial whisper after deciding to ignore his "you can fuck me" remark. That may have been a little cowardly, which was out of character for Priya, but she figured it was a smart move considering she was actually thinking of doing just that with him.

He looked at her as if he could tell she was lying or ready to tell the lie before the words could even escape. She felt like clamping her lips shut and keeping them that way, until he did that thing he'd done with his tongue again—oh, she'd definitely open her mouth the next time he did that.

Right, because sexual arousal was exactly what she should be thinking about in lieu of the e-mails she'd been receiving that threatened the lives of all the people she loved and cherished in this world. Thinking about taking this man up on his oh-so-enticing offer—especially since the self-imposed celibacy she'd endured for the last year was about to take its toll—was definitely more important than following her blackmailer's orders and saving her family. In some crazy twisted world, she thought with an inward sigh. She knew she had no choice here and for the billionth time tonight wondered how she was going to do what needed to be done, when the people involved were reputedly more powerful than the president himself.

"I'm a reporter from the *Washington Post*. I wanted to get a comment from Mr. Reynolds about President Reed's campaign," she blurted out. "There, satisfied now that you know why I'm here?"

He looked like he was anything but, still he'd released his hold on her, physically, that is. His eyes still bore into her as if he were performing some type of perverted X-ray of her body right in this hallway.

"You waited all night, the entire three and a half hours that Mr. Reynolds was downstairs in that ballroom to follow him to his room to ask for a statement?"

He lifted a brow in disbelief as he spoke. The slight rasp of his deep voice echoing around her as if forever planting itself in her memory, like she'd really forget being felt up by this guy, which was definitely not going to happen.

"It's my job," she told him with a shrug. "And since I'm assuming you're some type of bodyguard and not going to let me get that statement, I'll just be going."

Priya was more than shocked that he hadn't reached out to grab her again, to try and stop her from leaving.

Instead, she'd walked about three very uncomfortable steps because she knew he was staring at her ass as she did, before his voice stopped her.

"Have a drink with me?"

She turned. "What?"

He closed the space between them, taking her by her elbow, much more gently than he had touched her before, yet still sending electrifying spikes up her arm.

"We'll go down to the bar since having you in my room might lead us to other things besides a nice cordial drink." He continued as if she'd already accepted, walking them to the elevators at the far end of the hall that had brought her up here about fifteen minutes before.

Once they were inside the elevator and she felt like she needed to stop this impending train wreck, Priya turned to him and announced, "I'm not the reporter who sleeps with someone for a story."

He looked at her then, an amused grin on his face—amused and way too cocky for her, but still sexy as hell.

"Good, because I don't sleep with reporters. I do, however, take beautiful women to bed and give them a night they'll never forget. Tonight, however, I'll settle for a glass of wine."

Rebuffed and not sure whether or not she disliked it or felt relief, Priya kept her mouth shut. It wasn't an easy task since she'd always been inclined to ask questions, always searching for answers. Sometimes, however, the answers she found were more than she'd bargained for. That was part of the reason she was here tonight, on this foolhardy mission to uncover something she wasn't sure she believed herself.

Still, it was apparent that this man knew Reynolds personally. In the last two weeks Priya had interviewed everyone from a receptionist in Reynolds's office to the manager of the detail shop where his SUV was dropped off every Friday afternoon. Her file on the man was almost an inch thick with one glowing remark after another. He appeared so squeaky clean she'd felt sick each time she flipped through her notes. So, if having a glass of wine with this new person she'd seen with Reynolds could help get this task completed sooner, rather than later, she'd do it, and whatever else she had to, if it would save her family's life.

# Chapter 2

She took another sip of her wine, her glass almost empty. Bas was on his second glass, sitting in the circular booth toward the back of the hotel's bar at well past midnight.

He should be upstairs in his room, probably in bed since he knew there would be meetings tomorrow before his scheduled return to Sedona. All of the Faction Leaders had come for the meetings, to talk about what the Assembly's plan of action would be against the rogues and the killer drug they were filtering through the streets. Since that drug had claimed its first human lives here in D.C. and this was where the Assembly Leader lived, it was logical that they start here. The beginning was always a good place to start, he thought as he watched her take yet another sip, looking out the window toward the fading D.C. nightlife.

"How long have you been a reporter?" he asked her.

She'd already told him her name was Priya Drake and that she'd lived in D.C. all her life. Bas admitted, even if only to himself, he wanted to know more.

"A while," was her roundabout answer. "How long have you worked for Reynolds?"

So this was what they were going to do. He almost chuckled. Asking her to come down here for drinks had been a twofold mission for Bas. She'd admitted that she'd been coming to see Rome, but Bas hadn't believed her reason why. The stale stench of lies in the hallway as she'd spoken was the first giveaway and the way her eyes kept darting between him and the door to Rome's room was another. She needed to speak to Rome, like Bas had felt he needed to touch her, to get just a sample taste of her. That was a strong need that he figured went beyond wanting to know who a man was backing politically.

"I've known him for the better part of twenty years," Bas replied.

"I hear he's a bitch to work for, a perfectionist with a quick temper." She'd set her glass down on the black napkin, sitting back and letting her hands fall into her lap.

"On the contrary, he has a very mild temperament as long as you stay on his good side." As did some of the shifters who lived among the humans. They almost had no other choice but to be that way, it helped to keep their secret.

"And you stay on his good side, don't you?"

"I stay on my side," was Bas's instant response. "Why do you care who he backs politically? He's in the private sector so it doesn't matter who he decides to put his money behind."

"It matters," she said quickly, too quickly for this to be a simple political story, as he'd already surmised. There was a passion behind her words, an urgency that only continued to pique his interest.

He sat forward, placing both palms on the table and looked directly at her. "Why don't you tell me what you're really after?"

She opened her mouth to speak and Bas held up a hand to stop her.

"Tell me the truth and I'll see if there's a way I can help you. Lie to me again and this evening doesn't end as well as we both hope. Take your choice."

She didn't frown, but arched an elegant eyebrow and nodded. Right now she was probably thinking that she had an inside lead, that since she believed Bas worked for Rome, she could get him to provide the real information she wanted from Rome. That was not remotely possible, but Bas was enjoying the little light of excitement in her eyes at the possibility.

"I don't usually bow to threats," she replied after a short pause, and then immediately faltered.

It was quick, a blink of her eyes, a look toward the window, then back at him with her composure firmly in place. Fear, with its tangy citrus-like scent, filtered between them, and Bas was immediately concerned. Had someone else threatened her? Shadows possessed a very protective nature where females were concerned. That's why the feel of his cat pressing firmly against his human form was no surprise. It was rearing up, ready to defend if need be.

"At any rate," she began again with a sigh. "There've been some incidents in the past few months, the gruesome murder of Senator Baines and his daughter, a huge bank heist by supposed masked robbers, and the grisly and still unexplained death of a stripper at Athena's. All crimes unsolved."

Bas nodded. "It's a shame how much violence is still present in the world."

She tilted her head then, staring at him as if that remark had changed something in her mind. Then, with an almost imperceptible shrug, she continued. "There have been rumors, maybe you've heard them."

"I don't usually listen to rumors. They're rarely true," he told her.

She sat forward then, pushing her wineglass to the side and folding her arms on the table. Her voice lowered as she spoke. "Some say the bank robbers stood and walked tall like men, but had the looks of big cats. Eyes, sharp teeth, everything except walking on all fours and wagging a long tail."

Through their monthly and sometimes weekly conference calls, Bas had learned of the incidents that had taken place in D.C. even though he lived across the country. Each incident that she'd mentioned had been a concern for the Assembly as it threatened the exposure they wanted so desperately to avoid. Still, he kept his composure. "Some say I have cat's eyes," he replied lightly. "Are you accusing me of being a cat?"

She contemplated his words before replying. "That's not what I said. The way the senator and his daughter's bodies were mangled definitely leads toward a nonhuman killing except the bodies weren't found in an alley or in a wooded area, for that matter. And that stripper, she was just about ripped to pieces."

Bas didn't like to raise his voice or show much emotion. It gave the other person the upper hand, he thought. If someone knew what button to push to get a reaction out of him, they'd likely push it all the time. That act would surely get someone killed, there was no doubt. His cat teetered on the brink of rage and painful hunger.

"I thought the stripper was filled with some type of drug that may have actually been the cause of death."

She was instantly shaking her head. "There's no drug that will shred human skin like that. Something sharp and something vicious had to be involved. I saw the body myself! It was horrible," she exclaimed.

He wondered how she'd managed to see that body but remembered she was a reporter. The lengths to which the press went to get a story these days had long since ceased to amaze Bas—disgusted him, yes, but not amaze.

"And just how does this relate to Roman Reynolds and his political views?" Because that was the real question Bas wanted an answer to. The rest he would leave for her inquisitive mind to try and figure out, hoping that she never really would.

That's when she did it again, faltered. He had a feeling she didn't do that often, or at least tried not to. She didn't seem to like it judging from how fast she tried to rebound. This time it was with a slight shake of her head as if she were trying to clear it of some thought she'd rather not have. Bas was beyond intrigued now, he'd almost venture to say he was vested somehow in this female he'd just met and was insanely attracted to.

She cleared her throat before looking at him again. This time there was something missing in her eyes. The glow of excitement that had been there when she'd spoken of those murders, the tinge of outrage in her tone as she'd talked about the stripper, was now replaced by a sullen look that spoke of uncertainty.

"Some say Rome's friend Xavier is the one who killed the stripper. The FBI even investigated him for it. They didn't prove it but Xavier left the FBI. They say he was seen with one of the cat people in the alley behind Athena's one night," she told him in an even more hushed tone. Then she squared her shoulders and said with a little more clarity, a bit more force, "I want to know what Reynolds knows about the murders and the cat people."

And there it was, the dreaded ax that Bas had been praying wouldn't drop. The scenario the Elders of their tribe back in the Gungi Rainforest hundreds and hundreds of years ago had feared. It was one of the reasons some of the Elders refused to leave their jungle in Brazil—exposure.

"You should find another story to pursue. This one sounds preposterous and is most definitely a waste of your time. Does your editor know you're working on this? Why hasn't he tried to show you how far-fetched it is?" Why hasn't someone tried to stop her before she gets herself killed? His teeth clenched at that unspoken question.

"He doesn't know," she replied almost instantly. "I mean, I'll tell him when I have more to go on."

Bas didn't like that response any more than he liked the quick flash of lust that speared through him as his gaze dropped to the smooth mocha-toned skin between the mounds of her breasts.

"Come, I'll take you home," he said, standing. Reaching into his pocket he removed some bills from their gold clip and dropped them onto the table. He needed to get away from her before he did something he somehow knew he would regret.

She looked startled, then deflated. "I don't need you to take me home. I can get there on my own."

"I'm sure you can," Bas said, once again taking her elbow as she stood and moved from the booth. It was a mistake to touch her, the searing heat at the connection a stark reminder of that fact. Bas frowned. "But I'll take you anyway."

He liked touching her, a lot. She wasn't pulling away physically but was holding herself just out of reach mentally. He didn't know why that appealed to him.

Once outside she turned to him, a slight temper surfacing. "Look, thank you for the drink and thank you for not doing whatever it is you do with people who try to contact Mr. Reynolds that maybe shouldn't. I even appreciate you listening to my ramblings about work. But really, I don't know you well enough to let you take me home and as I stated before I'm not interested in having sex with you."

After a nod of his head to the valet who had immediately come into view as they'd exited the hotel, Bas returned his attention to Priya.

"First, you know my name is Sebastian Perry and that if I really meant you some harm I would have done it while I had you in that hallway alone. Second, by your synopsis of the current violence going on in this city, you know it's a lot safer to have me escort you home at this time of night than it is for you to hop in a cab and get there on your own.

And third, you didn't say you weren't interested in having sex with me, you said you didn't sleep with men for a story."

As she opened her mouth to reply an SUV pulled up to the curb. Bas opened the back door for her and waited for her to get in.

"You think you're so smooth," she quipped, coming closer to the door.

"What do you think?" he asked, loving the way that red dress hugged every one of her delectable curves, the material blowing alluringly against her bare legs in the slight night breeze.

She stood right in front of him then, her high heels almost bringing them eye to eye. "I think you may have a slightly overinflated ego," she stated decisively. Then added, "But that's not necessarily a bad thing."

Bas smiled and watched as she climbed into the car. Her ass was firm and plump and he remembered with startling clarity how it felt pressed against his still burgeoning arousal. "No, that's not a bad thing at all," he mumbled as he climbed into the backseat after her. "Not bad at all."

Forty-five minutes later, after Bas had warned Priya one more time to drop the foolish story of cat men, he was back in his suite. Rome, who was formerly the East Coast Faction Leader but had recently been elected the Assembly Leader, had rented him a suite. Actually he'd rented each of the three Faction Leaders a suite in the hotel where the fund-raiser for President Reed was being held. As a whole, the Assembly had agreed that this human was the best presidential candidate. Not only had he made terrific strides in his first four years in office, but they were confident that the next four years would prove even more effective. President Reed's grandmother was from Colombia, a fact that Rome also thought could work to their advantage should they ever need backup in the human world. Bas wasn't 100 percent certain the president would take their side based on that connection alone, but he stood behind the Assembly Leader wholeheartedly.

He'd known Rome much too long not to stand behind him. At some point in their lives all of the Faction Leaders had shown their loyalty to one another as well as to the Assembly. They weren't about to stop now.

That's why Bas now stood at the window looking out onto the D.C. night, holding his cell phone to his ear. A second later there was an answer on the other end and Bas spoke a simple phrase. "We may have a problem."

# Chapter 3

Pain seared through her so intensely Priya was jerked from her sleep, sitting up straight in the center of her bed. Her breathing was erratic, sweat drenching her forehead as she lifted a hand to her chest and slid the other between her legs.

All night long, she thought with a sigh, closing her eyes and remembering the all-too-vivid dreams she'd endured. He'd touched her, kissed her, taken her like no man had ever taken her before. And he'd done it with that sexy-as-hell grin on his face as if he'd known just how good he was giving it to her. Priya wanted to scream. Not because—opening one eye to peek at the clock on her nightstand—it was zero-dark-thirty, but because with all he'd done to her in her dreams she still felt like she was about to explode with pent-up desire.

Frustrated and horny as hell, she tossed off the sheets, mumbling as she jerked open the top drawer of her nightstand and pulled out an old friend. Celibacy had begun immediately after the breakup with Jonathan who had been a really nice financing director at the used-car dealership where she'd gone to purchase a newer vehicle. They'd dated for approximately three weeks while he'd worked on the financing for her car. Then one night he'd shown up at her apartment with roses and a bottle of wine. He ordered

Chinese food and they sat in candlelight—even though the only two candles she had in the house were mismatched, one from Christmas and the other something fragrant from the grocery store. It had been sweet and they'd topped off the night with sex—first with Jonathan on top, then with her bringing it home. "It" being the climax that had almost completely knocked Jonathan out, but had left Priya feeling a little bereft.

The next morning Jonathan awoke her with the bad news—she hadn't been approved for the car, and oh, he wasn't interested in seeing her again. Jerk!

Now, just about a year later she could go almost a few weeks without thinking about the sex she refused to allow herself, but only a couple of hours cursing the male population in general. Last night, after being with "him," she felt like all the cards she'd stacked so neatly in the lovely card castle of her dreams had come crashing down.

With a huff she lay back against her pillows, the small vibrator in one hand while her other arm lifted to fall over her eyes. She hadn't resorted to this in months, hadn't been so desperate for any type of relief that she thought she might actually scream in frustration in far too long. Normally when the urge struck she'd go to the gym, which didn't really work out for her since that type of physical exertion had never really been her forte. It was after the gym when she went to the ice cream shop on the corner—whose great idea had it been to put an ice cream shop about ten feet from the gym's entrance anyway?—that she really found her bliss.

This morning she didn't think cake batter ice cream mixed with waffle cone pieces was going to do the trick.

Pulling up her nightgown she cursed once more, all but saying his name but refusing as if it were some type of omen. Her finger pushed the ON button so hard she thought she may have broken the handheld device, but the low hum assured her it was ready and able to perform the task. She lifted her legs so that her knees were touching, then let them fall, not so gracefully, to the sides, bringing the heels of her feet together. Pushing her panties to the side because she was too irritated to simply pull them off, she placed the silver-topped apparatus to the throbbing hood between her legs and made a low humming sound that almost matched the toy's as it made the connection. No lubricant had been needed since her dreams had excited her sufficiently.

Biting her lower lip as she moved the bullet up and down and around the tightened bud of her clit, she closed her eyes and saw him once more.

Sebastian Perry.

His name echoed in her head even though she'd willed it not to. His eyes hungrily devoured her as they'd done something so cordial as share a drink in a bar. In the dream he'd slid around to the side of the booth where she'd been sitting. His hand had touched her thigh, sending spikes of heat to every pleasure point throughout her body simultaneously. She'd tried to be calm, taking another sip of her wine, but that had been futile. Clever fingers worked her dress up slowly, slipped between her thighs to find her waiting for him.

"Hot," he'd whispered against her ear as he slipped the first finger past her swollen lips. "So hot for me," he'd continued, his tongue licking over her lobe.

She'd kept her eyes open, acutely aware of the fact that they were in a public place where anyone could walk past and see them. They'd know instantly what was going on as the pad of his thumb pressed against her clit and she'd hissed, bucked, and closed her eyes to the pleasure.

At the vivid memory of the dream, Priya rubbed the bullet fiercely over her clit, loving the sensations rippling through her body, the fullness of her breasts, the stinging hardness of her nipples. She moaned louder, bit her lip to stop herself, then cursed and let out a long, low scream.

In the next dream Sebastian held her against the wall in the hallway at the Willard InterContinental. He'd lifted her feet from the plush forest-green carpet, wrapping her legs around his waist and clasping them there. In seconds he'd unzipped his pants to free his erection, pushing his engorged length into her waiting pussy with the gush of her already potent arousal. And then he'd gone to work.

Her hands moved frantically, one controlling the bullet between her legs, the other grabbing her breasts, squeezing until tears stung her eyes. Her breath was coming in loud gulps now, her head tilted as her back arched off the bed.

She could imagine him inside her, filling her, pleasing her, and she bucked her hips. A flash of thought and she almost tossed the vibrator and pushed her fingers into her aching center instead, but penetration was cheating, she'd often told herself. It was okay to bring herself to orgasm by stimulation alone, any type of penetration and she might as well kick the celibacy habit and go get laid.

In the dream he'd rammed into her so hard her head had snapped back, rapping soundly against the wall, but she hadn't cared. He'd grabbed her breasts, squeezing tightly, groaning as he looked down to see his efforts had pushed them over the rim of her dress. Her thighs clenched around him as her nails dug into his shoulders and when they both came it was like the grand finale at the Fourth of July fireworks display—exhilarating and extremely satisfying.

On the bed her thighs quivered, her head thrashing against the pillows until she moaned with the rush of release and finally lay slack against her now-damp sheets.

"Dammit!" she cursed, jumping off the bed and heading straight for the bathroom.

Leaving the apparatus on the side of the sink for later cleaning, she moved directly to the shower to switch on the hot water. Yanking the nightgown so hard she thought she may have heard it rip, she tossed the material to the floor then stepped out of her panties. In the next instant she was in the shower, letting her head fall back as the sting of the water hit her still-aroused body. She scrubbed herself as if she'd been touched by some sort of disease, raking her nails over her skin while muttering something about arrogant, too-fine men.

About a half hour and two cups of coffee later, Priya had regained some semblance of control, putting the dreams and the morning's escapade behind her as she sat down and powered up her laptop. Checking her e-mails was the last thing Priya wanted to do, dread settling quickly in the center of her chest as she pulled up her mailbox. So instead of checking them she composed one to Lolo, her computer-geek friend at the paper. She and Lolo had been the best of friends for the last two years, after she'd felt so bad about turning down his date request that she'd taken him out for a Big Mac meal that had been on special that week.

She sent Lolo the pictures she'd taken with her cell phone at last night's dinner and asked him to go through the databases to provide her with names and connections to Roman Reynolds. After sending off that e-mail she thought briefly about cleaning her apartment, then changed her mind in lieu of another cup of coffee. Oh, how she loved the convenience and quickness of her Keurig.

Then, as if it had been on the agenda all along, she sat back down in front of her laptop and typed his name into the search engine. She shouldn't have, she knew it and berated herself while waiting for links to appear. She didn't give a damn who Sebastian Perry was, he wasn't going to help her with this story, his parting words after he'd walked her to her door last night had said it all.

"Stay away from Roman Reynolds and forget about the notion of cat people. You'll be much better off if you take my advice," he'd said in a mellow tone that matched his reserved demeanor. He'd stood close to her as he always seemed to do, like at any minute he would reach out and touch her cheek, pull her closer, gently kiss her lips . . . no, no, NO!

Priya slammed her hands down on her desk and closed her eyes. "Do. Not. Think of him that way," she told herself sternly. "Just do not!"

When she opened her eyes again it was to more than a couple of hits on his name. Words like playboy, eccentric millionaire, and recluse were all mentioned in the descriptions of him. His bio explained why he was so arrogant— heir to a communications fortune and yet he'd earned his own fortune. The rich simply got richer. And good-looking rich guys showed up on the cover of *GQ*, multiple times. She groaned as she remembered assuming he was Reynolds's bodyguard last night. As arrogant as Perry was, he was probably thinking she had to be a colossal idiot not to know who he was.

Pictures of him with various women appeared on gossip pages, all with titles insinuating they were a "hot" item. Yet she never saw the same female twice. Perry's background seemed to personify some of the things Priya hated about men—entitled, conceited, and distracted. In the midst of all these things that she shouldn't give a damn about, she came across something important. While Perry owned his own string of resorts across the world, he seemed to be extremely close to Reynolds, Delgado, and Markland, all of whom lived right here in D.C. It was a picture of Perry and Markland at Perry's Sedona resort taken only a week before that night she'd seen Markland and the other men in the alley behind Athena's. To Perry she'd made it seem as if someone had given her that information, when in fact, she'd been there and had seen it for herself. She shivered at the memory of those eerie eyes. She and her photographer had been rushed out of the alley by a forceful and attitudinal female and warned not to come back. And the next morning Priya had received the first e-mail with instructions on how she would be the one to reveal the creatures living among them, she would be the one to take Reynolds and his crew down.

She'd been about to ask who was sending the e-mail and what gave them the right to order her around. The picture of her brother gagged and bound and bleeding from a gash in his head had been the only answer she'd needed.

Before Priya could think more about the man she'd met last night in connection with the man she was determined to get to, her phone rang. Instantly, she knew who it was and wondered if she should answer it. Nobody used her house phone besides her family, all her business contacts and Lolo used her cell. Prior to receiving that first e-mail, Priya may have ignored the ringing phone, at least for an hour or two until she was able to get some work done. Starting her day with the drama that inevitably came with the Drake family was not something she enjoyed doing. But now that had changed, the e-mails she'd begun receiving had changed how she dealt with her family. They had inextricably connected her family and her work so that this next story was literally do or die.

If the truth be told, her entire life had been do or die. Born the fourth in a succession of unplanned children to Karen Drake, one of Prince George's County's poster children for what *not* to do when you grew up, Priya had been working toward a better life for what seemed like forever. While her two sisters had followed in their mother's footsteps, dropping out of school and having babies faster than they could figure out names for them, her brother, Malik, the oldest of the Drake siblings, had been suffering from drug addiction for as long as Priya could remember. It seemed odd and slightly pitiful that as the youngest child who had worked drive-thru at Burger King to pay her way through college, she was the most responsible of the Drakes, the one everyone turned to when they were in trouble.

Reaching for the cordless phone that sat on the corner of her desk, she answered, "Hello?"

"Hey, baby," her mother replied.

"Good morning, Mama," she answered, closing her eyes and dreading what might come next. "What's going on?"

That was the first question because Karen never called just to say hello.

"I was just calling because I need a few things from the store. My prescriptions." She paused, coughed like she might stop breathing altogether in the next minute, and then began again. "I need my prescriptions. Malik was supposed to get everything for me but I don't know where he is. Haven't seen him in days."

Priya closed her eyes. No, she wouldn't have seen him in days. In fact, it had been more like weeks and Priya knew why.

"Just tell me what you need, Mama. I'll go to the store and bring everything over."

Karen gave her the list and Priya shut down her computer, going into her room to get dressed.

She was just about to head out the door when she saw the envelope that had been taped to it. She stopped, only able to stare at it for endless moments. When she figured that was stupid and beyond unproductive she took a couple of steps, reached out, and snatched it from the door. Willing her fingers not to shake she opened it and read. It was an address and a time and the words: The clock is ticking.

Angry and helpless to do anything about it, Priya was about to ball up the note and the envelope but stopped because there was something else inside. The black napkin from the bar last night where she'd had the drinks with Perry.

She looked around the apartment, saw everything was where she'd left it the day before and yet there was something different. She hadn't noticed anything when she'd come in last night, possibly because she'd been so wound up after being with Perry that she'd gone straight to bed. They would have had to come in after that or maybe just before she arrived home. At any rate, this confirmed someone was following her, just as she'd thought that night in the alley.

She had just enough time to deliver her mother's groceries and medications before she had to be downtown, before she had to approach Roman Reynolds.

# Chapter 4

"I thought you were working on the reporter. You said she didn't see anything." Dominick Delgado, Rome's Lead Enforcer's voice echoed throughout the spacious corner office of Reynolds and Delgado, LLC.

Nick, in addition to being Rome's partner in the law firm, handled all of the training for the Assembly. For almost eight years now Eli and Ezra Preston had been Lead Guards under Nick's immediate command, personally guarding Nick and Rome while doing an exceptional job of training the new recruits.

At this late-morning meeting, Ezra leaned forward, planting his elbows on the long conference room table on the far side of Rome's office. They'd all checked out of the Willard early this morning, after receiving the text from Rome to do so and to meet here. This weekend was supposed to be about figuring out a strategy against the rogues and solidifying their relationship with the nation's top leader. Now, the focus had turned to something they'd all thought was already handled.

"I did a full report and e-mailed it to all the FLs. The threat was classified as minimal since she doesn't even have a byline at the *Post*. Her stories are mostly editorials on things like what's the best coffeemaker to buy in the dwindling economy. She rents a small apartment on Georgia

Avenue and she's up to her neck in defaulted student loans," Ezra reported.

On one side of the table sat Rome, Nick, and Xavier, three of the highest ranking Assembly officials who often stuck together even outside of shifter business. Jace Maybon, the Pacific FL, and Cole Linden, the Central FL, accompanied Bas on the opposite side. The Lead Guards, Eli and Ezra sat at the two ends of the table.

"I saw the report," Rome added. "Since we hadn't seen anything in the paper immediately following the last killings I figured Ezra was right and she wasn't a threat."

"And now she's returned," Bas stated, sitting back in his chair.

"What does she know?" Nick asked in his usual agitated tone. This was the highly volatile leader that had guards and other shifters, as well as probably a good amount of humans he'd come in contact with deathly afraid of him.

Bas shrugged. "She says she has a source who saw a man whose face began to look like a cat's in an alley behind Athena's. The source also stated you were there."

With the mention of Athena's and Bas's obvious nod in his direction, all eyes went to Xavier, better known to the shifters as X. The muscled arms of this shifter who was built more like a WWF wrestler, were what everyone saw first. The fact that he was a computer genius who used to work for the FBI was secondary, and often unbelievable. X had been the one hanging out at Athena's. He'd also been accused of killing one of the strippers there who he'd been in contact with. And his *companheiro,* Caprise, had also danced there.

"There's no source, Drake was there in the alley and the next day she wrote a story about the raid on Athena's," X said definitively. "We were dealing with the whole Rolando situation. He was the one who was shifting when

Nivea dragged the reporter and the photographer out of the alley," he finished.

Rome squeezed the bridge of his nose. Nick cursed. And Bas shook his head, rubbing a hand casually over his jaw before replying. "It was dark in the alley. She'd just come out of a nightclub where there's known drug activity. As long as there's no one to corroborate the story we're fine," he told them in the nonchalant manner he was known for.

That was Bas's way, he was the cool-under-pressure FL, the relaxed and always composed owner who didn't take any crap from anybody but rarely had to get violent. He worked hard as hell to keep that persona as his general profile, preferring that over being considered the vain and superficial one in leadership. A low-level reporter—not even as hot as Priya Drake—could not rattle him because the alternative wasn't safe for anyone.

"So you denied everything she said?" X asked.

"You know he did," Jace added with a smirk. "And he did it with that smooth-ass smile of his. She probably couldn't remember what the hell he'd said because she was transfixed by his pretty-boy looks."

Bas smoothed down his low-cut mustache, shaking his head. "You have your way of dealing with problems, and I have mine. But I didn't give her any additional information, if that's what you're really asking."

"We're asking if your smoother-than-silk, lover-of-the-century plan is going to keep this female's mouth closed?" Nick inquired.

Bas didn't like the way X and Nick were looking at him, didn't like the implications that were floating around this room, but he didn't plan to address them either, not unless absolutely necessary. His hand moved to glide slowly down the length of his light blue Ferragamo tie. "She won't tell a soul what she saw until she's absolutely sure," he said with confidence. "And if she does, I'll fix it so that nobody believes a word she says."

Nick, who used to have his own reputation as the handsome and unattainable attorney, until he'd found his *companheiro* and had a *joining* ceremony, followed by a beautiful little daughter, only shook his head. "Where is she now?"

"Probably still in his bed," Jace quipped.

"You slept with her?" X asked, incredulous, because sometimes, even Bas's closest friends believed the hype of his notorious reputation.

Besides the image of Bas that had been created solely by the press, it was common knowledge among their tribe that shifters had an insatiable sexual appetite, especially when they found their *companheiros*. There was nothing more important to them during the *companheiro calor*. What none of the shifters in this room knew was how successful Bas had been in banking that desire to save his own sanity and to keep the guilt that ate at him daily with a voracious appetite from consuming him completely. But that wasn't for them to know, it was his business and the way he handled it was solely up to him.

"I did not sleep with her. I gave her a couple of drinks then took her home," he told them. "She's smart but I'm not certain she even believes what she thinks she saw." He almost said he wasn't sure she was pursuing this story because she wanted to, either, but he didn't. His concerns for the reporter, the ones he knew he shouldn't be having, were to be kept private, like so many other aspects of his life.

"Besides, nobody believes reporters half the time," Cole added, leaning forward in his chair. Cole led the Central Zone and lived in Dallas. He was an investment broker who focused on two things only—his money and his job as the FL. Female entanglements definitely took a backseat in Cole's world and he had no problem voicing his concerns over how the other sex could interfere with a man's life. To say he was bitter in that regard was an understatement.

"To the contrary," Jace, the wild card in the group of FLs added. "They believe them way too much. People are so predisposed to believe anyone with power—politicians, superstars, millionaires—are all natural-born liars and cheaters, that anything they find in print that corroborates those facts becomes the law to them."

Jace's words rang true, especially since he dealt with the press more than any of the other FLs in his line of work as the brash and opinionated talent agent and owner of Maybon Artist Management in Los Angeles.

"We have no connection to the bank robbery. That was all crazy-ass Sabar and his league of felines," Nick stated. "I'm so glad that bastard's dead."

"We're all glad he's out of the equation but that doesn't mean there aren't still rogues he had following him out there. And, we do have a connection to Athena's." Cole eyed X, an action that earned him a lethal glare from the former agent.

"Caprise is keeping a low profile at Athena's," X reported. His mate continued to dance at the club, using that as her cover while she kept a lookout for the rogues that had occupied the place like gangsters before.

"And I stay away from the place altogether," X continued tightly. There was no doubt how he felt about that fact.

"I think we may be seeing more in this than is necessary," Bas spoke up. "I reported it to you as a problem just so we would know what we're dealing with, but I don't think she has any more information than what's been floating around in the D.C. news for weeks."

"Maybe you're the one not seeing enough," Cole directed to Bas. "Did something else happen between you and this woman, because it almost seems as if you're defending her. Are you sure the two of you didn't have some type of personal connection?"

At that question Bas spun around. He was in Cole's face so fast it took a moment before Cole could stand to address him, and Nick and X could get close enough to both, one of them putting a hand on Bas's shoulder.

"What are you accusing me of, Linden?" Bas questioned the other FL, a low rumble building in his chest.

"Sit down," Rome ordered. "Both of you," he added since no one had moved.

Bas backed away, mentally kicking himself for losing his cool. He never did that and wasn't about to venture into why Cole was easily able to bait him this time. He wanted to storm out of the room, to go someplace to be alone, to try and figure out why this reporter and her inquisitive eyes and alluring scent had haunted him for the first half of the night and why during the other half he'd dreamed of her in the Gungi, her dead eyes looking up to him instead of Mariah's.

Instead, he took a steadying breath and sat down. When he looked at Rome again it was to find the leader watching him closely.

"You're right," Rome admitted. "We do already have history with Ms. Drake. But so far you're the first one of us to have personal contact with her, so tell me how you think she should be handled."

It wasn't out of the norm for Rome to consider their opinions, that's just the type of leader he was. He knew that keeping the Shadows safe and protecting the humans at the same time was a team effort and he'd acquired one hell of a team to see that through. Bas only hated that Rome's use of the word "handled" had succeeded in stroking a serious protective instinct in him that he knew the others would never understand.

Once again deciding that now was definitely not the place to let his personal feelings interfere, Bas spoke on what he knew from a strategic standpoint. "For now, I think the best plan of attack is no attack at all. Nobody's going to believe her ramblings, she'll discredit herself by even putting them in print. She has absolutely no evidence and I doubt the *Post* would be willing to take on the liability for printing anything about Rome without solid proof to back them up. They don't want the Lethal Litigator suing their asses," he ended, trying for a lighter mood.

Bas continued to look down the table at Rome, who readily acknowledged his reputation as a ruthless litigator in D.C., with a nod.

"The rogues should remain the priority," Bas added with finality.

Rome was quiet for a few moments, obviously contemplating what their next move would be. His mind would no doubt be on the issues that were now permeating the very fabric of the democracy he was trying to build for the shifters. His actions from this point forward would undoubtedly set the stage for how they would proceed, how their lives would go on in this world of humans who had no clue what they were.

"We'll keep her in our peripheral for the time being." Rome spoke decisively. "Right now, I want all of you to head back to your zones. Nick received a report this morning about a shipment possibly coming into Arizona tonight."

"Coming in from Mexico?" Bas asked immediately. The last shipment they'd intercepted in his zone had given them Felipe Hernandez, a former lieutenant in the Cortez Cartel. The man was still being held in the lower bunkers of Bas's resort where they'd locked him up after X had come to Sedona to question him.

"It's not Cortez," X offered, shaking his head. "No way they're going to send in another shipment after we captured the last one and their lieutenant at the same time. Not this soon."

"Whoever it is, there are two boats expected to dock at midnight mountain time," Nick reported.

"Where'd you get this intel?" Bas asked.

All eyes fell on Nick. "It was an anonymous e-mail sent to my work e-mail address. I didn't have a chance to give X a heads-up so he could do his computer mojo and find out where it originated from before coming into this little get-together. But we'll get on that trace right away."

"In the meantime, you need to head back to Sedona and get some guards down to that location," Rome told Bas.

He nodded. Understanding immediately what his priority was. The shifters were his life, right alongside his business. That was all he had in the world and, truth be told, all Bas wanted. This mating and joining crap wasn't for him. And having his mind messed with by a human female definitely wasn't in his repertoire.

"On my way to the airport now," he told Rome. "You cornballs coming with?" he asked Jace and Cole. The three often traveled together when it was time to meet with Rome and while all of the FLs kept in close contact, they seemed to have an even tighter bond since they'd always known Rome was destined for greater leadership than being a Faction Leader.

Cole hated Bas's laid-back ways with women and everything else, most likely because of his parents' bitter and very public divorce. Jace, on the other hand, took everything in stride as most L.A. transplants did. Life to him was lying out on the beach, tanning, and hunting—for new talent as his human job was as a high-profile Hollywood agent. Bas joked with both of them about their sense of style among other things, hence the reason he was now calling them cornballs.

"Whatever, even your pimp suit isn't hiding the fact that the human female struck a chord somewhere in that superficial soul of yours," Cole said, standing up and brushing imaginary lint from the jeans that were a staple of his wardrobe.

Bas decided to ignore those words because, yeah, there was a stitch of truth to them. Instead he simply nodded to Rome saying, "I'll be in touch."

# Chapter 5

"You're being followed."

Priya screamed, turning around with her Mace already in hand. The small container that hooked to her key chain came in handy just as her self-defense instructor had told her it would. Her arm was raised, finger on the nozzle, ready to fire when the man standing behind her gave her a lopsided grin instead of a knock on the head.

"Lolo, what the hell are you doing here?" she asked with an exasperated sigh. Lowering her arm she refrained from spraying him in the face but still scowled with agitation.

"I came by your place to give you the information you requested but you were running out the door when I pulled up," he began, looking over her shoulder every few seconds as he continued. "The minute you got into your car a black truck with tinted windows pulled up beside me, blocking me in so I couldn't get out. You took off and that truck took off behind you. So I followed the truck."

Priya shook her head. Lolo, short for Lowman Sheradon, stood at five feet eleven inches. He had chocolate-brown hair that he kept in shaggy disarray on top and tapered on the sides. His eyes matched his hair color, the deep dimple in his chin giving him an adorably cute look instead of boyishly handsome as he liked to claim.

"What are you doing following people? You're not a cop," she reminded him and tried to turn around, to head back toward the location that she was already late getting to.

"No, not a cop, but a concerned friend," he said, pulling her by the elbow to stop her movement.

"Not now, Lolo, I have someplace to be," she told him.

"That truck stayed parked at the corner of your mom's house the entire time you were inside, Priya," he told her earnestly.

Priya didn't try to pull away, but folded her arms over her chest at his words. "How did you know that was my mother's house?"

It was Lolo's turn to sigh and he did so with a genuinely apologetic look. "I know it's your mother's address because I've seen you go there before and I looked at all the names on the mailboxes. There's only one Drake listed."

She gave a nervous little chuckle, shaking her head. "So you're actually the one who's following me, not some stranger in a black truck." It was an attempt to take Lolo's words lightly when she knew he was telling the truth. She knew because whoever was following her had probably been doing so since that very first e-mail and just last night they'd taken the following to another level and had broken into her apartment, most likely while she was in bed asleep. All that, coupled with what had happened at her mother's house earlier, only proved she had to do what they said and she had to do it fast.

"No, I don't follow you around," Lolo stated but looked away instead of holding eye contact, which Priya instantly knew meant he was lying. He huffed. "Look, I'm just saying that someone is following you and those pictures you sent me, they have some pretty powerful people in them. So I'm a little worried that you may be getting yourself into some trouble here."

She shook her head again, refusing to let the concern in his voice deter her. "Who was in the pictures?" she asked somberly.

"Reynolds, Delgado, President Reed, and a few businessmen from the private sector. Major Randall Guthrie was also in the background of one of the pictures watching as the president and Reynolds talked. He didn't look happy."

"Guthrie's a natural-born killer given the permission to do his evil deeds by the commendations lined across the chest of his Marine uniform. He never looks happy," she quipped.

"And he never misses a kill," Lolo added. "Look, I know you don't want to tell me why you're looking into Reynolds or why this is so top secret, but I don't like it, Priya. I'm getting a bad feeling about it," he said, lifting a hand to his chest and rubbing as he looked up the street and then back down to where he'd come from.

"That's your acid reflux, Lolo. Take a pill, e-mail me all the names, and I'll call you later," she said, turning once again to head toward the Reynolds Building.

She'd taken only two steps when the glass doors to the front of the building opened and a line of men—no, they actually looked more like living gods—came filing out. She noticed them immediately and stood still, watching them. The first two had also been at the table with Reynolds last night at the reception. Their names she already knew, even without Lolo's assistance, thanks to her early-morning research on Perry. The first was Jace Maybon, a talent agent from L.A. with tall, dark, and sinfully delicious looks that would raise the brow of any breathing female. The second, not to be outdone by the first, was Cole Linden, slightly more low-key, brutal in the boardroom, and seemingly averse to females as noted by an article in *Forbes* that neatly outlined his portfolio and congratulated whatever lady was lucky enough to land him.

Both of them paled in comparison to who came out next. Her breath should not have hitched, her eyes widening. There should have been no surprise that he was close because her body had already begun to respond as it had only to his proximity. He was dressed in a suit, a dusky gray that she thought might actually match the color of his eyes. Sunlight caught the diamonds that circled his watch as he lifted his hands to pull his jacket together and button it.

He looked up instantly, as if he'd been expecting her to be standing there. His gaze locked on hers and she licked her now-dry lips, cursing the tingle of her nipples at the sight of him. Priya instinctively took a step back anyway. Linden and Maybon had already gotten inside a truck . . . a black SUV, to be exact. But Perry walked immediately toward her.

"What are you doing here?" he asked.

"Hello to you, too," she replied, taking a deep swallow but hoping he didn't notice. He towered over her today, his broad shoulders and chest blocking her vision, encompassing her without even touching her. "I see you still haven't worked on your greetings."

"Priya, we should go," she heard Lolo say from her left. He was pulling on her arm again.

Perry looked over at Lolo, a muscle ticking in the right side of his jaw. "Who is this?" he asked in a voice deeper, sterner than she'd previously heard from him.

"This is a man and he's with me," she said slowly as if she thought he might have trouble comprehending, especially since he'd taken on this master-of-the-universe stance demanding answers from her as if she actually owed them to him.

His gaze went to where Lolo's hand rested on her arm, then back to her face.

"You should not be here," he stated.

"It's a free country and I have a job to do," she insisted.

He shook his head. "Not here. Not now," he told her. "It is not safe."

"I told you," Lolo chimed in. "Let's go, now!"

Priya watched as Perry looked at Lolo once more. There was dislike and something else she couldn't quite place, but she shook that off. None of it mattered, only getting into that building mattered and she didn't have much time to do it. Burning a hole in the pocket of her jeans was a list of questions she'd been told to ask, even more prevalent in her memory was that those questions had been left taped to her mother's door.

"Listen to your friend and go," Sebastian told her, his voice taking on an urgent tinge. "Go or I'll have you physically removed. I don't think that's what you want."

"I want you to stop thinking you can tell me what to do, Mr. Perry," she said, squaring her shoulders and taking a step forward. There was no way she was letting him or anyone else stop her, no matter how big they were.

He reached out then, grabbing her by both shoulders. "Go. Home. This is not a game."

"We're going," Lolo said, pulling Priya so that Perry was no longer touching her.

She might have felt like a limp rag being tugged from one opponent to the next, but the warmth that had moved through her like a fine wine at Perry's touch was instantly missed and she almost called out for him to touch her again. She actually considered jerking away from Lolo to run back to him, back to the man she barely knew, but had dreamed about, in full-blown touch-a-vision color.

"Look, there's another one," Lolo yelled in her ear when she was still staring at Perry. She looked to her left, to the street where another black SUV was completing a quick U-turn, tires screeching. In seconds there were more men filing out of the Reynolds Building, all of them built

like super-soldiers, moving quickly to create some type
of formation surrounding the parked SUV. At the door
stood four men, covering the entrance, each of them holding big black guns down at their sides. Another one came
up behind Perry, touching a shoulder to his arm. Perry
didn't move, didn't even turn in the other man's direction,
but kept staring at Priya.

Lolo continued to pull her, but she never turned around.
She did the backward walk thing while keeping her gaze
locked on Perry. To her surprise and stroking her female
ego slightly, he held her gaze as well. Even when he finally
did move to the truck, he kept staring at her before mouth-
ing the words, "This is not a game" once more.

Bas thought about her while he was on the plane. Staring
out the window to the soft white stretch of clouds he let
his mind drift. To her.

He had seen many women before, had even slept with
his fair share, but none had ever been human. Not since
Mariah. And none had ever been one bit like Priya Drake.
She was sassy and bold and brash and clever and absolutely
clueless to what would happen if she pursued this story.
Rubbing a hand over his chin, Bas thought of how many
times he'd considered letting Jace and Cole go ahead to the
airport and going back to her apartment. He would tell her
again to stay away from Rome and anything that involved
him. He'd wanted to tell her to be safe, to keep living her
life the way she had been before that night in the alley behind that club. But somehow he knew she wouldn't be able
to do that. He'd sensed that urgency last night at the hotel
and again earlier today on the street. This was something
she had to do, he only wondered why.

Then Bas willed himself to stop wondering. It wasn't
his concern, *she* wasn't his concern. She couldn't be and
to some that might be a shame. To him, it was his life, his

world, the one he'd decided to live in after Mariah's brutal murder, the only one that allowed him any semblance of peace.

If Priya Drake didn't have the sense to heed his warnings, then so be it. Rome would deal with whatever came next where the tenacious reporter was concerned. He was the head of the Stateside Assembly for a reason. And Bas, well, he had enough to deal with when he returned home—a shipment of drugs to possibly intercept and the carriers to question. He did not have time to wonder about a female, about what it might have been like to sink his length into her warm flesh, to feel her clutching him tightly, whispering his name, needing him on a level he'd never thought possible.

And that was for the best, he reminded himself. Shifters remaining separate, but still a part, of the human world had long since been a goal of the Assembly. There was no way he would ever go against that.

Not even for her.

# Chapter 6

Bas was finally home.

Half an hour ago Jacques Germain, Bas's Lead Enforcer, had been at the private strip of land Bas had designated as shifter airspace, to pick him up. The jet was making its next-to-last stop before heading back to the East Coast to await Rome's next instruction. Jace would be dropped off last and then all the FLs would be back in their zones, back on the job of keeping the rogues at bay and protecting the humans from the danger that lurked just beyond the shadows.

The airspace was completely off the grid so the FAA had no way of tracking their jets to or from their destination. Just as below the basement floors of Perryville Resorts was yet another twenty-five feet dug into the earth, where the shifter labs and surveillance spaces where kept. The walls of the U-shaped bunker were lined with layer upon layer of reinforced steel and guarded by some of the most high-tech security equipment ever invented. Bas had consulted with Nick on most of the layout and what would be needed to keep the fortress both stable and secure. X had given his input on the technology and the general warfare.

Should, for whatever reason, their security somehow become breached, it was Bas's territory. He had teams of shifters designated by achievement levels in combat, lower levels—the yellow team—that did perimeter checks, and higher levels—the blue team—that worked discreetly among the citizens of Sedona. Bas's years as a Marine had provided the combat skills required to train hundreds of shifters to protect and safeguard their secret as well as their people. His college years had given him the education and sophistication he needed to rub elbows with the rich and elite of America. The fact that he was a shifter had given him the solid footing he needed to stay sane among everything else.

Sanity was exactly what Bas was thinking of as he climbed into the back of the mocha-and-steel Yukon Jacques drove. Behind the Yukon were four silver Jeep Wranglers—the official vehicle of the guards that had been redesigned and fitted with top-notch technology and warfare on Nick's orders. All the FLs traveled with what Bas considered a small army even though Sabar Tavares had been confirmed dead. The shifters knew Sabar had not worked alone. His known partner in crime, Darel Charles had not been seen or heard from since that night, so they had to consider that the rogue threat was still alive and possibly planning another attack. But for the moment Bas's attention needed to remain focused on the incoming shipment he would need to intercept.

"Nick sent me the e-mail," Jacques reported through the intercom link they all wore tucked discreetly into their ears and activated by small chips embedded in the collar of their shirts.

"Good. I want a blue team in place and ready to roll with me tonight," Bas instructed while looking through the truck's tinted windows.

He gazed at the familiar roads, winding around the

side of the mountain, traveling low into the valley where he'd built his masterpiece. Perryville Resorts Sedona was located near the secluded Boynton Canyon, sitting on more than eighty acres of natural terrain. Its structure was surrounded by red-rock buttes known for inspiring the mind, body, and spirit. This was the reason Bas stayed here year-round. While each of his resorts had a special place in his heart, a unique something that had drawn him to the locale, this one was his baby. From the moment he'd opened his first resort he knew he'd end up here. His plan was to expand Perryville until it touched every exotic locale in the world, but here, where he could stand on the balcony to his penthouse suite and look at the magnificent orange-and-fuchsia swirls in the sky as the sun set over the beautiful red rocks, was where he belonged.

"The team's already in place. I've scheduled a debriefing in an hour," Jacques continued.

Bas lifted an arm and glanced at his TAG Heuer Monaco to check the time. An hour would give him just enough time to shower and change clothes and to do a little more research before heading out.

"That's fine. Have Jewel bring all the mail from my office to my room and get me maps and blueprints to the buildings we'll be going to tonight," he told the shifter.

If there was a shipment coming in and they were going to intercept it, he wanted to know exactly where they were going and how they could get out quickly if need be. Because there was a good chance they could be walking into an ambush tonight. A damned good chance.

The minute the SUV drove slowly through the ten-foot gates linked together by the splitting halves of the Perryville Sedona logo, Bas rolled down the window. He inhaled the still and sultry Arizona air and felt strands of tension releasing slowly from his shoulder blades. It was like that here—for him, even the dry heat was a comfort, possibly giving him a taste of the Gungi on a daily basis. He stepped out of the truck the moment it stopped, ignoring the click of his loafers as he walked across the stone-tile driveway.

The front doors of the resort were glass, the logo that had been promised to brand his resorts throughout the world boldly displayed in gold swirls above the entrance. Inside the floors were marbled, leading to the granite-topped front desk.

With a nod of his head to his staff Bas headed toward the private elevators that were located past La Selva, the resort's signature restaurant, which featured an intricate mix of Spanish and Southwestern dishes, complete with its own wine bar and around the corner from Alma, the resort's spa that used Native American techniques to cater to the mind, body, and soul.

He pressed the button for himself, feeling the presence of Jacques to his right and two other guards to his left. No doubt there was another guard taking the service elevator up to his penthouse right now to sweep the premises before Bas arrived. When he finally made it up to his suite Bas immediately moved to the desk that sat in the far corner of the room to switch on his laptop.

His footsteps were quiet as he walked across the mahogany-colored carpet to the bar where he fixed himself a quick glass of wine while his computer booted. That's when he caught her scent. Perfume, a very generic brand, something soft, just a tad floral and most likely meant to be enticing. But she wore too much. There was a secondary scent, one Bas was sure no human would ever detect. But since he wasn't human, he'd lifted the aroma the moment they'd first met. The tangy, citrus smell of fear comingled with the floral perfume, creating a powerful mixture that often tickled Bas's nose in an annoying fashion. Then again, she very rarely spent long periods of time in his presence so there was never enough of it to annoy him. Still, he'd known it was there, the fear she carried with her like a cloak. And he'd wondered about it, but never asked. She was a human female and she worked for him, two reasons for Bas to always keep his distance. She was also a female in trouble, an even bigger reason for him to keep her close.

"Your mail, sir," Jewel announced in her quiet voice as she set the mail down on the corner of the mantel.

She faced him then and Bas stared into now familiar, but still a bit out of place brilliant green eyes and hair that fell to her shoulders in tight, fiery red curls. Her skin was tanned, couldn't help but be otherwise living out here, but the hair and eyes had never matched for Bas. Instinctively, he'd known they were the result of contact lenses and hair dye, but he'd never asked her why. The fact that she was afraid of something was all he'd needed to offer her a job and shelter. His need to protect the female had been strong from the start and even when he was away it didn't falter.

"Thanks, Jewel. How've you been?" he asked in the cordial manner he always spoke to her. There was nothing between them, no sexual desire and no intention to go beyond the employer and employee relationship, so unlike what Bas had felt with the other human female he'd just met.

"I'm well, thank you. How was your trip?" She spoke clearly and politely, always.

"Both pleasant and disturbing but isn't that the way of the world?" he replied, flipping through the mail he'd picked up.

She smiled at him. "I guess so."

Jewel never talked much. She answered him respectfully but never offered more than was required. Because this wasn't new and he had other things to do, Bas hurried to dismiss her. "Well, thanks for bringing me the mail.

I'm going to catch up on some things in here and will be down in the conference room around nine thirty. Tell Mrs. Ramirez I'll take a late dinner down there."

Jewel nodded and left the room as quietly as she'd entered. She would go directly to the kitchen where Maria Ramirez, his kitchen manager, could usually be found and deliver his message. Jewel was a good worker, which was another reason Bas had allowed her to stay at Perryville for the last few years.

He finished his glass of wine, which was excellent, a new blend he'd secured from two of Jace's actor clients who had taken the plunge into the winery business. He'd have to remember to send Jace an e-mail telling him how flavorful the wine was and order more. Bas undressed, then moved into the bathroom, opening the glass doors and stepping inside the marble-tiled shower beneath a cascade of hot water.

The hot spray slapped blissfully against his skin as he first moved so that it drenched his front and then his back. Flattening his palms on the tiles just beneath the shower head Bas stretched, elongating each vertebra along his spine. Inside there was more movement, more stretching and pushing, a low growl rolling through his chest.

It wanted out. The beast within wanted to run, it wanted to stretch and be free. Most of all, it wanted to fuck.

Inhaling deeply, searching for calm, for steady breathing, steady thoughts, Bas fought the hunger. It had been growing impatient these last few months, stalking him like a hunter, reminding him that regardless of the choice he'd made to live this solitary lifestyle, it yearned for something much more. Shaking his head, Bas denied it, again. His jaw clenched so tightly the rattling of his teeth echoed throughout the shower stall.

He could not have her. There was no question about that. If it were just a woman, the hard drive of a blatant carnal connection, then he could find someone and slake the burning need.

Searing pain streaked through his chest but Bas did not growl, he did not yell out in agony, because he was in charge. Not the cat, never the cat, he promised himself. The cat hadn't yelled this loud to save Mariah, it hadn't ripped through the human skin to save the innocent human whose only mistake had been falling for him and following him to a dangerous and unknown place even after he'd declared their relationship finished. It hadn't torn those other shifters to shreds to protect her the way it should have. So he'd be damned if he'd listen to the inner roaring now.

Priya Drake was off-limits and that was that.

Yanking his hands from the tiles and grabbing the soap, he proceeded with another thought, ignoring the movement, the hissing, the agitation as if it were nothing more than a nuisance that would hopefully go away. Switching off the spray of water when he'd finished he stepped out into the cooler room and prepared to dress, to make contact with the East Coast guards to ensure that the near-confrontation just as they'd stepped out of Rome's office building had been resolved.

Abruptly he stopped before pulling on his boxer briefs. His dick was so hard as to make the task uncomfortable, if not almost painful. Bas sighed, gripping his length in one palm and jerking so hard he half expected his release to come shooting out instantaneously. Then his memory betrayed him, her scent filtering through his nostrils as if she were standing directly in front of him. When he closed his eyes in exasperation it was only to find that she was there. In his mind he could see her face, see the alluring curve of her chin, the soft mound of her cheekbones, the length of her eyelashes. Her compact body wore jeans and a short-sleeved shirt as if they were custom-made.

He'd touched her. Bas growled, his hand growing tighter around his dick, teeth clenching once more.

No man could touch her. No other man could have her, could not fuck her. Because she was his.

"No," Bas hissed, "No,"

His hand moved of its own accord, jerking upward until the bulbous head burned with impending release. Sliding down his shaft and up roughly once more he cursed and cursed some more, until release finally came in rushing jets of white dripping to the floor so loudly his eyes shot open even as his head lulled back.

"No. Not her," he said on a hampered breath. "Not her."

# Chapter 7

*This is not a game.*

That's what he'd told her, even though she'd been fully aware of those facts from the first e-mail she'd received. This wasn't a game, and whoever it was that wanted her to uncover this secret Reynolds and his friends were harboring, were doing a damn good job of hammering that fact home. Right to Priya's doorstep, to the heart of who she was, to be exact.

This morning she'd walked up the familiar cracked steps to her mother's house, becoming instantly overwhelmed with all the memories that lived beyond that front door. Using her key she'd gone inside, walking through the vestibule, inhaling the scent of stale cigarette smoke and old grease. Her mother would be in the kitchen, no doubt, sitting at the old Formica table with its only two surviving chairs, across from the cracked counter that held the nineteen-inch television Priya had bought her two Christmases ago. She would be dressed in her robe, cotton and frayed at the collar and her hair, which she'd long ago cut short would be slicked down to her scalp with some gel concoction she was fond of. In one shaking, bony hand would be her ever-present cigarette, while her ankles crossed beneath the table, shaking as well.

"Mornin', Mama," she'd said.

"Hey there, you got my medicine?"

"Of course," Priya replied, putting the bag from the drugstore on the table within her grasp.

She went to the refrigerator, opened it, and unpacked the other bags she'd brought with her, the ones with the milk, eggs, butter, and Cap'n Crunch cereal her mother loved.

"I don't know where Malik is," Karen had said while Priya's back was still turned to her. "He never usually stays away this long."

Priya stilled. No, her older brother Malik never stayed away for weeks because in a matter of days he'd run through whatever money he'd been able to scrape up, getting high with all the drugs he'd been able to find. He always came back to Karen's though, because she always let him in. She cooked for him, and washed his clothes, and even gave him what pennies she had left out of her monthly check so that he could go right back out into the streets. Closing her eyes, Priya tried not to think about the endless circle of their lives. She tried not to think about the father who had walked out on them, thrusting Karen into the endless pit of depression and self-loathing that had created such a loving home for her to grow up in. At one point she almost covered her ears as she thought she could still hear Levi Drake's yelling and cursing as he beat Karen and Malik like they were rodents on the street. Priya and her sisters had escaped those beatings only because they stayed away from Levi and his deadly temper, out of his reach and sight as much as they possibly could. Malik had always protected Karen, always jumped in Levi's face whenever he struck her. One day all that violence ceased because Levi was gone, the no-good bastard.

"Malik will be home soon, Mama," she told her mother

as she leaned over to kiss her forehead. "He'll be home real soon, I promise."

"You'll bring him back, won't you?" Karen asked, her words stilling Priya instantly.

Her mother was asking her for something and it wasn't new. All her life Priya had felt like she'd been put on this earth to care for her family. She was the youngest and yet she was the strongest, the most dependable. She'd never let any of them down and they trusted in that fact. Even her sisters who had never been as close to her as Priya would have liked, knew who to call when their child support payments were late, or when one of her nieces or nephews needed new shoes. It was always Priya and she always came to the rescue.

"He's probably checked himself into another rehab," she said after taking the few minutes she needed to gather her thoughts. Some days there were things she wanted to say to her family, moments when she just wanted to scream for all of them to get their own lives together and leave her the hell alone. "You know how they have the blackout period when they first check in."

"No," Karen had said in a low whisper.

It was so low Priya had turned to her, leaning against the counter as she looked at the frail frame of a woman who at one time had a light in her eyes, a luster to her chocolate-brown skin.

"I think it's different this time," her mother had finished.

It was different, Priya thought sadly. It was something Priya had never imagined she'd be in the middle of, some sort of blackmail scheme that she couldn't walk away from.

"He'll be back, Mama. I promise," she told her mother as she moved to stand right beside her, rubbing a hand over her shoulder.

Karen surprised her by lifting one of her shaking hands

to touch her daughter's fingers where they rested on her robe. "You always keep your promises. You always do the right thing."

Priya didn't know what to say to those words. Karen had never been one for affection, not having anything left to spare after Levi had beat all the good out of her. Priya was used to that, they all were. Certain things just weren't expected from her mother—compassion, pride in her children, love in her eyes, were just among the few. But this touch, the sound of Karen's voice—she was right. It was different this time and Priya only prayed she could do what was necessary to give her mother what she wanted, once more.

"Yes, Mama, I keep my promises. Malik will come back," she told her without another second's hesitation.

And he would, Priya vowed. If she had to walk right up to the devil and shake his hand she would do it to bring her brother home to her mother. If she didn't, the idea that another man that Karen had loved with all her heart may have also walked out of her life would be too much for Karen to bear. And watching her mother deteriorate any more would be too much for Priya.

So now, she was officially broke. As she stepped through the doors of Sedona Airport and coughed into dry, stiff air she thought breathing was going to be quite difficult. With only her carry-on bag, laptop case, and her purse she proceeded to hail a cab praying that she still had enough cash in her purse to pay for transport to and from Perryville Resorts.

Her entire life savings, one thousand two hundred and eighty-five dollars, had quickly dwindled down to one hundred and fifty dollars after her round-trip airfare and the exorbitant nightly rates at the exclusive Perryville Resort. No wonder he wore Armani suits and Dolce & Gabbana silk ties, gouging people to stay at a simple hotel the way he did. She frowned as she climbed into the back of the cab and gave her destination. Sebastian Perry was quickly moving up her list of people she detested.

So why was she here? Why had she flown across the country when the notes had directed her to Reynolds? Because Sebastian Perry knew what she was after. He knew the secret Reynolds was hiding and she was going to get him to tell her. He'd warned her to stay away from Rome. Fine. Then he would be the one to tell her what she needed to know. It was that simple.

No, there was absolutely nothing simple about Perryville Resorts. The redbrick building was like a small fortress jutting up from the earth surrounded by nature's choice and not man's, by the most beautiful rock formations Priya had ever seen. Sure, she'd never been anywhere farther than Ocean City, Maryland, for a week in the summertime, so saying she hadn't seen many gorgeous feats of nature was a given. But that didn't stop her from recognizing the breathless wonder that was the Boynton Canyon and this magnificent display of modern décor that had been dropped inside of it like a penny in an old Coke bottle.

She stepped out of the cab, slipping her sunglasses off so she could see everything without any buffer. The sun had already set, night looming over the resort like a shadow, but even it couldn't hide the opulence. The front doors seemed much taller and wider than normal doors she'd walked through, gold handles and writing on them added grandeur. She wanted to go back home and slip into her red dress once more, to put on the shoes she'd paid only about a third of her weekly paycheck for at Macy's. Jennifer, her hair stylist who worked on Florida Avenue, would gladly squeeze her in for a quick wash and curl, and her manicure was still in acceptable condition. The jeans and black fitted T-shirt she wore did nothing to make her feel like she belonged in a place like this.

Still, her green money that held the same value as everyone else's had paid for a room, so Priya walked up to the front desk and checked in. She tried to ignore the soft music that sounded like a harp over dripping water that played overhead. This wasn't a vacation. She walked with her chin held high, her duffel bag growing a little heavier in her hand toward the elevators and once she finally stepped inside, let out the breath she'd been holding.

"Do or die?" she whispered to herself, shaking at how true that sentiment actually was in her case.

The elevator dinged, doors opened, and she hurriedly stepped out.

"Great. Big expensive resort and no signs to tell you which way to go to your room," she quipped then looked down at the key card in her hand. It had the number written in small green numbers beneath the gold-printed Perryville logo, the same one that was printed everywhere she'd looked in this building as if anyone would dare to forget where they were or who owned the place.

It took her another five minutes to realize she was on the wrong floor and to curse herself for being wrong once again. Slapping her palm against the UP button she waited impatiently for the elevator. All she wanted to do was talk to Perry again, get some information out of him this time, then go back home where she belonged. The elevator doors opened once more and she stepped inside determined to do her job as quickly as possible and not to enjoy a moment of this gorgeous place for fear that at any moment she might just get used to it.

Bas stopped where he stood. He waited a beat, his hand paused over the knob of the door leading to the conference room. He was late by about fifteen minutes and it couldn't have been helped. Maybe it could have had he not given into a basic need, a need that continued to claw at him. But he was here now and they were waiting for him. They had to pull out soon if they were going to make it in time for the drop-off.

Still, Bas didn't move.

He inhaled deeply, released it slowly, and felt a now-familiar tug inside. It was as if the beast had begun stalking the human, taunting him with what it thought was an inevitability. This time Bas would not give in, not even an inch. He pushed back, sending the beast an undeniable message.

*Not here. Not now.*

Bas had changed into dark khakis and a polo shirt, the closest he could get to dressing casually. On his feet were his black steel-toed Timberland boots, probably the most urban item he owned. In his front right pants pocket was his cell phone, in the left his keys. He focused on the here and now, the important things versus the unthinkable.

Then there was a sound. He looked down the hall to his left. Nothing.

Conference rooms were located on the second floor. They didn't book many conferences here as he preferred the place to be used as a serene getaway and not another place to work. There were no guest rooms or other amenities, just the conference rooms. And only one conference room was in use at the moment. So why did he believe someone else was there?

As quickly as the sense of . . . who, he wasn't quite sure, had appeared, it disappeared and Bas cursed softly under his breath. For the first time in he couldn't remember how long, Bas felt off, unbalanced, and uncertain of something as normal as walking down a hallway. He didn't like this feeling, not one bit.

"What if this is a setup?" Paolo, a guard with the deceptive looks of a teenager, spoke as Bas finally entered the room.

Paolo had been one of Bas's blue team members for the last two years and in that time the shifter had more than proven his worth. For that reason, and because he was active in the community as the head of a nonprofit that helped to keep wayward teens off the streets, Bas had a tremendous amount of respect for him.

"We're planning for that contingency," Bas chimed in, determined to keep his head in the game.

Jacques, who sat to Bas's left, ran his fingers slowly over the screen of his iPad. "I'm sending pictures to everyone's phone," he announced.

"These are the faces of the rogues who were reportedly at that warehouse in D.C. before it exploded," Bas told them. "But not after."

"So these are the ones we're looking for tonight?" Syfon, the blue team leader, asked from the far end of the room.

"We're looking for anyone who has something to do with that shipment. Whether it's a driver or a runner or the goddamned ringleader, I want him," Bas told them emphatically. "Preferably alive."

"Rogues don't come willingly," Syfon announced, as if it needed to be confirmed.

Paolo gave him a smirk. "And we don't ask politely."

"I want everyone to stay sharp out there. We have no idea who may have been given the grand task this time. And if these are the same synthetic drugs that have been killing off humans in D.C., I don't want them arriving on American soil on my watch. Am I understood?"

Jacques looked around the room to the legion of twenty guards he'd trained personally. When his gaze returned to Bas they both looked to Paolo whose stare was aimed directly at them. The three of them nodded and Syfon stood first.

"Understood, FL," he said, giving Bas another nod. Then he gave a motion with his right hand, two fingers up, turning in a small circle. The others around the table stood, giving the same signal—the blue team solidarity motion—and they headed out of the room.

"Paolo's a good soldier, albeit sometimes he can be a loose cannon," Jacques said when only he and Bas were left in the room.

Bas nodded. "He is. That's why I want you to keep him close." No other words were needed. Bas and Jacques had been together for a long time, Jacques being elevated to Lead Enforcer about ten seconds after Bas had been named FL. They were partners in this mission and damn good friends. So Jacques knew exactly why Bas wanted Paolo kept close and agreed with him wholeheartedly. It's also why Bas felt safe in what he was about to ask.

"Do you smell it?" he asked, his voice's timbre lower than it had been seconds ago.

Jacques nodded. "The adrenaline is high. They're ready to hunt in whatever form you command."

Bas shook his head. "I don't want any shifting," he told Jacques adamantly.

It was nothing new that Bas preferred his soldiers to fight as humans. Outside the canyon and the resort there was a small town of about two thousand residents. The last thing they needed was to believe that among all the other legends and folklore that went with the canyon's history, that there were also cat people living in the mountains.

But that had not been the scent Bas was referring to. And since it had been Jacques's first response that meant he likely had not picked up the scent Bas had. In all actuality Bas wasn't sure he'd actually picked up a scent. It was more like a feeling, a presence that brought with it the taste of a yearning he'd always dreaded.

# Chapter 8

**Nogales, Arizona**

They were late, Palermo Greer swore as he waited at the base of the tunnel. It was almost ten forty-five and they were supposed to do the pickup at ten a.m. sharp. He didn't pace, like Black, the six-foot-five-inch-tall shifter who was built like a running back and had the personality of the feral cat that he was.

"We wait ten more minutes," Palermo said solemnly. The hair along the base of his neck stood straight up, his cat pressing like a giant boulder against his spine, ready to break free for any reason. They were alone out here, standing in a building looking down a hole that went more than fifty feet down. The tunnels had taken two years to build and were perfected with a state-of-the-art ventilation system, beamed walls, and six-foot-high ceilings. It began at the back of a building at the border checkpoint in Mexico and ran the length of two football fields to this abandoned strip mall in Nogales. This was Palermo's first time being near one, but he'd seen the blueprints and knew exactly where the rogues bringing the shipment in would meet him and how they would use the rope and pulley to lift the drugs up into the building.

That's where they stood right now, at the top, waiting for the signal that the shipment was ready for transport.

"If they don't show we're fucking screwed," Black mumbled on another pass by the spot where Palermo was leaning against a wall.

"They'll show," Palermo stated, his eyes glued to the opening in the floor. Watching. Waiting.

"What if they don't?"

"They will," he grumbled.

Black slapped a beefy fist into the palm of his other hand. "They're late."

"I know," Palermo said with a nod.

"And you're not fucking pissed off? I am! They're wasting our time. We should be back in D.C. working with Darel to build our base."

The shifter was talking about Darel Charles, the rogue shifter who now thought he was running things after the cold-blooded way in which he'd cut Sabar out of the picture. Black was afraid of Darel. Palermo wasn't, because he knew that despite Darel's posturing and grandstanding he couldn't run this operation by himself. That had never been the plan. Unfortunately, Darel had no clue what was actually going on around him, and Palermo planned to keep it that way.

"They're here," he said finally, pushing from the wall he'd been leaning against and going to stand right over the hole in the floor.

Black joined him, breathing harder than was necessary but Palermo knew that wasn't from any type of exertion. Instead it was the rogue's adrenaline pumping. He was ready for anything and so was Palermo. Reaching behind his back he slipped out the UK semiautomatic rifle. The rifles were designed by Robert Slakeman at Slakeman Enterprises and were intended for use by the US military, or the military of some other country. Instead, for whatever reason, Slakeman had sold them to the highest bidder. And now they were in the hands of the rogues, an army of such warriors the humans could never have fathomed.

A golden light appeared at the bottom of the hole, it flashed four times, then went completely dark. Palermo looked up to Black then nodded. Black grabbed hold of the rope that had been tied and wrapped around a nail just beneath the entrance of the hole. The rogue then reached up with his thick arms, punching in one of the rectangular ceiling panels from its base. Overhead there was a metal drum that Black laced the rope over and around. He let the length of the rope fall down to the base of the hole. Minutes ticked by and Black looked from the hole up to the drum then back down to the hole again.

Palermo, however, looked in another direction. He looked at the door that they'd come through. They were in the center building of the strip mall, the place that used to be an old hardware store. The windows were intact, but they'd been spray-painted on just like the walls. The door was relatively new as they'd installed a keypad lock system to keep out unwanted guests. But that wasn't what Palermo was concerned with. What bothered him was the scent he'd just picked up, the musky rainforest fragrance that could only belong to one other species. With his finger on the trigger he stepped away from the hole.

"Where you going?" Black asked him. "We're about to get to work here."

Palermo ignored him initially until he was standing right in front of the windows looking out into the night. He saw nothing and yet he knew it was there, he knew *they* were there. Raising his arm, ready to fire at will, he whispered, "We've got company."

\* \* \*

"Are you sure this is where we're supposed to be?" Paolo asked Jacques as they stood in the parking lot of what looked like a totally abandoned strip mall.

Around them was nothing but deserted land, dirt, and dirt, and even more dirt. There was no humidity, just what felt like a fleece blanket draped over them so that each time they breathed it was stale air that clogged their lungs instead of helping to reinflate them. It was dark, no street, so no streetlights. Luckily for them shifters possessed night vision all the time. Still, as Bas looked around he frowned, because there was absolutely nothing to see.

What probably used to be a thriving mall was about eighty thousand square feet, half of that consisting of parking lot while the rest was dilapidated buildings. About ten miles down the road, back in the direction they'd just come from, was an abandoned trailer park, units still sitting on cinder blocks. Now there was no one, not in the trailer park and not at the mall. The idea of a mass evacuation sat like a rock in his chest and his fists clenched at his sides.

"This is where the e-mail said to come. The drop-off is being done here, tonight," Bas said solemnly.

"Well, there ain't nothing here for us to intercept now, is there?" A shifter by the name of Kaz, who acted like Paolo's personal shadow, asked with a chuckle, only to receive a scathing glare from both Bas and Jacques.

Paolo wasn't as subtle with his reprimand, punching Kaz squarely in the chest. "If the FL says this is the spot, this is the spot!"

Kaz nodded tightly.

"Take those five with you and go around that side, check every building, and yell if you see something," Bas instructed Syfon. "You," he said, pointing to Paolo, "start down that end and work your way into the center."

As the shifters dispersed Bas looked to Jacques, and continued. "You and I will take the back."

"Kaz, you come with us." Jacques snapped his fingers at the tall, muscled shifter and picked up his pace behind Bas who had already begun walking around to the back of the building.

Bas's plan tonight had been to come here and intercept the drug shipment, to hopefully grab the ones doing the drop and take them back to the bunker for questioning. By morning he would have a complete written report to send to Rome. Something, a tiny slither at the base of his spine, told Bas things weren't going to go according to his plan.

They walked slowly, each of them looking around. Bas could sense the other cats around him, all ready to break free and hunt by way of their true nature. But they knew it wasn't allowed. Bas preferred to fight in human form whenever possible. And after his latest stay in D.C. he was more than adamant about the nonshifting rule he'd implemented the moment he'd taken charge of his own zone. Jacques understood that rule just as well as Bas did and made sure to enforce it throughout the training of all new guards on their team.

"They're here," Jacques announced, interrupting Bas's thoughts.

"Where?" Bas asked, shaking off the memory of D.C. as best he could and looking in the direction of his Lead Guard.

Jacques inhaled deeply. "The rogue stench is strong and coming from that middle unit there."

Jacques nodded and Bas pulled out his M9, holding it by his side as he moved. Jacques carried a similar sidearm as they'd both at one point been Marines. Bas was more comfortable with the M110 semiautomatic sniper rifle and carried one in the back of his truck at all times. But tonight called for something a little less formal, or at least that's what he thought as he approached the building.

They were about ten feet away from the gleaming gray steel door that was totally out of place in the otherwise condemned building.

"Pretty state-of-the-art for one building among so many others that don't even have doors, don't you think?" Jacques asked.

"Complete with a control pad and if I'm guessing correctly, by looking at the cord running around the door and the windows, a security system as well," Bas observed.

From his side Jacques coughed and frowned. "And the stench grows worse. I'm calling for the others," he said, turning his face a little more to the right so he could speak directly into the com link in the collar of his shirt. "Back lot, center building. Now!"

"Too late!" Bas yelled, raising his arm to take aim about two seconds before a hail of bullets blasted through the front window of the building they'd been approaching.

There was no cover to take so instead Bas and Jacques dropped to the ground, rolling until they were close enough to the building to stand with their backs against the wall. In the distance the others came, Bas could hear them although he couldn't scent them. The aroma that filled his nostrils—even though they were in the midst of battle—wasn't of shifters. Still, he knew the matter at hand took priority and thus lifted his arm, aimed the gun, and jumped through the front window of the building.

Jacques was right behind him yelling, "This way!"

Inside was dark and damp, glass crunching beneath their booted feet as they moved farther back.

"There's a light," Bas yelled. It was a faint light but it was there and so were the shadows moving quickly in the distance.

"Go!" Jacques yelled, but Bas hadn't realized he'd stopped moving.

They both ran toward the light. Bas saw another shadow and finally picked up the scent. Rogue. With a growl he turned in the opposite direction of the shadow and fired. There was yelling now, coming from all directions. Urgent words in their native tongue of Portuguese, more in English.

"*Fixe os pacotes! Fixe os pactoes!*" someone yelled.

"Shoot their asses now!" came another deep command.

"*Mover-se! Mover-se! Mover-se!*"

"Not so fast," Bas murmured as he turned the corner where he'd tracked the voices. Two burly men stood over a hole, one pulling on a rope with all his strength. With one shot he took out the first guy's right kneecap. With the other—and because this fool had thought he was faster pulling a blade from the side of his leg, lifting his arm he prepared to throw it—Bas shot clean through his wrist, hearing the knife fall to the floor with a clank.

The rope slipped from his grip, a whirling sound catching Bas's attention. He looked up, then down and cursed. "The stash is down here, Jacques!"

More footsteps sounded behind him as Bas acted on pure impulse, jumping down into the hole without another word.

"Dammit, Bas. Hold up!" he heard Jacques say from behind.

The two of them landed on their feet even though Bas figured they'd gone about fifty feet down into the earth. Dust kicked up beside them but their eyes opened wide at the sight of brick after brick of what Bas knew was the savior drug, created by the infamous rogue, Sabar. But that wasn't all he saw. There were two more sealed crates with large red, white, and black labels on the side. Kneeling down, Bas wiped away some of the dust to see the name and post office address for Comastaz Labs. Cursing, he slapped his palm on the box, the other hand fisting at his side.

Months ago Bas had reported to Rome and the other FLs that Comastaz Labs, the government-run facility that processed official FBI data and DNA by day and worked on nuclear weapon research by night, had been broken into.

"I want all of this taken to the bunker. Now!" Bas informed Jacques. "And find out where this tunnel leads."

Using the rope that still dangled down the hole, Bas climbed up, coming to the top to see two of his guards cuffing the men he'd shot. Bas went to the one who screamed like a girl because his knee had been blown to shreds. He put his foot on his chest and applied pressure until the man lay flat on his back. He was definitely a man and not a rogue. Both of them were or they would have shifted by now.

"Where are the others?" he asked. "Who the hell are you working for at that lab?"

"Fuck you, man! You shot me!" was the glowing retort.

Bas pointed his weapon between the man's eyes, leaning in closer and whispering menacingly, "I'm going to shoot you again if you don't answer my questions."

"We don't know!" the other guy yelled from behind Bas.

His wrist was dripping blood but it hadn't stopped Kaz from pulling his arms behind his back and putting cuffs on him. The man's dirty face dripped with sweat, the army fatigues he wore dingy and about three sizes too big for his body.

"How did you know to come here then?" Bas asked. "Who paid you to come here and pick up these boxes?"

"We just got a text that said to be here and that we'd be paid when the shipment was on the way," Hole-in-the-wrist told him.

"Shut up, you stupid snitch! We're both dead if we talk."

The one-knee bandit had a lot of rage in him and a stupid sense of bravado.

"These *porcos* don't know nothing! Just keep your mouth shut until we can get a lawyer!"

Bas grabbed him by the collar of his Van Halen shirt, lifting the man right up off the floor and plastering his back to a wall with a loud thud.

"No lawyer and no police. I'm gonna kill you and leave your rotting body in this desert if you don't give me a name. You got that?" Bas told him by way of his final compromise.

The amount of drugs he'd seen down in that tunnel was enough to wipe out at least a couple of neighborhoods in a metropolitan city, or worse, the drugs that were laced with the herb damiana could create such psychopathic people they'd wipe out the infected and the innocent in the span of a couple of weeks. But those two instances, as bad as they seemed, weren't what really had Bas worried. The crates from Comastaz were. He needed to know what was in them, who had shipped them to this location, and why. What he was certain of at this point was that seeing the name of this lab again, only months after first receiving reports of questionable dealings going on at the government facility, was no coincidence.

"There are more out here!" someone yelled from behind Bas. "Move out!"

Bas cursed, dropping the one-knee guy onto the floor and running back through the building to the window where he'd made his entrance. There were more out front, two of them that were now surrounded by his shifters.

"Stand down!" Paolo ordered, pointing his semiautomatic at them. The others in the circle, six more, held their guns trained on the two in the center as well.

Bas moved closer, his spine tingling with each step, the ripple of his cat pacing impatiently just beneath his skin.

His ears were trained on the matter at hand, the sounds of running feet, painful yells, cursed demands. His eyes zoned in on the two in the circle, who stood back to back, knees bent, arms extended as if they were ready to pounce at any moment.

Paolo continued to yell at them, the two prisoners yelling back. Tension rose from the asphalt like a thick haze of smoke. Eyes glimmered in the night, changing, shifting. Bas cursed. He ran toward the circle, gun raised.

"Stand the fuck down!" Paolo yelled once more.

Then there was a growl, a deep guttural sound that signaled everything was about to change. One of the prisoners fell to the ground on his knuckles and knees and Bas knew what was coming next.

Paolo fired instantly, the others around him following suit, and the bodies crumpled on impact, muted roars echoing through the night.

Bas came to a stop, looking down at the carnage, blood staining the asphalt, human bodies with shifter eyes crumpled and dying. Paolo and the others passing high-fives like they'd won the damned lottery.

"Enough!" Bas yelled, his patience long since vacating the premises. They'd been about to shift, which would have in turn caused his soldiers to shift, and then there would have been an all-out catfight in the parking lot. And not the kind a man generally wanted to see.

"Clean this up. Load them in the truck and get inside to help pack up everything in that tunnel," he instructed Paolo, who he knew was the ringleader of this particular group. The shifter had a penchant for egging on confrontations and while he was a good soldier, Bas knew it was well past time to rein him in. He'd already said as much to Jacques. A meeting in the next couple of days was now a priority.

But for now, they needed to clean up and get out of

here. The likelihood that someone had heard the commotion or the gunshots was slim since they were in such a remote part of town. Still, he didn't like them being out in the open with the desire to hunt too fertile in the minds of his shifters. The sooner they got out of here and back to Perryville, the better.

His thoughts turning in circles, he intended to go back in that building and interrogate or intimidate those dumbass wannabe runners some more while his men packed up everything they'd seized from the tunnel. But just as he turned around something stopped him dead in his tracks. Something that had been nagging at him since they'd taken to the road on this trip, possibly even before he'd left Perryville. He inhaled deeply, felt every muscle in his body stiffen. Then his cat rose up, stretching languidly, purring almost softly. Bas looked around, his eyes hurriedly scanning the perimeter and then he cursed once more.

Priya's heart beat like a dozen racehorses as she was jostled back and forth along the back floor of the SUV.

"Stupid. Stupid. Stupid." Over and over she berated herself for the split-second decision she'd made at the resort.

After finally finding her room she'd wanted to waste no time getting to Perry. But she needed to find him first. Unlike back in D.C. she didn't have the opportunity to follow him upstairs on the elevator then walk right up to his room and knock. That had been her plan with Reynolds until Perry had intervened. Now she'd wondered how she could get a face-to-face with the owner of this lavish resort. Easy, she'd thought, make a complaint about this lavish resort then demand to see the owner as the only source of recovery for the acting management. It was a foolproof plan, or so she thought as she exited her room, slipping her key card into her back pocket and carrying nothing else but the key chain she'd impulsively purchased at the gift shop in the lobby. It was a bronze replica of the Per-ryville logo she'd seen when she'd visited the Web site online to make her reservation. Priya had no idea why she'd purchased it as this was not a vacation and she didn't need to take home any souvenirs—all she needed was to get the information they wanted, by the time they'd dictated, or her brother would die. Just as she was headed to the front desk to lodge her complaint she glanced out the doors to see a line of vehicles: a dark-colored SUV in front and several smaller silver ones behind. After Lolo's warning about the black truck following her in D.C. and the two she'd seen on the street—along with Perry and his fine-ass bossy self—she should be leery of these vehicles altogether. Instead she felt the thrill of a connection, a link to the direction she needed to follow.

Forgoing the front desk Priya headed directly through the main lobby's glass doors. The scene reminded her somewhat of standing outside of the Reynolds Building earlier today, except there were more trucks and more men. Still, she was certain this type of entourage could only be for one person. And wasn't it just like the smug, well-dressed millionaire to require such an elaborate motorcade for his travels. She frowned at the complete waste of money and effort just to prove he had more money than most of the human population.

She was just about to head for the first vehicle when it pulled off. The second one behind it followed suit. The lights to the third one came on and she saw the wheels turning as if it were ready to pull off. There was only one more vehicle still idling so she had about two seconds to decide what to do.

"Now or never," she whispered before running across the walkway, barely missing two other females in bikinis who must have been on their way to the pool. The last vehicle's driver was preoccupied by the two bathing-suit beauties.

Priya took that opportunity to open the back door, saying a silent thank you that it had been unlocked. She slipped inside, pulling the door closed as quickly and quietly as she could. The screech of tires ahead most likely muffled the sounds she made as she pulled her legs up so she could fit on the floor. On the seat above there were blankets and duffel bags. She pulled them down covering herself completely and waited, holding her breath and praying she didn't get caught. The driver's door closed and the vehicle pulled off in the next two seconds.

They drove for what seemed like forever and she struggled to remain still. It wasn't a strong point of hers, keeping still, that is. She'd always been active, always wanted to keep moving, for fear that if she kept still, her father would notice her and decide he had yet another punching bag.

Perhaps she could have fallen asleep, it seemed like they were in the truck for so long. But a little thing called fear of being caught kept Priya's eyes wide open until the moment the vehicle came to a stop. She actually held her breath while the driver stepped out of the truck and she could hear other doors slamming in the distance. Never in her life had she gone this far for a story. Sure, she'd camped outside of Senator Baines's offices after they'd found his daughter's and his mutilated bodies months ago, just to be the first one at her paper to get an actual quote from his administrative assistant. Unfortunately, Reid Clack, who was currently assigned to the political section of the paper, had already interviewed the brother-in-law and the daughter's boyfriend. All of which trumped the vague and rehearsed statement the ditzy admin had tossed her when Priya had just about accosted her as

she'd jumped from the bushes near the front porch of
Baines's midtown home.

Then again, that story hadn't been nearly as important as this one. It didn't directly involve her and her
family. If she allowed herself to even think beyond that
point she would admit that some of the things that were
going on in D.C. did mysteriously link back to Reynolds and now to Perry. But none of that was Priya's main
priority.

She sat up when she thought she could hear footsteps
moving away from the vehicle. Peeping over the console
between the two front seats she could see nothing through
the front window but darkness. Not a very good sign since
she had no idea where she was at the moment and had no
weapon to help her should she actually be in a dangerous
predicament—more dangerous than being caught in this
truck by Sebastian Perry? she wondered.

Priya couldn't even see the men who'd gotten out of the
vehicles, it was so dark. Cursing, she kicked at the duffle
bags and the blanket she'd pulled over herself, then decided on second thought to look around in the vehicle for
a flashlight because this darkness was not going to help her
one bit. The first duffle bag had clothes in it, men's clothes,
she thought. The second bag also had clothes, but beneath
them were handcuffs and rope. Holding the cool metal in
her hands, Priya frowned, wondering what these were used
for. A salacious thought entered her mind and she quickly
dropped the cuffs back into the bag, shaking her head.
"Not even gonna go there," she whispered and kept looking
through the bag. No flashlight.

Cursing again, she climbed into the front passenger
seat and opened the glove compartment. Surely everyone
kept a flashlight in there. Everyone but whoever owned
and drove this particular vehicle. Without another choice
she opened the door and stepped out into the night air.

She was in some type of parking lot, Priya surmised after looking around. Old condemned buildings across from her. Why would Perry drive all this way to come here? A dark, run-down place with nobody around. Whatever the reason it couldn't be good and she figured she had two options—get back in the car and wait out this entire scene then return to the resort and try to talk to Perry again, or walk around until she found him and his men and figured out what they were doing here.

The alley back in D.C. had been dark and the men there had no doubt figured the darkness would cloak what they didn't want anyone to see. Why wouldn't Perry think the same thing this go-around?

Her decision made, she started walking forward since she was almost positive the footsteps she'd heard had moved away from the vehicle. In no time there was more movement and she could see men dressed in all black running in different directions. She didn't know which way to follow but went with the ones closest to her, sticking close to the walls as they moved about. They seemed to be looking for something, going in and out of the buildings, kicking down doors, or breaking windows out. She prayed this whole trip hadn't been about vandalizing a vacant property, even though that would make a great human-interest story—rich real estate mogul trashes old buildings in his spare time. That would be one hell of a headline.

Her thoughts were interrupted when the men she'd been following all ran right past the building she'd ducked inside of for cover.

"They found them!" she heard one of them yell.

"Go! Go! Go!" another one yelled.

Okay, whatever was meant to go down apparently was. Priya took off running after the last man had passed her hiding place. She thought she'd waited too long, especially since she clearly did not run as fast as they did. She had a membership at the local YMCA but rarely used it; now that her lungs were on fire and her thighs screaming for mercy, she thought maybe she should make more of an effort to use the membership after all.

By the time she'd made it around to what she thought might be the back of the buildings, she was totally out of breath and she thought she'd heard gunshots. At first she didn't see anyone, then again her eyes were blurred with the sweat dripping from her brow. Then she heard them, yelling and cussing, threatening to kill someone. Fidgeting at her pockets she looked for her Mace, cursing because she hadn't brought her purse with her. Which also meant she didn't have her cell phone to call the police in the event someone actually did end up dead tonight.

Then all of a sudden, the shouting stopped. She ran ahead, still ducking in and out of the open doorways the others had left before her. Now she was actually appreciating their penchant for vandalism. She moved until she was one building away from where a group of them stood. Shadows of men were all she could make out, until he spoke.

"Enough!" he'd yelled.

And Priya froze. It was Perry. He hadn't spoken to her in this tone, still she recognized it instantly.

"Clean this up. Load them in the truck and get inside to help pack up everything in that tunnel," he continued and warmth flooded Priya's body.

Sure, it was really hot out in this dry night air and she'd just run what felt like a country mile so it was safe to say her body temperature was already running on high. But this was different, the heat swirled around and inside her, centering in strategic locations—at the tips of her breasts and deep in her center like its own pulsing heartbeat.

She swallowed, willing herself to get a grip. Her eyes

had zoomed in on a particular shadow, the taller one, with the broad shoulders and locked. It was him, she knew it even though she couldn't see the butter tone of his skin, the silkiness of his hair or his . . . eyes . . .

As if they were magnets drawn inexplicably to her, and even though she stood hidden in the shadows of that building, his eyes found hers and they were not human.

# Chapter 9

"No," Bas said, a low rumble vibrating from his chest as he walked toward what he prayed was not really there.

It wasn't Mariah, he knew this for two reasons: one, the scent was different and two, Mariah was dead. Still, it was a human, there was no doubt. The presence had been with him since he'd been back at the resort, in the distance but within reach, just like before.

All at once, or rather the moment their gazes locked, he knew exactly where both were coming from. This shit had been distracting him all damn night. He hadn't been able to focus entirely at the briefing or during the ride down here, his mind had constantly gone back to that feeling that someone else was near, watching him, waiting for him. Her scent was spicy and hovered like a thick cloud over him every waking moment since he'd first pulled her into the hotel room in D.C. But he hadn't believed for one moment she was in Sedona. Why would she be in Sedona? It was foolish to even consider that a possibility, even more foolish for him to entertain the thought that yet another female had followed him.

Still, the feeling persisted. The scent had permeated every part of him, inciting his highly trained-to-be-nonexistent cat into a not so gentle stalking. Bas had tried to ignore it, tried like hell to convince himself that he wasn't one of those shifters who got all caught up in one female's scent or craved her proximity. He'd never been that kind of shifter and wasn't about to start now and especially not for *this* goddamned female!

"Need some help, sir?" one of his soldiers asked from behind.

Bas shook his head, holding up a hand signaling the shifter to remain where he was. "I got this," was his tight reply.

Glass crunched beneath his booted feet as he stepped into the building where she still stood just inside the doorway. She hadn't tried to duck out of sight when he'd noticed her. Would he have turned away, dismissing these feelings once more if she had? Maybe, but that didn't matter now, since he was about three feet away from her and his fingers tingled to reach out and touch her. His jaw ticked with the effort of clenching his teeth the whole walk over here and now that he was this close, he felt like he was definitely going to get lockjaw if he didn't speak soon.

"What the hell are you doing here?" were his words of choice.

"Seeing exactly what you told me didn't exist," was her quick retort.

"First," Bas said, taking a step toward her. "You're not seeing anything out here in the dark. And second, this ridiculous crusade of yours is going to get you killed."

"Are you threatening me?"

He was right in her face now, only about an inch separating their bodies from touching. His hummed with an eerie anticipation for that connection to happen sooner rather than later, and her eyes filled with what Bas was positive was desire. Through her T-shirt her nipples had hardened, her arousal mixed with her already intoxicating scent was enough to make his human half feel more than a little weak at the knees, while his cat sat upright, roaring an unfamiliar call to Bas's ears.

Reaching out he grabbed her by the arm, pulling her flush against his chest. There was a moan somewhere in that space, from which one of them Bas couldn't be sure. "Not yet, Ms. Drake. But you're begging for it," he told her through clenched teeth.

"Sir, you ready to roll?" Jacques asked from the doorway Bas had just walked through.

Bas sensed the moment the shifter's eyes locked on the female and felt a glimmer of rage rippling through him.

"Where'd she come from? Was she with—"

Lifting an arm, his hand palm up to Jacques to silence the shifter's next words, Bas replied, "She's with me. Get the trucks loaded and let's go."

Years of service and friendship held Jacques silent, no doubt, still Bas knew he'd have to figure out how to explain Priya's arrival to his team. But first, he needed the nosy reporter to explain it to him.

Once Jacques had returned outside, Bas, his fingers still gripping Priya's arm, looked down at her. "You're going to ride back with me and keep your mouth shut. That is not a request, Ms. Drake."

He could see the conflict in her. She wanted to fight back, to shove him away and most likely curse him in that sharp, pinpointing way she had. But she was also smart enough to recognize her own predicament. If she'd followed them out here, which Bas doubted, but couldn't completely rule out, then how was she going to get back? And where was she going back to, Perryville or D.C.? That wasn't an easy question, but Bas had already decided on the answer, she was staying with him. He wasn't letting her out of his sight, in spite of the ravenous pacing his cat was presently doing.

"Lead the way, sir," she replied, sarcasm all but dripping

from the last word—the last word that had his dick jumping to immediate attention.

With an obvious frown and a low growl that he kept buried deep in his chest, Bas headed for the door, pulling her behind him. He didn't release his hold on her until he was back at his SUV and she was buckled in the seat right across from him.

The ride back was done mostly in silence. Bas remained deep in his own thoughts, more than aware of the female's presence just a few inches away from him. There was no possible way he could ignore her. His dick was so hard, his need for her so great he was having a hard enough time breathing. Clenching and unclenching his fingers at his sides he cursed inwardly at the urge to take her right on the backseat. His temples throbbed as he thought of having her out of those tight-ass jeans, his dick buried hilt-deep in her wet pussy in about ten seconds flat.

She'd been staring out the window, acting as if she were trying to figure out her next move, when Bas knew instinctively lust was driving a similar heat path up and down her spine. He could tell by how she shifted in her seat every few seconds, adjusting her legs, making sure her thighs rubbed together, no doubt applying as much pressure to her clit as she possibly could under the circumstances. He ached to help her out in that situation.

But his duty held him still.

"I told you this was not a game," he said finally, his words stilted by the intense heat radiating throughout his body.

"You have no idea what this is for me, Mr. Perry," she snapped back instantly.

Bas was quiet a moment, taking in what she'd said and knowing it was absolutely true.

"Then tell me," he insisted, his voice a little closer to normal. "Tell me why hours ago I watched you being dragged away by some guy on a street in D.C. and now you show up across the country snooping around where you don't belong. Tell me there's a good-ass explanation for why you insist on behaving so irrationally for a fucking story!"

Normal had lost its course somewhere along the way and now he was just plain angry.

"I don't have to tell you anything," she shot back.

Bas reached for her then, pulling her across the seat after snatching the seat belt free. She was just about in his lap as his hands gripped her shoulders tightly.

"Oh yes, Ms. Drake, you do have to tell me. Or so help me I'm going to fuck your tight little body in this backseat and then I'm going to take your ass to the airport and personally put you on the next plane back to D.C." He spoke through clenched teeth.

She opened her mouth to speak and Bas simply reacted. Leaning forward he took her lips, not in a kiss, but a heat suckle of first the top, then the bottom one which was only slightly plumper. As his dick throbbed with the intense pleasure he let his tongue trace a line around her mouth as she gasped.

"Tell me to and I'll stop," he whispered over her lips.

This time when she prepared to speak he pressed forward again, taking her tongue and sucking like his life depended solely on the sweetness of her. She squirmed beneath his grasp, her breasts pressing against his chest, her hips moving seductively over his engorged length.

When finally Bas pulled away, whispering urgently, "Tell me," once more, she turned her head, her breathing erratic.

"Stop," was her breathy reply. "Just stop. This is not what I want. It's not why I'm here."

Like a splash of cold water her words rained over Bas and he instantly released her. First and foremost, he had never forced himself on a female and never would. Even though her body screamed the exact opposite of her words, that's all Bas needed to hear.

"I can't help you if you don't trust me enough to tell me the truth."

"How can you ask me to trust you when I don't even know you?" she replied after moving back across the seat. "And it's not even about you, not directly, I mean." She sighed and then let her head fall back against the seat, closing her eyes momentarily. "I just need to get this story and I need to do it by the end of the month. Can you help with that, Mr. Perry?"

Bas didn't know what to say to that. He wanted to say yes, that he'd do whatever he could to help her with whatever she needed. But he didn't know if that was true.

She was a reporter. A damned tenacious, persistent, and sexy-as-hell reporter who was out to expose the shifters and he should simply kill her to remove that risk. He was almost positive if he called Rome that's what the Assembly Leader would order him to do. While the Stateside Assembly was a peaceful organization, trying to live in a world where humans believed they were the dominant species, they were also entering into a time of war. Exposure now could be more than detrimental to not just the shifters, but also the humans.

So, if she wanted his help to tell the world about his kind, no, he could not do that. He also knew that to say those words to her, right at this moment would not benefit either of them.

Luckily, the vehicle had come to a stop and Jacques now stood holding the door for Bas to get out.

\* \* \*

At Perryville Bas climbed out of the backseat first as Jacques stared at him expectantly.

"I'm taking her up to my suite. Secure the prisoners and the cargo. Don't question the detainees any more tonight, let them stew for a while. I want everything found in those crates photographed and identified. Schedule a conference call with the FLs for seven tomorrow morning. You and I will meet in the conference room at six thirty. I don't want to be disturbed until then," he finished, giving his Lead Enforcer a nod of his head.

Jacques returned the nod. "I'll walk you around to the back entrance."

Bas moved around the truck to the passenger side and opened the door for Priya.

She didn't hesitate but stepped her first leg out of the truck then followed with the next. When she stood in front of him she simply stared up into his eyes. A tilt of her head said what she saw wasn't what she'd been looking for. At that, Bas gave a small smile, before taking her arm once more.

As Bas and Priya walked, Jacques remained in front of them. The soldier never turned back to look at them or to say a word. There was a back entrance into Perryville for when they had detainees that needed to go to the bunker or just didn't want to be seen by the guests. Double steel doors that required a combination to get inside, opened at Jacques's command. Bas and Priya stepped inside and moved down the long hallway with its gray-painted cinder block walls and tiled floor.

Only when they were on the elevator heading up to his suite did Bas relax, minutely. A few seconds later when the elevator doors opened again, he guided Priya off, moving swiftly to the door that would let them into his suite. She followed silently. Until they were inside.

"Look," she began as soon as he released his grip on

her and she'd spun around to face him. "I don't know who you think you are, or who those drones out there have pumped you up to believe you are, but I'm not on your payroll. So the orders and the dragging me around stops here. You offered your help, but I get it if you cannot actually give it."

Bas didn't respond. Instead, he kept walking through the large living area, past the small office section, and straight back to the bedroom, knowing she would follow him. Once in his room he grabbed at the bottom of his shirt, pulling until it was free of his pants and up over his head. Tossing it onto one of the leather chairs that faced the floor-to-ceiling window across from his bed, he turned to face her.

"So you didn't come here to be ordered around," he said in a voice that was practiced calm and smooth edges. It was his seduction voice, the one he used on the rare instances when he'd needed the release of sex.

The pulse at the base of her neck quickened and she folded her arms over the delectable mounds of her chest. "No. I didn't," she replied in a much less confident voice.

Bas nodded and sat on one of the chairs. He lifted one foot and removed his boot, did the same with the other, all without looking up at her. She was nervous, the musky incense-like scent mixing with the spicy aroma she held naturally. Bas inhaled it all, letting it move through his body with slow efficiency, almost relishing the moment it touched his cat.

He stood then, removing his belt, and unfastening the buckle of his pants. Together with his boxer briefs he pushed all the material down his thighs, stepping out of them as they pooled at his feet. Then he stood tall, naked, and looked at her.

She sucked in a breath.

Good, he thought with an inward smile.

He walked across the room, then took her hands and unfolded her arms from her chest. Keeping his eyes locked on hers—she couldn't look away if she tried and Bas knew she wouldn't make that effort—he flattened her palms against his chest.

"I will help you," he stated softly. "You want to see if I'm really a cat beneath the human clothes?"

She licked her lips and Bas instinctively mimicked the motion.

"Do I feel like a cat, Priya?" he continued, taking a step closer to her, until his erection jutted forward, touching the soft cotton of her shirt just beneath her breasts.

The minute she opened her mouth to speak, Bas pounced, taking her mouth in a kiss so hungry his cat scratched at the surface, reaching for its own release instantaneously. She couldn't reply verbally, could only react physically and that reaction was not what Bas had expected. It was so much . . . more.

# Chapter 10

Priya felt like she was sinking. In her mind she thought of stepping into quicksand and going down, down, down, slowly, but most assuredly. Beneath her fingers and palms was the taut smoothness of his skin and beneath that, the steady heartbeat that rapped a quick rhythm almost matching her own.

His tongue scraped along hers as if he were tasting something he'd craved forever, and she moaned softly. Hands much stronger and much larger than she'd assumed had cupped her face about a second before his lips had begun their brutal assault. Now he held her in place, in truth he held her upright. Because with the very naked Sebastian Perry kissing her the way he was, Priya's entire body had turned to molten lava. Every part of her was on fire, her knees weak, her spine tingling, fingertips burning.

She moved her hands because if this was going to be her one shot at touching him all over she wanted to take full advantage. Or would he parade around naked in front of her again? She didn't believe that and didn't want to waste time considering it. Instead, she let her hands travel to his shoulders, broad and strong; she gripped him while tilting her head to deepen their kiss. Biceps roped with muscle greeted her next touch as her hands moved downward. Back up again she touched what she could of his back, but he was much broader than her arms were wide and she barely scraped the side of his shoulder blades. He radiated strength, all over, including the persistent punch of his thick arousal to her midsection.

She wanted to touch him there. The thought came quickly and she lost her breath with anticipation. Her hands moved to his torso then, thumbs rubbing along the sculpted board of his abs, down and back to tight buttocks. Then they were in front of him once more, moving of their own accord to where they wanted most to be. Her palms—shaking slightly but figuring it was too late to turn back—wrapped around his length, feeling the amazing heat that emanated from there.

Bas sucked in a breath at her touch and the connection of their lips was broken. For endless seconds they simply stared at each other, his gray gaze holding her plain old brown eyes captive.

"Put your hot little mouth there," he told her, dared her almost.

Priya wanted to pull away. He knew she wouldn't do it, knew without a doubt that she would not go to her knees and suck his thick hard dick, no matter how much she really wanted to. In that instant she added that to the list of things she was beginning to hate about Sebastian Perry: he knew too goddamned much.

Priya was no stranger to men. She'd cashed in her virginity card the night of the senior prom in a dismal initiation into adulthood. But none of her previous exploits, even the ones that had come much later in her adult life and ended with pretty strong orgasms on her part, could compare to the desire ripping through her body right now like a tropical storm.

Bas stood absolutely still, like a beautifully intricate sculpture of everything masculine, looking down at her with a smirk that all but called her a coward. She tightened her grip on him, holding firm at the base of his arousal as she glared up at him.

"And what will I get in return?" was her taunting question. It was probably a bad idea to play this game, with this man, but she didn't care. She wasn't in the mood to let him win another round.

The corners of his mouth tilted in a half smile as he lifted a hand to trace along the line of her lips. "It'll get you whatever you want, pretty girl."

On impulse her tongue snaked out to lick the tip of his finger on its trek across one more time. Bas's smile instantly disappeared. Emboldened by that reaction she licked around the pad of his finger before lowering her mouth, taking the digit in, sucking hard, then pulling back slowly. She watched him as she did this, his eyes growing darker, his dick pulsating in her hands, moisture seeping at the tip.

His hips thrust forward and she stroked his length, all the while suckling his finger. He pumped into her hand with more forcefulness, more rhythm and he reached up, clasping the back of her head, guiding her until they were totally in sync. Her nipples were so hard it was painful, her center throbbing, the lips of her vagina damp with desire.

"Pretty little Priya, with the hot-ass mouth. I wonder if the rest of you will be this hot," he whispered.

She would not try to respond, was positive she couldn't, considering her position and the fact that she just might tell him exactly what was hot on her right now.

"I wonder if I throw you on this bed if you'll open like a pretty flower for me and let me taste your sweet nectar."

She closed her eyes, couldn't help it. The choices were to either cut off the eye connection they had going on, or do as he said and lie on that bed, spreading her legs open wide for him. Closing her eyes didn't completely help since she was still licking his finger and palming his dick.

None of which were things she should have been doing, or had even considered doing when she'd boarded a plane to come out here.

"Do you want me to taste you, Priya?" he asked, pulling his hand slowly from her mouth. "Open your eyes and tell me what you want."

Priya opened her eyes. She saw the lust plainly in his darkening gaze, in the way he licked his lips as he watched her, circling his hips as she stroked him. Her thumb brushed over his tip, felt the dampness of his arousal and she clenched her teeth.

"No," she said with a snap, then yanked her hands away from his dick. Not so sure about her movements and not at all confident she wouldn't reach out for him again or actually fall on the bed and beg him to take her, she backed away.

"As I told you before, this is not why I'm here." Her hands were shaking and she rubbed them up and down her thighs in an effort to stabilize her raging hormones.

"Do you want me to get down on all fours?"

He was sarcastic and he was serious and she hated both of those facts. She did not believe Sebastian Perry was a cat. Hell, she didn't even know if she believed in the whole cat-and-man thing. Sure, she'd seen some weird-ass eyes in the alley, but that could easily have been attributed to contact lenses, they came in all colors now. As for the story about the bank robbery, she wasn't completely sold on that either. This is why she'd never thought to write a story on any of this, not until the e-mails started. Now, she had no other choice but to investigate, to uncover and to hopefully reveal whatever it was Roman Reynolds and his friends wanted kept a secret.

"If that's going to turn you into a cat, fine," she said wearily. "If not, you can answer my questions honestly and I can get out of your life forever. It's that easy."

"I'd rather we both get on all fours, naked, together," he continued.

He hadn't moved, still stood in front of her in all his naked glory. And dammit, it was definitely glorious. She wanted him inside her, his dick, his tongue, whatever, she wanted it. And she cursed herself for that weakness, even if she had no intention of ever acting on it.

"You're not as alluring as you think you are," she said, in direct contradiction to what her body was feeling.

"And you're not that smart," was his quick retort. "At least not as smart as I thought you were."

"Wait a goddamned minute," she began, anger slowly pressing arousal out of the picture. "You are not going to stand here and talk to me like that!"

"No. I'm not," he replied, turning away from her. "I'm going to take a shower and get ready for bed. I've had a long day."

"I'm not finished talking to you."

"Then we can finish the conversation in the shower," he told her nonchalantly just before his delicious body disappeared through an opening in the wall.

She was not taking a shower with him! Not even if her life depended on it. And she wasn't going to storm out of this room, closing the door with a slam behind her, telling Sebastian Perry to kiss her ass in the process—because Malik's life did depend on this.

With resignation she followed Perry through the opening in the wall because she did not see a door anywhere and wondered what he'd done to make this opening appear.

This was his bedroom and there was a big bed against a long wall, a silver duvet on top that looked almost too decadent to belong to a man. That had her turning to survey the entire room. The one she'd kind of ignored when she'd had to follow him back here and was then distracted by the . . . ah . . . nakedness.

Charcoal-gray, white, and red was the color scheme. A little different for a guy, she thought. The furniture was sleek, expensive, and contemporary. The king-sized platform bed had an ornate frame of leather and mirrors, red silk draped around its border. The bed was flanked by matching end tables with lamps that looked as if they were made of aluminum. The floor was a highly glossed mahogany tile. The walls consisted of charcoal-colored slates, some that opened as doors, like the one he went through to the bathroom and others that supported marble tabs that held statues and picture frames. She moved closer to one that wasn't too tall for her to reach and picked up one of the frames. Frowning, she surveyed the white background with the glob of black in its center that looked strangely like those cards a psychiatrist would flash, asking what's the first thing to come to your mind. This one in particular reminded her of a teardrop. Beneath it was a simple letter M. Priya ran a finger over the picture wondering at its true meaning.

Finishing with that little mind trip and wanting to complete her search of the room before he returned, she put the picture down and moved to the window that for some reason had been calling to her. Even in the dark the view was astonishing. The mountains in the distance looked close enough for her to reach out and touch. The resort was very well lit and probably guarded like a fortress, she thought, considering the men Bas traveled with.

The men, she recalled, hadn't entered the building with them. The men had been standing in a circle taking orders from Bas a few seconds before he turned to her with those eerie yellow eyes. That memory had her gasping for breath.

"Afraid of heights?" he asked from behind her.

Priya turned slowly, trying to prepare herself to see him again, praying with all she had inside that he wasn't still naked. When she looked at him her mind whispered, *thank you, thank you, thank you.*

He'd wrapped a towel around his waist, his shoulders still glistening with beads of moisture.

"I'm not afraid of heights, Mr. Perry, and I'm definitely not afraid of you," she retorted.

To her dismay he sighed. "No. You're not afraid of me. And you're not afraid to fly across the country and jump into one of my trucks to follow me to god knows where. You weren't afraid of trying to break into Rome's room and you're not afraid to stand in this room with me totally alone, trying to ignore what I want to do to you."

"All you have to do is answer my questions," she said, realizing his words were true and that she should be afraid.

Bas shook his head. "You're in my bedroom and I'm wearing a towel. I think you can call me Bas now. Mr. Perry is my father."

He moved to another one of those panels in the wall, touching it with the tips of his fingers then waiting as it shifted to the side and he could pull out a drawer. With his back to her he pulled a black tank top over his head. The towel hit the floor, tight buttocks flexed as he bent slightly, pulling black boxer briefs up until they were covered. When he faced her again all Priya could do was gulp. Even not-so-naked the sight of him was attempting its own brand of torture on her libido.

"I just need to know what's going on, Bas," she said quietly. The trip cross-country, the adrenaline of hiding in the back of that truck going who knew where, then finding a small army of men in the dark desert, was beginning to take its toll.

She wouldn't let kissing-the-naked-as-a-jaybird-sexy-guy take precedence in her exhaustion, even though the memory was still punctuated in her mind.

He moved to stand beside his bed then, reaching to

pull the duvet down. Red sheets, more like the dark crimson of blood were beneath the fancy silver material. He fluffed a pillow before looking back up at her.

"It's a story, that's all. My guess is that someone has you working on this story for whatever reason. That someone is not your boss, which puts you in a precarious situation. But you don't seem to mind putting yourself in that same predicament more than once. I offered you my help before. The offer still stands." Before she could reply he held up a hand. "It's not answers from me you need, Priya. That's not going to completely fix your situation and I think you know that."

She refused to believe that.

"Tonight, Bas, tell me what I saw tonight," she insisted.

Priya moved to stand directly across from him on the other side of the bed.

He raised a brow. "You're tenacious enough to chase this story, no matter what I say. I'm guessing that's why you were chosen over any other reporter at the *Post*. Tenacious and ambitious, two traits that could easily get you killed."

"Don't waste your time threatening me. If you were going to kill me you would have done it already, or had one of your goons do it for you." She sighed with exasperation because this was getting her nowhere and she was tired of running in circles with him. "You don't think we have a right to know if something else is out there? If we need to protect ourselves?" she asked.

"There were men out there tonight, just like you saw before. You flew all the way out here to see more men, when you could have stayed in D.C. and seen the same thing."

"Men with yellow eyes?"

"Ever heard of contact lenses, Priya? Your big story is riding on the sighting of a man wearing yellow contacts just like Michael Jackson wore in his music video and vampires wear on television and in the movies. I really don't see you making big headlines with that."

He climbed into bed then, reaching over to touch a tablet that had been sitting beside the telephone. When they'd been cast into darkness his voice sounded once more. "You can finish your searching in the other room and come to bed when you're finished. Unless you'd like to take the couch."

"I'm not staying here with you. I'm leaving," she announced, turning and extending her arms in front of herself to keep from bumping into anything as she made her way to the door.

She was just about to step out of his room when his words, spoken so quietly she almost missed them, stopped her. "I can't let you go."

No matter how much Bas hated it, his words had been absolutely true.

He couldn't let Priya Drake out of his suite, or out of Perryville for that matter, because she wasn't going to stop digging for this story. She wasn't going to stop trying to prove that cat people existed. The really bad part about the situation was that she was absolutely correct. Shifters did exist, which meant if she continued to dig she would eventually find exactly what she was looking for.

And when that happened, Bas would have only one choice.

He lay on his back, eyes closed, feeling her presence still in his suite and wondering what was going through her mind. He'd given her permission to look around and he knew she would do precisely that. But she wouldn't find anything, primarily because she didn't know where to look. Not only were the walls designed to give a sleek look to his private rooms, they were specially equipped to hide what Bas didn't want anyone walking inside to see.

His safe, his file cabinets, his private computer with all the files regarding the Mountain Zone's laws and progress reports and anything at all that connected him to the Gungi. All she was going to find out there was a desk with a computer that she would never hack into and even if she did, it had nothing but Perryville information on it. X had even installed an encrypting backup system to all the FLs' computers that wiped out the entire history of searched Web sites each time the computer was shut down. Hell, Bas didn't even have pictures of his family in there.

Inhaling deeply, Bas tried desperately to clear the last couple of days from his mind. At this moment he wanted anything other than to have spotted her watching him at that fund-raiser and then attempting to get into Rome's room. He wanted to have never met Priya Drake and he damn sure wanted to never have tasted her.

Her lips were soft and gave just a hint of the sweetness that dwelled within her. Sweetness he was sure had been hidden beneath her stubborn and prickly exterior. But it was there, banked beneath the fiery heat of her gaze, the soft whimper of her voice when his tongue had stroked along hers. And when she'd touched him . . . damn! His hands clenched into fists.

"It makes sense to send me into the other room when you know there's nothing for me to find," she stated from the doorway a short while after she'd left.

"It was your choice to look anyway," Bas replied, lifting his fingers to squeeze the bridge of his nose. He didn't want to inhale too deeply now, she was entirely too close. Any more of her scent in his lungs and he was going to pick her up and fuck her where she stood.

"Then why not offer me the choice to leave?" she pressed.

How could he tell her that wasn't possible, without explaining why and without admitting to himself that the "why" was beyond even the threat of the shifters' exposure?

"Then you really would have come all this way for nothing." When she didn't reply he continued. "Are you going to sleep here or in the living room?"

*Living room. Living room.* Please, if there was a high deity and it was likely to grant wishes to even the shifter species, he prayed for her to sleep in the living room.

"I didn't come all the way here to become another notch on your sexual-conquest post," she replied tartly.

"And I'm not asking you for sex." No matter how much he and the cat waiting impatiently within wanted exactly that from her. "Sleep is high on my itinerary right now," he continued. Sleep or another shower where he would no doubt ease himself of the pounding ache his erection had become.

She didn't speak again until she was lying on the bed, stiff as a board and making absolutely sure to stay as far away from him as possible. Her clothes remained on, he knew, even though he didn't turn to verify. He'd heard her shoes hit the floor and the exhale of the breath that meant she was making this decision under duress.

"If you wanted a female in your bed I doubt seriously that you had to resort to kidnapping," she whispered into the darkness.

"You came to Perryville of your own accord. You followed me and my men on a business trip and then you accompanied me up here to my suite. Not sure how that translates to kidnapping but remind me to give Nick a call in the morning to check the law on this issue."

"How can we protect ourselves if we don't know what we're up against?"

Bas didn't reply. For once in his life, he didn't know how to.

She sighed and the room grew silent once more.

Bas heard each breath she took, he imagined the rise
and fall of her breasts as she did so and slipped his hand
beneath the sheet, cupping his length in his own hand this
time, jerking hard before cursing himself. There was no
way he was going to jerk off while lying right next to her,
no goddamned way.

"If they exist, the truth will come out. Now, or later, it
will come out," she said quietly.

It was his turn to go still, his teeth gritting so hard his
temples throbbed, because she was absolutely right.

# Chapter 11

The dream had come again, like a thief to steal his night's rest. Six shifters had circled her, moving each time she did, growling each time she screamed. It was a standoff, one they knew they would win. As for her, she had no idea what she was looking at or how they would hurt her. All she knew was fear, instinctive and so potent it pounded against her chest. Tears blurred her eyes but didn't fall.

He thought that maybe she'd cried out louder before, maybe her face had been streaked with tears, but no, not this time.

She didn't cry and she did not try to run, probably knew it was futile. Instead she squared her shoulders and shouted something to one of them. The shifter lunged forward as if to take her right then, but it was stopped by a bigger cat, a stronger jaguar with more years of hunting experience. This one moved closer to her and she watched it in anticipation. He could see the moment she resigned herself to her fate and the exact second she decided to fight instead of succumb. She jumped at the cat, knife in hand, bringing it down with an aim to the shifter's head. Unfortunately, the cat was faster and it moved so that the knife slid almost painlessly down its flanks. Then it came up on its hind legs and wrapped its powerful jaws around her neck.

She didn't have a moment to scream and no tear ever fell from her eyes—her brown eyes.

It wasn't Mariah, Bas thought with a start, his eyes jerking open while the rest of his body remained still in his bed. It was still night—early morning he guessed—and her eyes still flashed in front of him, now along with the rest of her face being pelted by the rain as he'd had to bury her body once more. How many times would he have to do this, would he have to relive this? But this time was different, he reminded himself. This time it had been Priya's body.

As if somehow aware that he was thinking so intently about her, she turned over onto her side, hands cradling her face so that she looked innocent against the pillows of his bed. She was here, in his bed, Bas thought momentarily, trying to play catch-up from the real world to the dream then back to reality once more.

He touched a finger to her cheek, let it slide down to the line of her jaw, watched it shake as it moved and he sighed heavily. She couldn't stay here, he thought to himself. And he couldn't let her leave. Rome would have her killed because she was a threat to them, and whoever it was that had put her up to this would probably do the same if she didn't deliver. He had no other choice.

It felt good to have a reason behind his actions, an excuse to do what was becoming all too natural where she was concerned. Bas moved closer to her, being as careful as possible as he scooped her body into his, wrapping his arms tightly around her. She made a noise and he held his breath, knowing that in about two seconds she might hurl some sarcastic remark at him. Instead, to his shock and pleasure, she snuggled closer into him, her palms flattening on his bare chest, her cheek following as she rested her head against him. Bas kissed the top of her head, inhaled her scent deeply and actually felt it permeate his bloodstream.

She would not leave Perryville and nobody would hurt her, not even his Assembly Leader.

Later that morning, Bas sat quietly at the head of the conference table. He'd turned his chair so he could look out the window while he waited for the early morning meeting to get underway. In the chair to his right, where he always sat during meetings was Jacques, looking contemplative and mildly concerned.

Jacques was a quiet shifter; he kept his opinions to himself and generally dealt only with the facts. Jacques had stayed in the Marines longer than Bas had, completing two tours of duty including Desert Storm. He'd come from a large family where both parents were still alive and strong in the shifter community. And yet Jacques hadn't left Sedona in the ten years he'd been there with Bas. He was a six-foot-three-and-a-half-inch-tall man with mixed heritage as his father was French and had migrated to the U.S. a few years after World War II. Armil Germain had met and married Renee Jones, a beautiful African-American shifter after meeting her during a protest in Washington, D.C. Now, the Germains resided in Maryland while Armil worked with the Department of Justice. Armil and Rome were working very closely together to help shape the Stateside Assembly. But Jacques preferred to keep himself separate from his parents' endeavors. Actually, there were times when Bas thought Jacques was keeping himself separate from the entire world.

"What are you going to do with her?" Jacques asked in his monotone manner, interrupting Bas's thoughts.

Bas didn't immediately respond because he didn't have an answer to that question. Or rather he did but wasn't quite ready to discuss it, even with his second in command. "For now she stays here," was his reply. "And nobody needs to know that she's here."

The last was said as Bas turned, meeting Jacques's gaze.

Jacques didn't even blink. "Is that wise?"

Bas wanted to shrug but he usually shied away from the callous response. "It is how I want it to be."

Jacques nodded. "She booked a room and used her credit card to secure it. If someone begins looking for her she'll be easy to trace here."

Flattening one hand on the table, his other on the arm of the leather high-backed chair he sat in, Bas agreed. "Check her out of the room before noon today and book her on a flight back to D.C."

Again, Bas looked to the window where the sun was beginning its glorious appearance. The sky was absolutely brilliant with color, gold and orange spheres spreading over the red buttes that stretched to the mountains. This moment of the day had always been Bas's favorite. Each morning he awoke in time to sit on his deck and enjoy the solitary glory. It reenergized him, giving him purpose to continue on another day, when it would have been so easy to sleep through it all.

This morning he'd left his room earlier than was necessary, disturbed by the pure bliss he'd been experiencing in the hours before with Priya wrapped tightly in his arms. He enjoyed the feel of her softness against him, the warmth of her breath over his skin, and of course her scent. He was enjoying that way too much, he thought with finality. For a brief moment he'd thought of cancelling all his morning meetings and staying with her, keeping an eye and hopefully his hands on her. But Bas had never shirked his duty before and wasn't about to start now. Correction, he thought glumly, he'd only shirked his duty once and had sworn to never let that happen again.

"Put a trace on her cell," he said to Jacques as an afterthought. "I want to know who she's calling or texting every second of the day. She has a laptop in her bag, and I want to know what she's doing on that as well."

Jacques didn't flinch at the directives, but he did go a step further. "GPS?"

Bas nodded. "Yes." Even though he didn't plan to let Priya out of his sight until they both decided how this situation would end. His motto had always been to plan for the best, but be prepared for the worst.

"Dialing the others," a female voice echoed through the intercom that was perched in the center of the conference table.

Within the next five minutes each FL was on the speakerphone, all of them probably sitting in a similar room in their offices across the U.S.

Bas began immediately. "It was a setup," he announced. "By the time we arrived the bulk of the shipment had been moved. We recovered less than one hundred pounds of product and detained three men. Not. Shifters." The last was stated with emphasis.

The collective curses throughout the line confirmed the others felt just as pissed off about this as Bas had been last night.

"The three we detained were pretty low on the totem pole and broke relatively easily," Bas continued. "So we now have a name. Palermo Greer was the lead on this shipment. He and another they say was called Black did the initial pickup."

"Then where the fuck are they now?" Cole was the first to interject.

"That's how we know this was a setup," Bas continued, trying like hell to ignore the bitter taste in his mouth after saying that particular name. The fact that he knew Palermo Greer and actually had a gruesome history with the man, was nobody's business but his own. "Nick's message said an eleven o'clock drop, correct?"

Nick's voice echoed through the room. "Right. I'm looking at the e-mail now. Eleven MST."

"We arrived around eleven ten. They weren't out in the open so we had to find the drop spot. It was a tunnel down under the buildings. One guy was in the tunnel loading the crates, the two others were in the building taking the product and putting it in trash bags."

"But you said it was a small score?" Jace inquired.

"Very small," Bas said, nodding. "Last time there were thousands of pounds."

"So what happened to the rest?" Rome asked, his voice serious and grim.

"One of the guys said the drop was scheduled for ten o'clock. The delivery was actually late so they didn't get started until a quarter to eleven. Palermo and his guy worked them hard to hurry and get their truck loaded. Then they took off, about ten minutes before we arrived, without the complete shipment."

"Send us a message about a drop with a time that guarantees we'll miss them completely," Nick was saying. "Why?"

"To let us know they're one step ahead of us," Jace said. "They want us to know that they're going to keep doing what they want and we can't stop them."

"What kind of product was it?" Rome asked.

Bas replied, "The savior drug. That same shield marking was on each of the blocks. And that's not all we brought back. There were guns, Rome. Really sophisticated automatic weapons with some sort of heat-seeking mechanism that Jacques and my team here are still trying to identify. And . . ." Bas paused, looking over to Jacques who nodded in agreement while sharing this last bit of information. "There were two crates, inside were lined coolers and eighty packets of human blood."

"What the fuck?" Nick exclaimed through the phone line.

"That's not all," Bas added.

"Fuck! There's more than blood and drugs?" Jace snapped. "What the hell is going on out there?"

Bas wished he had an answer to that question, on more accounts than either of the persons in this meeting knew.

"The crates were from Comastaz Labs here in Sedona," he said with a finality that rested on the ears of each of them.

"You're telling me that Comastaz Labs, a United States government facility, had a shipment of blood samples mixed in with a shipment of the savior drug and this shipment was facilitated by rogues?" Rome asked in a tone that may have signaled for no one to answer for fear of not saying what the Assembly Leader really wanted to hear.

As the lab and this shipment fell squarely under Bas's jurisdiction, he spoke first. "Yes, that's what it looks like. We know the circle the drugs are running, there's no big mystery there. Sabar brought this drug over from the Gungi, he put it on the streets through Athena's with the plan to branch out. Darel Charles took over after Sabar's untimely demise. Palermo's most likely heading up the West Coast division of rogues while Darel takes care of the East."

He took a deep breath and exhaled slowly.

"The Comastaz connection is the problem. Why blood samples and why with this shipment?" he asked.

Rome spoke up next, his tone representing the authority he held over the group. "So let's deal with this Palermo Greer, first," he said.

X spoke up then, no doubt he and Nick were at Rome's side, most likely in Rome's private conference room in his suite at Havenway. It was early so the First Female,

Kalina, may not have been in on the meeting, but there was also no doubt that Rome would fill her in immediately. They were a very close couple, Bas thought, even more so than the norm for joined shifters. But it wasn't like Bas was some type of expert on that, just something he'd observed.

"First and foremost," X began. "Greer hasn't been in the States for a while. Nobody's seen him in years. Some say he was also one of Boden's boys."

"Boden Estevez, the first rogue who was eventually beheaded," Cole stated.

"Allegedly beheaded," Jace added.

Rome interjected then. "What do you mean 'allegedly'? Is there some proof otherwise?"

"I'm sending you all a picture on your cell," Jace told them. "It came across my desk a few weeks ago as someone seeking representation."

Jace owned Maybon Artist Management, one of the top five talent agencies in Los Angeles. He worked with A-list actors, supermodels, and best-selling authors, both foreign and domestic. He was renowned and well known for his sharp candor and killer instinct—if the humans he worked with only knew.

There was silence as everyone checked their cell phones and then some grumbling as the picture appeared on each of their screens.

"She's hot, but now is really not the time," Cole replied with a chuckle.

"She's Bianca Adani," Jace continued seriously.

"Boden's mate," X added.

Silence throughout the room again.

"So now we have Palermo—one of Boden's boys, and Bianca, Boden's mate, here in the States," Rome stated. "After years of both of them being away."

"Not a coincidence," Jace replied.

Bas was already shaking his head. "I don't believe in coincidences." No, there was absolutely no way Palermo Greer running around this close to Perryville was by chance. There was a reason he was here, a reason beyond the revenge Bas had vowed fourteen years ago, that one of the men that had slaughtered Mariah was neatly placed within his reach.

"Neither do I," Rome said. "If you've gotten all you can out of the detainees, turn them over to the cops."

"Whoa, the cops?" Cole questioned, something which normally wouldn't go over well with any other leader of a tribe of shape-shifters. But Rome was different. He respected everyone's opinions and to that end didn't mind hearing feedback—to a certain extent.

With Cole, everyone knew he was still carrying a chip the size of Texas on his shoulder after his parents' divorce, so that was taken into consideration whenever they had to deal with him.

"Take them to the cops and say what? We just happened to roll up on these dudes during a drug transaction? How do we explain being there in the first place without bringing heat on ourselves? The last thing we need is more exposure and possibly another reporter running some insane story about cat people."

The last was obviously directed at Bas, but he wasn't biting, especially since he had his own little reporter lying upstairs in his bed.

"None of my team shifted. We all remained in human form throughout the entire exchange. But I have to agree with Cole, here," Bas admitted, albeit reluctantly. "If I take them in, the question is going to be what we were doing all the way in Nogales in the middle of the night at a deserted strip mall."

Rome was quiet for a moment. "Then what do you suggest?"

"Well, I'm guessing they're illegals so we can always turn them over to border control. They won't ask questions because they don't give a damn why they were here, they'll just ship them back to Mexico." He told Rome what he and Jacques had already discussed.

"Fine," Rome replied after some contemplation. "X will gather more intel on Darel and Palermo. Bas, you work on those weapons, find out what they are, who made them, and how these low-level dealers got their hands on them. I'm meeting with the president's advisors this week to talk about their position on the war on drugs and gun control so all the information you can get me on this new drug and these guns will help."

"He's running for a second term, Rome, and I know you want to stay in his corner, but do you really think he gives a crap about what's going on in the streets when he's got all that international bullshit to deal with?" Cole inquired.

"I think it's important that I build a relationship with the highest political party in the United States, especially since I am the highest party in the Stateside Assembly." Nobody commented on the fact that the president of the United States had no idea he was taking personal meetings, in addition to monetary campaign donations, from the leader of a shape-shifter tribe that had planted roots on U.S. soil.

"Wilson Reed and I have known each other since the days when he and his wife hung out with my parents. He was a highly respected attorney in D.C. before I even passed the bar and I consider him a good family friend. So the answer to your question, Cole, is yes. I believe he cares very deeply about what's going on in the streets of the city he grew up in as well as across the world," Rome stated firmly. "Jace, you follow up on Bianca. Find out what's she's doing here and who she's hooking up with.

And Cole, I want you to keep an eye on your borders too. This is the second takedown in your zone, Bas. They may not try to go in there again. Nick's got eyes down in Florida, so I want you to be on alert as well. Finally, Bas, I want you to find out what the hell is going on at Comastaz and do it fast!"

After their leader had spoken, none of the other FLs dared speak again, except to say good-bye.

# Chapter 12

"I just need you to keep an eye on my mother for me," Priya said to Lolo as she sat on the couch in Bas's suite.

"Where are you?" Lolo asked. He was outside, she could hear the cars going by and the noise of the streets. A brief glance at her watch and she figured he was on his way to lunch. He'd most likely go to the Subway on the corner three blocks down and order the teriyaki chicken with spinach, pickles, and mozzarella cheese. Her stomach churned at the thought, just as it did each time she was with him and he made the order. Man, she wished she were there.

"I'm following up on a lead," she said, taking a deep breath and focusing on speaking like she was normal, like all was well, even though it wasn't.

Her lead had led her right into a wall—a very sexy and very perplexing wall. Sebastian Perry wanted to sleep with her, there was no doubt about that, but he didn't want to tell her his secrets. Could she blame him? She wasn't about to tell him hers.

"Dammit, Priya, tell me you're not still on this Roman Reynolds trip," Lolo argued. "I don't think there's anything there. And Maury was not pleased that you weren't in this morning. He's going to go ape-shit when he finds out you're working on something behind his back."

She shook her head, even though she knew Lolo couldn't see her. "He's not going to find out because you're not going to tell him."

"I'm not going to tell him that you're following up on leads to prove something that nobody is going to believe and I'm definitely not going to tell him that you're staking out Roman Reynolds. But I'll tell you what *is* going to happen, Priya. Reynolds is going to have you arrested, or worse. His friend Xavier still has connections to the FBI even though he's no longer working there. You know the Feds can make people disappear faster than the Mob."

"Melodramatic much?" she quipped. "Look, I have some leave time. I'll e-mail Maury this afternoon and tell him I'm taking a vacation. I just need you to watch my mom until I return."

"This is crazy; how do you think you're going to get any of them to talk to you? They don't talk to anyone but each other, everybody knows that."

Men talk to their lovers, Priya thought. Last night, or rather this morning she'd awakened wrapped in Bas's arms. A mistake? He had most likely been dreaming about one of his other conquests, and she'd just happened to be there, in his bed. But while he'd held her she'd distinctly heard him say, "I will protect you." Again, she had no reason to believe he was speaking to her directly, why would he be? He hardly even knew her. Still, the entire episode convinced Priya that now, more than ever, she needed to stay as close to Bas as possible. He would lead her to the answers she required, she had no doubt. She also had no concrete reason to believe this, especially since he'd been adamant about her not moving forward with this story, but something inside, something deep inside told her this was where she needed to be.

"I have it under control. In a couple of days I'll have

everything I need. So if you could just watch out for my mom, that would be great."

"Watch her do what? Where are you and why can't you watch her?"

Priya sighed, not wanting to give Lolo any more information than was absolutely necessary. He would stay safe that way, he wouldn't be involved, and he wouldn't suffer if she messed up.

"I'm out of town and that's all you need to know. Look, I have to go," she told him. "I'll text you later."

Priya hung up before Lolo could ask another question, which was clearly his intent as she could hear him talking as she hit the END button. Tiny spikes of guilt pricked her temples, initiating the start of what she knew would be one of her marathon migraines.

Now she was sitting on the soft leather couch, legs crossed, drumming her fingers on her knee as she tried to think of what to do next. They wanted her to expose Roman and his friends, to report on the catlike people, but Priya needed evidence. The story would never make it to print without something concrete to back it up. Maury, her editor, was a stickler for having all his ducks in a row and he would give her hell if she cut any corners. They wanted the report out by the first of next month, twenty-two days away.

What they didn't know was that she was also trying to figure out who the hell they were, in the hopes that she could get to her brother first. With that thought in mind she riffled through her purse until she found what she was looking for. Holding the business card in her hand she read over the name and the telephone number: Dorian Wilson, DEA. The last time Malik had been arrested he'd cut a deal with the Feds in exchange for a lighter sentence. They apparently were going to do an even bigger favor for him by putting him back on the streets, as their informant.

Now, Malik was gone. Priya's first instinct after receiving the e-mail had been to contact Agent Wilson to tell him what was going on. It was like her e-mail stalker could see into her mind because another message had come through with the simple words: *Tell anyone and he dies right now.* So she hadn't told. But she'd had Lolo trying to trace that damned IP address each time a new message surfaced.

Still, she had nothing, on either end, and she was getting damned frustrated by that fact.

"Hello," a female voice sounded and Priya nearly jumped off the sofa. Instead her movement knocked her purse onto the floor and as she scrambled to retrieve it she noticed a really great pair of red shoes. Instantly switching to her wannabe-fashionista mode, Priya sat back on the couch and looked at the complete package. Around five-foot-three- or four-inches tall in the flat red patent leather shoes, skinny jeans, and a paisley-print silk tunic. Hair and eyes that said hey-look-at-me and a smile that said I'm-not-really-this-outgoing, quite an amazing contradiction, Priya thought to herself.

"I'm sorry if I frightened you," the female said in a gentle voice that only added to Priya's assessment.

Standing finally, Priya extended her hand. "No, it's no problem. Just daydreaming, I guess. I'm Priya Drake and you are . . . ?"

She accepted Priya's hand in a quick shake. "I'm Jewel. I work here at Perryville. I was told to bring you breakfast."

"Oh. Well. Thank you," Priya said for lack of another suitable comment. She was thinking this was one fancy outfit for staff when Jewel moved to a tray she'd obviously brought in with her.

As Priya followed her across the room she thought she'd have to work on being much more observant if she expected to find information. This woman had come into the room with a tray of food and Priya hadn't heard a sound.

"I didn't know what you like so I told them to give you a variety." She talked while removing the chrome domes from plate after plate.

Priya wasn't a picky eater by any stretch of the imagination; blame that on living in a household where you ate whatever was provided, never really developing a palate for anything special, because there was rarely ever anything special.

She reached over, grabbing a slice of bacon and taking a bite. "So you work here?"

"Yes," Jewel replied.

"How long have you worked here?"

"About three years."

"And you're allowed to come and go in the owner's suite as you please?"

Jewel's head tilted a bit, her green eyes surveying Priya. She folded her hands in front of her and took a slow breath. "I'm Jacques's assistant. Jacques works very closely with Mr. Perry. So if Mr. Perry asks me to do something, I do it."

Did everyone do what Mr. Perry asked? Priya wondered.

"Really?"

"Yes. Really. You should have no worries that there is something personal between Mr. Perry and I. I'm just an employee."

Priya laughed at that, a sound that obviously shocked Jewel. "Oh honey, you're the one who doesn't have to worry. There's nothing personal between Bas and myself. I'm just here . . ." Priya paused, catching herself as she figured it probably wasn't a good idea to tell everyone who she was and why she was really here.

"We're just acquaintances," she finished.

"Oh," Jewel said with a nod. "Right."

The woman didn't believe her but Priya didn't really care. She was still trying to figure out if Jewel could help her.

"Actually, I just met him a few days ago. I don't really know that much about him," she began, grabbing an English muffin and buttering it as she talked.

"Would you like to sit down?" Jewel asked.

Priya shook her head, dropping the knife and taking a bite. When she finished chewing she continued. "Does he bring a lot of women here?" The question came out even though that wasn't what she really wanted to know. Okay, she sort of did want to know that, but only in the sense that maybe the type of woman he preferred would lead her to the type of man, or animal, he really was.

"I haven't seen any," was Jewel's reply.

"That's strange."

Jewel looked confused. "Why do you say that?"

Priya shrugged. "I just figure a real important man like Bas, with all the security he travels with and all these high-tech gadgets in this place, that he must be a hot commodity."

Jewel waited a beat before replying this time. "He's a wealthy man, if that's what you mean. And he has a lot of people working for him."

And I'm not about to tell you any more, was what Jewel hadn't said with words but conveyed quite successfully by looking away from Priya.

Luckily, that action hadn't deterred Priya at all. "Perryville Resorts are renowned all over the world. He seems to have found his niche," she began. "Funny, I would have never pegged him for a politician, though."

Jewel blinked before shaking her head. "I don't think Mr. Perry is into politics."

"Well, his friend Roman Reynolds is," Priya replied easily. "I saw them at a fund-raiser for the president in

D.C. a couple of days ago. Good to know where their support lies."

"Mr. Reynolds is a nice man, as well," was her stilted reply.

"So you've met Reynolds. How about Delgado and Markland? Do they all come here a lot?"

The woman paused. Her hands dropped from in front of her and she traced a finger along the rim of the cart that stood between them. It was an absentminded sort of gesture that at the same time should have told Priya a lot about who she was talking to.

"I don't know them," Jewel answered eventually.

Yet her beautifully arched eyebrows had lifted at the mention of their names. Priya finished the English muffin and sipped from the glass of orange juice, all the while watching the pretty woman standing across from her, the one who wasn't saying as much as Priya figured she could. There was definitely something going on with her, something deeper than the red of her shoes and hair, but Priya wasn't here to psychoanalyze this woman. She wasn't a part of her story. This quiet, jittery woman did not possess the same confidence as Bas and his friends so Priya didn't think she was one of them. Still, she wasn't dismissing that she could be helpful—at least Priya was fairly sure of that fact.

"So what do you do for fun around here, Jewel? I'm not sure when I'll be leaving so I guess I should enjoy myself while I'm here." And you would be just the one to show me around, Priya thought. This woman worked for the man who worked closely with Bas, most likely one of those goons he'd been with last night. What better way to find out what was really going on than to spend some time with her? In the next moment Priya knew that wasn't meant to be.

\* \* \*

"I'll be in charge of your entertainment during your stay."

Priya didn't even bother to turn at the sound of his voice. She knew who it was and what she would find if she did, so she simply stood still. Jewel, on the other hand, tensed immediately.

"I was just finishing here, Mr. Perry," she told him, moving hurriedly to get away from Priya and as close to the door as she could.

"It was nice meeting you," she yelled to Jewel, receiving no reply.

"Well," she said, finally turning to face him. "I see I'm not the only female in your harem."

The words were easy enough to say, but looking at him was much more difficult. She couldn't help thinking that this story might come a lot easier if he weren't so damned good-looking.

Bas took a couple of steps, closing the gap between them in slow, confident strides. Everything about him breathed assurance and masculinity. To say that he was too damned fine for his own good somehow seemed like an understatement. As a matter of fact, all of them were too damned fine, Reynolds, Delgado, and Markland. She was beginning to think that couldn't just be a coincidence.

"We'll start with a tour of the resort and some of the local sights, and then we'll have dinner at La Selva," he told her without wavering.

"And then I'll be locked in this room again," she added to his self-made agenda.

He took a seat in one of the leather chairs, crossing an ankle over his knee. The gaze he gave her was one of patience, of kindness to what might have been the mentally ill and Priya bristled instantly.

"I am not kidnapping you, nor am I keeping you under lock and key. You are free to roam about as you will. In fact, I encourage you to take full advantage of the resort's amenities. We're especially proud of our spa and its holistic Native American treatments."

He sounded like a commercial, a very smooth and cleverly rehearsed one.

"Look, why don't I make this easier for both of us," she said, sitting on the couch across from him. "We can tour your resort and your sights and then we'll have dinner. At which time I'll ask my questions and you'll give me straight answers. Then I can pack my bags and get out of your hair. You'll be free to do . . ." she hesitated, "whatever it is you do around here without me snooping around."

With his arms outstretched on the sides of the chair, Bas asked, "What makes you think I haven't given you straight answers already?"

"Because I can sense when someone's not being completely honest with me. I think you know something about what I saw but for whatever reason you don't want to tell me."

His expression never changed. "Did it ever occur to you that when people don't give you the answers you want, it's for a reason? Mainly, because they don't know what you're talking about."

Priya immediately shook her head, not at all appreciating his smooth rebuff. "No. That never occurred to me."

He actually smiled at her reply. It was a slow spread of his lips that put a light in his eyes and sent a punch of lust through her gut.

"I'll get my purse and we can get this tour underway," she said, standing up and hurrying to put as much distance between them as possible.

# Chapter 13

**Phoenix, AZ**

"They never showed up," Black told Palermo. "And I went back to the site this morning. The tunnel's completely cleaned out."

"So they stole the rest of our shipment?" Palermo leaned his tall, lanky body against the side of the hotel they'd spent the night at in Phoenix. They'd been scheduled to leave Arizona today and head back to Albuquerque where a house had already been purchased to store their stash. That was thanks to Sabar's master plan to rule the world. Seems more than one person and/or shifter could have the same plan but execute it in an entirely different manner. Palermo had come into the scenario in the later stages and through channels that nobody, not even Darel, knew about. So his agenda was his own, and he planned to keep it that way. As long as everyone did the things he needed them to do.

He'd hated the fact that he and Black had to bail on the drop last night before everything was done, but he'd lifted the scent of shadows and didn't want to battle with the other shifter while making such a sensitive exchange. That, Palermo now realized, had been a colossal mistake.

The three humans that had been hired by one of Darel's contacts to help them get set up were now mysteriously missing. And with them was a total of a quarter of a million dollars' worth of drugs and guns that were to be used to set up their dealers and get the money rolling in. And the special packages that only Palermo knew were going to be included in the shipment. Those were the ones that worried him the most at the moment.

"I'm not so sure it was their plan to take the goods and run," Black offered.

Palermo wasn't so sure of that. Still, he doubted the dumbass humans had a clue as to what had been in those other two crates or how important they were to some very powerful people.

Frowning, he looked at the shifter that he'd had no choice but to bring along on this part of the mission. They were supposed to keep a low profile while they were here. The people that Palermo was working with did not want to be identified or connected in any way to what he was doing. Unfortunately, Black wasn't one for being discreet. His physical attributes almost made that completely impossible, with his larger-than-normal frame, and all-black clothes covering just about every inch of his skin even in the hot Southwestern climate. The locals had been staring each time Black had walked through the hotel lobby, no doubt taking in every detail of this stranger in town.

"What do you mean? My shit's gone and so are those *ladrões*!" Palermo exclaimed, trying like hell not to lose his temper even though somebody obviously thought he could be played for a fool.

Black shook his head, his thick neck looking as if it were trapped inside the material of the shirt collar wrapped tightly at his throat.

"When I was in the tunnel I picked up a scent. Shadows," the big shifter stated simply.

He hadn't needed the other shifter to tell him what he already knew. Still, Palermo cursed long and fluently at that point. He pulled out his cell phone and dialed quickly.

"We've got a problem," he announced immediately when the line was answered. "Tell me again, which one of those bastard FLs are in charge out here?" he spoke into the phone.

When he received the answer, Palermo nodded, then he smiled, a slow and very satisfied smile. "No. I don't need you to send me any information on this one. We go way back."

Because he wouldn't hang up until he did, Palermo gave a brief synopsis of their situation, and then felt his smile turning into a frown as he listened to the bullshit threats coming from the other end of the phone, before thankfully clicking it off and stuffing it back into his pocket. The immediate order was to kill the FL of the Mountain Zone, but that was the least of Palermo's worries. He wanted his stash back, needed desperately to find those damned crates from Comastaz. Then he would take care of Sebastian Perry, with more pleasure than he'd allowed himself in ages.

"What's doing?" Black asked, his big beefy arms folded over his chest.

"We're taking a little side trip," Palermo told him. "To a place called Perryville."

## Sedona

The original plan had been to take her away from Perryville for a while, to give Jacques time to do his background check on her and plant all his devices to track her. There were some favorite places Bas wanted to take her even though he'd never taken any other female to those particular spots before. He didn't bother to question why, it would only land in the pile of growing questions he had where Priya Drake was concerned. So he'd ignored it, taking her from the room and guiding her along the halls of the resort he was beyond proud of owning and operating.

She hadn't asked any questions during the tour of the resort. Well, at least not any questions about the story she was after. Instead they'd shared small talk that had him admiring her even more than he'd been afraid he already did.

The change in her mood had come quickly even though she'd tried to hide it. Luckily, Bas was very perceptive; okay, his shifter senses were more the culprit in this instance. Her excitement was a burst of hibiscus and jasmine that sifted through his nostrils with the stark memory of his visits to the rainforest. That would be the only other place that Bas could safely identify with scents like hibiscus and jasmine. There was a place just at the base of the Gungi where he'd made sure to visit each time he was there. The ground was cushioned with damp foliage, the canopy providing heavy shade above so that it almost appeared the world in the jungle was in a perpetual darkness.

The atmosphere rang with the endless drone of cicadas and crickets. In the distance there was a waterfall, its rush of activity giving a semblance of relief from the heavy damp air. Tree ferns burst from the ground, branches spreading like eagle's wings, tiny leaves soft as dewdrops to the touch. Just north of the ferns a gentle clearing was invaded by jagged rock, ghostly wisps of white spray rolling downward, kickback from the waterfall.

This woman, this reporter that he didn't want to give in to, reminded him of this place. Her smile, her thirst for information, and undoubtedly her fresh and exuberant scent took him back to the Gungi in a way that made Bas more than nervous.

It made him wonder.

Presently—because that's where Bas's mind needed to focus—the sun was beaming brightly over smooth red clay-covered walls as they walked first through the outside area of the Alma spa. There was a side entrance as well as an entrance directly through the resort. Since they'd come out of the front door and walked around they had used the side entrance, which opened at the pool. Slate-colored lounge chairs were perfectly aligned around the six-foot-deep, pebble-lined pool that stretched from one end of the deck area to the other, about twenty feet.

"I love to swim," was her first genuine comment. "This looks absolutely refreshing."

The water did look tempting as the heat of early afternoon had begun to settle upon them. She walked a little ahead of him and his gaze was immediately drawn to the tight pull of denim across her delectable ass. She had a compact little body that moved with the same energy as her mind. He was still thinking of how much courage it took for her to leave her home and travel across the country for a story. Then again, reporters did this every day. They worked tenaciously, sometimes methodically, to uncover every fact they could to support their story. What most reporters didn't do was attend a five-hundred-dollar ticketed political fund-raiser wearing a dress with the price tag still attached, nor did they make sloppy attempts to break into a private suite of a prominent businessman. And no reporter had ever followed him across the country in an attempt to expose the one thing that Bas lived to protect.

"We didn't swim a lot when I was younger," she'd been saying as she stooped down to put her fingers in the water.

The statement brought a plunge in her mood, a shadow of hurt and pain clouding the bright flowery scent of her previous excitement. It was a lightning-fast change, one that concerned Bas and irritated the hell out of his cat.

"Really? The summer months get pretty hot in D.C.," he commented, assuming that was where she'd been born and raised. By the time Bas returned to his office, Jacques would have a complete background report on Priya Drake and Bas would know all he needed to know to make a decision on how he would deal with her. At least he hoped so.

"Our only option was the public pool, which was a couple of miles away from where we lived and had usually reached its capacity by the time we got there, which was normally late afternoon. My mother wasn't a morning person."

Her voice had held a desolate tone as she talked, her gaze still focused on the water.

"You didn't have any siblings that could take you?" Bas asked, suddenly very interested in the woman, not the reporter.

Priya nodded. "My sisters are older and always had more important things to do. And my brother . . ." She paused, staring out at the water with the saddest look Bas had ever seen on her face. "He was busy a lot too," she finally finished.

"That sucks," he stated before he could stop himself. It was a knee-jerk reaction and what he'd really been referring to was that it sounded as if her childhood may have been the source of her past pain. That bothered him more than it should have.

She flicked her fingers then and stood, giving him a quick gaze. "Not everyone was lucky enough to be born rich and to grow up to become even richer. We didn't have a lot and what we had was split four ways so that meant no indulgences like lavish summer vacations, enticing swimming pools, or whatever else a very active imagination could dream of. It was a long time ago. I got over it. No big deal," she stated quickly and turned to walk away from him.

Right, or rather wrong. She obviously hadn't gotten over it, not in the least bit. If there was one thing he could sense through his human side, more so than the shifter, it was the remnants of a painful past. Most likely because he still carried his around like old luggage.

"We're going inside," he said, once again abruptly as he'd just decided to change his plans.

He took her hand and was moving before she could reply. When he thought she might have argued, she didn't, simply walked along behind him. For some reason that too, bothered him.

A few minutes at the front desk, a nod from one of the ladies he employed, and then they were on their way down the marbled floor hallway. The attendant stopped in front of a door, painted a warm coral shade with a gold knob, which she turned to let them inside.

"You can undress in there and come out with this robe on. Dana will be with you momentarily," the attendant said with a polite smile as she handed a white terry cloth robe to a now-perplexed-looking Priya.

"What?"

"That will be fine, thank you," Bas interrupted after Priya's question. He dismissed the attendant, waited until she'd closed the door behind her, leaving them alone before turning to her. Her stance had changed, her shoulders squared, one eyebrow arched in that way she did when she was about to fire off with a bout of questions. Funny how he'd memorized her actions, her moods, and the slight dimple that appeared at the right corner of her mouth when she smiled.

"Before you argue, look at it as an indulgence that you're way overdue for. You're about to receive a top-notch massage from one of the world's most talented massage therapists. You can thank me later," he told her while reaching for her shoulders and turning her toward the door to the bathroom.

"I don't want a massage," she snapped, tossing a look over her shoulder that should have had the effect of daggers shooting into his skull, but actually felt like a lightning bolt to his groin.

"You're going to love it, Dana is the best," was his cordial reply.

"I'll bet you know how good she is firsthand," she added when he'd opened the door and scooted her inside.

Bas smiled as the scent of jealousy wafted slowly between them. "Dana's a man."

She arched a brow. "Then I'm almost positive you know he's the best."

Had his smile ever faded so fast, Bas wasn't sure, but her words were a pinprick to his infamous ego. "He's the best because I pay him more than I pay some of the top management staff. Now get undressed."

He closed the door before she could speak again and walked out of the room to answer the cell phone that had been vibrating in his pocket.

She'd never had a massage, never thought it was worth spending her money on. Things like rent, gas for the car, and food sort of took precedence.

So it was with a few hesitant steps that Priya emerged from the bathroom wrapped in a robe so soft she wanted to purr as her bare feet were cushioned by equally soft carpet in a warm beige color. The walls in here were painted the same coral as outside with a beige-and-gold-flecked border. Two tables were positioned in the center of the room, covered in white sheets and what she thought might actually be a mattress beneath, they looked so comfortable. Atop the white sheets were peach-colored rose petals. Priya lifted one, rubbing her fingers over the smoothness as she continued to look around.

Directly across from the head of the table about eight feet away were two steps and a tub. Above the tub was a fountain that looked like a sheet of banged aluminum. Water slipped quietly over the tin surface to drip into a narrow drain. When she'd first come into the room, overhead fluorescent lighting had been on. Now, there were candles, short fat ones, tall skinny ones, all white, all emitting a light earthy fragrance throughout the room.

Turning around once more she let her hand rub along the length of one of the tables, looking around and wondering how she came to be here. She shouldn't be in this luxurious place about to experience her first massage when she had no idea where her brother was and if he was still alive. With a curse she was about to go into the bathroom and change back into her clothes when the door opened and in walked what could only be described as a Greek god—if she were the type to believe they actually existed, which she didn't think she was. Until now, of course.

"Hi, I'm Dana," he said. "You can take this table right here and I'll be back to get started."

Swallowing deeply, Priya watched as the over six-foot-tall, olive-complexioned, bald-headed man who seemed to be squeezing all his magnificent body parts into white pants and a white T-shirt, flashed her a gorgeous smile then turned to leave the room before she could reply.

In the next instant Priya pulled that robe off so fast she thought she might have ripped it. Yanking back the rose-petal-covered sheet she didn't even mind that those pretty flowers were now falling silently to the floor as she climbed up onto the table. It took a second of adjustment as she made sure the sheets covered her naked body, then she lay there, like a kid at Christmas, waiting, anticipating.

When the door opened again she wanted to turn around and get another look at Mr. Dana, but for once in her life didn't have the guts. Instead she closed her eyes in an effort to calm the rampant beat of her heart, her mind wandering with thoughts of Dana and his highly paid hands.

The sheet moved and was tucked at her waist. Priya bit her bottom lip, wondering if he would massage her entire body. Would he want her to turn over so he could touch her breasts? What about her thighs? She knew there was tension there, especially around her inner thighs. That thought had her frowning because in the same instant she realized that it wasn't Dana that she wanted between her thighs. Inhaling deeply, Priya forced herself to remain still. Seconds later there was a sound, like something opening, a tube or a bottle, hands clasping together, rubbing against each other. She let another breath out slowly, waiting, figuring she could get through this. She had to because there was no way she was going to tell the ever-confident Sebastian Perry that he'd ruined her for another man's touch, even a simple massage.

Then strong hands touched her shoulders, softly at first, just the tips of fingers running rhythmically over her shoulders. Instantly, heat flowed from that point down, just like the fountain above the tub. His hands were oiled, she realized as she sighed, when they flattened on her back. His fingers gripping her shoulders, pinching nerves, uncoiling muscles, and soliciting a deep moan from her.

Now her breasts did tingle, the lips of her vagina were throbbing. His hands moved down, fingers fanning over her sides, drumming over her rib cage. She couldn't help it, she sighed again. Then his thumbs were at the base of her spine, rotating, pressing inward until she actually gasped.

Her entire body tingled, nerves on end in anticipation of his next touch.

"You ready to thank me yet?" he whispered into her ear.

If she hadn't already experienced the rush of heat and complete shift from not-really aroused to OMG-definitely aroused, Priya might have questioned who was actually giving her the massage, at least before he spoke. But she knew who it was, knew damned well who was touching her, who was driving her crazy once again with his touch.

"No. This is a breach of contract. I'm supposed to have Dana, the highest paid massage therapist in the world. Not you," she replied, the complaint not matching her breathless tone.

He had the audacity to chuckle, arrogant jerk. But his hands were a godsend, as he pushed past the towel to cup her buttocks, kneading each mound with tender efficiency. She wanted to rear back, to lift her hips from the table, or get up on her knees and let him inside. Priya closed her eyes then, thinking of how long it had been and how it seemed like forever since she'd really been sexually satisfied. Too damn long was apparent.

She heard the opening and closing of a tube once more, sighed as she felt the splash of warm oil slapping directly against her skin this time. His hands slid sinuously over her buttocks once more and Priya sucked in a breath. Heated spikes soared through her body, landing with sharp intensity at her clit and she silently wished for her bullet so she could find some relief.

As if he'd heard her prayer Bas's hands slid lower down her crease, dipping inside, coming out, then going inside once more. It was a tease, her teeth gritted in response, a vicious and painful tease.

"I know how to make you thank me," he said, his voice going deep, his fingers following to touch the tight ring of her anus.

"I do too. You can go get Dana and then get lost. Thank you very much." Sarcasm came naturally even as erotic tingles performed a little dance at the base of her spine. He wasn't going to touch her there, he couldn't.

And yet he did. The pad of one finger pressing with gentle force until it breached the entrance and Priya moaned.

"Uh uh, that's not what I'm going to do," he replied just before pushing the sheet down a little farther.

With pleasure so intense she had to catch her breath, Priya bucked up off the table at the touch.

"Relax. If you don't like what I do to you, I'll run right out and get Dana. I promise."

"Like I'm going to believe that," she said on a soft moan and then tensed as that finger went deeper. It was a wicked sort of pleasure, a no-please-don't and yes-don't-stop type of enjoyment that she never imagined she'd experience.

He startled her when he stilled, his voice serious and a bit forceful. "You can trust me, Priya. If I say I'm going to do something, I'll do it."

Why those words meant anything to her Priya had no idea, but they did and she murmured, "I know," before pressing back against his hand in search of the mysterious delight.

"Open for me," he told her after a few minutes. "Let me all the way in."

Oh, god, she was not doing this. She never imagined in her wildest dreams doing something such as this. And yet, her legs parted, her muscles relaxing as she waited, anticipated, hungered.

When his other hand slipped from her cheek, which he'd been holding securely, she sighed. His talented fingers slipped right past the first hand to plunge deep into her core and she gasped, her own fingers clenching in the pillow beneath her. Bas worked both fingers inside different entrances, simultaneously. Everything around her became a blur as she floated through the haze created by Bas's erotic massage.

"Did you know that when you become sexually excited your pupils dilate?" he asked, pulling out of her center with one finger and pressing deeper into her anus, with another. "Not a lot so that you look like you're frightened or possibly injured. But enough so that I know there's a change in you. Your breathing changes, coming in shorter hitches."

Kind of like she was doing now. Priya bit her bottom lip so hard she thought she might indeed draw blood.

"I can also smell your arousal. As the wetness coats your lips a smell so fucking sweet fills my head and I can hardly concentrate." Two oiled fingers sank deep into her center this time, while one eased slowly from her anus. "That's never happened to me before, Priya. I'm always in control of my mind, my body, everything."

His words floated somewhere around her as Priya fought to hold onto her sanity while his fingers dismantled everything else about her. She needed him inside her at this moment, needed all of him, whether it be his fingers or his dick, she simply needed more than she ever had in her life. Moving, she rubbed her taut nipples against the sheets, resisting the urge to slip her hand between her legs to work her clit.

"I was always in control, until you showed up," he continued, as he dipped the fingers from both hands inside of her once more, until it felt as if they were both rubbing against each other deep inside of her.

Her thighs shook as his name slipped from her lips, her eyes closing, opening, her body fighting for release.

Her hips bucked involuntarily and he pulled his fingers out halfway until they created a rhythm. A rhythm that was making breathing harder, talking almost impossible, and hating Sebastian Perry outrageously contradictory.

"Will you lose control with me? Will you let go and let me please you? Damn, I want to please you, Priya. I want to please every inch of you, pretty girl."

He'd moved so that his lips were once again at her ear, his fingers deep inside of her. His tongue snaked out, licking her lobe once, then twice, until she gasped.

"Will you please just hurry?" was her response. "Goddammit, just hurry!"

He pumped her faster, licked her in long, hot strokes as he did and Priya thought she was going to explode. Instead she pressed her knees against the table, coming up slightly to increase the pressure of his strokes. She was almost there, her arms even shook now, her breath coming in deep pants as he worked her thoroughly, his tongue tracing a hot path along her skin, delving deep into her ear. She felt like Bas was completely covering her, as if she were a prized instrument and he was playing the hell out of her. She strained against the pain that rippled right along the sweet edges of impending ecstasy as she remembered who he was and why she was here. The thought was so powerful, the realization of how wrong they were and how right this felt, warring inside her like true rivals, she gasped, shaking her head and closing her eyes. Lowering her head to the pillow she waited, it was coming, that fall over the cliff of ecstasy was in sight. Just a few more strokes, just another lick of his tongue, another whisper in her ear and . . .

"What did you just say?"

"Where? I'll be right there."

What the hell? Priya turned back, wondering at Bas's words, at the complete stilling of both his hands. He was talking to someone and it clearly was not her. His brow wrinkled, his lips stretching into a straight line as he listened, to what or who Priya had no idea. In the next instant he was pulling his hands away from her, cursing as he turned to grab a towel from the other table.

"Get dressed and go straight to my room," he told her.

By now she was sitting up on the table, staring at him in disbelief. "What the hell are you talking about? And where are you going?" she asked, watching in complete incredulity as he moved toward the door.

"Do what I said, Priya. Go to my room and stay there until I come get you."

He was gone then and Priya cursed like she'd only ever heard a drunken Levi Drake do before.

# Chapter 14

The control room was on the level just above the bunkers, encased in cinder blocks and bulletproof steel doors on the front and around the corner on the side. Not only was a code required to obtain entrance, but there was a specially made key to fit each door. The key had been made by a shadow whose day job was as a locksmith—kudos to the shifter database that X created and routinely updated. The only persons with keys to this room were Bas, Jacques, and Syfon, the leader of the blue team.

When Bas let himself in, Jacques was already there, seated in one of the tall control chairs, staring at the many closed-circuit monitors that climbed the wall in front of him. The monitors covered every hallway in the resort and the elevators on a regular basis. There were cameras everywhere, so with a few keystrokes the view could be switched to outside a specific suite in the spa or the storage room in the kitchen. There was nothing at Perryville that Bas could not see at any moment he desired to do so. Right now, Jacques was scanning the complete perimeter, which consisted of a three-mile radius immediately surrounding the resort, as well as the extended acreage under his ownership, going deep into the forested end of the canyon. While the building itself was kitted with an electric alarm system, there was also an underground trigger system in place for the outdoor areas. Atop the roof of the main building were sniper points for five of their best trained to take a first look.

"Nothing," Jacques replied to Bas's yet unasked question.

"Where's the team?" Bas continued, standing beside the seat he usually took for himself when he was there. He couldn't sit, could barely focus as two powerful entities battled for his attention—the rogues vs. Priya.

"Five up high, four in the front, six in the back," Jacques began, giving Bas the rundown. "Two on the humans we caught last night because I'm thinking that's who they're coming for."

Bas nodded in agreement. "We took some of their drugs, their guns, and their mules."

"And let's not forget their blood," Jacques added dryly. "I guess now they want it back."

"Now that's certainly not going to happen," Bas added with a wry chuckle. "Let's try to take them alive. I have a feeling this is circling back to the explosion in Rome's zone."

For the first time since he'd come into the room, Jacques looked away from the monitors to stare directly at Bas. "What makes you think that?"

"A man by the name of Ralph Kensington's body was found in that building. One of Nick's earlier reports was that Kensington was in cahoots with Robert Slakeman who owned that building and Slakeman Enterprises. Did you get a look at the serial number on one of those guns we retrieved from the tunnel?"

Jacques shook his head. "Not really, no. I was more concerned with how many there were in comparison to the small amount of drugs that had been left behind and those other two crates that I still can't explain."

Which was also a question that needed an answer,

sooner rather than later. But more urgent was that serial number. Bas had seen that combination of numbers before.

"The serial number was UK79865 and right behind that were the initials, RSE," Bas told him. He'd always had an eidetic memory, which totally conflicted with his laid-back, gigolo reputation. It wasn't something he broadcasted along with other details of his life, but it came in handy, especially at times like this.

"Robert Slakeman Enterprises," Jacques said slowly. "Arrogant bastard wants everyone to know his handiwork."

"I'm not surprised. The UK5—the weapon's nickname as it had been listed in those documents we found when we raided that truck Hernandez was traveling in—is Slakeman's most coveted creation. The government didn't want it because of its instability and Slakeman's sky-high price," Bas added with a frown. "So Rome's theory of Slakeman and Kensington selling firearms to the rogues was dead-on, they're not only expanding their army of dealers, they're arming them pretty damn sophisticatedly as well."

"And the expansion starts here," Jacques muttered.

"No the hell it doesn't," Bas said solemnly. "The minute you get a trace on them I want to know. This is one round of questioning I plan to handle myself." Whoever had the guts to come at Bas head-on was no mule.

Jacques was nodding, moving his body so that the chair swiveled a bit from side to side. "Where is the reporter?" he asked.

That question threw Bas for a moment since he'd been so focused on the guns, drugs, and bastard rogues and exacting a modicum of revenge. "She's in my room where she's going to stay, especially now that we may have company."

"You know I don't normally question you or what you do in your personal life," Jacques began, letting his words drift slowly.

Bas looked at him long and hard this time, noticed the recession of his hairline just before the dreadlocks he kept bound at the base of his neck with a black band, snaked backward. He noted the concern in the corners of his eyes and the set of his shoulders, which translated to the fact the man was fully prepared to say whatever it was he wouldn't normally say. Bas had to respect the guy for that type of honesty, and if truth be told, boldness. For all that Bas liked to dress well and live lavishly, he was a cold-blooded killer and if anybody knew that, Jacques did.

Still, the man he'd known for years continued to hold Bas's stare as he spoke. "She's bad news, Bas. Keeping her here is not a good idea, especially under these new circumstances. What if she sees something or hears something? Hell, she might have seen or heard something last night before you even realized she was there. And as a matter of fact, when exactly did you realize she was there?"

"Stop!" Bas snapped, not loudly, but sternly enough that Jacques's lips clapped shut immediately. "I know what I'm doing."

"Do you?" Jacques asked. "Because when Rome finds out he's going to send the order to kill her. Does your plan include that?"

He was asking if Bas would kill Priya when Rome ordered it. Bas had asked himself that question more than once since meeting her and still hadn't come up with an answer.

"It's not going to come to that."

"There's no alternate ending here, Bas," Jacques warned.

At that Bas growled, his cat fighting the words as vehemently as the man intended to. "I said I know what I'm doing! I'll handle her and I'll deal with Rome."

"He's the head of the Stateside Assembly. Just how do you plan to *deal* with him?"

That question was meant to leave a stinging impact on Bas. What it did in actuality was piss him off just a little more. "I said I'd deal with it and I will," was his final retort. "What you need to do is find those rogues and let me know the moment we're ready to head out and bring those fuckers back to the bunker. Are we clear on that?"

Jacques turned from him then, focusing his gaze on the monitors once more. "Clear as ice, sir," was his stony reply.

Bas didn't slam the door to his office, that would have been futile. He didn't swipe all the papers from his desk, curse a blue streak, or even growl like his kind was used to doing. As angered as he was by Jacques's words of killing Priya, he wouldn't let it show. He couldn't.

Sitting at his desk, he switched on his computer and waited. Elbows planted on the desk blotter, hands folded, he let his forehead fall into his palms. In and out, he breathed slowly, not counting down from one hundred because that tended to irritate him more than help. Instead he focused on the air around him, the intake and expulsion, his lungs inflating and deflating. Focus.

On that last intake of breath his teeth clenched. He could still smell her. Not the jasmine or hibiscus or the simply alluring scent he'd first lifted from her that night in the hotel, but her essence. It was the barest, most primal part of her and he could still smell it on his hands even though he'd stopped to wash them after leaving her in the spa. Inhaling deeply he let the scent waft through him and closed his eyes.

"Dammit!"

His palms flattened on the desk loudly.

Focus, he reminded himself. Just fucking focus.

His fingers moved quickly over the keyboard until his e-mail box was up displaying over one hundred unread messages. The first one he clicked on was from Jacques.

It was Priya's background report. He read it word for word, twice. Then cursed again.

None of this was news to him. She was a reporter, the youngest of four children, struggling financially, but living the life she'd always wanted to live. Or so it appeared. There had to be something, a big-ass something that would make her act recklessly enough to pursue a story that wasn't authorized by her boss and to risk her life.

There were three more attachments to the e-mail, one that was a list of IP addresses and locations. Another that showed an e-mail that had been sent to primetimepriya227@venicemail.net from Nedob.sonroter@urauk.org.

They must be exposed. Deadline: 60 days

Bas looked away from the computer to the desk calendar and counted from the date of the e-mail forward. Twenty-two days left. Now there was a rumble in his chest, his fingers curled into a fist, and his temples throbbed. Somebody was threatening her to expose them, the question was who and why.

Just as he was about to dedicate some time to trying to figure that out there was a knock at his door.

"Come in," Bas said, pressing a button to clear his computer screen.

"Got something for you, boss," Dana Booth said as he stepped into his office.

The massage therapist was also a shadow shifter and a damn good researcher as well.

Bas signaled him to come in and waited until he was seated across from him before replying, "What did you find?"

"The shipment came from the lab, just like the labels said. As far as I could trace they left the Comastaz facility one week ago; the refrigeration apparatus built into the crates was only good for seven days. The samples needed to make it to their destination by then or risk contamination."

"So they're no good now?" Bas asked, not sure why but not altogether pleased by that assessment.

Dana shook his head. "No good now. But somebody at that lab put a trace on those crates. See, at first they were shipped through UPS to an address in Mexico. Then back to the US with the drugs and guns."

"Why?" Bas asked immediately. "Why ship crates of blood from the US to Mexico then back to the US again?"

"That's where I come up short. My thought is we need to get somebody into Comastaz to get some definitive answers. Unless one of those buttheads in the bunker starts giving up some real information."

Bas was almost positive he'd gotten all the information he was going to get from them. They couldn't tell what they didn't know and it made sense that they weren't trusted with all the pertinent information. After dismissing Dana and thanking him for the information, Bas sat back in his chair, thinking about how fucked up things were becoming on the shifter front and how one woman was once again turning him inside out. He let loose a roar that may have startled the resort guests if he hadn't ensured that his office was sound-proof and situated at the farthest end of the floor.

Inside his cat paced impatiently and Bas, against the training he'd implemented years before, let it roam. He allowed the pushing and felt the crack of bones as the partial shift took over. It wasn't something they did often, but his restraint and patience had taught the cat this type of obedience, this yielding to the human form that Bas had required after Mariah's death.

His elongated teeth pricked his bottom lip, eyes dilated until he knew they were no longer gray but golden yellow. He roared again, pushing away from his desk to go and stand at the window. It was growing dark outside even though he had no idea how long he'd been closed in here. The cat wanted to run, it wanted to hunt, to kill whoever was threatening Priya. Bas needed to find out who that was first, he needed to find that out before he did anything else, before she found proof of their existence and before Rome ordered her death.

# Chapter 15

She was in his room, again. Locked in, even if discreetly and it was partially her fault this time. After Bas had left her naked and unfulfilled on the table in the spa she'd hurriedly dressed and opened the door to go after him. Only to run face-first into the wide, hard chest of a man with a squared jaw and a tribal tattoo wrapped around his neck.

"I'll take you upstairs, ma'am," he'd said in a robotic tone.

"No, thank you. I know my way," she'd said, then tried to move around him. She should have known that wasn't going to work since he almost blocked the entire doorway with his spread-leg stance and bodybuilder-like physique. A body that should have aroused her, considering the nerve-wracking point she had approached with her celibacy endeavor. But there was nothing, only the low hum of being jilted by the infamous Sebastian Perry.

"I will take you," he continued as he stepped to the side to let her pass, and then quickly moved to stand beside her once she was in the hallway. "Mr. Perry's orders."

Of course, she thought, frowning at his words. "You follow all of Mr. Perry's orders?" Everybody around here seemed to do whatever that man said.

He nodded. "Yes, ma'am, I do."

"Why?" she demanded, then softened her voice a little. "I mean, do you work for the resort or Mr. Perry personally?"

There was no immediate response and Priya thought he might not answer her at all. When she looked over to him he seemed to be contemplating what to say.

"Does Mr. Perry dictate your answers too?"

He did something then that shocked her. He smiled, a wide toothy grin that gave this large muscled man a mischievous little-boy look that reminded her of Malik.

"He does not dictate anything. I just do my job," he told her.

"And right now your job is to escort me up to his room and lock me inside. Am I correct?" she continued when they'd walked through the reception area of the spa, out the double doors that led into the resort.

"My job is to make sure you are safe until he returns."

"Oh, like a bodyguard? I've never had my own private bodyguard before." Her fake exuberance did not appear to be lost on him, but it obviously did not change his course.

He shook his head. "Then I guess I'm honored."

Once inside the elevator she looked the man up and down once more. He wasn't her enemy, she thought drably. He wasn't the man who'd driven her desire up so high and so fast she thought she might actually die when the release finally hit her, then left her there looking and feeling like a fool. He was just doing his job and she was taking her sexual frustrations out on him.

"What's your name?" she asked. "Or are you allowed to tell me?"

"I'm Paolo."

He spoke like he wanted to say more but was maybe being forced not to. That might be taking things a little too far, she thought, since there was no one here to actually stop him from talking.

"Nice to meet you, Paolo," was her simple reply.

From there Priya had chosen not to fire off any more questions about Bas or the staff. Mostly because she knew he wasn't going to give her any of the answers she hoped for. The fact was Bas was clearly the boss here at Perryville. He was the boss and he was the only man that had ever aroused her and left her hanging, which she feared was a bigger issue than his staff refusing to give up any dirt about him.

Still, she'd been amused as they approached the door to Bas's suite and she wondered how they would get in. Standing close and watching his every move, she asked, "Don't tell me you don't have a key," she quipped.

Paolo turned to her then, giving her a breathtaking smile that might have stopped the heart of another woman, but paled in comparison to Bas's reserved allure. "I have a temporary code," was his reply.

Priya nodded as he turned his attention back to the control panel, watching every button he pushed, filing the information away for later use.

Now, here she was once again in the room that had secret doors and computers with basically no information on them. Light switches she couldn't find, windows that had no latches, automatic mini-blinds that worked on anyone else's command but hers. And just because she was already thinking that things couldn't get any worse, her cell phone chirped.

A few seconds later Priya was mumbling something to herself, dropping her head into her hands, and sighing. Lolo couldn't trace the e-mails, not even the one she'd received just yesterday. So she still had no idea who was blackmailing her. Two weeks ago they'd sent her a picture of Malik. He'd looked okay, disgruntled and probably angry as hell at being held captive. But she had no idea where he was.

Coming here was supposed to help him. It was supposed to lead her to the answers they wanted. Instead, courtesy of the reputed playboy, she'd been sucked into his spell, letting him touch her and take her to higher heights than she'd ever reached before. She'd thought it would help break down his barriers, but she didn't know any more now than she'd known before. Obviously she wasn't good at the sex-in-exchange-for-information work ethic, either.

In twenty-two days her brother would be killed and her mother would be devastated. Priya would be a failure both on the professional and the familial fronts. And then what?

"Dammit!" she cursed, replying to Lolo's text with quick keystrokes.

Pausing, she reached farther into her purse and pulled out that business card. She was texting him the e-mail address and telephone number of Agent Dorian Wilson. She wanted him to send the e-mail message to the FBI. If she couldn't save Malik, maybe the Feds could.

With that done, Priya also admitted that it was time for her to leave Perryville. Bas wasn't going to give her any information she needed, no matter his "trust me, I can help you" routine. It was all a part of his seduction. It was that reputed seduction that had garnered him so many women and his infamous reputation. Besides that, he would never betray Roman Reynolds, the same way none of his employees here would ever betray him. She found her other bag and pulled out some clean clothes. The first thing she needed to do, desperately because this scent that hovered over her was driving her mad with rage, was take a hot shower to rinse his traitorous touch from her skin. Then, she was getting the hell out of this room; if she had to break through a window to get someone's attention, she was leaving Perryville Resorts tonight!

\* \* \*

It was quiet in his room when Bas returned, blissfully
so. During the entire ride up the five floors to his penthouse suite his mind had buzzed with words like *human,
rogue, breasts, guns, blood, sweet, wet, drugs,* until he
was sure his fist would connect with the wall at any moment. Squeezing the bridge of his nose as he stepped off
the elevator, Bas reached for focus once more, for balance. Two things that had been hard as hell to come by in
the years since he'd returned from the Gungi.

Memories of that night had assailed him on a regular
basis, and then, each time he opened or closed his eyes
he'd see hers—blue eyes, light and helpless, and soulless
because of him. On the heels of his parents' divorce, not
being able to save Mariah had been devastating to Bas. It
had also been the catalyst to his rebirth, or should he say
the emergence of the man he was today. The fearless and
shrewd businessman who never took no for an answer
and never did anything half-assed. On a good day he was
flawless, on a bad one, he was still better than the vast
majority of ass-kissing backstabbers in the business. As
far as the Assembly went, he was a hell of a fighter and a
leader, as recognized by his appointment to Faction Leader.
He was also a loyal friend to Rome and had pledged his
allegiance to him eternally.

Or until the moment the leader asked him to kill Priya.

Then, they were definitely going to have problems.

As he walked into the suite he couldn't come up with
the words to explain why he felt so protective of her, or
why he wanted so desperately to harbor the one person on
this earth at the moment that could do the most harm to
his people. She could destroy them all with one story, one
revelation, and then where would they be? The staunchest
and fiercest rule of the *Ètica* was their autonomy, because
it not only prevented the shifters from having to go into a
defensive mode among the human world but it also pro-

tected the humans from the unknown that would surely be the death of them. With that said, was it fair not to give them the heads-up that there was another race living amongst them, a very deadly-if-provoked race at that? Priya had posed that question to him last night and Bas had been haunted by her words ever since.

*You don't think we have a right to know if something else is out there? If we need to protect ourselves?*

Everyone had a right to protect themselves, Bas thought. He just never really considered the fact that the humans would need to protect themselves from the shadows because a huge part of Rome's platform as leader was for their kind to live peacefully amongst the humans. Which, Bas had to figure, would make it slightly harder for Rome to immediately order Priya's death. They would be knowingly killing a human. Even if that act would save their tribe. His temples throbbed as he sympathized with each party in this argument. Unfortunately, his birthright dictated he reside confidently on one side over the other.

When he arrived in his suite he realized Priya was in the tub. And for Bas, at that very moment, nothing else seemed to matter. He moved through his private living space based on memory alone as he wasn't actually seeing anything that was there, just moving until he stopped at the bathroom door. It was open because he was sure she didn't know how to close it. Everything in his rooms operated on a remote that responded only to his touch. Jace and Cole had thought the innovative technology was over the top and vain, just as they often described him, but Bas had implemented it for the security and privacy benefits. Maybe he'd had the forethought that there would come a time when someone would be in his personal space looking for any damning information they could find on him.

When he'd had the bathroom designed Bas had thought going with the stained concrete floors and floating cabinets was a great idea. The marble sink and countertops had been one of his favorite aspects of the room. But tonight, none of those amenities fazed him. Seeing her just a few feet away sitting in the spacious, oversized spa bathtub that adorned each of the suites in Perryville, surrounded by big fluffy bubbles was the absolute highlight of this space. Folding his arms over his chest, Bas leaned against the counter, settling in to watch her until . . . well, until that became too much torture to bear.

She seemed not to notice his arrival as she lifted a mocha-toned leg into the air, using a loofa sponge to pour water over that limb. Bas swallowed deeply. When she did the same with the next leg, he lifted a hand to rub a finger along the line of his jaw. Next came her arms, one first, then the other, water cascading down over her shoulders and neck in lovely rivulets that made Bas more than a little envious. Her head tilted back as she held that sponge above her neck and squeezed so that a splash of water drizzled down the long, enticing curve of skin.

His dick was rock hard, pressing painfully against the zipper of his pants. At his sides his fingers, sans the claws that had been there only about thirty minutes ago as he'd stood in his office, clenched and unclenched with the desperate need to touch her. The scented bubbly water did nothing to ease the intensity of her personal aroma and on each inhale desire filtrated throughout his body.

She knew he was there, knew he was watching. That knowledge came quick, like a slap, to be followed up by a smirk.

"Look all you want," she spoke finally. "But your touching privileges are revoked. Permanently," she continued with a stony look over her shoulder.

"Get dressed," was all he said to her. "I ordered dinner to be brought to the room."

She stopped bathing and stared at him incredulously. "I'm not staying."

Another slap to his face. Bas was not having a good night and when he didn't have a good night, his cat didn't have a good night and that could lead to all types of chaos. So he gritted his teeth and looked at her—at her dark brown eyes and firmly set lips. He did not look to the remnants of soap and bubbles running down her shoulders and her chest, creating a path between the plump globes of her breasts.

"We're having dinner and we'll talk about you staying." That was the best he could do. Especially since what he really wanted to do was grab her from that tub and slip his dick deep into her pussy, which he knew was still hot and waiting for him.

This was not working for him. Being this close and not touching her, not tasting her was harder than not breathing. So instead of continuing what he thought was a pointless conversation with her, he turned and walked out of the bathroom. All the while he breathed a sigh of relief that she hadn't stood up to confront him. All his blessed control and focus would have surely been lost at that point.

Priya smiled at his retreating back. He'd been watching her. She'd heard the moment he stepped into the bathroom and thought she couldn't have planned that little performance any better. Once she knew she had an audience—a very captive one at that—she'd given him a little show. He deserved to be teased after he'd done that and then some in the spa.

Unfortunately, he'd bailed before the grand finale, but that was fine, her leaving Perryville could have the same effect. If she thought for one crazy moment that she meant anything more to Sebastian Perry than the nuisance reporter that wanted to know his secrets, she was in for a rude awakening. Luckily for her she didn't think that, it was crazy to assume, to even consider that a man like Bas would want . . .

He didn't want anything from her and neither did she from him. That's what she told herself while toweling off and reaching for the simple paisley-print sundress that she slipped over her head and shimmied past her hips. It wasn't Vera Wang but it was cute and it hugged her in all the right places. If she were trying to catch the infamous Mr. Perry, she could give some of those fancy-schooled and even fancier-dressed women a run for their money, easily.

"Good thing I'm not trying," she quipped then looked into the mirror, fluffing the top of her hair. The sides were beginning to grow out so she switched on the water to wet the tips of her fingers then patted it down. After a resolute sigh she reminded herself that this was all pointless; she wasn't here to seduce Bas, and she definitely wasn't going to stick around long enough for him to finish seducing her. With that thought in mind she headed out of the bathroom.

Right into an empty bedroom.

And an empty living room.

Where the hell had he gone?

She was just about to head back into the bedroom when a whooshing sound signaled one of the floor-to-ceiling windows sliding open. This entire space was full of gadgets, secret doors, lights illuminating on some silent command. It all made her think of a man with too much money to spend and too much time on his hands. Or an obsessively irritating version of both.

"What do you have against doorknobs and well, real doors?" she asked because the whole Bruce Wayne vibe she was getting from his resort to his private living quarters was beginning to rub her the wrong way.

He wore dark gray slacks and leather shoes, the shirt a

pullover this time, yet it still lay over his broad shoulders and muscled biceps as if the designer knew Bas was going to be the one wearing it.

"I've set dinner up outside. It's a nice night and I thought you'd like to enjoy it," he told her.

"That would sound nice if I planned to stay for dinner. But I'm not. I'm leaving," Priya replied, rubbing her hands together as she moved toward where he stood.

He sighed as if he were tired even though his body didn't give way to any of the usual exhaustion symptoms— slumped shoulders, weary eyes, slight frown. No, he still looked perfect, damn him. "Can we just have dinner first? If you still want to leave after that, we'll work something out."

This was new, she thought. It wasn't an order, but a request, and it was sincere and almost humble. He'd never spoken to her that way, never looked to her the way he was right now. "Why?" she asked.

He rubbed a hand over his light mustache, down around his chin. "I'd like to have dinner with you, Priya. Would you please join me?"

Damn, she should have had her cell on record or she should have had her tape recorder out to memorialize this moment. She was sure none of those other females had ever been asked to dinner like this by him, or at least telling herself that made her a little giddy.

"My flight leaves at ten thirty," was her lame response.

He nodded and came to stand directly in front of her. "We've got time," he said.

Priya swallowed, loving the scent that always seemed to surround him. It was musky, and earthy and fresh and just damned arousing.

"And for the record . . ." He leaned forward and whispered into her ear, "There are plenty of doors in this room, you just have to know where to look to find them."

"Yes," she said on an exhale of breath that she'd held since the second he came close to her. "And that's normal, right?" she asked, just before stepping out into the night air.

She wouldn't go so far as to say it was cool, but the air wasn't as stiff as it had been when she was out with him earlier. This part of the balcony she'd seen through the window, the same redbrick tile that was on the deck at the spa. A clay-colored wall with a white iron bar atop for support and safety, she figured. What she didn't see was the table and the dinner he'd mentioned.

"Do we play hide-and-seek for the dinner table as well?"

With a smile that practically glided through the air and smacked her in the face, sending spikes of heat straight to her core, he replied, "This way."

Priya let him take her by the arm. She followed him as they rounded the side of a wall and walked up three steps. Then she was shocked into silence, which for her was just like keeping still, not something she was very good at. There was a pool—it was the first thing she noticed—a big pool, longer and wider than the one at the spa and it glowed. Yes, the water was a brilliant turquoise that illuminated the entire deck, including the table covered in a black tablecloth with two long, slim candles and flowers in its center. The flowers were also blue, several different shades of the color that seemed to radiate against the crystal glasses and the silver trim of the china plates. She couldn't help it, she gasped.

"I took the liberty of selecting our meal," Bas began, talking as he escorted her to the table. His tone was sort of like, "I know you're amazed at this gorgeous display I've laid out for you, but please, don't drool."

In the alternative, Priya took a deep breath, released it on a slow exhale, and promised herself she wouldn't do something so belittling. But she did sneak another gaze at the pool before taking the seat Bas offered, wondering if she'd have the opportunity for a swim before leaving this resort.

"Grilled pork chops, buttered asparagus tips, and garlic mashed potatoes. It wasn't Mrs. Ramirez's first choice, but I told her you were a pretty special guest."

He sat across from her, lifting his napkin and settling it in his lap. Priya had already done the same and when he looked up at her she couldn't help but smile. "I'm special, huh?"

"Yes, because I've never fed a woman on my patio before."

"Where do you normally feed them?" she asked for a lack of anything better to say because his "special" remark had caught her off guard.

He paused for a moment before replying, "I usually take my dates to restaurants."

Priya simply nodded, regaining a little of her composure. "Well, I'm not a date," she told him matter-of-factly. "And this is not some romantic night. I came here for a story and you refused to give it to me. Case closed."

"I said I would help and I will," he added in agreement, uncovering the dishes of food and reaching for her plate, ignoring her references to them not being on a date.

"You'll tell me what I want to know about Reynolds?" she asked hopefully. "I'll write a good solid story, I'll make sure I tell his side completely. I just need you to tell me everything."

He stopped fixing their plates then and looked up at her. "I need you to tell me everything," he said quietly. "Who is Malik and why is someone threatening to kill him?"

Priya had just picked up her fork, was about to touch it to her plate so she could eat, but she paused. That was an understatement, she just about froze. "What did you say?"

"I asked you who Malik was and why has the threat of his death made you risk your life for a story?"

"How do you know that?" she asked, her heartbeat racing. "How the hell do you know that?" She slammed the fork down then, her fingers shaking.

He looked as if he might not tell her the truth, like he might try to lie, but then he didn't.

"I saw the e-mails. I know they're threatening to kill Malik if you don't deliver this story."

Priya shook her head. "No," she whispered, her throat suddenly feeling clogged. "No. I'm a reporter, I'm just following a story. A story this big could jump-start my career. It could make national headlines. That's always been my goal," she told him, swallowing every few words, trying to keep her composure, trying to keep from crying.

"You had no idea these things were connected. You were content to write the stories you'd always been writing, letting your career take its natural course. They changed the game and now you're playing by their rules."

"I'm not playing," she said and then pushed back from the table. "I'm not playing, I'm working and you're not helping! You lie and you don't keep your word. You are not helping, goddamned you, Sebastian!"

# Chapter 16

Pain and fear engulfed her and stabbed at Bas like searing hot blades. She'd stood up and was about to walk away from the table, from him, when he stood and grabbed her. He pulled her body back to him, wrapping his arms around her to keep her still.

"Let me go! I have to go! I have to get back." Her words were cut off. She choked and tried again. "I have to get back to save him," was her quiet cry.

Bas held her close, hearing her words, hearing the despair in her voice, feeling the pain of her helplessness because he'd been there once before. He'd watched someone die when he could have acted. They were the same. No, Priya was different because she wasn't willing to just watch, to wait. She wanted to act. Unfortunately, Bas knew he couldn't let her do that, not alone.

"I said I would help you and I will. Tell me who they are and I will fix this. I will get Malik back for you." Even if it's a man she loves and wants to spend the rest of her life with. Those words didn't slip from his lips and he had to swallow hard to keep them back.

She turned then, still in his embrace, and looked up to him, eyes brimming with tears: "Who are you? Who are they? Please, tell me."

Bas knew what she was asking, he knew what she

wanted to know. But he couldn't tell her. No matter how much he wanted to help her, he couldn't tell her about his people. What he could do, however, was to help her forget, even if just for a little while. He could help her focus on the good things in this world, things she'd missed in her life, things that would make her smile and feel good about herself.

"Let's go for a swim," he suggested impulsively. The look on her face said the question stunned her too. He didn't give her a moment to think about why the request seemed out of the blue and possibly ludicrous considering their situation. He let his hands slide down her arms until he clasped her fingers. "Come, the water awaits."

"I'm not prepared to go swimming," she told him as they came closer to the edge of the pool.

There was no customary lip that clearly defined the end of the walkway and the entrance of a pool, but a smooth transition of the tiled flooring to the glowing water. That's where Bas stopped walking, turning her so that she faced him. He looked deep into her eyes, so deep that Priya blinked and attempted to turn away. The feeling that he could see something inside her, something she wasn't willing to reveal to this man of many mysteries himself, was unnerving.

"I have a plane to catch."

He shook his head, keeping their bodies close as he looked down at her intently. His gaze was so deep, so absorbing she actually shivered beneath it.

"Let's not think about the plane or the story or anything right now. The water is cool and it's waiting. Let's just take a swim."

"A swim? Is that all we're doing? Taking a swim?" she asked, not necessarily believing him and not quite accepting that he would lie to her at this moment.

"We're doing what's necessary," was his reply. "Very necessary for both of us."

He cupped her face then, turning her so that she was once again gazing up into his eyes. The reflection of the pool and the candlelight both had the same striking effect to his gray orbs, it made them seem translucent. And that intrigued her.

"You are a very attractive man," she admitted. It wasn't a lie but on a normal date she probably wouldn't have been so up-front about her admiration of a man's looks.

That may also be attributed to the fact that she'd never had a normal date with a man that looked like Bas, or had his bank account, for that matter.

"And you are a very alluring woman," was his reply.

After those words his suggestion didn't sound so out of the question. Her first instinct was to argue, to run like hell out of here and catch that plane home. To do what exactly? Without Bas's help she had no story. Without his touch she only had her vibrator.

"What will I wear for this swim?"

It was a brazen question, even to her ears, and obviously to the peaks of her breasts that hardened instantly. He leaned forward then, his thumbs rubbing along her cheekbones, lowering slightly until they scraped the edge of her jaw.

"We'll both wear the same thing," he whispered, so close to her now his wine-tinged breath fanned warmly over her face. "Nothing."

His lips brushed against hers as the last syllable of the word was spoken and Priya drifted willingly into his kiss. Their lips melded in a soft connection, tongues snaking out gently at first to be reacquainted. If she'd thought she'd been warm before whenever he'd only looked at her, or touched her, there was no comparison to now as his mouth seduced her slowly, methodically, inevitably.

She was on her tiptoes now, wrapping her arms around his neck, pulling him down closer, attempting to take their kiss deeper. His hands moved from her face to her sides, dragging slowly down the length of her torso to her hips. When he cupped her buttocks she moaned, nipping his bottom lip between her teeth. He groaned in return and she felt the material of her dress being grabbed into his hands. In a rough move that both shocked and aroused her, he pushed her back slightly, breaking the kiss, but lifting her dress up at the same time. Later, much later, Priya would tell herself that she'd had no choice, that once the die had been cast there was no turning back. Well, that die had surely been cast the moment Bas walked her out onto this balcony with this gorgeous pool and the candlelit dinner. And the second his tongue had so lavishly and seductively stroked hers she knew there was no turning back.

She lifted her arms, allowing him to completely pull the dress up and over her head. Her underwear wasn't of the sexy Victoria's Secret variety, instead she wore simple cotton royal-blue boy shorts. In light of the thin straps on her dress she'd worn no bra and the night air instantly tickled her already puckered nipples.

He stood there then, for what felt like endless moments, staring at her. His eyes roamed from the top of her head over her breasts and hips, down her thighs and to her toes, in a swooping assessment that had her feeling just a bit edgy. When he lifted his hands to cup her breasts, she sucked in a breath. His touch was so dominating, so completely enticing she could barely inhale. Maybe it was because she hadn't been overly blessed in the breast department and his large hands made that alarmingly clear. Or was it the smooth, heated feel of his palms pressing against the swollen mounds, his fingers clenching to grip her beneath them, or the breath he sucked in as he did so.

Her eyes flew to his face at that moment, her heart

skittering around in her chest at the knowledge that he was just as aroused as she was. There'd been a tightening to the features of his face, a muscle actually ticked in his jaw, his lips were only slightly parted, just enough to release a breath so he wouldn't suffocate. For a few seconds Priya allowed the power of femininity to wash over her. She hadn't come to this dinner tonight dressed in expensive clothes, drenched in diamonds, or cooing like some simpering socialite looking for a leg up in the world. And yet, he was touching her and looking at her as if she were the only female in existence. Floating on that knowledge, she lifted her hands to the three buttons at the neck of his shirt, releasing them each slowly.

He watched her. She'd seen the shift in his eyes as her hands moved and he followed every movement of her fingers. When she had the buttons undone and flattened, her palms over his taut pectorals, he tensed beneath her. With a painfully slow movement she touched his biceps, then ran her fingers along the length of his arms until she reached his wrists. His hands still cupped her breasts and for a second she paused, not wanting to break that contact. Then she sucked in a breath and pushed his hands away from her body. His head snapped upward, his gaze quickly capturing hers.

"We'll swim together," she whispered. "My body, with your body."

While she spoke she grabbed the hem of his shirt, pushing it up over his sculpted abs and muscled chest. He lifted his arms, pulling it the rest of the way over his head because she might have needed a stepladder to achieve that feat. Bas was more than six feet tall so he towered over her five-foot-five height and yet their bodies still seemed to fit perfectly, at least for the moment.

"Finish it," he murmured as he tossed his shirt in the same direction her dress had gone only moments before.

That was a command, there was no doubt about it, and as much as Priya hated men that thought they could tell her what to do and when to do it, she undid the buckle of his belt and pants, pushing them along with his slacks down his muscled thighs. Stepping out of her sandals quickly, she even knelt down and waited while he stepped out of his leather loafers to push the clothes free of his legs totally. But before she could rise all the way up, she was being scooped into his arms, then soaring through the air as he jumped with her in tow, into the glistening water.

The coolness was a blissful release as they broke the surface, Bas's arms still wrapped tightly around her.

"Nice," he said, smiling down at her, water dripping from his face.

Priya shook her head and wiped her eyes, then let her hands fall to his shoulders as she acclimated herself to their naked bodies touching—well not totally naked, the material of her panties rubbed annoyingly against her skin. With a start she realized she wanted them off. She wanted to wrap her legs around Bas's waist and feel him sinking his thick length deep inside of her. The thought made her gasp and before she could speak, Bas's lips were on hers once more. This kiss was hungry and rough, his teeth scraping over her lips almost to the point of being painful. His hands gripped her bottom, fingers slipping beneath the rim of her underwear. He parted her cheeks, thrusting a finger into her moistness and Priya bucked against him. In and out he stroked her until her breathing was coming in pants and she reluctantly pulled her mouth away from his so she could catch another breath. His teeth moved to her jawline as her head lolled back, down the line of her throat where he nipped and licked, licked and nipped. As she moved against the ministrations of his finger her nipples scraped along the cool wetness of his chest;

the friction was erotic and had her thighs bucking and her voice screaming out his name as a tremendous release rippled through her body.

She felt weightless when Bas unwrapped her legs from around his waist, and not just because they were in a pool. That release had been just like the one she'd brought on herself in her apartment, the morning after first meeting Bas. It was exhilarating and yet she wanted more, needed another desperately. Bas continued to hold her close with one arm as he swam to the side of the pool then shifted so that her back was to the wall.

"You enjoying our swim?" he asked, a salacious smile spreading across his face.

Priya cleared her throat and her mind of the greedy thoughts. "It's nice," she finally mumbled. "I mean, the pool is really nice. How do you get the water to glow like this?"

For a moment he looked as if she'd said the wrong thing. Priya ignored that look, she needed a moment to regroup, to find the stability required to continue acting like the mature woman she was, and not some wide-eyed, naïve schoolgirl who'd just had an amazing orgasm.

"The pool has a pebbled finish called beveled turquoise. Together with the inground lighting it produces the glowing effect. I thought it was a very romantic touch," he told her, all while resting his hands on the wall behind her and pressing his body closer to hers.

She could have done without the touching, or benefited more if it were in strategic locations. Instead of making that known, she kept her arms to her sides beneath the cool water and gave thanks that they'd moved to a lower depth in the pool so at least her feet were now touching the bottom, providing just the stability she needed.

"It's probably a bit more than romantic," she finally admitted. "But then I'm sure that was your plan."

"You think I had a plan to get you into my pool?" he asked, moving so close now her nipples brushed against his chiseled chest.

"Not me," she replied after swallowing deeply. "Any female."

He shook his head, cupping a hand to the back of her neck. "Never 'any female,' Priya," he whispered. "Only you."

He was lowering his head to hers and try as she might Priya just didn't have the strength—or the good sense, whichever the case may be—to move.

"Uh huh," she whispered.

"Do you believe me?" he asked.

"Uh huh," she replied, not entirely sure of what he was saying, only knowing that his lips were close to hers, his arousal rubbing devilishly against her thigh.

"Do you trust me?"

"Uh huh," she moaned as his tongue traced her bottom lip.

"Do you need me?" was his next question.

She had to swallow again, close her eyes, then reopen them to make sure she wasn't dreaming. "Yes," she whispered, this time because the burning deep inside for him could only be described as need.

"I need you too, Priya. I don't know why or how this came to be, but goddammit, I need to be inside you."

That admission was chased by his hands going below the water, grabbing her underwear at both sides, then ripping them off. Her thighs moved of their own accord as she whimpered, "I need you, Bas. I need you right now!"

Bas couldn't stop now if all of the Elders were lined around this pool dressed in Speedos and holding scrolls with specific rules of the *Ètica* written in neon-green highlighter for him to see. He was all in, or rather, in a few seconds he was going to be all in . . . no matter the consequences.

He grabbed Priya's pliant legs, wrapping them around his waist once more. Then he reached for her arms, lacing them around his neck because he loved the feel of her holding him, trapping him, so to speak. When she leaned forward and took one pebbled nipple into her mouth, his cat roared, loud and strong; it stood on all fours, mouth open, intention set. Bas grabbed hold of her hips, positioning himself so that his dick nudged her tight opening.

"Do that again," he instructed her in a hoarse tone.

When she obliged he closed his eyes, pulled his hips back slightly, and thrust forward quickly. Slow just wasn't on the list of options right now. He'd been starving for this connection, his cat begging for it and now that it was here, well, it was simpler to just say, there was no stopping him.

She gasped as he thrust his full length inside her. She was tight, her grip on his dick like a stranglehold. He almost came instantly. For seconds and with all the strength he could muster, Bas held absolutely still, giving her a minute to acclimate herself to his size. Her head had dropped to his chest as she tried to steady her breathing.

Lowering his mouth to her ear, he asked, "More?"

She lifted her head, licking her now-swollen lower lip and whispered, "More."

Pulling back then thrusting deep once more, Bas sighed with pleasure. Out, then in, out then in. Her legs tightened around his back, fingernails digging into his shoulders. He pounded into her, losing himself instantly in the warmth of her abyss. She moved with him, giving as well as she was getting. Inside his cat paced and purred, lifting a paw to swipe at nothing and then at him for not giving in to this sooner, for not obliging their mutual needs.

Her head lolled back and he stared down at the line of her neck, that hollow that he'd adored since day one.

Leaning forward, he licked her there, over and over as his hips undulated forcefully. Her mouth opened as she screamed his name.

"Sebastian! Sebastian!" she yelled and he shivered all over.

Each time she said it Bas felt vibrations from the lobes of his ears straight down to the tip of his dick. His thighs shook as he continued to work in and out of her, his mind warring with the mind of his cat, his body fighting to control all three. He gripped the side of the pool for leverage as Priya held onto him. Around them water coated their bodies, lapped at the motion they made, coaxing and encouraging their release.

"More, Sebastian! More!" she yelled and Bas breathlessly obliged.

He reached for her legs, pulling them from around his waist but keeping them spread wide beneath the water. Pulling back until only his tip was inside her, he demanded she look at him as he thrust back in deeply.

"Yes!" she encouraged him. "Yes!"

Bas could hear nothing but the sound of her voice, could see nothing but the deep brown of her eyes, feel nothing but the heated moistness of her body. His incisors sharpened as a familiar rippling along his spine tempted another part of him. He closed his eyes in an effort to keep the cat at bay. But the more she called his name, the more the cat struggled to break free.

"Look at me, Sebastian! Look at me!"

Dammit, she was encouraging him again. Saying his name, telling him what she wanted, demanding what she needed as he pumped harder, more fiercely than he'd ever felt his hips move before.

"Yes!"

This time the guttural moan was his own. "Dammit all, yes!"

His hands went to her hips then, holding her perfectly still as he speared his length in and out of her again and again. Her thighs shook, her teeth sinking into her lower lip as she kept her eyes on him.

"Yes!" she said between clenched teeth. "Yes!"

Feeling her come this time was infinitely sweeter than the first. The strength with which her inner walls grasped his dick and spasmed with her release was enough to push him right over the edge. He released her hips, letting his palms rest over her breasts as he took two more pumps before growing absolutely still, growling into the nape of her neck as his own release burst free.

Seconds later, when Bas thought he could at least breathe steadily again, he pulled slightly away from her. Not enough so that their connection was broken, but just enough so he could look down at her.

"This wasn't supposed to happen," he told her.

She nodded immediately and agreed, "I know."

"But it did."

She nodded again. "So what now?"

He thought about that question for a minute, thought about the implications it proposed and fought like hell for a reasonable answer. With any other female it would have been simple, get dressed and leave. With another shifter the arrangements would have already been stated before getting to this point. In any other business arrangement he would state his terms and advise they be accepted or declined.

But this was totally different. He knew it as his dick pulsated inside her warmth once more, as her gaze held his intently and even more so as she rubbed her hands along his back, along the tribal tattoo and the length of his cat depicted there.

"Now, we sleep," he told her before slipping out of her slowly then helping her out of the pool.

They didn't speak again, Bas sensing that neither of them knew exactly what to say. All her questions had taken a backseat to what had transpired between them, just as had all, or rather, most of his reservations. Even though consequences and repercussions ran rampant through his mind, Bas would not speak them, not tonight. Instead he gently dried her off when they were in his bedroom, then he pulled back the duvet and sheet and guided her into the bed. Initially, she paused and stood beside his bed looking up at him as if she wanted to say something. Bas prayed that she wouldn't. If she did it would be about her story or her brother or how he planned to help and Bas just didn't know. He didn't know why he'd felt compelled to help her or to protect her from Rome and anyone else out to harm her. For the very first time in his life, Bas didn't have all the answers and for a shifter like him, that wasn't an easy revelation to deal with.

Finally, after about a million excruciating seconds, she silently climbed into the bed, rolling onto her back to look up at him once more. When she lifted a hand, reaching for him, Bas thanked every deity in the world and climbed in beside her without hesitation.

He pulled her close to him, his chin resting on the top of her head, her still-damp hair tickling his skin. He held her close and tight, feeling like if he didn't she might disappear for good. In his mind he vowed to keep her right here, safe in his arms forever.

The impossibility of that scenario wouldn't completely filter through his mind until hours later.

# Chapter 17

It wasn't a loud noise but more like a vibration that shook the table on Bas's side of the bed. Priya had been lying over his chest, her leg entwined between his, both of them sound asleep. Or rather, he'd been sound asleep while she'd been lying there, loving the feel of the rise and fall of his chest and the intoxicating scent of masculinity. It all felt so right and yet, she knew it was terribly wrong.

She didn't belong with a man like Sebastian Perry in a place like Perryville. Sure, she'd been working her entire adult life to get ahead and to leave her past behind her, but never in a million years had she imagined she'd be surrounded by things like expensive watches, designer ties, or a home in a place that was like a small remote town with as much technology as a *Star Wars* movie. This just wasn't where she'd imagined herself at twenty-seven years old, and it definitely wasn't where she'd imagined herself when she'd spent the last of her life's savings to chase this man and his secrets across the country.

Bas stirred immediately upon hearing the muted sound. He probably would have jumped straight up if she hadn't been sprawled so wantonly across his body. Instead, he adjusted her with gentle hands until he managed to slip from beneath her, letting her head be softly cradled by the pillow and pulling the sheet up to her neck.

Priya remained perfectly still, lying on her stomach, keeping her eyes closed. He moved through the darkness with hardly any sound, the bathroom door sliding open with an almost imperceptible whishing noise. Moments later she heard the belt buckle clinking as he slipped on his pants and chose that moment to do a mock yawn, turn, and resettle amongst the sheets. Through barely slit lids she watched as Bas froze, standing at the foot of the bed, watching her intently. She could feel the heat of his gaze as she'd flipped over onto her back, letting the sheets slip down just far enough so that her breasts were bared.

After a few seconds of staring and most likely contemplating, he turned away and Priya opened her eyes completely. She watched him move to the door and tap the spot about level with his right shoulder. Lights from the tiny control pad were revealed, a red one, green one, and yellow one. She couldn't see which one he pushed but the green light began blinking about two seconds before the door opened. He walked through and didn't close the door behind him. But he didn't need to, she'd seen all she needed to see. Her heart pounding with that knowledge, she waited, estimating in her mind how long it should take him to get to the front door and exit the room.

Sixty seconds later Priya was kicking the sheets off the bed. She moved as fast as her still-languid limbs would take her to her bag where she pulled on underwear, shorts, and a tank top. Her tennis shoes were near the wall where she'd seen Bas obtain his underwear just yesterday. Stuffing her feet into them she hurried through the bedroom door and didn't stop until she was in front of the wall where she knew the front door was located. Taking a deep breath she wiped her now-damp palms down her thighs.

"Do or die, Drake," she told herself, then reached up to a spot that aligned with her eyes.

When she stood in front of Bas and didn't look up, the top of her head came to his shoulders. Subtracting for the height she gained when wearing the small-heeled sandals she'd had on last night, she guessed somewhere near her eyes was more accurate. After taking a deep breath, she pressed there on the wall and waited.

Nothing.

"Dammit," she hissed.

Then slowly she traced a finger along the same area, not yet willing to give up. The smooth, almost feltlike material that covered the walls didn't give any indication that she was either hot or cold in her search. And just when she was about to give up and curse Sebastian Perry to hell and back, a piece of the wall shifted. She hurriedly pulled her hand back for fear it would get swallowed up and she'd be held prisoner by the cyber guard until Bas came back. The wall peeled back and a control panel was revealed.

"Bingo!" she said excitedly as she pushed the green button.

The front door opened and she faced the cool hallway with a pride she could barely contain. Now all she had to do was find her way to the floor he'd walked her through two days ago. Whatever type of alarm it was that had awakened him was meant to be covert.

For that reason she had to figure it wasn't a resort problem, and since earlier today when they were in the spa, Bas had apparently been talking to someone other than her, Priya was almost certain he wouldn't be heading to the front desk. Boarding the elevator she pushed the button marked B, she presumed for basement, and waited.

But the minute the elevator doors opened and she was about to step out Priya received a surprise she wasn't counting on.

\* \* \*

"They're on the grounds," Jacques said, checking the firearm he held then slipping it into the holster at his knee. When he stood up straight he pulled the one from the back band of his pants and checked it.

"Not for long, they're not," Bas added from across the control room. He'd already gone to the weapons vault on the far side of the room to retrieve his M-40A3, the newest sniper rifle used by the corps. He'd secured his weapons through his former captain who had now moved up in the ranks to hold the position of commandant, and who was also a shadow.

"I'm going out with Syfon and his five," Jacques told him.

Bas nodded as they both moved for the door. "I'll go up with Paolo and Kaz. I want those two close just in case they get the dumbassed idea to shift."

Jacques nodded and the two separated. Bas didn't look back, just headed for the side stairway and ran like he was back on the combat field. Thoughts of what they might find tonight filtered through his mind as adrenaline pumped through his veins like gas into a fuel tank. He took the steps three at a time, his muscles bunching with the effort. Along his spine the stretch of his cat joined him, elongated muscles making the run seem more like a glide upward and around, twining about the dwelling until he burst through the rooftop door.

Paolo and Kaz were both at either side, having been dispatched to this location already. About twenty feet forward were two other shifters, their sniper rifles trained toward the trees that lined the west side of the resort.

"One down below, fast approaching," Kaz informed Bas.

"There's another one closer near the parking garage," Paolo added. "One's a cat."

Fuck! His mind roared, the curse never falling from

his lips, his finger twitching on the trigger. "Let's stop that bastard first!" he instructed, then yelled to the others up ahead, "Get a bead on him and shoot."

This one they would most likely have to kill, the threat to his guests wasn't worth the risk. Through his com link he could hear Jacques directing his crew around the back end of the building to where the rogue had been sighted.

Going to the edge of the roof Bas crouched low, lifted his rifle to rest on his shoulder, and stared through the scope. That was all for the human side; to hunt this cat he needed more. His eyes adjusted to the night, filtering through the trees like a laser. Inhaling deeply he picked up the scent, felt the rush of the animal on the move, and followed his gut. He moved slightly to the right, about two inches at first, then another five. In seconds the cat burst through the opening of trees just beyond the tennis courts. A low growl escaped, Bas's sharp teeth elongated to prick his lower lip. His finger squeezed the trigger only slightly.

"Got 'em!" he heard someone mumble.

"I got that sonofabitch too! Let's light him up!" Paolo added in a louder voice.

"Hold tight," Bas whispered. "Don't rush the shot."

As if his words had never been spoken, the first bullets exploded with the muted sound of their silenced weapons. From above, spewing dirt from the ground where they'd hit speared upward. The cat roared as it was hit in its hindquarters, then it ran faster, like a blur of black fur streaking forward, heading directly for the resort.

Bas was up in seconds, moving like lightning to kick the gun out of Paolo's clutches. "I said hold tight!"

"I had the shot," Paolo argued.

"You had nothing, you idiot!" He wanted to say more, wanted actually to punch the cocky bastard in his jaw for missing the shot completely, but had other matters to deal with. "Fall in and don't shoot until I tell you to or the next bullet flying's gonna tag your dumb ass!"

Paolo's facial expression said he wasn't happy with that order; the clench of his teeth and squaring of his shoulders said he recognized he didn't have a choice. Bas led the way down from the roof, shouting orders through the com link that a cat was on the loose.

"You shouldn't be here," Jewel whispered, grabbing Priya by the arm and pulling her off the elevator.

"Well, hello to you too," Priya said, trying to keep from falling on her face while the woman moved quickly in front of her.

"This space is off-limits to guests. It's off-limits to everyone," Jewel continued.

They were heading down the hallway that Priya recognized from when she'd been dragged upstairs. It seemed everyone thought that was her preferred mode of travel. Not! She pulled roughly out of Jewel's grasp. The other woman stopped, turning to face Priya with a worried frown.

"We need to get back upstairs. They won't like it if they find us down here," she told Priya.

"Who won't like it and why not? It's just a basement. What do they have down here besides probably old furniture and supplies?" Priya quipped, looking around the space.

It felt like a maze. A cement maze that twisted and turned in all directions with no discerning features to give even a hint of guidance. Yet, Jewel seemed to know exactly where she was going.

"Why are you down here if it's not allowed?" Priya asked.

The other woman folded her arms over her chest, a deep frown marring her otherwise pretty face. Her riotous curls had been pulled back on top into a ponytail that gave her a childlike quality, her eyes blinking furiously as they glared at Priya.

"That's none of your business," was her sharp retort.

Priya nodded. "Okay, I could give you that except you just grabbed me from the elevator, running me down this hallway like you knew where you were taking me. As for me, I'll gladly admit I have no idea what's down here, but I'm awfully curious now that I'm not alone in my quest."

Jewel sighed. "You're not going to go back upstairs, are you?"

"Are you?"

The woman made a frustrated sound. "You're going to mess up everything for me."

Priya was not deterred by the anxiety in Jewel's voice, but rather more intrigued. "And everything would be what, exactly?"

Their conversation was interrupted by the sound of footsteps, running footsteps that were coming closer in their direction.

"Quick, down here!" Jewel yelled, reaching for Priya's arm and pulling her along once more.

Priya was getting damned tired of people pulling her around like she was nothing more than a rag doll. Still, she ran with the woman because she had no clue who was running up behind them. About six feet ahead was a set of double doors. Jewel hesitated momentarily as they came to a four-way section and she tried to figure out which way to go. Priya, who again had no clue where she was going, took the lead. This time she dragged Jewel behind her and felt a spurt of enjoyment at having done so. Until she pushed against those double doors and they both tumbled out into the night.

Falling face-first onto the ground, they both grunted. Priya scrambled to get up even though her chest was throbbing with the breast-to-dirt-ground contact. She was on her hands and knees when she heard a sound that shook the world around her. Everything in her stilled, everything besides her heart which beat a rhythm that echoed almost as loudly as the horrific roar she knew she'd just heard.

In the next second she was grabbed around the waist and yanked from the spot where she'd been rooted. Her back hit the wall this time with a sickening thump as she was tossed behind whoever had come up from behind and grabbed her. When she thought her lungs were ready to cooperate—screw her legs because they just weren't in the mood to move at the moment—she opened her mouth, prepared to scream a few choice expletives at someone. Then there were gunshots and more growling. Male voices yelled as a flurry of action seemed to break out around her. Looking to the side she tried to find Jewel, but didn't see her. Figuring this couldn't get any worse, she took a step and was prepared to run back inside the building when a body blocked that move.

She didn't have to look up because she knew who that someone was, knew instinctively as the molten heat began to flood her body. But Priya did look up, there didn't seem to be any other option. Bas was seething mad. No, that probably didn't even begin to describe the look on his face, the glint in his crystalline-looking eyes or the snarl that marred the bottom half of his face. She opened her mouth to speak, not knowing for sure what was going to come out—an apology, a curse, a hi, how you doing?

It didn't matter because he grabbed her by the front of her T-shirt, pulling her so close she came up on her tiptoes. "You stay behind me, do you hear? Don't try anything stupid, just stay the fuck behind me!"

Priya nodded like one of those dingy cartoon females that had damsel-in-distress written all over them. Her head bobbed up and down like she was a mute and when he released her, she did exactly as she'd been told. Because while Priya had always been independent, stubborn, and just a little bit on the hyperactive side, she'd never considered herself to be stupid by any stretch of the word.

Bas moved back inside the building, mumbling something into his shoulder as he did. She couldn't hear his words because her ears were still echoing from the roaring and being in close range of the gunshots. She hadn't seen who'd been shot. Hell, she hadn't even seen Jewel who just minutes ago had been within arm's reach of her. Now they were moving through those damned light-gray-painted hallways that made her feel like now she might be in some kind of prison. Or at least, a warped-ass nightmare, the kind you had after staying up half the night eating Crunch 'n Munch, drinking chocolate milk, and watching a *Walking Dead* marathon.

They'd just rounded another corner when they came face-to-face with another man. Or at least Priya thought he was a man, even though right about now he looked like some sort of big-assed machine—"big" being the operative word.

"Well, if it ain't the fuckin' FL," the man snarled at Bas. "And what do we have here?" he continued.

Bas's left arm came backward, cupping Priya and tucking her even closer behind him. In his right hand, she'd just noticed, had to be the biggest, blackest gun she'd ever had the pleasure of seeing close-up.

"You don't belong here," Bas said in a steely tone Priya had never heard him use before. "I'm going to give you five seconds to walk the fuck away."

Priya leaned around Bas's muscled body to get another look at the guy/machine and cringed when she did. He'd thrown his head back and laughed in response to Bas's directive. His teeth almost seemed as black as the sweaty skin on his face and he was built like a freakin' boulder.

When one of his creepy-ass eyes locked on hers she moved quickly, slipping behind Bas's cover once more.

Then the man inhaled. She could actually hear him taking a deep breath and its exaggerated exhale.

"You got yourself a mate, FL? Weak-assed shadows," he grumbled. "I'm gonna take pleasure in killing you both. Palermo'll thank me later."

"Or I'll kill you now, take your choice," Bas replied, his gun arm lifting, aiming.

"I'm gonna rip your throat out, FL!" the man shouted, then roared.

Yes, he roared, long and clear as those freshly painted walls that surrounded her. The sound was pure animal, killer animal, she corrected. She shook all over, her fingers grasping the material of Bas's T-shirt, her teeth bearing down into her bottom lip to keep from screaming.

Bas fired, one, two, three . . . and more and more shots until Priya couldn't hear anymore. She covered her ears, her mouth opened wide releasing a scream that was even silent to her. Then Priya did something she'd never, in all her life done before. As if she had that dingy cartoon damsel-in-distress female tattooed on her forehead, she fainted.

# Chapter 18

"He's gonna kill you for sure now," announced the slow-talking shifter sitting across the table with his arms and legs shackled.

No, Bas thought, his temples still throbbing from the events of the night. Whoever "he" was, he would certainly kill this character before anyone else for the way he was running off at the mouth. Not that Bas was complaining, oh no, he was more than happy to sit across from him with Jacques standing to the right of them, listening to this idiot tell them everything he knew.

"Why does he want to kill me?" Bas asked.

Beside him Jacques growled, resting his hands on his hips, the right one closer to the gun he had holstered there.

Idiot shifter's nose had begun to run, right after he'd shed the first round of tears. Jacques and his team had found this one after he'd walked right through the front door of the resort. In human form, dressed in a golf outfit—complete with the most ridiculous hat ever—no warning bells had gone off with the security down there. Not until his scent sifted throughout the lower floors, but by then he'd disappeared down there and the cat that had traveled with him had been spotted. Then the alarm had gone off and they'd set out to catch the intruders.

"You took something he wants really bad."

"The drugs," Bas stated with a nod.

"Yeah, those too. They need to sell that, got lots of buyers chompin' around for this hot new stuff. But that's not all, there was something else down there in those caves, something he says is a big fuckin' deal to some pretty dangerous humans." He sneezed then and turned his head to his shoulder in an attempt to wipe his nose on the collar of his lemon drop-yellow shirt.

"Who is he?" was Bas's next question even though— thanks to the cat he'd killed in the bunker—he had a pretty good idea who he was dealing with. He also had no doubt those pretty dangerous humans the rogue mentioned were connected to the Comastaz Labs.

Idiot golfing shifter sniffed and shrugged. "Goes by Mr. P."

"Creative," Jacques said with a smirk. "Who was the cat?"

"That's Black. He came with Mr. P from the East Coast. They got a lot of plans for the operation here. I'm new, just started yesterday."

That's great, his resume would be short and sweet. Bas leaned forward, flattening his palms on the table. "I've got a message for you to take back to Mr. P," Bas told him with a smirk.

The shifter shrugged again and Bas resisted the urge to punch him just for being the idiot snitch for these devious bastards. Instead, he was going to send Mr. P, also known as Palermo Greer, a nice little care package, one that would warn him in no uncertain terms not to fuck with Bas again.

Minutes later Bas was leaving the bunker with Jacques right behind him. "Burn that cat and put his ashes in a box with their signature mark on it. Send the box to Greer, with a message."

Jacques nodded, probably reading Bas's mind as to what the message should say.

"Tell him if he wants me, to grow some balls and come get me himself." Bas stalked away, slamming his palm into the elevator button.

But as he waited he changed his mind. Upstairs was just one more issue for him to deal with and dammit, he was bone tired. The rush of adrenaline at hunting shifters combined with the general irritation with two of his soldiers then the surprise arrival of his sexy-as-hell, nosy little reporter.

His temples throbbed as he leaned backward to stretch his back. That action only fueled an already burning fire. He'd been trying like hell to ignore the persistent rustling at his spine, the pressure in his temples that was more than just tension. His shoulders burned, even though he'd tried rotating them a few times in search of release. The partial shift he'd allowed earlier in his office hadn't helped. It wanted out and Bas was too damned tired to stop it any longer.

On a long curse, just as the elevator door opened, he turned away and headed for the double doors leading outside.

Down the small incline there was a path that Bas had purposely kept flanked by tall trees to provide much more than just shade. The path followed a winding uphill passage to the balcony of his room. In the opposite direction it led right into the forested area that was otherwise gated off from the resort guests. The walk was too long and the brush there too thick for any of them to ever try exploring even if they ignored the restricted area signs.

That's where Bas was headed. And once he reached the fence he unlatched it and stripped. A box that looked like it held electrical wires and such opened at his touch and key-code entry and he placed his clothes in there. Then Bas dropped to his knees, lifted his head, and allowed his cat the freedom it requested.

The cracking of bones was a welcome sound as his spine expanded, his limbs thinning, yet growing even stronger. Like a shiver moving from head to toe, soft golden fur rippled through every pore. Night air reached its nose and there was a muted sneeze, then a brunt chuffing that announced the cat's arrival. Remnants of the rogues that had invaded this area still lingered in the air, fueling the cat's fire, so to speak. It took off into the darkness without further thought, running upward, upward over the red butte rocks it was accustomed to, through the trees and draped by the darkness of night. It ran free, ran long and hard all the while still yearning for more.

From her.

Priya awoke alone in the center of Bas's bed surrounded by darkness. She sat straight up in the bed, looking around to no avail. He wasn't here. She knew that without even getting out of the bed to inspect the rest of the rooms.

Folding her legs beneath her she rested her elbows on her thighs and replayed the events of the night. Bas's touch was electrifying. His kisses were smoldering. The feel of his strength and experience between her legs was . . . well, mind-blowing. A gentle tugging at her center seconded that emotion.

But that wasn't the part of the evening she wanted to replay. Priya had had questions before. Those questions had been the sole reason for her coming across the country. That original question was further corroborated by another glimpse of those strange eyes that night out in the desert. But tonight, tonight there had been so much more. By way of questions, that is. Why had Jewel been down in the basement and where had she gone to after they'd made it outside? And who had made that roaring sound? Priya was positive it had been a who and not a what, or quite possibly a what that could also be a who. The final question, or the most alarming realization of the night was that Sebastian Perry was a killer. He was gorgeous, rich, and one hell of a lover and he was also a coldhearted killer.

Closing her eyes, she jolted at the memory of him shooting that big man, shooting him so many times he could be nothing else but dead. And she was now a witness to that illegal act.

On a groan she fell back against the pillows, letting her arms drop over her eyes. She'd done it this time, she'd gone way beyond the boundaries of what she should have. And it was all to save her brother who had never done anything in his life to save himself.

To say she'd failed dismally was an understatement.

All she had was an instant replay of a murder and a persistent ache at her center that she feared only one man would ever be able to soothe again. And if she stayed in this place a moment longer the situation would probably only worsen. She should have left earlier, she shouldn't have been swayed by his smooth deep voice, his seductive eyes, or that goddamned pool.

Shaking her head she got out of the bed and fumbled until she found her purse and cell phone. Using the flashlight app she'd downloaded, she searched around until she found every piece of her clothing, stuffing them into her bag. Remembering how to open the door, she let herself out of the bedroom and moved into the living room. She was a few steps from the front door when she heard a sound coming from the balcony. The blinds were still drawn but the door they'd come through earlier this evening after their dinner and . . . well, after all that, was still revealed. Meaning the blinds to hide it hadn't retracted so she had a glimpse of outside.

There was another sound, like furniture being moved and she stilled. Priya looked at the door to the balcony once more then turned to head toward the door that would take her out of here instead. And that's when she heard the next weird sound. It wasn't a growl, she instantly told herself, more like a muted gruff, or a really, really, deep-throated groan.

*Go, Priya. Just turn around and go home,* she told herself but "herself" obviously wasn't listening as she moved to the balcony door instead.

*Okay then, just take a peek then you can go. There's nothing for you here, nobody that can help Malik but you, just like always.*

Her words to herself really were falling on deaf ears when she looked down to her hand as it pushed at the glass on the door, searching for a way to open it. After pushing it all around the base with no success, she sighed.

*See, it's fate telling you to get out while the getting's good.*

But just as she took another step there was another sound. This, she knew without a second thought. It was a deep and painful sound and it was coming from the balcony. Fear was a funny thing. In the normal world, to normal people, it usually caused an instant fight-or-flight reaction. When it came to animals versus people the consensus rang true with flight. But not with Priya. Not tonight.

She banged on the glass so hard with her fists she thought she might actually break through it. Instead a slow beeping started on the wall and right beside her one of those control pads were revealed. Cursing, she pressed the green button so hard her finger burned. As soon as the glass door slid to the side she stepped outside. The sound was gone and she cursed.

Again, there was a part of her brain that said she should have chosen the flight response about three minutes ago, but alas, she ignored it. Following her instincts she walked around the balcony to where she remembered the stairs leading to the pool. Running up the few steps, she continued to survey the area, not really knowing why but looking for those ominous glowing eyes. What she found was so much more.

It came out of nowhere, teeth bared, a roar echoing in the night. A huge cat, cheetah or leopard or something. Even without a positive identification or introduction Priya could do nothing but scream. And when it charged at her she screamed again, backing up until she fell right into the pool. Priya fought her way to the surface, swimming to the opposite side of the pool as fast as she could. Then she climbed out because in the pool she was definitely a sitting duck—no pun intended.

Dripping wet, she looked around for the animal but didn't see it. Good! she sighed to herself then headed back the way she'd come. She was getting the hell out of this place. Big cats, big men being shot to death, sexy men giving her more orgasms than she'd ever had in one night, it was all too damned much for one woman to take.

The minute she cleared those three steps and turned that corner, Priya's thoughts immediately took another turn. The cat was sitting in front of the door and when it looked at her this time a spark of recognition soared through her body, resting immediately between her legs.

"No," she whispered, her head shaking from side to side. "Bas?"

# Chapter 19

**Perryville**

The cat took a step forward.

Priya swallowed hard, clenching and unclenching her fingers at her sides. Her mind whispered for her to take a step forward, but the message failed to be transmitted to her feet. She backed up instead. She was dripping wet, her heartbeat echoing in her ears as her conscience screamed, *Run! Run! Run!*

The cat came closer, its back hunching with every move. Its mouth was closed, a deep growling sound accompanying its movements. She tried to look at the eyes; they were golden, not glowing as she'd witnessed before, just gold and staring at her as it drew closer.

Yeah, it was coming closer.

Priya backed up again and remembered the last time she'd continued on this course it had ended with her falling into the pool. So this time she turned and ran, realizing too late that she had nowhere to go because she was on the balcony. But then how did this cat appear out of nowhere? If it could get onto the balcony, could she get off? She ran back up the steps and headed in the direction from which she'd seen the cat emerge.

The cat must have figured the same thing as it leaped

past her, rounding in front of her once more. She came to an immediate stop, so immediate that it threw off her balance and she fell backward, landing on her butt with a loud smack against the concrete.

Priya cursed, crab-walking backward this time in an effort to get away. But there was no getting away, she thought dismally. The cat approached. More like stalked right in front of her. Not bothering with the swift kill, just taking its time, taunting her, watching her. That thought brought her gaze back to its eyes and she stopped moving entirely.

There was something there, something very familiar that she couldn't outrun even if her feet were fast enough or there were some divine intervention strong enough to get her the hell out of here.

"It can't be," she whispered, knowing that the words were in direct contradiction to the reason she was here in the first place.

She closed her eyes, thought about counting to ten and hoping to wake up from this horrific dream. Instead, when she reopened them the cat was standing right beside her, its huge head only inches away from her face. Priya opened her mouth to scream for help. But instead, "Bas?" was the name that tumbled free.

A sound that could be construed as a hoarse sort of bark—if it were a dog, she thought with a mental kick to the clearly erroneous comparison—came from the animal. It was a cat, not a dog—a big-assed cat that was now towering over her. Her heartbeat was still fast and loud, signaling that at least some part of her realized she should be scared as hell right at this moment.

Other parts of her, the very female and totally traitorous parts, pushed her to reach out, to touch *him*—not *it*.

"No," she whispered, shaking her head and moving back again. She stopped suddenly, had no choice really when the top of her head met the wall. She yelped and lifted a hand to her head.

The cat was there in an instant, moving so quietly she would have never known it moved at all had she not seen it. She hurried to sit up straight, to have both her hands free just in case.

But as she lowered her hand from her head the cat dipped its large crown so that her fingers brushed over its fur, its soft-as-silk fur. Priya gasped but she didn't pull away, she let shaking fingers linger over the path downward to its nose. It sniffed her and she didn't recoil. Instead, her nipples hardened.

"You're Sebastian," she stated.

There was no question in her voice, none in her mind as she continued to look down into those eyes. Lifting her other hand, she cupped the head of the big cat as if she were its trainer or something other than an enormously foolish person. But she wasn't foolish and she—miraculously—wasn't afraid.

The cat moved in closer, lowering its front legs, resting its head on her thighs like a baby. It had been breathing heavily; she could see its flanks moving up and down in a rapid fashion that almost matched the beat of her heart. But now, as it rested on her lap, the heart rate slowed, both their heart rates slowed. She rubbed along its back, letting more of its fur ruffle through her fingers as the revelation truly hit her. There were cat people in this world and she'd had sex with one of them.

Bas's shift back was slow so as not to startle Priya. Well, not to startle her any more than he already had. The fact that he was now a naked human laying his head in her lap didn't really make things much better.

She gasped and jumped a little so that his head lolled and almost connected with the concrete. Then her hands went to his shoulders, stilling him instantly. Tentative fingers ran along his shoulder blades slowly, down farther. Warmth spread immediately, swirling at every inch of his skin that she touched. Inside his cat purred as her fingers moved over the tribal tat that occupied his entire back. It was a very large, artistic display of the tribe he'd dedicated his life to, the cat he wouldn't be here without. And Priya was touching it, she was looking at it and wondering. There were questions in her mind and her eyes, but there was no fear.

Sure her heart beat rapidly, her breathing hitching as she looked at him completely naked, after seeing what he could become. But there was no fear, the scent she held was drastically different and his body instantly responded.

Giving up the warmth she'd been offering his cat and the exploration she took of the man, Bas rolled away, coming to a sitting position beside her. He lifted his knees so his obvious nudity wasn't bursting onto the scene the way his cat had.

"Now you know," he commented with a resigned sigh.

Beside him she grappled for words, opening and closing her mouth so loudly he heard her teeth clicking. He couldn't help but chuckle.

"Ever since I first met you you've been asking one question after another, assuming one thing or something else. The only time you weren't on your interrogation spree was . . ." He hesitated as his body warmed with the thought. "And now, you're silent."

Priya cleared her throat. "I'm not silent," she insisted. "Just trying to gather my thoughts before I speak."

"Is that new for you?" he asked. "That's why it's taking you so long."

She elbowed him. "You're not funny."

No, it wasn't funny. Bas had just broken the biggest law of the *Ètica*. He'd just betrayed his entire tribe. But instead of him feeling like a colossal ass, or going into soldier mode and coming up with a plan to neutralize this situation, he was getting a hard-on from the simple brush of her skin against his.

"I'm not trying to be. Look, this is a new situation for both of us. Why don't we just get on with the preliminaries," he said, shifting a little so he could face her, but not give away his very obvious and slightly painful arousal.

"And what would the preliminaries be in this particular situation?" she asked incredulously, pushing wet strands of hair from her forehead.

"Questions and answers," was Bas's quick reply. The solution, or rather a temporary one, had just come to him, his new plan of sorts.

She arched an eyebrow, the left side of her mouth tilting upward in a half smile. "Now you're speaking my language. I'll go first," she said, already geared up for her first question.

He put a finger to her lips to stop her and wanted to lean over and lick every droplet of water off her instead of this ridiculous talking idea he'd come up with. Quickly pulling his hand away, he began, "You ask a question. I answer. Then I ask a question and you answer. Deal?"

Priya drew her lips into a tight line, then sighed. "Deal."

Bas nodded. "Go."

"What are you?"

Damn, he knew that was coming.

"I am a *Topètenia*." Saying the words filled him with a mixture of pride and regret. In all his life he'd never once thought of the moment when he would have to explain what and who he was. "We are a tribe of jaguar shifters originating from the Gungi Rainforest in the Amazon. And we live among humans." He finished with a look in her direction to survey the damage of his admission.

She looked right back at him, as if she'd already known what his explanation was going to be, but still needed a second to process it. Instead of speaking, which he clearly expected her to do, Priya reached out and touched a hand to his chin. She traced a line along his jaw to the left, up to his cheekbone, over his nose, up to his eyebrows.

"I knew there was something about your eyes," she whispered. "The moment I first saw you sitting in that ballroom, I knew you were different. Even from Roman and the others, you were different."

Now was probably the best time to tell her about Rome and the others, about the democracy they were building here, that they weren't a danger to humans. Yet, he remained silent. Bas kept his lips tightly drawn as he enjoyed the warmth of her touch, the soft tone of her voice. She wasn't judging him, wasn't even condemning him or what he'd told her he was. A very small part of Bas had always wondered if that would be the human reaction to their race, if fear of the unknown would ultimately produce ignorance and intolerance. The woman sitting across from him gave no indication of that being true. But Bas was no fool, in the end—and once he moved past the erection she inspired and the lust that boiled in the center of his gut like a coveted recipe for love—she was a human. And sadly, humans had proven time and time again that whatever they feared, they destroyed.

"Who are you?" he asked on impulse, reaching his hand out to mimic her actions.

Her bone structure was infinitely softer, a sleek jawline, high cheekbones, pert nose, and delectable lips. He wanted to kiss her right now, to climb on top of her and slip his thick length inside of her. His body strained with that thought, but Bas refrained.

She tilted her head in response, rubbing her cheek along

the palm of his hand. In that second all Bas could see was her, all he could feel was desire and need punching forcefully against him and everything he believed.

"I'm just a woman," was her whispered reply. "Just a woman who . . ." Her words trailed off.

Bas moved closer, cupping her face now with both hands. "You're just a beautiful woman, with the softest mouth and the sweetest tongue. You're what I've dreamed of," he admitted, lowering his face so that his nose brushed the tip of hers. "So help me, you're what I'm most afraid of." He said the last so softly he barely heard the words himself.

Then there were no more words, no more thinking, no more wondering. His lips touched hers, a quick brush and instant punch of lust so potent that if they were standing, they might have both fallen. In the next instant Bas's hands were at her waist as he lifted her onto his lap where she willingly straddled him. Her clothes were wet, sticking to her body in an annoying fashion that solicited a low growl from his cat. With his mouth working frantically over hers, his hands went to work ridding her of the wet articles. He ripped at the flimsy cotton of her shirt, broke the snap on her bra, and yanked at the shorts that barely skimmed her thighs until they were in two separate pieces falling wherever he tossed them on the ground.

When she was blissfully naked, Bas ran his hands along her spine, down to her buttocks where he cupped the soft cheeks.

"This wasn't part of the plan," she whispered over his mouth.

Bas nipped her bottom lip, holding it gently between his teeth, then releasing the plump fold to suckle it quickly into his mouth. "I know," he admitted, his hands slipping between the crease of her backside. One finger pausing at the tight ring of her sphincter, while the other hand moved farther until her moistened center all but sucked his digits into the warm depths. "But I can't stop," were the strained words falling from his lips as he closed his eyes to the pleasure of feeling her.

Priya bucked at his touch, reaching between their bodies to wrap her hot little hands around his length. With one hand planted firmly at his base she stroked upward with her other hand, letting her thumb rub along the sensitive tip. "Neither can I," she replied, the tremble in her voice and touch of her hands prompting Bas to lift his hips in response.

There were other things going on, other concerns, other issues that needed addressing, but none of it mattered to Bas at this moment. Nothing but her, the sound of her voice, the feel of her heat against his skin, the touch of her hands, her tongue as she leaned forward to lick a scathing line from his earlobe down his neck. Everything was about this moment and this moment was about them, this man and this woman—and the cat that lingered, hungry and ready to possess.

Bas pressed two fingers into her scorching center with a deep thrust, swirling them around so that her moistness dripped down onto his hand. Farther back, the pad of his middle finger pressed gently past the tight rim, stretching her slowly. She worked his dick like her hands were her mouth—and yeah, Bas was thinking that her mouth would be so much better. At the same time she rocked back and forth, working each of his fingers deeper inside. Her breasts bounced, nipples rubbing teasingly past his chin until he turned his face and with his mouth open wide, sucked one right inside. His tongue rolled over the taut bud, cheeks hollowing as he tried to pull the entire mound inside like dessert after a fine meal. She arched back and Bas groaned hungrily.

Reluctantly, he pulled his mouth away from her when the sweet torture threatened to kill him. With heaving

breaths he shifted, slipping his hands from her and waiting until her fingers uncoiled themselves from around his
dick. Said body part throbbed its disapproval but Bas was
sure he had something infinitely better in mind. Coming to
a stand he lifted Priya up into his arms, walking slowly—
because he wasn't going to be able to totally keep from
touching and tasting her—and kissing her as he moved
them toward the patio door.

It seemed like a long walk, but not really, as their tongues
dueled during the process. Her arms wrapped tightly around
his neck, breasts pressing into his chest. Bas wanted her in
the bed, he wanted to lay her down, spread her wide, and
take her slow. But that wasn't going to happen. It couldn't
happen, not this time, because he didn't have that type of
patience.

He fell onto the couch, repositioning Priya on top of
him, spreading her legs wide and aiming his thick length
upward until the tip pressed into her dripping center. She
grasped his shoulders, gripping him so tightly her blunt
nails cut into his skin. In the next instant she slammed her
hips down so hard and so fast Bas could do nothing more
than let his head loll back as a growl rippled through his
chest to echo into the dark room. She pulled back and
sank down in rapid succession that heated every inch of
Bas's body. When he finally licked his lips and swallowed,
his mind wrapping around the rise in body temperature
and sure-as-hell ride to orgasm, he gripped her hips and
joined in the fun.

She was so slick and so tight at the same time, her scent
mixing with his own to create something foreign and yet
exotic. He guided the strokes now, controlled the depth,
the retraction, the connection and she screamed with excitement. Her back was arched, her teeth sinking into her
lower lip, breasts moving with their exertion. Leaning forward he licked her there, right down the center of her chest

where a light sheen of sweat had appeared. The scent exploded into the air, stinging his nostrils, running in slow rivulets down his spine.

"It's too much! Too much!" she screamed, her head shaking back and forth wildly,

Bas completely agreed. The feelings soaring through him, the scent, her voice, the feel of his flesh running right alongside hers like a perfectly oiled machine was just too damned much. More than he'd ever experienced with anyone else, ever.

"I've got you, babe," he replied with a guttural groan, his hands moving from her hips to grip the cheeks of her buttocks tightly.

He spread her wider, loved the feel of unobstructed entrance into and out of her. Slipping his fingers through her crevice he sighed heavily at the instant warmth of her desire that coated them. He touched her there again, the tight entrance he'd explored before. His molars ached, his dick hardening to the point of making his vision blurry.

"Dammit!" he cursed for wanting her there so badly. Needing to shift their position so he could ride her with all the ferocity he was feeling, he attempted to adjust but failed dismally as Priya's release took charge.

Her body locked over his, her head dropping so that she was staring down at him.

"Sebastian!" she said through gritted teeth. "Sebastian!"

He kissed her then, taking her mouth roughly, loving the helpless whimpers that matched the constriction of her sugar-coated walls around his dick. When she sagged against him Bas thought again to readjust their position but his body overruled his mind and instead he speared into her deeper and deeper, holding her still by her hips, moving with frequent, powerful thrusts that rendered him speechless until his release ripped free and with it a part of that wall he'd built securely around his heart.

# Chapter 20

"How many of you are there?" was Priya's first question as they lay in Bas's bed, neither of them sleeping.

He hesitated and Priya held her breath. She prayed he wasn't going to go all tight-lipped on her now. If so, there was going to be trouble. Sure, she'd not too long ago had the most mind-numbing orgasm she'd ever experienced and he was the sole person responsible for said spectacular orgasm. But the fact still remained that he was not human. The repercussions of her having sex with him were momentarily taking a backseat to finding out everything she could about his . . . species, for lack of a better word.

"There are more tribes," he said, his voice deep, but low in the dark of the room. "All across the world, but most specifically in the rainforests and we've been here for hundreds of years. We're not a threat to humans."

Well, that was good to know, sort of. Priya moved slightly, still lying on her back but pulling the sheets up higher, creasing them beneath her arms. She looked up at the ceiling only to see more darkness. The automatic blinds on the windows in the bedroom sealed the room completely from any light. Not that there was light just yet as she was thinking it was somewhere in the vicinity of three a.m.

"But you can certainly be a danger to us, right? I mean you are huge and menacing and . . . and . . ." She paused

because what she was about to say next had absolutely
nothing to do with the unknown species versus the humans.
Clearing her throat, she tried again. "I mean, it's obvious
that you're more powerful than humans even though you
look just like us."

Her words sounded as if she should be getting the hell
out of here instead of lying in this bed naked beside him.
But she hadn't run. Not once she realized she was staring
into familiar, yet unfamiliar eyes and that the big beautiful
cat was the man she was beginning to believe she couldn't
stay away from.

"We could be a danger," he replied tightly. "But we're
not. At least it's not our plan to be, hence the secrecy. It's
a lot easier to remain neutral in a world that's not afraid of
you or misunderstands you, when nobody knows exactly
who or what you really are."

Priya hated that there was logic to his words. Hated it
so much she ignored it.

"But if someone were to tell your story, to explain why
it is you're here and what your plans are . . ."

"We're not aliens, Priya!" he roared, sitting up straight
in the bed.

She gasped but sucked it in, moving until she could sit
up next to him.

"That's not what I meant," she admitted quietly.

"But that's how it sounds. And if you print that story
people are instantly going to go into prepare-for-the-
alien-invasion mode. They're going to stop going to work
and go out and buy guns instead. They're going to take a
defensive posture against everyone because they won't be
able to tell who is what. Some of them, the boldest ones,
are going to attempt to hunt us down, to save the earth from
our kind. And that's when things are going to get really
bad." Bas shook his head at the vehemence in his words.
He hadn't meant to talk to her that way, hadn't meant to

make things sound so dour, but he had and actually, they
were.

"No, Bas," she replied quietly. "I want to save my
brother's life."

Bas paused then, feeling like a total ass at having momentarily forgotten how it was she came to be here with
him.

"Malik is your brother?"

She nodded. "He's my drug-addicted brother who steals
from my mother to get high and has never held a job in
his life." She stopped, took a deep breath, and continued,
"He's my older brother, the one that fixed the chain on an
old bike that someone had thrown away so I could have
one of my own. When I was in college and was stupid
enough to go to a frat party, get drunk, and leave with one
of the pledges, Malik was right there in the parking lot
when the jerk-off tried to fuck me right there against my
old beat-up car.

"Malik's not the best guy in the world. He's not even a
nice guy on his forced sober days. But he's my brother
and he's all my mother has left and if she loses him she
just might die of grief. And if I lose them both . . ." Her
words halted as she blinked faster and faster, fingers
clenching together before she turned away.

Bas waited a second, gave her that short span of time
to inhale shakily and exhale before he touched her shoulders, turning her back to face him.

"I won't let you lose your brother, Priya. I will find
them and I will make sure your brother is safe, without
you having to write this story," he promised.

"Will you kill them too?" She cleared her throat. "You
killed him or it without blinking. How many others have
you killed?"

Her question was valid, her words true yet they still
managed to make Bas feel like a monster. Standing from

the bed, he reached up a hand to touch the tiny button beside one of the wireless black filigree sconces above the bed. Then he was standing on the other side of the bed where she lay. He didn't touch her like he wanted to, but sat beside her instead.

"I killed an intruder. He and another broke into the resort and posed a danger to my staff and our guests. I did what was necessary." He purposely left out the part about doing what was natural.

She visibly gulped and then nodded. "You've done that before?"

He didn't even blink. "Yes. I'm a former United States Marine and a jaguar Shadow Shifter."

"And you'll do it again? Those people sound serious. They showed me a picture of Malik and his head was bleeding. If I don't do this story and you go after them, you'll kill them, won't you?"

"I want you to tell me everything they've ever said to you, in addition to the e-mails. I will find them and I will . . ." He hesitated. "I will handle them. That's all you need to know."

She looked up at him, her hair tousled, lips still swollen from his kisses and Bas knew they weren't finished. He knew that whatever this was between them was not passing. He wasn't going to send Priya on her way and never see her again. He couldn't.

**Washington, D.C.**

Three sets of eyes stared at the e-mail that had been delivered to Nick's personal inbox. Each of them read those simple sentences:

**They know WHAT you are.**
**They know WHAT you do.**

**And now, THEY can do it too.**

And it was signed, **CL, Sedona, Arizona**

"What the fuck does that mean?" Nick spat, slapping a hand onto the glass top of his desk.

"You tracing this?" Rome asked X, who was standing on the other side of Nick.

When they'd been called into Nick's office for the second time this week, X had automatically known to bring his laptop. It still amazed Rome how fast and smooth his big, bulky fingers moved over the keyboard. X had already run a cord from his laptop to Nick's and had been steadily typing while they read the message for the third time.

"Tracing the IP address now," X replied.

Rome folded one arm over his chest, using his other hand to rub along the freshly cut goatee at his chin. "Someone's trying to tell us something," he said, more to himself than to the others in the room.

"No shit." Nick breathed enough tension into the room to cause Rome's cat to sit up and take notice.

It was the norm, this was just how a shifter was genetically predisposed—fight now, answer the questions later. Rome, thank all that was holy and good in the world, was the exact opposite. He thought about everything, from the moment of conception to when the plan of attack was put into action. That was why he had been named the Stateside Assembly Leader. It was also why, of the three friends in this room, he'd always been the one with good grades and good behavior growing up.

Rome also knew that Nick had other things on his mind that were only being agitated by these cryptic e-mails that someone had taken to sending them. Shya, Nick's three-month-old daughter, had been sick the last few days. Dr. Frank Papplin, the shifter doctor that pulled double duty at a human hospital in D.C. and at Havenway, the Stateside

Headquarters in Virginia, had assured Nick and Ary that it was a simple cold, possibly brought on by the change in seasons. But Nick and Ary were still on edge, as Rome thought any good parent would be about their newborn. For what it was worth, Rome wanted Nick to be at home with his *companheiro* and child, but things were going on in their world that could adversely affect them all, even young Shya. And because their newfound pen pal had decided that Nick would be their contact, Rome had no choice but to require his friend be here with them instead.

"Someone's trying to tell us something, again," X added without looking up from his laptop.

Rome nodded. "Precisely."

Nick sat back in his chair, dragging his hands down his face in one of his signature exasperated moves. He took a deep breath and even without looking at him Rome knew he was calming down. It took a moment, but Rome was patient. Usually.

"This is the third message. It's from a different e-mail address but it's giving us the heads-up about something," Nick concluded.

"Something that I'm betting concerns one of our goals," Rome added.

"Goal one was to get rid of Sabar and his crazy death drug. Partial check," X said.

"Uh huh," Nick added. "Goal number two was to stop the next shipment that was coming into the States. Another partial, but still a hit."

Rome nodded again, pieces to this puzzle slowly shifting into place. "Goal three, establish the Assembly and the new Stateside democracy."

They were all silent a moment.

"Damn!" X yelled, his fingers moving slowly on the keyboard. "It came from Sedona."

Nick sighed. "It says that at the end of the e-mail. Duh."

Rome knew instinctively that little bit of sarcasm was not going to go over well.

X shifted in his chair, turning his laptop around so they all could look at it. "No, jerk-off, the e-mail originated from Sedona. The Comastaz Laboratories, to be exact."

Rome looked from one computer screen to the next. "CL, Sedona, Comastaz Laboratories. Dammit!" he swore.

"Those crates Bas pulled out of that tunnel were post-marked from Comastaz," X stated.

"Coincidence?" Nick asked.

"No such thing," Rome replied.

"Hell no," X added. "Something's definitely going down out there, something we should probably find out about before whoever 'they' are prove what this message says."

Rome let his arms fall to his sides, fists clenching and unclenching. "Get Bas on the phone right now! I want someone in that lab, someone we trust without any question."

"I'll go," a voice sounded from the doorway, surprising the three shifters as they turned to see its owner.


## Sedona

"This came for you."

Palermo turned around slowly. He'd been standing on the balcony of the cheap-ass hotel they'd booked in the small town just outside of Perryville. It was still early, not even noon yet. Black and Sye, the younger rogue he'd sent into Perryville, had still not returned.

Their assignment had been to sneak inside, find out where the drugs and guns were, and get his shit back. Palermo had a sinking suspicion that had not happened. In fact, he had a lump in his stomach the size of a sizzling hot lava ball. Bad mojo for goddamned sure.

"What the hell is it?" he asked looking down at the box Rube offered him.

This was another young rogue, one of the recruits he'd made to help execute this part of his assignment. The instructions he'd been given were clear. While Darel Charles sat in D.C. building his drug empire and dishing out orders under false pretenses, Palermo's job was more serious and much more dangerous. He was dealing with a madman and a sadistic shifter, both of whom had their own agendas, prime reasons why securing the rest of this shipment was so important.

Rube shrugged, thin shoulders slapping against earlobes stretched by some round object to the point where the shifter looked almost alien with the two gigantic holes on each side of his face. He had other piercings, bars through both eyebrows, one through his lower lip and chin, and when he talked a ball and ring were visible from the center of his tongue. His nubby fingernails were painted black, with silver rings on each finger. To say he blended in with some of the humans Palermo had seen since he'd been back in the States was an understatement.

"Don't know. Sye just came back with it."

Palermo's head jerked up, his gaze moving from the box to Rube in one quick motion. "Sye's back and you didn't tell me?"

Rube blinked, confusion clear on his thin face. "Just did."

"Where is he and where's Black?" Palermo asked, moving past the stupid-ass rogue and the box he still held to pull the door open.

He looked up and down the hall but didn't see anyone. "Where the fuck are they?"

Rube shook his head. "Sye just said to give this to you. He didn't look too good. Like he'd took a beatin', limping and shit, bleeding from his lip."

Palermo slammed the door, turning back to face this guy he'd willingly put in his employ. He'd have to come up with a better way of running background checks.

Moving quickly, Palermo ignored the other questions rumbling through his mind, for the first time inhaling deeply and picking up a scent. It wasn't a good scent, not at all. He snatched the box out of Rube's hands, dropping it onto the bed before ripping the top off.

"Fuck!" He roared at the sight. "Fuck!" Repeat, rewind, and repeat again, because once or twice just didn't seem like enough.

Rube came over to the bed, looked down, and made a heaving sound. He covered his mouth, which might have been the smartest thing the asshole had done so far today.

"What else did Sye say when he dropped this off?" Palermo asked, taking one final look at the pile of ashes that reeked of shifter scent. On top of the ashes was a sheet of paper and the big-ass diamond ring that Black always wore on his pinky finger.

"Said those shifters told him to give you that box and that the leader guy said to come and get him yourself."

"Pick that shit up," he told Rube as he pointed into the box. "Now!"

"Really? Man, there's dead-ass ashes in that box. They burned his ass good," Rube complained, still inching his way back from the bed.

Palermo reached a hand behind his back, pulled out the .45 he kept in the band of his pants, and pointed it directly at Rube's temple. "Pick up the piece of paper and read it or die right this fucking minute, you pussy-ass punk!"

Rube swallowed, the sound loud in the quiet of the room, the scent of fear almost overtaking the scent of dead burnt shifter. Almost.

He took another huge swallow and stepped toward the box. Reaching in with one eye closed—as if that was going to make the shit a little less gross—he picked up the paper, holding it by the tips of two pale-ass fingertips.

"Says, 'come and get me, bitch!'" He read the slip of paper, his voice cracking with nervousness.

Palermo lowered his arm, let the weight of the gun rest in his hand against his thigh as he returned to the window once more. From there he could look to the west, upward toward the sky and see the tips of the mountains where just below a little town buzzed with activity. It buzzed with life, human and shifter. All of which would fall at his command.

"You don't have to ask me twice, you bastard-assed Faction Leader. You don't have to fucking ask twice," he mumbled, lips turning up into a snarl, canines and claws extending.

# Chapter 21

Jewel jumped at the sound of his voice. Her heart hammering against her chest, teeth clenching. A feeling she was all too familiar with encompassing her, all too quickly. For the years that she'd been in Perryville she'd tried valiantly to tamp down the fear that had just about smothered her before. Last night it had come back in full force. This morning she felt like she was drowning in it, struggling just to keep her head above water and give in to total defeat.

"I asked you a question," Jacques repeated.

He was a formidable man, even if his build was on the slender side. There was strength in his long arms and piano fingers that Jewel knew instinctively could be deadly. Today he was dressed similarly to his usual style, casual but stylish in chocolate-brown khaki pants, which were perfectly creased over leather tie-up, low-cut boots, a soft, beige, knit sweater without wrinkle or lint hanging perfectly over a toned chest. The brown tones should have blended to the point of dullness over his almond-bark skin tone, instead it accentuated the deep hue. He spoke with the faintest hint of an accent that she'd never been able to place and he took a step closer, signaling she still hadn't responded to his question.

She cleared her throat, willed her hands to remain still at her sides while squaring her shoulders.

"I saw you and some of the others chasing a man in the back gated area," she replied, familiar with this scenario.

Jacques's face remained a blank mask, his eyes cool as he surveyed everything about her. It was strange but Jewel figured he could probably see right through the white linen pants and matching sleeveless top she wore.

"And what else?" he prodded.

Jewel lifted a hand to tuck a few wayward curls back behind her ear. She'd used a coral-colored headband to hold the riotous mass back today. It matched the beads on top of her soft leather mules.

"Nothing. Your men grabbed me and carried me back into the building. I've been here in my room ever since." Which was only a partial truth.

She had no doubt been brought up to her room and ordered to stay inside. But she'd seen plenty before and after the chase. Jewel had seen plenty in the three years she'd been at Perryville, but she knew it was imperative that she keep that knowledge to herself. Another task she was more than used to.

"Why were you and that woman down in the bunkers? You know that is a restricted area," he continued.

Jacques always smelled good. It wasn't a cologne, she knew, but a scent that he and some of the others carried—a musky sort of outdoors scent that Jewel had immediately begun to think was embedded in their skin.

"I caught her heading down there and I tried to bring her back." Which was true enough, she supposed.

Priya Drake was a nice-looking woman, smooth mocha-toned skin, bright inquisitive eyes, high cheekbones, and what men would call a sumptuous mouth. She used that mouth to talk a lot, Jewel had surmised from their first meeting. Question after question, seeking information Jewel was not prepared to give—not that she didn't possess it. If Jewel thought it was strange that Sebastian Perry had a woman locked in his private space after years of never seeing him anywhere with his dates beyond the guest floors where suites occupied the space, she was smart enough not to mention it, to Jacques or to Priya.

"That means you had to be in that space too." Jacques stood directly in front of her now. "Do not attempt to lie to me, Jewel. I will know."

He was a fool, just like most men. The way a person could sometimes pass a lie detector test was the same way she looked up into his eyes and repeated, "I was on my way back from a late snack and speaking with Mrs. Ramirez in the kitchen when I saw her boarding the elevators. She was heading downstairs and I attempted to stop her. When my words were not enough and she took off into the hallways of the bunker, I followed her in an attempt to steer her back up to Mr. Perry's room. It did not work. She's a very stubborn female."

The story was delivered as Jewel had practiced it all night so that now it was what she firmly believed. And as long as she believed she was telling the truth . . .

"You are not telling the truth," Jacques countered.

Dammit. Well, there was always a first time for something not to work and Jewel always had a plan B.

"If you know all then why bother to ask?" No matter how much she feared what might happen next, Jacques did not need to know. No man would ever have that upper hand over her again. They would not scare her into submission or manipulate her into doing their bidding, no questions asked. Never, ever again.

"I know that this is not the first time you have seen something here you should not have."

She didn't even blink. "If you have a problem with my services, then let me go." It was clearly bravado speaking, but hell, it sounded good even to her. Jewel had nowhere to go if she was forced to leave Perryville, nowhere else to hide.

"No, my dear," he said, lifting a hand to toy with strands of her hair. "That is precisely why I've let you stay."

He had never touched her, not sexually or casually, even though he made a habit of standing in her personal space more often than not. He would touch her hair, or a scarf she wore or even a bracelet once, but never her skin, never her person. For that, Jewel was supremely grateful.

"Now, however, our arrangement must change," he finished then stepped away from her heading to the door.

Jewel's heart beat faster, panic soaring through her like a ravaging disease. She took a step toward Jacques, fists clenched at her sides and blurted out before thinking, "What are you going to do with me? Are you sending me away?"

Jacques paused at the door, his hand on the handle. The look he gave her over his shoulder was new, a different expression that she couldn't quite explain, and she gasped.

"Wouldn't you like to know?" was his parting retort before he opened the door, stepped through, and closed it with a resounding click behind him.

It was morning, well past, Bas thought as he lay on his stomach, still in bed. He opened his eyes, felt the annoying itch that said he could probably sleep another hour or so, then closed them again. Next, he inhaled deeply and confirmed the lump of dread that had formed in the center of his chest.

Priya was still here.

Priya knew who and what he was.

Damn.

With a resigned sigh he was about to roll over, to reach for her but then he felt her touch. The soft inside of her thighs brushed over his buttocks as she straddled him. Shaking fingers traced the lines of his tattoo and Bas waited. She would have more questions, she always did. No matter that he'd told her too damned much last night, he knew he would answer her, no matter how much he didn't want to.

"I can see it now," she said softly. "I didn't really see it clearly that first night and then last night, well, I wasn't really paying that much attention to it. But now I see it clearly."

Bas continued to take steady, slow breaths. The warmth of her center resting against his skin was a huge distraction from the sound of her voice. She was wet and hot and he craved her once more. Always, it seemed.

"It's a cat," she continued. "Your cat."

He neither confirmed nor denied. It was weak, he knew. At some point Bas was going to have to make a decision about this new situation he found himself in. He was going to have to decide what to do with Priya now that she knew. But for the moment all he could think about was the sweet scent of her arousal, the soft feel of her body against his.

"It's the shield of the *Topètenia* tribe."

"All of you have it?" she continued. "It's beautiful."

She leaned forward, her fingers moving across the blades of his shoulders, down to the center of his spine were he knew the face of his cat began.

"Yes," he murmured just before her lips touched his skin.

Then it was her tongue as she traced an outline around the center of the tattoo. The eyes of the cat. Heat spread from that spot throughout the entire upper portion of his body like spilled water.

"You're beautiful," she whispered, her breath draping over him in warm waves. "Absolutely beautiful."

Bas's teeth clenched, his entire body tightening with her words. He turned easily beneath her, reaching out his hands to hold her in place atop him as he now lay on his back. She was gorgeous, hair sleep-tousled, eyes already dulled with desire, lips still slightly swollen from his hungry kisses only hours before. Her blessedly naked body was before him and Bas didn't hesitate to reach out to touch her. Pert breasts fit perfectly in the palms of his hands as he cupped them, squeezed, and purred.

Her eyes shot up to him at the sound and he licked his lips in response. "Come to me, Priya. Come to me," he whispered.

With slightly parted lips she leaned forward into him, lifting her chest so that they would be more aligned with his mouth. He took her immediately, one hard nipple and soft curve into his mouth, sucking deeply as if he were a babe at feeding. His other hand held firm to its twin, squeezing even as his tongue flicked over the hard nipple. She sucked in a breath and bowed her body over him. His cat roared inside, pressed closer to the surface, hunger clawing at it.

Giving her other breast the same attention as the first, Bas sucked and licked and groaned as his erection grew harder still, a drop of pre-release dampening its tip. He wanted to be inside her more than he wanted his next breath and by the sound of her whimpers she was in the exact same place. And yet, he couldn't resist another urge tapping against him persistently.

Since the first day he'd been intrigued by Priya's scent, sucked into her endless questions and infinite suspicions from the first second they'd made eye contact. And every time thereafter it was her scent that he always recognized first. It seemed to call to him and try as he might, Bas had never been able to ignore it. Now, he wanted to taste it, to have all of her, claim all of her as his own.

He moved again, this time placing his hands at her hips, looking up into her half-closed eyes. "Come to me. Bring all that sweetness to me," he whispered hoarsely.

With the words he lifted her until her knees were now planted on either side of his face.

"Hold on," he instructed her as he tightened his hold on her hips, pulling her center down until it was like a desired dessert only inches away from being devoured.

She was warm to the touch, hot plump vulva lips drenched in her nectar. The sweetest taste to ever touch his tongue, he licked her once again, loving the soft dampness moving over his tongue. Deep in his chest something pulled and swirled like a brewing storm but Bas ignored it and licked her again. Her legs were spread wide as she bucked above him, breath hissing out of her. He licked inside her lips this time, noting the even softer contrast, the warmer center. All the while inhaling deeply, exhaling slowly. It was all over him now, her scent that is, like a heavy blanket covering him, coddling him. Another lick, a suckle that pulled one plump fold into his mouth and Bas dug his fingers into her hips. A growl rumbled in his chest as he released her, licked again, sucked some more. She bucked over him, rocking her hips in encouragement. He speared his tongue into her center, moving in and out as his hips mimicked that same motion. He couldn't get enough of her and hungrily angled his head to take more.

Above him Priya held onto the top of the bed frame, riding his mouth as she'd previously ridden his dick. Bas's hands slid back to cup her buttocks, spreading her wider. He touched her rim, couldn't resist the urge his cat had to join into this moment. Pressing inside the tight warmth made his mouth water and move quicker over her juncture, her sweetness coating his tongue and slipping in hot rivulets down his throat.

As she came she yelled his name, her thighs clenched, holding his head tightly, assuring he did not stop what he knew had to be a sweet kind of torture. And as Bas's tongue speared inside her, his own release broke free, hips tightening and lifting from the bed, spurts going up then dripping down onto him. He couldn't whisper her name, couldn't thank her for a momentary end to the agony of desiring her. All Bas could do was hold her as her body continued to spasm, lick every drop of her essence as her body released, and he loved every goddamned second of it.

The hot water was a blessing, the big fluffy bubbles that smelled of honey and musk a luscious treat, the man sitting behind her using a loofa sponge to send rivulets of water cascading down her shoulders an unexpected, yet desperately needed distraction.

Priya sighed, letting her head loll back and rest on Bas's shoulder. Closing her eyes, she tried not to think about the cat he'd become, the one he wore on his back and carried deep inside him. She tried not to think about the fact that the cat was a deadly creature and that she should have run like hell to get away from it and this place. But what Priya really tried not to think about was how good the night had actually turned out to be.

Each time Bas touched her, licked her, caressed her, Priya felt inches of herself giving over to him, to this power that he had over women. On one level it was degrading as hell. Bas was an overconfident, too-slick womanizer, or at least that was what he appeared to be at first glance. Upon a little deeper reflection—and on a purely physical level—he was downright mesmerizing in bed. She couldn't deny that even if she wanted to.

On yet another level Priya felt like something else was going on between her and Bas, something just a little more serious than she figured either of them could have ever imagined. As they lay in the darkness of his room last night each of them had drifted into their own thoughts. She knew full well what her thoughts had entailed but really had no idea about his. Stunningly enough, she wanted to know. If she were being drawn to this man—not the story of his other half or their species and not simply the best sex she'd ever had in her life—but if this man were somehow pulling her closer to him, she wanted to know if her feelings were at least reciprocated.

"Tell me what you're thinking," she whispered without thinking twice about broaching this subject with him.

He remained quiet at first. Priya expected nothing less. In the time she'd known him she'd noticed how he contemplated all of his responses before giving them. Whereas she was the exact opposite, saying what she wanted the moment she wanted, sometimes to her own detriment.

"You don't really want to know what I'm thinking," he replied finally, moving so that the thick rigid length of his erection now rested beneath her buttocks.

"That's the obvious, Bas. I know you can do better than that." He was also damned good at attempting to deflect her attention away from what she really wanted to discuss. He'd tried this each time she'd asked about the cat people and for the most part it had worked, up until she'd come face to face with his cat. This time she wasn't going to be swayed, couldn't be because there was still too much at stake.

"So it's not more sex that you want," he continued with a lightness to his tone.

Priya turned then. It was perhaps not the smartest move since water and bubbles sloshed over the lip of the tub, landing with a messy splatter on the marble floor. She didn't care, she wanted Bas to look her right in her eye and deny what was really happening between them. Or at least, she wanted him to try.

"I want to know how you plan to save my brother. I have no idea who they are or why they're holding him, or why they chose me. Lolo, that's my friend from work, the one you saw that day on the street. He's been trying to track the IP address but hasn't been able to do it and—"

He touched two fingers lightly to her mouth. Priya closed her lips after her tongue had swiped quickly over his skin. A jolt of heat speared straight through to her center and she swallowed hard.

"I have equipment here that I'm positive is years beyond what your friend Lolo has. I ran the IP addresses through a thorough search last night before I came up here. As soon as you discontinue the Q-and-A and let me out of this tub I'll go to my office and find out where the e-mails originated."

His fingers had traced a heated path around her lips, over the line of her jaw, down to caress her neck. Tiny pricks of heat covered the surface of her skin. Priya wanted to shiver even though she wasn't cold. She wanted to lift slightly, adjusting herself so that she was aimed directly over his thick length. She wanted him again. It was crazy and it was intense, like an addiction, she thought with an inner sigh.

"Malik hasn't always made the right decisions," she told him. "He's always been controlled by the drugs. No matter how many rehab programs I convinced him to join. It's always been his crutch. I don't know how to fix that." It was the first time she'd said that aloud, the first time she'd admitted that she could not fix everything that was wrong with her family.

"We are not responsible for our family or the decisions they make," he told her. "It took me years to figure out that my parents' divorce was their own doing, their own decision. We can only hold ourselves responsible for our own actions and decisions. Malik's addiction is not your fault, neither is it your job to cure."

"But if he dies . . ."

Bas shook his head, reaching up to cup her face with both hands. "I'm not going to let him die. I don't think I could watch you endure that amount of hurt."

She didn't know what to say to that, didn't know how to respond. As it turned out she didn't have to because he was kissing her by then, his mouth working slowly and most assuredly over hers.

His hands moved down to rub over her shoulders, down her bare back to cup her cheeks. Priya let herself drift into the kiss, loving the stroke of his tongue over hers. As his tub was much wider and longer and more sumptuous than the one in her apartment she was able to spread her legs wider, her hands gripping his shoulders as she moved into his touch.

His touch that slowly slipped between her crease, the pad of one finger resting against her tight sphincter.

"You have a great ass," he whispered when he'd moved to kissing her jaw and then her ear. "I watched you that night at the fund-raiser. Every time you got up and walked around I watched you. I wanted you in this position from the first time I saw you."

Sex talk had never been high on Priya's list, then again, foreplay had been condensed to kissing, minimal touching, and then the actual act. In these last few days with Bas she'd learned just how much her sex life had been lacking, before the self-imposed celibacy.

"I was celibate," she said without thought.

He pulled back to look at her quizzically. "Celibate?"

"Yeah, long story short, it just wasn't worth the headache."

Bas nodded as if he understood, gripping one cheek with one hand, pressing that other finger inside to breach her. Priya gasped with the pressure and the flow of new sensations.

"Never pain, Priya," he whispered as they locked gazes. "Nothing I do to you will ever hurt you."

She wanted to believe that, desperately needed to have a silver lining to all that had gone wrong in her life, but he was just a man and his reputation . . .

Bas's other hand slipped between her legs, finding her clit and massaging until she moaned.

"Never pain," she heard herself say, dropping her forehead to his and biting her lip. The pressure of his finger sinking deeper into her rear while he expertly titillated her clit was intense and overwhelming and deliciously naughty all at once. She lifted her hips, felt her thighs shake, and she moaned.

"Only pleasure, pretty girl," he said and then nipped her chin. "Only pleasure."

"Yes," was Priya's reply, the only one she could manage.

The first orgasm came with a rush as she tightened like a bow above him. The moment she assumed she might manage a coherent thought Bas removed both hands, replacing the pleasure they'd evoked with the thick fullness of his dick, stretching her, filling her until she mumbled his name.

"I want you like this every day, every night," he told her. "I love you in this position."

She loved her in this position, or rather she loved how deeply he penetrated her from this position. Empowered by his words she lifted until she was sitting up straight, her back arched and she began to ride. Holding onto the sides of the tub for leverage she worked her hips over him, loved the look on his face as she lifted slightly then lowered down onto his length. His face didn't contort like her previous lovers, but stayed in its perfect and gorgeous state. Only his eyes told of the intense pleasure he was receiving. They'd darkened until they were almost black, his lips drawn into a thin line as she continued to move.

On impulse Priya planted her toes on the floor of the tub, pushing upward until only the tip of his dick remained at the base of her core. Bas hissed, a deep purr rumbling from his chest.

"Priya." He whispered her name, drawing it out until it was more like a moan.

He grabbed her hips then and his eyes shifted. No longer dark, they were now a golden yellow, with tiny black slits down the center. His cat's eyes. She didn't know what she was about to say but she opened her mouth, only to swallow the words when Bas pulled her down hard on his dick. More water sloshed over the rim of the tub as he began pumping mercilessly inside of her. Her teeth chattered at the force, her breasts jiggling their own protests and Priya cried out.

The next orgasm was even stronger than the first and Priya fell against Bas, out of breath and out of coherent responses. He held her tightly against him as his own release ripped free, caressing his hands up and down her back.

"I didn't plan for this," he said quietly after they'd sat for too long in the now-tepid water.

She'd turned her head so that her cheek rested on his shoulder. "Neither did I. And now I'm not so sure it was one of my smartest ideas."

"Impulsive, tenacious, and stubborn as hell," he replied.

"I don't think criticizing me is one of your smartest ideas," she quipped.

He had the audacity to chuckle.

"My father used to tell my mother she had a stubborn jaw and that she'd poke it out each time they argued. Considering how frequently that was, I was privileged enough to see that jaw more than I cared to. It looked just like yours," he finished.

Priya didn't reply. Okay, she didn't really know what to say to that. Bas had never talked about his parents to her before and she'd certainly never thought he would compare her to his mother.

"Then they were divorced and I didn't see either of them again," he finished.

"My father left, then my mother had so many men in and out of our tiny apartment I never knew what marriage was until I watched a few sitcoms on television," she added.

His fingers were making lazy circles along her spine. "I doubt my parents planned for their divorce and your mother probably didn't plan to have all those short-lived relationships."

"But that's how it ended," she replied, thinking she already knew where this was leading.

"Neither of us planned for this, we've already admitted that," he said.

She was getting a bad feeling. The mood had definitely shifted and not in her favor, she suspected. What the hell happened to the afterglow of sex? She didn't want to sound needy or desperate or whatever, but she couldn't help saying, "But it is now."

He nodded. "So it is."

She sat up then, covering her breasts because now she felt chilly and exposed. "And how will this end, Bas?"

At first he looked at her as if he wasn't really sure of what to say. Then the Bas she'd seen that first night, the one that stared back at her each time she Googled his name and the one that ran this resort with ease stared back at her.

"It will end, these things always do. The how and why doesn't really matter," was his aloof response.

And that was that, his close-lipped appearance seemed to say. He'd answered her question in another one of those roundabout ways and he had no intention of continuing with this conversation. Most men chose this moment to walk out of the room, to put some distance between them so the overly emotional female could have time to cry in private. Well, Bas was not most men. Besides, he couldn't move as she was still sitting in his lap. And Priya, well, she'd never considered herself a woman who needed a man to complete her. All her life she'd told herself she didn't need a man, didn't want one if it meant she'd end up like her mother, pregnant every other year and dead broke every day. No, she had bigger and brighter plans for herself and up until the moment she'd been thrust into Bas's world, she'd been living them out just fine. There was no way in hell she was going to let him change any of that. No matter how much the tightening around her heart threatened to choke her.

"Well said," she replied flippantly. "And now that we've gotten that out of the way, I'd like to find my brother and save his life, so I can get on with mine."

She moved as she talked, scooping up the loofa sponge and soaping it up once more. Priya didn't talk any more as she soaped and washed her body, ignoring the fact that Bas was still in the tub with her and that he was once again powerfully aroused.

In the next few minutes Priya was out of the tub, reaching for a thick soft towel from the gleaming silver rack by the door. Wrapping it around herself, she went to the sink and brushed her teeth before turning back to Bas. A small bubble of triumph floated through her as she saw him still in the same position, watching her quizzically.

"If you leave me the directions, I will meet you in your office," she told him.

He looked like he'd swallowed that loofa sponge she'd just washed with. His gray eyes giving her a cool glint, his fingers gripping the sides of the tub. When she thought he was going to continue with his brooding silent treatment she opened her mouth to speak again. Bas stopped her with a raised hand.

"I'll send for you when I'm ready."

She thought about telling him she wasn't his captive, again. Then she thought about the clutching pain in her chest—the freakin' emotions she hadn't intended to develop—and figured distance might be the best decision here, it might actually keep her heart from breaking in front of him. "Right. I'll be ready."

# Chapter 22

"I need you," Bas spoke into the phone.

He'd locked the door to his office and immediately booted up his computer. After printing all the e-mails Jacques had sent him from Priya's account and the new list of her most recent text messages, he'd forwarded that e-mail and placed a very important phone call to Washington, D.C.

"What's going on out there? Rome and his two side-kicks have been in a closed meeting all morning. Training of the new soldiers is on a fast track and everybody's on edge about what might happen next," she told him.

There was immediate concern in her voice, but no fear, never fear. Nivea Cannon was one of the toughest Shadow Shifters Bas knew. She was also the closest thing he'd ever had to a sibling. Bas's parents and Nivea's parents had known each other through their social circles in New York. As those social circles often included humans, Bas, Nivea, and her two sisters spent a lot of time together as the only shifters amongst the other kids their age. Bas was so proud when Nivea decided to leave New York and join Rome and his team in their work for the Assembly. And just recently he'd warned Nick to take extra special care of Nivea as she'd been given a very high-level assignment.

"It's probably about that shipment we intercepted a few days ago," he told her. "How's your other assignment going?"

There was a moment of silence on the phone line that concerned Bas.

"It's going slow. If Agent Wilson was still looking into Rome and his dealings he's decided to lay low for a while. I've been tracking him for weeks and keep coming up empty."

"But that's not what's worrying you, is it?" he asked, knowing that on the other end of the line Nivea was probably running her fingers through her shoulder-length hair in exasperation.

"It's nothing I can't handle," she said with a quick sigh. "So what's up with you? What do you need?"

He could probe a little more and maybe she would tell him what was really bothering her. Or he could relax, be patient, and expect a call from her when she was ready to confide, as she always did.

"I just sent you some e-mails and a printout of text messages. I need you to follow up and see what you can find. The human's name is Malik Drake, he's thirty-five years old, African American, two hundred and thirty-seven pounds, last seen at the Sullivan-Minster Rehabilitation Center. Send me whatever information you come up with immediately."

"Drake? Does this have something to do with that reporter? I heard about what happened at the hotel. She's still on this story, isn't she?" Nivea asked.

Bas turned in his chair, staring out the window to the mountains once more, wondering just how much he should tell Nivea. She lived at Havenway with Rome and Kalina. She saw the Assembly Leader on a daily basis, had meetings with him to discuss the status of her own assignments. How could he trust her with what he was doing here when he knew Rome's position on the matter? Because Nivea was like his sister, how could he not?

"He's her brother," he said after a few seconds of silence. "She's tracking the story to save his life. I need you to find out where he is."

"Wait a minute, I'm scrolling through the e-mail and attachments now," Nivea said, then paused. "How do you know all this?"

"She told me," he stated simply. "Priya Drake told me that someone's been e-mailing her, forcing her to follow this story. They want her to expose us, even gave her a time limit that I do not see the significance of. If she doesn't do what they say, they'll kill her brother."

"And you want to be the white knight to come in and save the day. Again. I swear the press would have a field day if they knew how chivalrous and romantic you really are."

Bas shook his head. "I don't give a damn about the press or what they think of me."

"I know. I know. But the world should know what a great guy you are, what a loyal and devoted friend and protector you can be."

"It wouldn't matter. In the end they would still see me as a threat. I'd still be a Shadow Shifter." Today, for Bas, that was a bitter pill to swallow.

"Wait a minute, what's his name doing here?"

"Whose name?" he asked, the serious switch in her tone causing him to sit straight up in his chair.

"Dorian Wilson," she told him. "Page three of the text messages. He's an FBI agent. The one Rome has me tailing night and day."

Turning back to his desk, Bas flipped through the printed pages, found the one Nivea was referencing and frowned. "This text is to her friend Lolo, he works at the paper and he knows about the threats to Priya."

"But how does she know Wilson? And why is she tell-ing this Lolo person to send the e-mails to him?"

Bas contemplated her question. "Her brother's had some run-ins with the law over the years, maybe that's the connection."

"Maybe," she said contemplatively. "I'll get started on this right away. I'll call you when I get something."

"Call me on my cell the minute you find something," he instructed. "And Nivea, let's just keep this between us."

"You didn't have to tell me that, Bas. We're family, this is what we do. Now, sit tight, I'll call you later."

Disconnecting the call with a slight smile on his face, Bas replayed her words—they were family and they did stick together. Priya was dedicated to her family the same way, if not with a closer connection. For that, he couldn't blame her for searching so hard for this story. He couldn't blame her, but at the same time, he couldn't let her print a word of what she knew.

"She's staying in his private suite. First time I've seen that since I've been here."

Palermo nodded as he listened to the voice on the other end of the phone.

"The bunker is the most protected part of the whole resort, so attacking through that route is like suicide. I tried to tell Black and Sye that the other night but they didn't listen. Perry and his sidekick keep that place wrapped so tight and guarded so heavily it's like walking right into the line of fire."

"So I'll walk in the front door," Palermo stated un-flinchingly.

"Just like you've got a reservation, which by the way you do. I made it this morning after your text. You can check-in by three tomorrow afternoon. Your room's on the

floor just below Perry's. All you have to do after that is
wait for him to come out and bam, you've got him!"

The bloodthirsty excitement coming from the other
line may have been infectious to others, but to Palermo it
was foolish and a sign of the untrained. Never underesti-
mate an enemy is what he'd been taught. Never assume
victory was another. So many things had been drilled into
his head in his years growing up in the West African
town of Etinosa. Words about fighting and claiming what
was rightfully theirs, along with strategies to eventually
turn the shadows' weak-minded and idealistic goals into
dust, were all Palermo heard growing up. And all he'd
ever felt was pain and disgrace.

Now was his chance to break free of those bindings, to
involve himself in something bigger and better, to finally
tell Boden Estevez to go to hell where his dark, perverted
soul belonged.

Paolo Melo had been with Bas and the blue team for going
on three years now. He'd come straight from training with
his father who had been one of Cole's lead guards. He was
twenty-five years old with a thick build, a quick laugh, and
murder in his eyes. His father had been concerned about his
son's temper and thought after an unsuccessful stint in college and a run-in with the law that it was time his son did
something different. He'd trained well, was a natural-born
fighter, but had a lot of growing up to do.

There was an edginess to the young cat that Bas recognized from the years immediately following his parents'
divorce. He'd wanted nothing more than to inflict some
kind of pain, anything that would resemble what he was
going through, on someone else. That urge had led him to
the jungle, to that night when he'd frozen completely. It was
also that urge and that night that sobered Bas and made
him into the shifter and leader he was today. He wanted

desperately to believe that Paolo only needed to get to that same point in his life.

Unfortunately, he wasn't so sure the shifter was going about it in the right way.

Jacques opened the door the moment a light knock sounded. He'd already called for Paolo to meet with them so they could discuss what had happened last night. Now the two watched as the young shifter walked into the room. He wore gray sweatpants and a hoodie, white tennis shoes, and a slight frown—he looked like someone out of a rap video or a college dorm. What he did not look like was a soldier being called to his superiors.

"You wanted to see me," he said to Bas after he'd taken a seat in one of the guest chairs across from Bas's desk.

They were in Bas's offices about an hour and a half after his conversation with Nivea. Jacques took a seat in the remaining guest chair, looking to Bas to see which one of them would answer the youngster.

With all that had happened with the intruders, the threat confessed by the one they'd captured, and of course, the fact that he'd revealed himself and what he really was to Priya, Bas was in no mood for chitchat or to tiptoe around what had become a big issue among their team. So he spoke first. "You were given a direct order last night and you disobeyed it."

Paolo sucked his teeth like an insolent child. "I had the shot," he continued to claim.

"And yet the rogue got away," Jacques added.

Paolo shot the guard a seething look and sat back in his chair. He lifted his arms, letting them drop back to his lap. "What do you want me to say?"

"I want you to stop walking around here acting like we owe you something," Bas told the talented shifter.

Sitting up in his chair, he let his elbows fall to the desk as he continued to hold Paolo's gaze. "Your father is a great guard. You want to know why? Because he knows how to listen, how to watch and wait and learn. He's not a hothead trying to make a name for himself in the field at the cost of either hurting someone else or, as last night proves, letting a rogue get away and get even closer to our property."

"We got him in the end," was Paolo's retort. "And I'm not my father."

Bas could definitely relate to that comment. He'd been compared to his father after he'd opened Perryville Bali and made it onto Forbes's Top Earning Entrepreneurs list. There had even been a number of his father's colleagues calling to offer their own investments in his resorts, which Bas respectfully declined.

"No. You're not," Bas told him tightly. "But what you are and what you will keep in mind the next time Jacques or I or any officer of higher rank than you in the Assembly gives you orders, is that you are a guard. You are here to protect and to serve and the moment you feel like you can no longer do that job, I will personally direct you to the door. Last night was the last bit of insubordination you will show while you are in our employ. Do I make myself clear?"

There was a moment of silence in which Bas thought he might actually have to relieve the shifter of his duties. That was a phone call he did not want to make to Paolo's father, but he would if it became necessary.

Paolo gave a half shrug, stopped only when Jacques made a noise like he was clearing his throat, then sat up straighter in the chair. "I got you," he murmured.

Bas raised a brow. "Excuse me?"

"I understand, sir," Paolo said in a clearer, louder voice.

Seconds later he was dismissed and Jacques and Bas sat alone in the office. Bas's temples throbbed as he sat back in his chair, rubbing a hand over his chin.

"The package went out as you requested," Jacques was saying before there was another knock on the door.

Bas frowned. "It's like Grand Central Station in here today. Come in," he bellowed, not really expecting who would walk in and what cheery news they would have for him this afternoon.

# Chapter 23

"I doubt very seriously he has to check with you before he makes a move," Ezra said the moment Bas shot him a chilly glare. That remark was met with a growl from both Bas and his sidekick, Jacques. Normally Ezra's reply would have been a big fuck you to both the shifters as he clearly planned to go through with the job he'd been assigned, no matter how much they got their panties in a wad. But Bas was a Faction Leader, he was the commander of the Mountain Zone, and thus deserved Ezra's respect as a Lead Guard. In other words, the two were not on equal terms, no matter that they both stood up to piss, put their pants on one leg at a time, and shifted into the same form of killer jaguar.

"Look, that new e-mail was some cryptic type of threat. We need to neutralize it as soon as possible. Your teams are stretched here trying to deal with the invasion of that savior drug and now the weapons that are attached to them. We're on the same side and I'm just here to do a job," Ezra said to both men as they sat in Bas's office.

"I just received a copy of this e-mail message about fifteen minutes before you showed up," Bas began, rubbing a hand over his clean-shaven jaw. "Last I spoke with Rome I was going to work on finding out what was going on at Comastaz, and he was going to continue his work with the president."

Ezra nodded. "Then this came and I guess the priorities shifted a bit. Look, you can see how bad this looks. I'm just going to go in and see what I can find out from the inside."

"You don't know a thing about that lab or what they do. How does he suppose we just get you on the inside?" Jacques asked.

Bas nodded. "Precisely. Besides that, I already have Dana looking into Comastaz. He found out there was blood being transported in those crates. We're tracking where it went before it arrived in those tunnels."

Ezra rested his elbows on the arms of the chair. "X is creating a resume and references for me. I've got an interview scheduled for tomorrow morning. I'll be in by the end of the week, out by next week with all the intel we need. In the meantime, Dana can continue to see what he can come up with on his end. We're all in this together, remember?"

Yes, Bas remembered, but he was almost positive that none of the other shifters in this room, or anyone else in the Assembly was going through what he was right now. A fact that only proved they were not all in this together. "Then what?" Bas inquired, feeling as if he wanted to explode from all the new developments in his life these past weeks.

"Then we proceed however is necessary. Somebody out there knows something," Ezra told him, holding the shifter's gaze solidly. "And what they know can adversely affect us. So we don't have time for a pissing match, we have to get in and find out what's going on before they come after us with whatever it is they know."

Refusing to show the turmoil that raged inside of him, the FL took a deep breath, rubbed his hand across his chin again as he sat back in his chair. "You're right," Bas finally conceded. "I'm not arguing that. It's just a matter of respect and common courtesy. But that's not your issue.

Jacques will get you situated in a room to work out of here, but you should probably get a hotel room outside of Perryville as well. Comastaz is run by the government so they're liable to do some background checking. I don't think it's going to look good if you're staying here."

Ezra nodded. "You're probably right."

"What do you think this message means?" Jacques asked after rising to collect the paper as it slipped from the printer on command from Bas's computer.

"I think it's about exposure," Ezra said immediately. "Everything now seems to be pointing at exposing the fact that shifters are here."

Jacques cursed and Bas looked back at his computer. It wasn't a subject any of them wanted to discuss so he understood the instant silence.

"Sabar didn't give a damn about humans finding out about us. In fact, I think the bastard instigated most of his attacks for the sole purpose of letting the humans know we were here," Ezra added.

"Then why not simply show them himself?" Bas asked. "At any point in time Sabar could have gone to the press or anyone within the government and shown them who and what we are. Why didn't he?"

"We don't have any reason to believe that wasn't his ultimate goal, I mean, before he was blown to pieces. The bank robbery, the fight on the street that night with rogue cats already shifted. He no doubt wanted to let them know we were here and that they should be very afraid."

"But we're not here to hurt them, never have been," Bas continued. "Fear in the humans will only spawn another war and soon we'll be fighting humans and rogues. It's going to be a fucking mess!"

"I concur," Ezra said. "A mess that we all would like to prevent if at all possible. That means we need to keep the humans from finding out we exist."

"Or we can simply kill the bastard rogues that put us in this position in the first place," Bas suggested.

Ezra smiled slowly. "I'm game for doing both."

Jacques balled up the paper, tossing it into the trash can as he moved to the door. "Then let's get this shit done," the shifter stated without an ounce of remorse or hesitation in his tone.

Priya's cell phone vibrated again as she walked down the hallway toward a room that had taken her most of the afternoon to find. She knew exactly who it was and what they wanted, but she wasn't ready to respond. Lolo had apparently wasted no time in contacting Agent Wilson to deliver the e-mails to him and Agent Wilson had wasted no time contacting her. He wanted her to send any information on Reynolds and the cat people she had ASAP, then he wanted her to board the first flight she could to get back to D.C. In his words, he couldn't "protect her from all the way across the US." She didn't know why not since he was the FBI, but then again, Priya wasn't so sure she needed more protecting at this stage of the game.

Things had changed drastically since she'd sent that text to Lolo and if she'd known how they would change she might not have told Lolo to contact Agent Wilson at all. Last night she'd been desperate and ready to put an end to Malik's suffering, no matter what the cost. Today, she knew that cat people, or Shadow Shifters as they were called, did truly exist and from what she could tell from Bas's still cryptic words, they walked the earth right alongside the humans. Only the humans had no clue. It was a huge discovery, a story that would no doubt land her in the national headlines. Her career would be set, her brother would be released alive, her mother could go right back to the life she'd been content to live with her son by her side.

But what about Bas and his people? What would happen to them if she released that story?

All she'd had to do was push SEND, she thought as she continued down the hall, ignoring the cell phone completely.

The story was written, or at least the first of what she figured might lead to a long line of revealing stories about the Shadow Shifters. She could touch on what they were doing here, how long they'd been here, and discuss the secrecy. How many more were there, where did they all live, there were so many angles this story could take. She'd make a ton of money, most of which would go to her overdue student loans and finding another rehab center for Malik. For a long time she'd wanted to buy her mother a house, to get her out of the run-down and drug-infested neighborhood she was in. Maybe she'd be able to do that sooner, rather than later, with her newfound fame.

Bas had more homes than he needed, four top-rated resorts with hundreds of rooms in each. He had cars and lavish penthouse suites all decked out with technological gadgets like he was the next James Bond. He had thousand-dollar watches and suits and let's not forget the ties. He had everything and controlled everything around him.

Priya didn't want him controlling her and Bas apparently had no plans to add her to the list of things he had. So they were even, she'd thought when he'd left her in his suite alone, with instructions to stay there until he returned. Of course she hadn't listened, and he shouldn't have expected her to because she wasn't in his employ and she wasn't his . . . what? What did she want to be to Sebastian Perry? More than a passing fling, she surmised with a pang to her chest.

"This will end," he'd told her. And it would, Priya knew. He would walk away and so would she. The question of whether or not the secret would remain intact was what had her temples throbbing. And it shouldn't be that way. Her goal had been clear from the start, the job was done. Malik would be safe and her life would go on without Sebastian Perry. It sounded even more clear-cut the more she played it over and over in her mind.

Unfortunately, her mind wasn't the problem. Her body and her emotions seemed to be taking over and she had no clue what to do about that fact. So she stopped thinking about it and lifted a hand to knock on the resort room door she'd been headed to.

A few seconds later the door was opened. Priya was holding up a hand before the woman on the other side could speak.

"I know, I know, you told me not to go downstairs. You told me it wasn't a good idea to be in the bunker and I didn't listen."

Jewel folded her arms over her chest and frowned. "I told you it was dangerous down there."

Yes, she had, Priya thought. Jewel had tried to tell her so much more and Priya wondered if she would get all that information from the woman now.

"I know, and I apologize for being so pigheaded and reckless." She hadn't really thought she was both those things but had been told so in the past so just went with it.

It was apparently a good assumption to go with since Jewel actually looked a little more relaxed after the comment.

"What do you want now, Priya?" she asked impatiently.

"I want to talk to you about what's going on here. About what I think you know."

The woman shook her head, dangling silver crescent earrings moving with the motion. "I don't know what you're talking about."

"I think you do."

Jewel tilted her head, her eyes narrowing just a bit before she gave a slight nod. "You want to confirm that I'm not romantically involved with Mr. Perry." She sighed heavily. "I told you before there's nothing going on between him and me. As a matter of fact, I'd venture to say that considering you're still here and not kicked out on your butt, that he must be pretty into you. So there should be no worries on your part."

Priya started to say something, started to deny but stopped. Growing up, she'd had two older sisters who had their own forays with the opposite sex, and of course, there was her mother. Funny how none of the females in the Drake family had ever been exceptionally close, so when Priya had experienced her first date and the next and the next, it had been a very private affair. Even throughout high school and college she'd never been able to forge any close or lasting bonds, especially not with females. That didn't mean she was averse to them, just hadn't found the right one, she supposed, kind of like she'd never found the right guy.

"I'm not worried," she replied slowly.

Jewel nodded as if she really didn't believe her. "Okay, good, then, I think you should leave."

Priya raised a brow. "Why? Did someone tell you not to talk to me?"

With a heavy sigh Jewel lifted her hands and massaged her temples. "Why are you here? What do you want from me?"

Trying desperately to ignore Jewel's comment about Bas being into her, Priya still wanted answers about other things. She suspected that Jewel knew this and was wrestling with whether or not to cooperate with her. Priya wanted that cooperation badly, she needed it. There were questions she had that even Bas couldn't answer, but she had a feeling Jewel could. Alienating the woman definitely wasn't going to work in her favor so she quickly decided on another tack.

"You wanna go downstairs and have a drink?" she offered. That's what girlfriends did, or so she thought. They had drinks together, they talked, shared, answered each other's questions, maybe?

Jewel looked at her closely for a moment and then the woman did something that was absolutely abnormal, and more confirming than Priya could have ever hoped for. Jewel took a step forward and looked up the hallway, then down, then back at Priya again.

"Fine," she said tightly. "Let me get my keys."

Twenty minutes later the two women were sitting in La Selva sipping mojitos and talking about nothing more than the décor and the food.

"It's Spanish-inspired just like everything else here at Perryville. I think Mr. Perry's parents were from Brazil or something like that," Jewel said as she toyed with the ends of her napkin.

"I can see that," Priya commented, looking around the restaurant.

What she really saw were tourists enjoying their vacations. Across the room was a family of six—mom, dad, and four kids that looked to range in age from fifteen all the way down to five. The two younger kids touched each other repeatedly, earning baleful looks from mom and reproachful ones from dad. While the two older ones took to more verbal altercations that finally had dad elbowing the older boy and the girl he'd been arguing with smiling in triumph. The scene might have touched a spot in Priya's heart except Levi Drake had never been a real father, so she had no idea what the complete family experience felt like. Adding to that dismal thought was the fact that she would most likely never have a husband, or four kids that they needed to reprimand while on vacation.

"So Bas is from Brazil?" she asked even though that wasn't the question she'd planned.

"His parents are. He was born in New York."

"Yes, I remember reading that somewhere online," she said a little absently as she tried to figure out why she wasn't asking questions about the shifters, but was focusing solely on Bas now.

"You shouldn't believe everything you read online, reporters are biased," Jewel commented before picking up her glass to take a sip. "They tell the stories they want to tell, regardless of the effects it will have on other people."

Now that comment hit home, reminding Priya of the story she'd written but had yet to send to anyone. "Good reporters get the facts first," she defended herself. "I like to deal with facts, such as, Sebastian Perry is a bit of a recluse, living out here in his own little world, doing his own thing."

"Is that bad?" Jewel asked. "Not doing what everyone else wants you to do, being your own person, taking charge of your own life. Is there something so wrong about that?"

"No," Priya replied immediately, thinking back to the day she'd moved out of her mother's house and into the college dorm. She'd only been able to stay there for one year before the small scholarships she'd received had run out. Working as a waitress and living in the basement of an older woman whose husband had been a journalist gave her the inspiration to push further. And when she'd managed to transfer from the community college to Howard University where she eventually graduated with a journalism degree, Priya had been beyond proud for making her own decisions and pursuing the life she'd always wanted for herself.

Of course, her old life still had a hold on her and kept her returning to her mother's house to help out whenever she could.

"Why do you stay here?" she asked Jewel abruptly. "I mean, you can be an administrative assistant anywhere. I'm guessing that's what your title is, right? Why do you stay in Perryville?"

Jewel looked up with such sadness Priya almost reached out to touch the woman's hand. Something told her that wasn't what the other female wanted and Priya understood completely. Pity was not an emotion she wanted to be on the receiving end of, ever.

"It's a good place to be," was Jewel's slow response. "And after a while you just want to be in a good place, with good people."

"Are they good people here? Perry and his sidekicks, are they good people?" That was the question that had bothered her throughout the night.

Bas said the Shadow Shifters were good, that they were creating a democracy for themselves, living amongst the humans in peace. So far she had to believe that was true, if she didn't think about the bank robbery or the murders back in D.C. He'd said they didn't wish to harm humans or anyone else for that matter. But he'd killed a man right in front of her. Priya couldn't forget that, nor could she ignore Bas's unapologetic demeanor when she'd mentioned it to him. True, the larger-than-life man had been an intruder so she could look at the death as self-defense, but something deep down told her it was more than that. Just as something told her there was more to Bas and his people than he'd told her.

"You ask a lot of questions. Have you always been this inquisitive?" was Jewel's response.

Priya shrugged. "I guess so. Nobody ever gave me real answers growing up so when I was old enough I was determined to find them, to never not be in the know again. That's why I became a journalist."

If Priya wanted the look on Jewel's face to change instantaneously, drastically, she would have made that announcement much sooner. But really it looked like the woman wanted to bolt instead of finish their drink.

"You're a reporter. What are you doing here? What are you writing?" she asked in what Priya instantly recognized was a nervous voice.

"Whoa. Whoa. Wait a minute," Priya said, this time reaching out to touch Jewel's arm as the woman was about to leave. "I'll tell you why I'm here, just have a seat."

Jewel hesitated. She looked around the restaurant, then out the window, then back to Priya as if she really had no choice.

"It's not about you," she said on instinct. The fear that had entered Jewel's eyes the moment she said she was a reporter, coupled with the pounding heart rate she'd felt as she grabbed her wrist, meant the woman was probably on the run from something. Now, the look of relief that was slowly taking over assured Priya that it wasn't a situation she wanted to get into. Jewel could rest assured there would be no question-and-answer session aimed at her past, not from Priya at least.

"I just want to know more about them. Perry and the legions of men he has following him around like he's some kind of mobster or something."

"They're his guards," Jewel said softly. "They are sworn to protect him and they don't deserve you spreading lies about them."

Priya shook her head. "No, that's not what I want to do," she stated emphatically, for the first time since this whole thing had begun, really thinking about what those people were asking her to do. "I don't want to spread lies about them, I just want to understand better." And then she would make a decision on releasing the story.

Jewel flattened her hands on the table, then as if nervous about something, picked up a napkin and absently played with the edges. "You asked before if they were good. Yes, they are. They let me stay here without any questions. I do my job and I live my life here with them, knowing that I'm safe because of them."

Right, Priya thought without posing another question. Being safe was important, especially when fear of whatever is chasing you outside of Perryville has a stranglehold on you and your life. For the first time in her life Priya felt connected to someone, to a female. She felt like she and Jewel had a lot in common even though neither of them had actually confessed the truth about themselves. Jewel was afraid of something, just as she was, and both of them had ended up here, in Perryville, with Bas and his friends, and that had to mean something.

It meant that was the end of the interview, Priya concluded. She'd never had a real friend, besides Lolo, and wasn't certain she could count Jewel as one just yet. What she did know for sure was that the thought of Priya being there to question her had made Jewel so afraid she'd paled. For the first time in a long time, Priya felt like crap about her job. Or rather, her time with Jewel had magnified the niggling doubt she'd had just before leaving her room. Suddenly, she was glad she hadn't hit SEND on the e-mail to Agent Wilson.

Ezra Preston had been born and raised the first twelve years of his life in the Gungi. He spoke fluent Portuguese, English, and a bit of Italian—if the female was fine enough to warrant the taxing on his brain to remember the melodious language. The first son of Aran and Gena Preston, his father was a leader in warrior training for the *Topètenia* tribe, and he'd grown up learning everything there was to know about fighting as a Shadow Shifter, in human and cat form. His twin brother, Eli, younger by two and a half minutes, had learned right beside him, almost as if the two had been born conjoined instead of identical.

On their thirteenth birthday the twins had been sent to
the States to attend a prestigious private school, a gift
from their maternal grandfather who sternly believed in
the integration of shifters and humans. They studied
American culture by day and were allowed to roam as
cats along their grandparents' vast estate in the mountains of Pennsylvania by night. At seventeen they were
flown to Sierra Leone to train with exiled warriors from
the *Lormenia* and *Serfin* tribes. It was important to their
grandfather that they know as much about each shifter
tribe as possible. Hector Preston wanted his grandsons to
be highly intelligent as well as thoroughly trained in defense amongst the shifter world and the human one. But
two years later when the twins were slated to join the
army, they'd performed their first revolt from the tyranny
that had been their life.

Eli had actually been the first to comment on the path
their lives were taking, while Ezra had been somewhat
content to continue learning about battle strategies and
weak points within each tribe. The idea to support their
tribe by becoming more active in the newly formed Stateside Assembly and possibly more like their human side
than the loincloth-wearing warrior *Topètenia* had been
Eli's as well. It hadn't taken much for Ezra to agree—in
fact, it had taken the first human female in his bed to convince him there was so much more to the world than just
the Shadow Shifters.

Ten years later they were Lead Guards to the Head of
the Stateside Assembly, positions of stature and great im-
portance that impressed their parents and grandparents—
who had been a little harder to convince. They were still
fighting side by side and leading with the same attention
to loyalty and strength as they'd been taught.

It was those teachings that had drawn Ezra to a complete

stop as he'd walked into La Selva and noticed the two females sitting at a table near the windows.

The first female, who faced him as he moved slowly to
the table the waitress led him to, caught his attention for
many reasons. Of course there were the obvious ones,
the intense red shade of her hair and the brilliant green
of her eyes—attention getters if ever he'd seen any. But
they neither impressed nor encouraged him to continue
staring even after he was seated, menu slipped between
his fingers.

He was two tables away from them and could see her
as if she were sitting only a foot or so away. Pert lips
moved as she spoke; slim, blunt-nailed fingers feath-
ered through her hair just before her head lowered, then
lifted again, concern etched plainly across her face.
She wasn't a skin-and-bones type of female even though
the half-eaten salad in front of her would have instantly
given that impression. But her face was full, her arms
shapely, not frail. Ezra would bet the extraordinary salary he received from the Stateside Assembly that she
was neatly curvy in shape and as alluring all over as
her face.

She lifted her glass to her lips and his dick twitched.
No, the clever bastard didn't just twitch, it rose to stand at
complete attention, ready, willing, and able to begin the
process which would undoubtedly lead to a happy and
satisfying ending. Ezra dropped his menu and let one
hand fall to his thigh where his length had extended. His
other hand lifted his own glass of water, putting it to his
lips so he could take a gulp, then another as he realized
her lips were now as wet as his own. Until she licked
them, then the hand on his thigh had no other choice but
to rub along his thick erection, a deep purr rumbling in
his chest.

In the next instant, as if she'd heard his gratitude for her simple act of drinking water, she looked directly at him. If he had not been wearing True Religion jeans, steel-toed boots, and a long-sleeved Under Armour shirt, he might have felt exposed himself. He might have assumed she could see his naked body, hot and hard for her. He also might have considered that the next swipe of her tongue across her bottom lip meant she was ready, willing, and able to give him the ride of his life—reverse cowgirl style just the way he liked it.

Instead her look slowly shifted to concern, maybe even fear, Ezra decided as he inhaled deeply, then exhaled with agitation. His body chilled as if she'd picked up a hose and doused him with ice-cold water. Fear from a female was neither attractive nor tolerated by Ezra—or any of the shadows for that matter. Bred into them as viciously as their warrior instincts and the laws of the *Ètica,* was the staunch rule to protect their females, at all costs. Ezra—who had never given a thought to being mated, but absolutely loved the female race, human and shifter— took that extremely seriously.

Setting down his glass he leaned forward in his seat, prepared to do what, exactly, he had no clue. He didn't know this woman, had no idea what had frightened her or what now had her head lowering once more, her lips moving frantically as she spoke to the female accompanying her.

The female, Ezra noticed with a jolt, who was oddly familiar.

They'd been sitting at a table with four chairs, the redhead with her back to the window, facing the front entrance—hence grabbing Ezra's attention immediately. Her companion was sitting right beside her, instead of across the table, so that now that he'd decided to stop drooling over the redhead, Ezra could see her face as well. And his body stiffened for an entirely different reason.

Priya Drake, the reporter from the *Washington Post,* sat comfortably in Perryville Resorts as if she were an invited guest.

"Shit!" Ezra cursed. "What the hell is she doing here?" His lips drawn, he immediately pulled out his cell phone to dial a stored number.

"Delgado," came the answer on the other end.

"We've got a serious problem out here," Ezra said immediately.

"With the lab?" Nick asked.

"No. With that nosy reporter from the *Post* who's sitting in Bas's restaurant like he sent her a personal invitation to do so."

"What the hell?"

Ezra kept his gaze on Priya. "That's exactly what I said."

"Don't let her out of your sight," Nick instructed. "I'm getting Rome and we're gonna find out what the hell is going on out there in sunny Sedona."

Disconnecting the phone, Ezra nodded. "Yeah, I'm gonna find out a few things for myself before this trip is over," he mumbled, letting his gaze shift from Priya to her luscious companion then back to Priya the second she looked up and caught his gaze.

Here there was no fear, no hesitation, and no apologies. In fact, she lifted her glass and offered him a smile, which had Ezra's cat chuffing in anger. But he wasn't about to shift right in the middle of this restaurant, no matter how much he thought that simple act would scare the hell out of the tenacious female. No, he wouldn't compromise himself or his tribe that way, but damn if he didn't want to put her in her place and send her packing once and for all. Sitting there continuing to watch her, he wondered why Bas hadn't done that as well. What Ezra really wondered was why the Mountain Faction Leader had brought the reporter to his resort and had neglected to tell Rome about it. That was going to be the million-dollar question tonight, Ezra was absolutely sure.

# Chapter 24

"If she figured out how to get out of the room, she's going to figure out much more," Jacques told Bas as they sat in the control room.

They were each in a chair, seemingly looking at the screens that reflected motion around the resort, and each thinking of something totally different. Bas had been pre-occupied all afternoon. Sure he'd come to life the moment Ezra waltzed in with orders from the Assembly Leader to get him into Comastaz and he'd acted with his usual efficiency after Ezra left and they'd begun to pull the necessary strings for the operation. But now, locked in this room with only Jacques, Bas was different.

He was at ease. At least enough to let the real weight that was bearing down on his shoulders show.

"Opening a door is not rocket science," Bas replied without much emotion. His hand moved over the cordless mouse to switch the screen he was watching to a different angle.

Jacques continued, unfettered. "She's still texting and sending e-mails. I talked to someone at the paper and they think she's on vacation, but with the presidential candidates being announced and campaigning hitting full swing, her editor wants every available reporter there. This story could cause her career to skyrocket. Otherwise she is nothing."

Bas bristled, his hand tightening on the mouse, his words tempered. "She's an intelligent and strong woman who pulled herself up out of the misery that was her upbringing to get where she is today. Do. Not. Call. Her. *Nothing*."

And there it was, no matter how practiced and seemingly calm. The reaction that Jacques knew he'd get if he poked hard enough. He couldn't say the confirmation made him happy, but at least he knew precisely what they were dealing with now.

"She's a human who can bring a lot of unwanted heat down on us, that's who she is. You need to remember that."

"No. You need to remember which one of us is in charge here," Bas said through clenched teeth. He took a deep breath, released it, and then followed with, "I know what I'm doing."

Jacques was quiet for a few consecutive heartbeats. "If you tell her what we are she will tell the world. She's a human and so the moment she finds out what we are she will either fear you or despise you. Falling for her is not a good strategic move."

"And sending her away is? She has questions, she's seen things. None of that will change if I send her packing. She'll just look for answers somewhere else."

"But she won't find them, ever, because nobody will tell her," Jacques countered. "Letting her stay in your room is a bad idea, she's getting too close."

"Keep your friends close and your enemies even closer, ever heard of that saying, Jacques?"

"Don't shit where you sleep, ever heard of that one?"

Bas slammed both hands on the console, his head turning slightly so that he was now staring right at Jacques. It was a deathly stare, one he'd seen only when Bas had his rifle drawn, target in line. He probably should have flinched but he was banking on their long friendship, his dedication to this tribe and Bas's dedication to the same, to keep him alive. Actually, he prayed like hell that it would.

"I've got this under control," Bas told him.

"I'm going to keep an eye on her and her text messages while you work this out. But mark my words, with Ezra here, if he sees her or gets one whiff of her out here, Rome is going to be all over this place. He's going to order her killed, Bas. So do us both a favor, if you're developing some type of feelings for her, cut that shit off now and get her the hell out of here while she's still breathing. Your continued guilt trip over the death of one human female is more than enough for both of us to live with."

"Are you finished?" Bas asked, standing and pushing the chair back so hard it banged against the wall, rattling the printer and fax machine on the table it was closest to.

Jacques's reply was a simple shrug. He didn't know what else or how else to say it to the shifter without crossing the line. And Jacques didn't want to do that, not unless he absolutely had to.

Bas rubbed a finger over his jaw and took another deep breath. He straightened, squared his shoulders, and then spoke as if they'd just walked into this room to have a little chat about the weather.

"That shifter I shot in the bunker, he knew where he was going. He wasn't lost even though those hallways are designed to be a big maze, from the color to the length, as you well know. But when he came around that corner it was with slow deliberation, like he'd been waiting for us to walk down that very hallway."

Jacques sat up in his chair, instantly alert to what Bas was saying, the scene replaying in his mind.

"The only thing down the end of that hall is the elevator that leads upstairs," Jacques told him.

Bas nodded. "The elevator that leads up to my private suite."

"There are no complete blueprints of this resort on any public file. According to the zoning board the bunkers don't even exist, just an unfinished space for storage." Jacques and Bas had discussed this repeatedly during construction, it was for their safety as well as the humans that booked rooms with them.

"Which means someone on the inside told him where to come and how to get around," Bas said tightly. "They were looking for the items we took from that tunnel. Somebody told them we have it stashed in the bunker."

It was Jacques's turn to nod this time because he was following Bas's line of thought step for step and coming to the same disturbing conclusion—they had a traitor in their midst.

Bas felt like running. He felt like heading out onto the balcony, down the path that led to his personal running spot, and stripping down to the barest part of himself. His bones ached; carrying the weight of all his worries and the cat that wanted to be free all day long was taking its toll. Knowing that he would enter his room and she would be there was something else he couldn't describe.

On the one hand he'd needed her all day. He hadn't felt complete, like something integral was missing as he'd moved from one meeting to another, even when he was down in the kitchen talking to his banquet manager about an upcoming event happening the first of the year, he hadn't felt like himself. He'd longed for her, to touch her, kiss her, sink inside her once more. That was basic, lust came naturally to the shifters and being with Priya had been as good as he'd thought it would be. Yet, Bas knew that wasn't all.

He actually ached inside at not seeing her, not scenting her close by. If he thought about her, the familiar scent that seemed to linger on both of them would resurface, but it was too far away, she was too far way. He needed her here, with him, right now.

And that was problematic, just as Jacques had warned.

Letting himself into the room, Bas tried not to think too hard on Jacques's words or on the truth to them that still had Bas's heart pounding. *Rome is going to order her killed.* And Bas was going to protect her with his own life if need be, there was no question about that. Then what? Would Rome order both of them killed? Bas would like to see him try it.

He would also like to see Priya, but she wasn't in the living room area. Right beside the door, where she'd left them last night he supposed, was her duffle bag and her purse. She'd been ready to leave Perryville, to leave him. Bas hadn't liked that thought the first time she'd said it to him and he liked it even less now.

His head lifted abruptly as he forgot about the bags and looked around the room for her. Along his spine a slither of worry worked its way up to his shoulders and he proceeded slowly into the bedroom. A part of him knew she wouldn't be here. The cat knew and was instantly on alert. He was about to walk out of the room, to go out onto the balcony to see if she was taking a swim when he stopped and looked back at the bed.

It was neatly made, pillows piled on one side—the right side where she'd slept last night—as if she'd been sitting there propped up. Working on her laptop he figured, as his gaze rested on the computer. Dread sliced through him like an iron-hot blade as he moved to the bed. The screen was black, but the flashing light on its side said it was still on and Bas touched the mouse pad to bring it back to life.

An e-mail message came up on the screen. A message to Dorian Wilson, the FBI agent that Nivea had been following. With a frown Bas read Priya's unfinished message telling the agent that her story on the cat people was attached.

His fingers felt like lead weights as he moved them over the keyboard to open the attachment.

> They live in the shadows—part man,
> Part animal—hiding their true nature

He read on, each word making his temples pound more, his chest aching with the betrayal he'd known was forthcoming.

By the time he made it to the end of the article Bas was ready to throw the laptop out the nearest window. He was going to storm out of this room and search every inch of this resort himself to find the author of the article and then what? What was he going to do to Priya Drake for doing exactly what she'd told him she would do? What she *had* to do to save her brother's life.

The alarm system beeped as the front door was accessed and Bas frowned. He didn't want to deal with Jacques right now and there was no one else that knew the access code to enter his suite. The one thing he really didn't need was for Jacques to come back here looking for him and to somehow see what was on the screen and to have confirmation that he was absolutely right about Priya Drake. Bas had just closed the laptop and taken a step toward the bedroom door when Priya walked in.

"You're back," she said immediately upon seeing him, looking as surprised to see him as he was to see her.

"And you were out," he said evenly. "I told you to stay here until I came back for you."

"I had to see someone," she told him like that was going to be reason enough and shut him up in the process.

"How did you get back in and who did you have to see? You don't know anyone here."

She sighed, clearly not happy with his questioning but Bas didn't give a damn. They'd officially crossed into another, less predictable aspect of their relationship, and he didn't like it. He would definitely deal with it, but he didn't like it at all.

"I'm going to shock us both and answer your questions without arguing that I don't have to do what you say or answer to you," she said simply as she sat on the bed.

Right beside the infamous laptop.

She continued when Bas failed to respond. "I went to check on Jewel to make sure she was all right. We were downstairs together last night and then she was gone."

"So you wanted to make sure I didn't kill her too?" he asked, his voice hoarse with the still raw emotion soaring through him.

Priya blinked, and Bas figured she was surprised at his tone or his question, either-or, it didn't really matter.

"I wanted to make sure she wasn't hurt or hadn't gotten into any trouble because of me," she replied, watching him carefully. "As for your other question, I watched Paolo when he brought me upstairs yesterday. You know, after you left me high and dry in the spa."

She'd wiggled her eyebrows at that and Bas's frown deepened. His chest felt like a killer whale had landed on it, his temples throbbing like drums as fury boiled inside of him. How could she write that story? How could she tell the world about them, when he'd told her what would happen if she did?

The fact that she was sending the story to an FBI agent and not whoever it was that had been e-mailing her about her brother was even more dangerous in Bas's mind. The United States government was the absolute last group of humans that needed to know about the shadows. Fear and domination would be the tools they would resort to in their effort to try and contain the unknown group. The shadows were not going to be contained no matter how much diplomacy—which he did not think would be much—came into play. It was simply a disaster waiting to happen.

"Bas, are you all right?"

Priya had stood from the bed and was now about a foot away from him. She reached up to touch him and Bas took a step back. "We're going to dinner," he announced abruptly. "Get yourself together and meet me in the lobby."

He didn't wait for a response, couldn't stand there in front of her without wanting to do something—but what? Shake her, yell at her, question her, berate her? What was he going to do with an adult human that had a job to do, not to mention a life to save? How was he going to contain the secret he'd so foolishly handed her? Bas didn't have the answers. He didn't have the control he normally possessed and he was very uncomfortable with his urge to shake some sense into Priya or toss her on the bed and sink himself so deep inside her nothing or nobody else mattered to either of them anymore.

Half an hour later, they were in the truck, Priya sitting all the way to one side of the backseat and Bas on the other. Tonight, Kaz was his driver instead of Jacques. Bas hadn't wanted any more of the man's advice on what he should and should not be doing and with whom he should be doing it, so he'd sought out Syfon to ride with him and Priya. Syfon hadn't been available and Paolo, who Bas would have liked to have close to him again, especially after their latest conversation, was mysteriously nowhere to be found. So Kaz had been next in line and since it wasn't as if he were heading out for a top-secret mission, Bas figured it was okay.

What wasn't okay was the guilt eating at him. It seemed this was his favorite emotion, only this time the female he felt guilty about was different. Staring out the window as scenery darkened by the fall of night, he thought about how angry he'd been upon seeing the article she'd written. The article that had depicted the shifters, not as a new species about to claim their differences from the humans, but as a group of people united and committed to having a life amongst the humans. And wasn't that exactly what they were? Wasn't that what Rome and the Assembly were trying to build for them? Still, the sight of those words on her computer had sparked the first tingles of fear in him, an emotion he hadn't felt in years and one he didn't like feeling at all. But could that fear be placed solely at Priya's feet? Or could it, as it was hundreds of years ago with the humans, be a simple result of impending evolution?

Squeezing the bridge of his nose, Bas wondered how long the Elders had actually expected to keep their existence a secret, especially with the rogues determined to wreak havoc regardless of the *Ètica* or anyone else's rules.

"I think you're probably causing more tension than releasing it," she said into the silence.

Pulling his hand down quickly from his face, Bas looked over to her. "I'm not tense."

She made some sound that seemed sarcastic and Bas decided to ignore it. The last thing he wanted was to get into another debate with her. It seemed every second they weren't ripping each other's clothes off and dying to get inside each other, they were engaged in a gentle tug of war, her on one side and he on the other. Just another reason why things between them were destined to fail.

"How do you suggest I relieve my tension?" he asked for the sake of keeping conversation going, but avoiding confrontation.

She shifted quickly, turning sideways in her seat. "I sing the alphabet song," she told him.

When he didn't immediately respond, she began to sing it. By the time she hit Q Bas was undoing his seat belt. Somewhere around U or V he was sliding across the seat, pulling her into his arms.

"What are you doing?" she asked after a startled note about Z fell from her lips.

"I'm relieving my tension," was all he said before dipping his head to lick the skin that had been exposed through the low-cut top of her dress.

He'd tried. Nobody could say that he hadn't, but damn if there wasn't something continuously pulling them together. Whatever it was proved stronger than all the arguments Bas proposed in his head, even than the control he had over his cat that was now purring with pleasure as his tongue moved over her soft skin.

"We're not supposed to do this, remember?"

Her voice was a breathy whisper, her hands cupping the back of his head, guiding him over slightly to the right. He followed her lead, letting his tongue stroke the curve of her breast. Her dress buttoned up the front and Bas's fingers worked quickly to undo the first few. Pushing the material and her bra aside he cupped the mound, letting the tight little nipple rub alluringly over the pad of his tongue. She hissed and Bas growled, pulling her even closer, sucking her into his mouth hungrily.

Priya held his head in place, arching her back beneath him as her breathing hitched. She wanted him just as much as he wanted her, perhaps more based on the way she was breast-feeding him. Bas's nostrils flared as a thick sweet scent infiltrated. With each inhale his body grew warmer, his dick harder. If he didn't get inside her soon he was going to hurt somebody or something.

Instead he fumbled between their bodies for a second longer than he wanted until his finger finally pressed into the godforsaken seat belt clasp. The moment it clicked he pulled his mouth away from Priya long enough for her to whisk her arms free and for him to grab her by the waist, turning her so that she was now kneeling on the backseat. The additional enhancements he'd ordered for his Yukon had added to the other FLs teasing how self-centered and eccentric he was. But right at this moment, Bas was grateful for the leather bench and extended floor space in the back of his truck.

They weren't supposed to do this. He wasn't supposed to be with a human and the human wasn't supposed to tell anyone who he really was. But as Bas undid his zipper, freeing his thick erection, he realized he didn't give a damn about what should and should not be—not at this moment. As this moment, as he pushed her dress up over her hips, rubbing his hands over the rounded globes of her delectable ass, he knew what mattered most to him.

"Bas," she whispered. "This is insane." But she didn't pull away, didn't stop him when he slipped his fingers beneath the rim of her underwear to touch her bare flesh.

Bas shook his head, not willing to struggle to think of an excuse. "It just is," he finally managed, the heady scent of her all but drowning him as he continued to rub her backside, mesmerized by her.

"I want you all the time," she admitted.

The words were like an echo to what Bas had already been thinking. He licked his lips, all but panting at the sight of her bent over and ready for him. "You want me here, pretty girl? Tell me you want me right here and now," he insisted.

Bas needed to hear those words. He needed to know this woman wanted him, not the rich resort owner, and even though she knew about his cat, he needed to hear her say the words that no other female had ever said to him before.

"I . . ." She hissed and arched back as his fingers

slipped between her crease, down to her heated center, spreading her dewy essence. "I, oh god, I need you right now!"

It wasn't enough, her words, her willing body, they didn't seem to be enough, not this time. Shaking his head and moving so that he was ready to sink inside, Bas planned to ignore what was still missing. He planned to fuck her right here and now regardless of the fact he was feeling something pretty strange between them. Then, as if his own feelings weren't bad enough, he inhaled and it hit him so hard he almost faltered.

Grabbing his shaft at the base, Bas guided his length to her, tapping the bulbous head against her plump cheeks. She moaned and pushed back, rushing him. With his other hand Bas pulled her apart, licked his lips once more at the sight of her plump folds, dampened by her arousal. He groaned at seeing how tight her ass really looked, after only feeling it up to this point. He couldn't decide what he wanted more, which he needed to feel the most. When she groaned his name he pushed forward, pressing the head of his engorged cock into her waiting center until he was completely buried inside her.

A new scent surrounded them, neither hers nor his own, but theirs. Bas clenched his teeth at the thought, then pulled out of her until he was almost completely clear of her warmth. Looking down to her essence glistening on his arousal he cursed, sinking back inside her once more. It couldn't be, he thought as he thrust again and again, keeping his eyes closed as if that would stop what he knew was happening.

He pumped slowly and she gyrated wildly as if she knew he was trying to get away, trying to save them both from a path that led to a dead end. It couldn't lead anywhere else, not for him. None of that mating and joining bullshit was for him, his parents and then Mariah's death had seen to that. Connections of the emotional sort weren't worth it, not for a shifter like Sebastian Perry.

Even knowing all this, Bas wanted more. Clasping her hips, holding her still as he rammed in and out of her, he knew he wanted it all. Everything she had, everything she was. He wanted to claim her, to mark her as his and to dare anyone to disagree with those facts.

Without another thought he did just that, leaning forward and sinking his sharp teeth into the nape of her neck. She let out a scream, simultaneously clenching her thighs around him as her release ripped through her fiercely. The increase of that foreign scent, her tightening around him, her scream, the deepness of his thrust, all of the above pushed Bas right over the brink and he let loose what had to be the most powerful release of all his life.

"Sweet," she whispered after they'd been still but for their racing hearts for a couple of minutes.

Bas had pulled out of her, moving back to his seat near the window, watching as she did the same. "Excuse me?" he asked when he realized she'd spoken.

She stopped buttoning her dress to look over at him. "It smells so sweet in here. Maybe we're at the bakery or the mall has a Cinnabon shop." She groaned. "I love Cinnabon."

If Bas thought it was strange that she was talking about Cinnabons after a very intense and possibly game-changing round of sex, he didn't say it, because something else had grabbed his attention.

The moment he'd climbed into the truck he'd activated the privacy window that blocked the front seat from seeing or hearing anything that was going on in the back, another enhancement which was actually in all the FL vehicles. So Kaz had no idea what they'd been doing back here for the last . . . how long had it been?

Yet the shifter had continued to drive.

Lifting his arm, Bas looked down at his watch. They should have been in town ten minutes ago. The truck should have been parked and Kaz should have either called him through the com link or knocked on the back door to get them out.

Instead, the truck was still moving.

"I need you to be very quiet," Bas told Priya after he'd adjusted his clothes. Reaching forward, he opened a compartment just beneath the privacy window. There was a small plastic packet in there and he retrieved it, holding it up so she could see it. "Clean yourself up and do not get out of this truck."

The calm that was in her eyes just seconds before was replaced by the slight edge of panic and Bas felt ready to kill. Instead he shook his head, returning to the seat and reaching out to touch her. "No. Nothing is going to happen to you. Nothing at all. I just need you to stay here until I come back for you. Do you understand?"

She nodded her head and Bas released his grip on her. She immediately took the packet of wipes from his hand and he moved across the seat to the window where he'd been before. Reaching beneath that seat Bas retrieved his gun, removed the safety, and spoke into his com link.

"Kaz, what's our ETA?"

There was no response.

"I said, what's our ETA?" Bas repeated.

A few seconds later there was still no response.

Bas cursed just as the truck swerved, jerking both him and Priya around on the backseat.

# Chapter 25

"Press pound three and say code blue," Priya whispered to herself as she held Bas's cell phone in her hands like it was her lifeline. He'd thrust the phone into her hands just before opening the door and leaving her in the back of the truck by herself. She pressed a button on the phone and watched it light up. If he wasn't back in seven and a half minutes, she was to call that number and hopefully help would come.

In the meantime, she thought with fear snaking along her spine, she'd just wait here, like a sitting duck. Looking out the window she saw immediate darkness and what looked like it could be streetlights in the distance. She pressed the button she'd watched Bas press when they climbed into the car and waited while the privacy partition was lowered.

"Dammit!"

The driver was gone. It hadn't been the same driver she'd seen the first night, the one she now knew from Jewel was Bas's best friend. This was a younger guy who had stared at her breasts much longer than was polite and gave a salacious smile when he'd held the door as she climbed inside. He'd had a creepy look about him but Priya was used to that. She hadn't come from the best neighborhood in D.C. so she was used to dealing with scumbags and jerk-offs, only she hadn't thought she would be faced with them in Bas's quaint little resort town.

It was deathly quiet now. The word "deathly" echoing in her mind as soon as she'd thought it and her heart hammered in her chest.

Why was she sitting here waiting for something bad to happen? Wasn't she more of a proactive than a reactive woman?

*Nothing is going to happen to you. Nothing at all.*

That's what Bas had said.

*I just need you to stay here until I come back for you.*

Yeah, or wait until somebody or something else comes back for her. To hell with that!

Priya reached for the door handle just as it was pulled from the other side. She stumbled a bit, keeping a grip on the cell phone and looking up into the deadliest eyes she'd ever seen.

Bas chased Kaz down the stretch of road before he turned off into a copse of trees. He could have shot him, could have just shot that bastard traitor in the back but they weren't in a private location.

Kaz had stopped the truck about a quarter mile away from a cul-de-sac town house development. If he fired his gun the neighbors would surely hear and call the cops. Cursing, he stopped running and turned back toward the truck. Priya was there alone. He had to get back to her and call Jacques to tell him what was going on. He had to . . .

The scream ricocheted off the trees, cutting through Bas like a heated blade. Inside his cat roared, his human feet picked up, and he ran full-on toward the truck only to come up short when he saw Priya . . . and the two full-grown male jaguars standing on either side of her. From behind the truck came a man that possibly matched Bas in height and weight; the glow of his eyes and the foul stench that rested heavily against the dry air branded him a shifter, a rogue shifter.

One of the cats knocked its head against the back of Priya's legs and she fell to her knees. Bas moved in and the one still in human form stepped in front of him.

"We meet again, Sebastian," Palermo Greer said, a wicked gleam in his cat's eyes. "This time you have something that belongs to me and I have something that belongs to you. You wanna trade?"

The last was said as if the words tasted like a dead fowl on his lips and were followed by a laugh that echoed in the night. Bas didn't flinch and he didn't give a damn what he had that Palermo thought belonged to him, Priya was not a part of this, not now and not ever.

"Let her go and I won't kill your sorry ass," was his response.

The rogue tossed back his head and laughed again, showing the tattoos on his long, dark, orange skin-toned neck.

"Like you did all those years ago when we were in the forest? Oh, wait, you didn't do anything that time and look what happened." Both cats, already shifted and standing just behind Palermo, replied with open-mouthed growls that echoed off the mountaintops.

Bas wanted to shift and break Palermo's spine with his bare teeth. He wanted to rip the bastard shifter apart the same way he'd watched him and his cohorts kill Mariah. But this wasn't Mariah. She was dead. This was Priya and his chest ached with the possibility that she could suffer the same fate, because of him.

"I'm not that man anymore," Bas told him steadily.

"You're not a man at all, are you? Or maybe you didn't tell your lovely little human mate about your true nature?" Palermo continued.

Oh but he had, Bas thought fleetingly. "This is not going

to end the way you want it to, Greer. I'm not giving you back the blood."

There was an endless second of silence while Bas's words were digested. "Then I'll just have to take hers," Palermo finally spat, his teeth elongating, head tilting as he leaned in closer to Priya's head.

Bas's gaze rested on Priya, who had only made a slight gasp as Palermo pulled her up around the waist, pushing her head forward. He would go for the back of her neck, paralyzing her before he actually killed her, just like he'd done with Mariah. But Priya was different—a fact Bas had already discovered—she wasn't crying even though fear engulfed her . . . no wait, anger was mixed with that fear. And as Bas looked even closer, he saw what she held in her hand, his cell phone and the screen was lit indicating she'd made a call.

Unfortunately, having Jacques on his way wasn't going to get that mangy rogue's hands off her and for Bas that was priority number one.

Returning his gaze to Greer, Bas moved slightly, aimed, and fired, hitting the filthy rogue in the shoulder. The sound of the gunshot brought the cats behind Greer into full action and they both lunged past Priya toward him. Bas had maybe two seconds to decide whether he was going to use all his bullets trying to shoot the cats down then take out their leader, or simply shift and kill all the bastards. Shifting would mean exposure, but Priya had already seen him and right about now he didn't give a flying fuck who saw him. She was the priority, saving her was all he cared about. A repeat of fourteen years ago with him burying a dead human body so that no one would ever find it was not going to happen, not this time.

He shifted, falling to his haunches instantly and the second the first cat approached, Bas jumped upward and bit deep into its skull. The second one attacked him from behind, but he twisted with the animal, pounding at it with his paws.

Priya moved quickly the second she heard the gunshot. The man holding her had faltered and she'd fallen to the ground once more, almost on her face. Not hesitating, she rolled over and came to a standing position, calling on her year of self-defense and kickboxing training at the Y. The man fell against the truck holding his shoulder and she went at him instantly. Fists balled, arms raised, she stepped toward him, angled her body, then put all her weight on her left leg, swinging her right leg into the air. The heel of her foot caught the man on his chin. His head jerked back and she moved in closer, punching him in the throat and taking away whatever air he had left.

He crumpled to his knees and she stepped away, looking over to where the cats were battling. The sounds were horrendous, the pounding against their massive bodies, the growls and roars. It all played in horrific stereo that only amplified the sight before her. These were vicious animals fighting possibly to the death and Bas, the man she'd been sleeping with these past couple of days, was one of them.

With her heart beating way too fast to be normal, Priya ran toward the cats, falling to her knees just a few feet away from the truck where Bas had dropped his gun. Once she had the cool metal in her hands, she fumbled through her mind to figure out how to use it. She'd taken self-defense classes, not classes at the gun range. But Malik had never been a stranger to guns or how to use them, so this wasn't the first time she'd held one in her hands. It was, however, the first time she held one with the intention of actually shooting someone.

Later she would wonder how she heard him, how she knew he was coming for her again but right now Priya turned quickly, gun raised, and pulled the trigger. The huge black cat that had been lunging for her hit the ground with a horrendous thump. Kickback from the gun pushed at her until she fell on her ass and in the next instant she was staring up into the face of one angry-ass big cat, teeth bared and ready to strike.

# Chapter 26

**Washington, D.C.**

Agent Dorian Wilson was nowhere to be found. Nivea had gone to his apartment once more, she'd waited hours for him to leave, but he hadn't. Sure, because of Bas's call she'd been an hour late getting to his apartment near the D.C. and northern Virginia border, but he wasn't due into work for another forty-five minutes, so she'd thought she still had time. Now, at almost ten o'clock in the morning, she knew something was wrong. A search of the parking garage where he held a monthly pass, proved her point. Wilson's car wasn't there.

Cursing to herself as she drove out onto the street once more, she reached for her cell phone, which was based on the dashboard and pressed for a stored number to be dialed. Before the number could be connected and she could speak through her Bluetooth, reporting her location and current situation to the guards at Havenway, she received an incoming text that read:

Search complete. IP location: 909½ 29th street NW.

With the call back to base completely disregarded, Nivea punched the address into her GPS and drove with every intention of finding out who was holding Malik Drake hostage and threatening the shifters at the same time.

Forty minutes later she parked her car directly in front of a brownstone that displayed the same address as the one in her phone. Grabbing her phone off the dash, sticking it in her back pocket, and checking the weapon under her right pants leg, she climbed out of the car and headed up the steps. Three presses to the doorbell but there was no answer. Two sturdy knocks and even an attempted yell through the door that she was with the utility company, and still no answer, but there was a scent.

Closing her eyes, Nivea pressed her forehead to the door and took a deep inhale. Cars drove by on the street behind her, somewhere in the distance a dog barked, and above the sun shone like a beacon. Nivea, however, remained perfectly still as she focused totally on the scent tickling her nose.

It was a human, a bleeding human and it was coming from inside this house. She didn't think beyond that, couldn't really, as her adrenaline kicked immediately into action. Pulling a pin from her ponytail she went to work on the lock, disengaging it about ten seconds after she'd first touched it. The knob turned at her command and in the next instant Nivea was inside the house. The scent instantly intensified and she stopped only long enough to pull her gun from its holster before fully moving in. Letting her senses guide her, Nivea moved through what looked like a very well-to-do person's house with its crystal-and-gold chandelier gleaming from above, plush carpets, and lavish furniture. She ignored all that in pursuit of the aroma, passing the living and dining rooms, coming to a pause at a door. With no one there to stop her, Nivea opened that door and hurried down the steps only to be welcomed by the ring of gunshots.

Ducking quickly behind an old armoire she extended her arm and returned the fire, seeing two men standing in front of a third man tied to a chair—the bleeding human.

A hail of bullets rained down at that moment and Nivea didn't dare peek out from behind the armoire again. Her heart thumped wildly in her chest as she finally cursed herself for not making the call to Havenway, for not asking for backup before entering this damned house. Now she was trapped with dismal chances of getting herself, let alone the bleeding human out of here alive.

"Here kitty, kitty, kitty," a male voice taunted when the shooting subsided. "Come out and play with us."

Dammit, a rogue.

Why hadn't she smelled them first? Why had she only scented the human? It didn't matter now, they weren't shooting so now was her chance. With her back to the armoire she gripped her gun and got low, coming around the side aiming and shooting the one rogue right in the balls. The other received a shot between his eyes and another squarely in the center of his chest. But those shots hadn't come from her. Whirling around she saw immediately who had fired.

"What the hell are you doing here?" she asked.

"Saving your simple ass," was Eli Preston's quick retort.

"Wait a goddamned—" Nivea had started, only to be cut off by Eli and that cocky-ass swagger of his walking right past her as if he had heard all he wanted to hear.

"Save it," he told her as he continued to move across the room. "Let's get him out of here before the owners of this house are notified we're here by the alarm you set off when you broke in."

There hadn't been an alarm. Had there? Nivea stood, holding her gun down as she walked over to where Eli was. He clicked the safety on his gun, tucking it into his back waistband and pulling a knife from his front pocket.

Kneeling down, he went to work on the ropes binding the human. The very bloody and unconscious, but still alive, human that Nivea was almost positive was Malik Drake. Next, and as if she weren't even standing there, Eli lifted the man over his shoulder and headed for the back door.

"Text your boyfriend Bas that we're taking his human to George Washington Hospital and don't forget to tell him he owes me one for saving your ass."

Gritting her teeth, Nivea had no choice but to follow him out. If she had triggered an alarm, the company had no doubt already contacted the police and the owners. They had to move fast. Faster than it would take for her to cuss Eli Preston out for following her and then to be-grudgingly thank him for, yes, saving her ass.

## Sedona, Arizona

Bas covered her body with his to shield her from any more of the fighting. Even though he'd taken out the two cats on his side, Palermo had shifted before she got off her shot and could possibly get up again. Or not. He had no idea where the cat had been shot, or if the bullet had hit the animal at all. And right at this moment it didn't matter. What mattered was getting Priya to safety. Palermo's words, his threats to do to Priya what he had done to Mariah, still echoed in Bas's head, spurring on a rage that ran so deep he'd come to believe it was an intricate part of the man and the cat.

He'd been outnumbered just as he was that night in the Gungi and at one point they'd had Priya surrounded. She could be dead right at this moment. The thought roared through his mind like a hurricane and his cat bared its teeth, yelling into the night once again. Then there was movement and he looked down into her face, saw that she was breathing rapidly, her eyes so wide they'd completely bulge out any minute now.

In the next moments Bas shifted, returning to his human form. He moved off of her but stayed close, helping her into a sitting position

"Are you okay?" he asked, raking his eyes over every part of Priya's body to be sure she wasn't hurt in any way.

"F—fine," she mumbled, brushing off the front of her dress and standing up. "I'm okay but you need to get dressed."

She was right. It was night but the altercation had been noisy. As Bas stood and looked around for his clothes he noticed the carcasses of the two cats he'd taken out and the one that Priya had shot. Looking back to where she'd been lying, he retrieved his gun and moved closer to the lead cat. It wasn't moving.

"Grab my phone," Bas instructed Priya while he went back into the truck to pull out the duffle bag stored in the trunk for occasions just as this. After pulling on jeans and a T-shirt, he circled back around to find his shoes.

It was then that he heard the other vehicles approaching and instantly went on alert once again. The scene was a mess, a questionable mess for any human. Bas was just about to run for his shoes and to get Priya when his heart stopped completely. Later tonight, he would think of how everything from that second on moved in slow motion, how his heart that had once beat rhythmically in his chest had stuttered to a slow, staggered beat, and how everything he'd ever worked for, every goal he'd reached, every moment he'd hated the collapse of his parents' marriage and the disappointment of the two most important people in his life, all paled in comparison to watching that damned cat rise from the ground, shift into human form, and reach out to grab Priya as she stood with her back to it.

"Nooo!" he yelled, charging forward.

Palermo turned at the sound of Bas's voice, his bloody arm around Priya's neck, a gun at her temple.

Bas's feet skidded to a stop as glinting eyes stared back at him, mouth twisted in an angry smirk.

"Like I said before, you got my stash and I got your mate, now we're even!" he taunted Bas.

"Let. Her. Go," Bas said, sounding like a man in complete control of his emotions. In all actuality his cat was ready to burst free once more, killing the only action on its agenda.

"Not a fuckin' chance! You can kiss her sweet ass good-bye unless you're ready to make an exchange."

"Bas," Priya yelled.

The sound of her voice, the fear in her eyes, the stench of dead cats on the humid night's air, had Bas seeing red. Rage and every other dark emotion he'd kept stored inside him came rushing to the surface. He took one step, and then another, and when the man's eyes glittered once more, his arm lifting higher as he aimed that gun at Priya's temple, Bas fell to the ground, grabbing the gun from the back waistband of the jeans he'd just slipped on. He aimed and fired.

Priya screamed just as light flooded the area while Bas's heart beat so frantically he thought it might rip right through his chest. He stood, quickly moving to where he'd last seen her being held at gunpoint. She'd fallen down on her knees while Palermo had fallen flat on his back. Bas pulled her into his arms. He sat with his knees on the dirt road with Priya cradled tightly in his arms, rocking her as she wept.

An hour later there was a flurry of activity at Perryville Resorts. News about some type of altercation just outside the resort had spread like wildfire and the guests were understandably nervous. The media had set up like they planned to tailgate in the parking lot and the staff answered inquiries from guests as calmly as they possibly could. Two police cars were parked at the front entrance as officers waited to speak to anyone who might have possibly been witness to what happened.

Upstairs, on the second floor in the largest conference room at the far west end, a room full of shifters sat pondering what their next move would be.

"Three rogues, and one of them, the one Bas capped right between the eyes, was Palermo Greer," Syfon reported, his face a mask of pure rage and fury. The shifter's broad shoulders were still bunched as if he were ready to shift and kill at any moment. At his side a Glock was holstered, beneath his right pants leg was another gun, and beneath the left was a knife that would cut through flesh as cleanly and quickly as if it were butter.

He continued speaking with Jacques's permission. "Greer arrived in the States a couple months back, immediately hooking up with our favorite group of rogues—Sabar and company. My cousin out in Seattle says they also have pictures of Greer with some human military men.

"Then he showed up on the East Coast the night of that explosion. Next thing we know he's out here setting up headquarters for that wannabe Darel Charles. We have no idea where that headquarters is exactly or how many they had in their employ already," Syfon finished.

"I had Syfon search Kaz's room the minute we returned. Everything's gone. Just like we thought, they had someone on the inside feeding them information. He must have informed them Bas was going out," Jacques added and the reaction was like dropping a match into a glass of gasoline.

"How did he manage to pull off driving the FL?" one shifter asked. "He never drives him."

Jacques spoke up for himself. "I was not aware that the

FL was going out and so was indisposed. Syfon says he
was never notified either."

"I got a text from Kaz about two hours ago saying he
had some things to take care of in town," Paolo volun-
teered. "So Kaz was working with the rogues all along,
that rat bastard."

Shifters all around the room cursed and argued and
praised Bas for killing the traitors—at least three of them
since Kaz had clearly gotten away. Bas wasn't feeling terribly upset over the loss. Since the plan to either get rid of
him or get their drugs back hadn't worked, Bas was almost certain Kaz's role as an informant had sealed the
shifter's fate. What he was still concerned by was the fact
that the rogue running the show in his area was one of the
same fucking killers that he'd crossed fourteen years ago.
That, in Bas's mind, was no coincidence.

Still, with all this going on around him, with the urge
to shift and hunt riding dangerously close to the surface
of all his men, Bas only listened with half an ear. His attention in this room was limited to his physical presence.
His mind was elsewhere, his emotions sifting through a
dark funnel cloud as realization finally began to set in.
Upstairs in his suite, in the bed he'd slept in alone for as
long as it had been there, was a woman who had only
been trying to save her brother. The fact that her agenda
had punctured a gaping hole into his world was just one
of those things that happened, something called fate, Bas
figured glumly. That fate should be such a cruel bastard
was another story entirely.

He'd left Priya in Jewel's care because he had duties to
attend to, priorities in his life that did not include her—
had never even anticipated a "her" was more like it. He
probably should have said something to her, consoled her
in some way, but he hadn't. After putting a bullet between
the eyes of the man who'd tried to orchestrate the killing

of an innocent human, it had been all Bas could do to hold her in his arms, to relish in the fact that she was very much alive. Priya had crumpled instantly to the ground, moving so fast that Bas thought for a split second that he may have hit her instead. He'd fallen to the ground beside her and she'd sunk instantly into his arms.

She'd cried then, like Bas had never heard a person cry before. The sound had torn through his skull like a knife, ripping through the memories and the pain he'd stored there. From the moment he'd met her Priya had been strong, courageous, tenacious. She hadn't cowered when he'd caught her trying to break into Rome's room or when she'd shown up in Nogales. Each time he'd confronted her about the story or why she was here, she'd stood up to him, squaring her shoulders and answering him in that sarcastic way of hers. In the wake of a very real threat against her brother's life, she'd decided to be the one to save him, was determined to do so. Never in all his life had Bas seen that type of selfless courage. Now, tonight, she'd cried in his arms like a baby.

Minutes later Jacques and the rest of the team had arrived. Unaware that Bas was leaving the resort, when Jacques had found his leader missing he'd instantly tracked the SUV through its GPS. He'd tried Bas's cell but had initially received no answer, because Bas had given it to Priya. They were in their own vehicles on their way to the location when Jacques received the call from Bas's phone and heard the commotion on the other end. Priya had only been able to push the CALL button while being watched by those cats before being grabbed by Palermo.

Once the team had arrived and secured the scene, Bas had lifted Priya and put her into the back of his SUV. He'd held her on his lap the entire ride back to the resort then carried her into his room and laid her down. She hadn't spoken a word in all that time, which for Priya was monumental. It also told Bas that she'd seen too much and experienced far more tonight than he'd ever wish on anyone.

Guilt was gripping him so tightly, holding him hostage when he should have been actively participating in the discussion going on around him. His chest was tight, his brow furrowed—he could tell because his head was beginning to pound—fingers clenching and unclenching as he tried to figure out what the next step should be. How could he make this up to her? How could he prevent it from ever happening again? And why hadn't he sent her away before now, before it was too late?

Bas was so deep inside his thoughts that he barely registered the sound of a door opening behind him then the quick hush that fell over the room. But at the sound of his name he did turn. Shock and alarm both were checked as Bas locked gazes with the Leader of the Stateside Assembly.

Squaring his shoulders, Bas looked to his men with a nod. "Syfon, you and the team should head downstairs to keep an eye on the situation with the authorities. The resort managers on duty down there will take care of the guests, but I want your eyes and ears open to what they're all saying about tonight's events. Make sure the yellow team is in position around the perimeter," he told the shifter solemnly.

Paolo stood immediately, ready to follow Syfon out into the hallway. For a split second while he and Jacques had considered the possibility of someone from Perryville feeding Palermo inside information, the young shifter had crossed his mind. His insubordinations and testy attitude made him the prime candidate for switching sides. Bas had never felt better about being wrong in his life. The young shifter's father would have been devastated if his son had done such a thing.

"Yes, sir," was Syfon's response and within the next few

seconds the members of the blue team, all except Jacques, had filed out, leaving only the higher-ranking shifters in the room.

"Assembly Leader, welcome to Perryville," Jacques said, rising from his seat and motioning for Rome to take his place at the head of the room.

Bas moved slowly so that when Rome walked across the room and stopped behind one of the chairs at the table, he was right there, ready to shake his commanding officer's hand. Rome took his outstretched hand, their eyes meeting, holding, saying so much in those few silent seconds.

This wasn't going to be good, Bas thought as they released each other. Bas relinquished his seat at the head of the table to Rome. When he was seated, Nick and X immediately moved to stand behind him. The First Female, Kalina, touched a hand to Bas's shoulder and Bas leaned in to kiss her cheek. He pulled out the chair to the right of her *companheiro* and helped her into it. Jax, Kalina's guard, sat right beside her, with Ezra sitting next to him. Moving to the other side of the table, Bas took the seat to the left of Rome and Jacques sat down beside him.

The ten-foot-long, glass-covered conference table had never appeared so cold and foreboding in this room of dark charcoal and black as it did tonight. The blinds had not been drawn so the evening sky provided a picture-perfect backdrop, with its vague twinkle of stars looking almost as lost as Bas felt at this precise moment.

"What happened tonight?" Rome asked, his palms flattening on the table.

Jacques gave the rundown after Bas nodded for him to do so.

"So he's dead? This Palermo Greer person that was setting up the rogue operation on the West Coast? Has his body been disposed of?" Nick asked.

Jacques shook his head. "Not yet. We have all three

shifter bodies in the bunker. We're waiting until the resort is clear of all law officials before taking action."

"Good move. But as long as they don't have a search warrant they can't go anywhere on this property you don't want them to," Nick continued.

"I'd rather not draw any more attention than absolutely necessary," Bas spoke up. "The disposal will be completed before dawn."

"I want DNA samples first," X told him. "The database should be updated with rogues as well."

Bas nodded. "Absolutely."

"And all this is because of that shipment you intercepted? The drugs, guns, and the blood from Comastaz?" Rome asked.

The tension settling over the room was palpable, yet Bas didn't falter. He sat up straight, shoulders squared, representing his zone and his team and taking responsibility for all that had occurred here like the leader he was. "Yes. He said as much when we were out on that road. He was pissed that I took them and pissed that I killed one of his minions."

Rome nodded. "X said Greer was a high-level official with ties to the rogues as far back as Boden Estevez, which connects perfectly to him hooking up with Sabar the moment he returned to the States."

Bas was not surprised to hear that fact. If Palermo Greer was connected in any way to Boden, Mariah's gruesome death had been just a game to him. The same game he was eagerly willing to play with Priya's life.

"So we scratch him off the list of most wanted," Rome continued. "We still have those crates to figure out and with that latest e-mail, that needs to become our top priority."

"And because they're the gift that just keeps on fucking giving, let's not totally count out Darel. He'll want to finish the setup out here himself now," X noted.

Rome shook his head. "I doubt that. He'll want to stay close to his current money flow, that's why he sent Palermo out here in the first place. What he will do is find someone else to do the job as quickly as possible."

Nick nodded his agreement. "That's why we need to nip his ass in the bud too."

"There are quite a few things that need to be nipped in the bud," Rome continued. "One in particular that I thought we'd already settled."

And here it was, Bas thought, the real reason behind the Assembly Leader's surprise visit to Perryville. Tonight's activities had happened only about an hour and a half ago, not nearly enough time for Rome and his crew to make the trip all the way from D.C. No, the leader had been called earlier, much earlier and Bas was fuming at the possibility that his second in command had been the one to make that call.

"Is there something you want to tell us, Bas?" the leader asked.

Bas looked to Jacques, who with the slightest motion of his head told him that he hadn't said a word. Then he looked to Rome. "The reporter from the *Post* showed up here a week ago. She's still here now."

There wasn't another sound in the room as Rome sat back in his chair.

"You mean she's still looking for her story? The one where she exposes the Shadow Shifters," he said slowly, succinctly.

The thought of lying never crossed Bas's mind. The situation was what it was, Priya had a goal just as all of them did in their own lives. She had a family that she cared about just as much as Rome cared about his mate and the Stateside Shifters. In the most basic of ways, she was no different from them.

"She has a job to do," Bas replied simply even though he knew this situation was anything but.

"And what happens when she finds out the truth? What happens when the existence of the shadows is revealed to the world? Whose job will it be then to deal with the consequences?" was Rome's next question.

"How long were we realistically going to stay a secret, Rome?" was Bas's quick comeback.

He hadn't even known he'd planned to say it until the words tumbled free. The already chilly aura surrounding them grew downright frigid as angry eyes bore down on Bas while he spoke.

"Our law states . . ." Rome began.

"Fuck that law!" was Bas's immediate outburst. Rarely, just about never, had any of the shifters in this room heard Bas take this tone, a fact evidenced by the stunned looks around the room. On the table in front of him, his hands remained quiet, the rest of his body giving away none of the fury roiling through him at this very moment. Only his tone and his words had exposed him.

While Rome still sat quietly, his demeanor never wavering—most likely because Kalina had reached out a hand to touch his arm immediately following the outburst—Bas spoke again, with only a slightly less agitated tone.

"I know that we're not supposed to purposely expose ourselves to the humans nor are we supposed to pull one up off the streets and tell them about our tribe. I've lived according to those laws all my life, sacrificing my own needs and desires to keep that exposure from happening. Hell, my teams are trained explicitly in taking down the enemy without shifting, period. So I don't need you to fly all the way out here to tell me what the goddamned laws are."

This was where friendship came into play, because from the standpoint of the leadership hierarchy, Rome could have stripped Bas of all his duties and inflicted whatever other type of punishment he could think of on him and he would have been well within his authority to do so. And everyone in that room knew this and they all remained silent to see if that would be the next event on their impromptu agenda.

Instead of adding to the drama, Rome simply sat there, staring at Bas, not actually in surprise, but with another look that had Bas's temples throbbing even more incessantly.

Then a softer voice spoke, a spirit almost as composed as her *companheiro*'s. "What happened to change your mind about the laws, Bas?" Kalina asked.

Bas took a breath as he looked at the First Lady. "Nothing happened," he told her. "I'm just saying that the laws were created in a different time, a different place. It was a lot easier to keep us a secret when we only populated the rainforest. We could hide within the trees and for the most part never be discovered by humans. But even then the shamans knew and they talked. And anyone superstitious enough to believe them knew about us. Don't you see, it's never really been a well-kept secret? There are some out there who knew and have known for centuries."

Even though this was the first time Bas had spoken the words, he knew firsthand how true they were. It was after he'd buried Mariah in the forest all those years ago, when he'd stood in the rain, his body numb to its moistness, his mind in a frenzy over what had just happened, that he'd felt the presence. Standing at the base of a tree, buttress root snaking along the ground so that it looked as if it held him captive, was Yuri, the old shaman who lived just outside the forest. The tall, wiry man had looked on with weary but knowing eyes and had never said a word. Not even when Bas had turned and walked away from the site. Throughout the years, Yuri continued to keep the secret, even when he came to the States and had tormented Nick's mate. But he knew just the same.

"You're right," Kalina said quietly. "There are some who are bound to know and there are more who suspect."

Once that was said, Kalina looked to Rome who caught his *companheiro*'s glance and apparently her meaning as he began to shake his head.

"Thinking you know something, thinking that you've seen something is entirely different from actually *knowing* anything," Rome said vehemently. "Giving this reporter proof is dangerous, Bas. Letting her stay here especially now when all this unsettled business is being taken care of, is a mistake. Not to mention the fact that you kept it a secret. You should have told me immediately!"

It was Bas's turn to nod. "Because we can keep our secret from an entire world, but I cannot have one to myself."

"I don't think that's what he's trying to say, Bas," X interjected. "The safety of the entire tribe needs to be considered."

Bas looked over Rome's shoulder to the Assembly Leader's Lead Enforcer. The man stood more than six feet tall and was built like a wide receiver, his tattooed arms bared by the short-sleeved shirt he wore.

"I've put this tribe and its safety first all my life. Why do you think I put the Mountain Zone's headquarters all the way out here in the desert? I could have had a penthouse in a thriving city with women falling at my feet, ready to heed my every command," Bas replied.

"She's no fool, this reporter," Nick spoke up. "I figured she wasn't going to give up. We shouldn't have underestimated her, we should have taken her sooner."

"We're not kidnappers," Bas objected.

Rome shook his head. "No, we're not."

"And we don't kill humans just for the hell of it, or because they think they know something," Bas continued, looking directly at Rome. It was imperative to everything that Bas had been taught to believe, to the man that he'd become, that the friend and the leader he followed agreed with him on this point. Bas didn't even want to consider what he was going to feel compelled to do if Rome said anything to the contrary.

"No," Rome said, holding Bas's gaze, "we do not."

Even though nobody moved or spoke for the next few seconds there seemed to be a collective sigh among them. No doubt this was still a problem, one more to be added to their growing pile.

"So what do we do now?" Jacques prompted, but nobody seemed in a hurry to toss out a solution.

Until she walked in.

# Chapter 27

Priya looked taller as she entered the conference room, closing the door quietly behind herself. She'd changed into jeans and a pink T-shirt that displayed the resort's name and logo in tiny rhinestone letters. Her short hair was damp, curling at the top and slicked down at the sides. She wore no makeup, no jewelry, nothing, as if she'd just slipped on her clothes after showering and left the room.

Bas stood immediately. Nick and X moved in closer to Rome. Ezra and Jacques looked equally stunned and on alert and Jax rushed to stand as Kalina was already up and on her way across the room to stop where Priya now stood.

"Hello," Kalina said with a warm smile, extending her hand to Priya. "I'm Kalina Reynolds."

Without hesitation Priya accepted Kalina's hand, offering a tentative smile of her own. "I'm Priya Drake."

"Yes," Kalina replied. "It's a pleasure to meet you, Ms. Drake."

"You can call me Priya."

With a slight tilt of her head Kalina continued, "And you can call me Kalina."

"I told you I would be back," Bas said, coming to stand beside Priya, instinctively touching his hand to her elbow.

"I can help you," she told him then looked to Kalina

and to everyone assembled at the table behind her. "I can help all of you."

"We can talk about this later," Bas told her. "You should go back and lie down."

"No," she replied adamantly. "I want to tell you how I can help."

"It's not necessary," Bas insisted.

"I want to hear what she has to say," Rome interrupted.

Bas frowned but knew any further argument was futile. Short of tossing a kicking and screaming Priya over his shoulder to the dismay of his First Lady, he really had no other choice. But he would not leave her side, Bas vowed, and guided her over to where he'd been seated.

As she sat, Bas wavered, for only a second, but he stood completely still, his eyes riveted on the back of Priya's head. Inside of him there was movement, no, it might be better described as an awakening.

"Are you all right, Bas?" Kalina asked him.

He looked up immediately at the sound of her voice. Clearing his throat and trying like hell to ignore this new feeling, Bas stood up straight. Jacques had vacated the seat right next to Priya, so Bas sat there.

"Fine. Let's just get this over with," he replied quickly.

"This is a surprise seeing you again, Ms. Drake," Rome said to her.

Priya didn't look at all nervous. In fact, she sat forward in her chair, arms resting on the table. For all intents and purposes she looked as if she were a part of this meeting, as if she actually belonged here.

"What happened tonight is going to be all over the media, if it's not already," she began immediately. "I'm sure that growling and roaring could be heard for miles beyond where we were standing. Everything echoes off those mountains. So why not use my connection with the paper to put your own spin on what happened, you know, sort of do some damage control," she said in what seemed like one complete breath.

Bas sat back in his chair waiting for the proverbial other shoe to drop as Priya had basically just informed everyone in this room that not only did she know what they were, but that she was willing to help them hide it. Well, actually, she hadn't said it in those exact words, but he knew that's what she meant. He kept his own query of why to himself as he looked around the room to assess everyone else's reaction.

"You want to distribute a public statement for us?" Rome asked. "What makes you think we need a statement?"

"Nobody wants bad press," she said. "The resort would definitely lose business. Or worse, you'd have all sorts of crazies booking rooms just to see if they too would hear the weird sounds or get caught up in some type of other-worldly drama. I'm proposing that we get a proactive jump on the media frenzy that is no doubt about to begin on the West Coast, since the East Coast buzz has already made its debut."

"You're referring to the rumors of cat people robbing a bank and the supposed sightings of men dressed as cats at the museum," X stated, it seemed for clarification, but he was looking at Priya strangely.

Bas had to think of something quickly, he had to put a stop to what was going on before it was too late.

"I'll write a statement and let the resort manager issue it to the press in the morning. The police will leave shortly because they'll have received all the answers they could get from everyone here. I have an entire marketing team that will no doubt come up with some sort of incentive package that will counter any lost bookings due to this incident. We'll rise above this and in a few weeks it will be old news," he said as if it were actually as simple as his spoken words.

He didn't want Priya involved in this, no more than she already had been. He definitely did not want her and Rome in the same room, not until he had a chance to tell the Assembly Leader that she was off-limits. Things seemed to be continuously spiraling out of control here, in the place that was once his safe haven. Now, it was up to him to stop it.

"I think Priya has a good point," Kalina began. "She's a notable reporter, even if so far it's only been in print. Why not utilize her skills and her very generous offer to our advantage?"

"Because I'm not one hundred percent certain we can trust what she'll say," Rome countered. "Not too long ago, she was writing stories in an effort to expose some sort of conspiracy. Now, we find her here, in the midst of more trouble, and I've got to wonder if this is not somehow working out the way she planned."

"That's out of line," Bas interrupted. "And it's not why she's here."

Bas would have said more but shaking her head, Priya put a hand up to stop him, then she looked to Rome.

"That's not how I operate, Mr. Reynolds. I am a reporter and I am committed to bringing accurate and meaningful stories to the American public. I was there tonight so what I report will be more accurate than anything Bas's manager could possibly come up with."

"So you plan to tell the American people everything you saw or think you saw tonight?" Jacques asked from his seat down the table.

"I plan to tell the American people that there is no need to fear any malicious beings in this area. Other than the normal murderers that skulk the streets in any other city. This statement is not about exposure, it's about damage control. You need damage control right now more than you need to be afraid of me revealing any of your secrets. Keeping a good reputation will be helpful if or when there is ever genuine exposure."

"It makes sense," X interjected.

Kalina sat back in her chair, smiling at Priya then looking up at Bas to give him the same response. "It makes a lot of sense. And frankly, I don't see how we can turn down her offer."

That last sentence was directed to Kalina's *companheiro* who had continued to stare at Priya, until her last comment at which time his gaze had gone directly to Bas.

"Get your people to set it up for first thing tomorrow morning. Until then nobody from this room will leave this resort. Is that clear?" Rome stated.

"I will leave after the press release," Priya announced, somewhat defiantly, before standing to leave.

Bas took a step back and moved with her. "Jacques will handle the specifics and I will make sure Priya is at the designated space in the morning."

"Bas," Rome called to him.

He and Priya were almost to the door when Bas stopped and turned to face the Assembly Leader. He knew that Rome wasn't finished talking to him, knew that the revelation that Priya knew about them wasn't finished being discussed, but he'd decided it would be finished for tonight. It had to be.

Kalina had stood as well and moved to her mate's side quickly, putting a hand on his shoulder as she stood on tiptoe to whisper something in his ear.

Rome cleared his throat a couple of seconds later and continued, "We'll see you at the press release," he finished with an obvious frown.

Bas nodded his agreement and led Priya out of the conference room and hopefully out of the line of fire—or was that the position he was in himself? It didn't matter.

All that mattered for tonight was that Priya was safe. That's all he was going to allow himself to think about.

"Does he know?" Rome asked as he took his seat at the head of the table once more, clasping his hands together.

"I've come to believe that with some male shifters it isn't so much knowing as it is accepting," Kalina told her *companheiro* as she stood behind him massaging the tenseness from his shoulders.

The others had filed out of the room with their assignments clear. Jacques would first secure rooms for the Leader and his *companheiro,* then for the visiting guards. Then he would work on the arrangements for the press conference. In the meantime, Nick, X, and Ezra would join Bas's teams in securing the resort and keeping watch for any new intruders. Jax would remain close to Kalina, most likely standing right outside the door of the conference room. And Kalina would do her best to convince her husband that Priya Drake was now one of them regardless of her human status; it was clear as day the woman was in love with Bas and had offered to help them because of that love.

"She's a human, Kalina. As long as she knows we exist she has the power to destroy everything we've built," Rome told her.

Kalina sighed. "Or she has the power to take us to that other level you talk about so much. What if she really is our ally, Rome? What if she's appointed our public relations spokesperson? She could counter all the swirling accusations, and there will be more. You know this as well as I do because the rogues aren't finished, they're just getting started."

He lowered his head then and Kalina knelt down beside him. Running the Stateside Assembly had been a huge undertaking for Rome, a responsibility that everyone assumed he was born to handle. Kalina didn't for one moment doubt her mate's ability to lead and she'd vowed, the moment he was elected, that she would do everything in her power to make this job as easy for him as she possibly could. Even if that meant telling him things he didn't actually want to hear.

She touched a hand to his cheek, rubbed the smoothness there, then let her fingers travel down to the neatly trimmed goatee as she turned his face toward hers.

"Priya is Bas's *companheiro,* darling. There's nothing you or I can do about that. Their *companheiro calor* was strong enough to fill this entire room. And I suspect that if the shadows are going to continue to live amongst the humans in so-called harmony, there are going to be more of these unions. As the leader of this tribe you need to be prepared for that. We're evolving just as every other species on this earth has at one time or another."

Rome stared at her for what seemed like endless moments before admitting, "This isn't the first time it's happened. It's not the first time a shadow has fallen for a human. But the shifters were much younger than Bas, much less experienced. I didn't like having to make the decisions I did where they were concerned."

Kalina held back her surprise because it was just as she'd stated, they were evolving and short of taking them all back to the forest and staying there forever, there was no way this forward movement was going to stop, no matter what complications it imposed.

"What the hell was that?" Bas asked the moment he and Priya were alone in his suite.

After switching on the lights, Priya moved to the couch and took a seat, feeling almost at home. It hadn't been

long since she'd first been escorted into this space and
introduced to this man, and yet, she felt like she'd been
here forever, almost as if this was where she belonged.
Deciding against this line of thought she reached over to
the table beside the couch and retrieved Bas's cell phone.

"You got a text," she said, extending her arm and the
phone in his direction. "They found Malik."

Priya had almost forgotten that she had Bas's cell phone
until she was lying across his bed—crying like a four-
year-old in Jewel's lap—when it suddenly vibrated. When
Bas had yelled for her to pick it up while they were on the
road she'd stuffed it into her bra about three seconds before
that madman had grabbed her from behind. It had stayed
there until she pulled it out in Jewel's company.

His text message light was flashing and the next time it
vibrated—which was about a minute later—the screen lit
up with the name of the person sending the message and
the first few words.

Malik Drake is in stable condition.

Priya had pressed every button she could imagine so she
could see every message. Luckily, Bas had disengaged the
lock feature on his phone the first time he'd given it to her
in the truck. Excitement and relief had soared through her
as she read. Her brother was alive and safe because Bas
had contacted someone he knew. She'd presumed another
shifter from some of the terms used, like rogue and scents.
She'd heard Bas and Jacques say these things out on the
road tonight.

"Thank you so much for all your help," she said with
another relieved sigh. "I didn't believe you'd be able to do
anything to help. Actually, I thought you were just saying
that to get me into bed. But you came through, you kept

your word, and you saved Malik." Her smile was giddy and she clasped her hands together to hold in her excitement.

It had taken all the control she could muster to shower and get down to that meeting room as fast as she could, thanks to Jewel for telling her where to go. Once inside, the mood was tense and unsteady. She'd seen Roman Reynolds immediately and knew that running and jumping into Bas's arms was completely out of the question. Even at this point, she still felt the need to reserve her excitement and any expression of gratitude. Basically because Bas was looking at her as if she'd just killed his puppy.

He'd taken the phone from her hands but he hadn't sat down. No, he stood just a couple feet away from her, rubbing his thumb over the phone, not checking any of the messages, but looking at her. "So because I saved your brother you think you have to repay me by conducting a press conference on our behalf?"

He didn't look or sound happy, but that was usually the case with Bas. Priya didn't know if she'd ever seen a genuine smile on his face, or felt like he had any sense of enjoyment in his life. That thought made her sad because he had everything a person in her position could want—money, power, and respect. He'd never gone to bed hungry, never worn hand-me-down clothes, never had to stay up half the night after working the late shift at the restaurant to study for final exams because she needed that college degree like she'd needed her next breath. He was living the dream and he didn't seem to appreciate it; that made her about 90 percent sad and 10 percent angry as hell.

"It's the least I can do," she told him with a shrug. "That Nivea person said they'd found Malik being held by rogues. That doesn't make sense to me for so many reasons."

He nodded as if he'd been thinking the same thing.

"You're wondering, if shifters were the ones behind this all along, then why make you expose us? Why not do it themselves?"

"Right, that's what I was trying to figure out," she told him.

"Wrong," Bas said, shaking his head. "None of this is for you to try to figure out. It's done. Your brother is safe and the threat is lifted and that's all. You can go back to your life now. You can move on."

He'd hesitated at the last words but Priya was already primed with a comeback. "How do you know? I still didn't do what they said and that seemed pretty damned important to them. Besides, I'd like to know why they chose me. How do we know they won't just try again? We have to find out who they are and stop them."

He sat down beside her then. "You reported on the night you saw those eyes in the alley behind Athena's. That's probably what made you a prime candidate for them."

"You're right," she agreed. "The first e-mail came the day after that story ran in the paper."

Bas shook his head then, looking as tired as Priya actually felt. The spurt of energy after finding out Malik was alive was beginning to ebb.

"Look, Priya, you do not have to do anything. Including this press release. I don't need your thanks. I'm happy enough knowing that you are out of danger."

And yet he still neither sounded nor looked happy. Her 10 percent angry elevated.

"Because Sebastian Perry doesn't need anyone or anything, right?" she asked, her voice dangerously quiet. "You have everything you want and yet you would prefer to stay locked up in this desert haven you've built, away from anyone or anything that might demand more from you."

"You don't know what you're talking about," he told her. "You don't know me."

Priya shook her head. "You're right, I don't. And it was never your intention for me to know you."

He looked down at the floor then. "We already discussed that this thing between us was never supposed to happen."

But it had happened and Priya, for one foolish moment, had believed that maybe the dream of meeting a good man and falling madly in love was possible. How wrong she'd been. Bas refused to be a good man, or rather he refused to let anyone believe that he was one.

"We did discuss it," she conceded. "And I want to thank you for your honesty. But I like to repay my debts. So I'll do the one press release and then I'll be out of your way. You can go back to living your solitary life since it seems to be what you want most of all."

There was more she wanted to say, a pitch for why she felt they belonged together came to mind. But the words would never fall from her lips. Tenacious, a tad bit hyper, and maybe just a little reckless were words Priya felt accurately described her. Desperate and pleading were not.

She stood up then, refusing to say more, knowing it would fall on deaf ears. Bas liked to be in control. He'd told her that before. Sure, she shook him up on a physical level, but that was nothing compared to the way he'd lived his life for so long. Her words wouldn't change him. She, the poor little human female from D.C. with the drug addict brother and food stamp sisters and mother one sneeze away from a nervous breakdown, was not going to change the enigmatic Sebastian Perry. He'd saved Malik, that had been the one miracle of her lifetime. She was smart enough not to wish for any more.

"I know this is your place but this is my last night here," she started, her voice much stronger than she was feeling at the moment. "I'd like for you to take the couch, if that's not too much to ask."

He sat there with his elbows resting on his knees, his

head down for five seconds before it snapped up and his intense gray gaze held hers. He didn't answer her, simply stared and Priya felt like she was stripped completely bare. Not just naked, but revealed, to this man who didn't give a damn what was inside of her. She wanted to weep with the magnitude of the mistake she'd made, the error in judgment she always had where men were concerned. It should be a crime to roll craps so many times in one life. But here she was and here he was and no matter what either of them said or did, there was no going back.

"No."

The sound of his voice startled her slightly and she blinked away the dismal thoughts that had tears pooling in her eyes once again. She breathed heavily, hating the thought of crying over this man, over this situation, after all she'd been through.

"It's not too much to ask," he continued. "You go on in the bedroom and get some rest."

She nodded, didn't speak, because what was she going to tell him next? That he was breaking her heart? That his absolute control, serious-as-a-heart-attack demeanor was causing her much more pain than that asshole half-cat had when he held that gun to her head?

Priya wouldn't tell him that. Instead, she walked away, slamming her palm on the control panel once she was in the bedroom. When it didn't work she slapped her hand on it again and again, until finally there was a click and the door slid closed. Then the tears fell and she gulped heavy sobs to keep Bas from hearing her, from knowing how big of an impact he'd had on her in such a short period of time.

# Chapter 28

She opened the door, Bas thought as he watched his bed-room door close. He'd gotten up from the couch, going over to help her when she couldn't get it to activate. For endless seconds after she was blocked off from him, Bas simply stood there, staring at the smooth panels. To any-one but him there were no visible breaks, no indication that there was a door here. It was his design, assuring his safety and privacy in his own space.

And Priya Drake had opened it.

Finally, he turned away, walking the few steps until he stood in the middle of the living room and looked around. Every control pad in this room was operated on Bas's command only—his fingerprints, his body temperature, his knowledge, with technology designed by X, per Bas's specific instructions. When they'd first returned to the suite tonight she'd immediately switched on the lights in the living room. There were no light switches in the room and no control panel to power them, just a sensor located on the sides of each sconce. They were only illuminated by his body temperature, the movement of his hand on either side.

And yet, Priya had moved her hands along each side, turning them on.

Her bags still remained packed but had moved from

near the door where they'd been earlier in the day, to closer to the windows where the blinds had been opened. After their return, before leaving her and Jewel in the room, he'd specifically closed them because he hadn't wanted any cops or other intruders to see inside.

Priya had been the one to open them, Bas knew without a doubt. Because she was connected to him, they had been intimate, had been in near-death situations together and now, dammit, all of that was more serious than even he'd considered. Shifter *companheiros* had a connection that grew emotionally and physically, similar to human relationships. The continued intimacy between the couple also triggered some type of biological connection that over time combined things like their shared scent, known as the *companheiro calor*. But Priya was a human, she should not have the same reactions. Bas hated to admit that she obviously did, and was experiencing them on a much more accelerated rate than two shifters together.

"How long are you going to deny that she's your *companheiro*?"

Feeling slightly overwhelmed, Bas turned slowly to find Jacques standing just inside the front doorway. He didn't startle, didn't even berate himself for not being alert enough to hear the other shifter's approach. This night had been too long and too eventful and seemed as if it would never end.

"There's nothing to deny. She's going back to D.C. tomorrow after the press conference," he replied to Jacques.

For security purposes, Jacques was the only one, other than Bas, who had a key to get into his room. Even though the sensors and control panels were innovative and good ideas for inside his suite, Bas had readily agreed with X that a specially made key was the safer option to enter the area and that only one other person should have access to that key. Jacques had been the obvious and only choice.

"The press conference is scheduled for nine thirty in the morning. I thought it would signify our commitment to the town and to the guests of Perryville that we're devoted to their safety and well-being by setting up in the side atrium. The sun won't be at its hottest that early in the morning and the scenery is calming, relaxing, hopefully enough to keep their minds off the danger that may still loom," Jacques reported.

"Palermo was here because of me," Bas said simply.

"He was here because he's working for someone that wants to take us down. Don't make what happened tonight personal."

"It was personal!" Bas yelled. "That motherfucker taunted me with killing Mariah. He looked me in the eye and wanted me to know he would kill Priya the same way if I didn't give him those crates back."

"She was not planned," Jacques said with a shake of his head. "Nobody, none of us, not even you would have ever thought a woman like her would enter your life and change things the way she did, especially not that asshole Palermo."

"But she did. She came into my life, into my home, my . . ." He hesitated. "She was not supposed to be here and now she's at the center of everything."

Bas moved to the window then, looking out at the darkness. The rogue had been out there, all of them had been out there, lurking, waiting for the moment they needed to strike. They'd stalked his resort and the innocent people who'd stayed here. And Bas hadn't been able to catch them in time. His fists clenched. He hadn't been able to stop them from causing some sort of exposure, just as he hadn't been able to stop himself from telling and showing Priya all that he was.

"I didn't at first," Jacques continued. "But now, I think we can trust her."

Bas waited a beat, sighed with the admission from his best friend. "Lucky for us Rome thinks the same. Or at least Kalina does. Her word goes a long way with the State-side Leader."

"That's because she's his mate. His partner, the other half of his whole." Jacques's comment sounded strangely reminiscent of one of the Elders.

Bas gave a wry chuckle, without turning to look at his friend. "What are you, reading from some ancient scroll?"

"I'm telling you what I know. Once a shadow finds his *companheiro,* they are completed. We were specifically designed to be half of one cohesive unit, one strength that cannot be broken once it is joined. I believe that wholeheartedly."

Bas's lips drew into a thin line. "Then I'll dance at your joining when you find your other half." He turned to face him. "In the meantime, I need a shower and then I have work to do."

Jacques didn't move at all. He stood with his arms behind his back, legs spread slightly. His dreads were pulled back away from his face, and the gold chain around his neck glistened.

"No other female will take her place. From this point on whoever you attempt to be with intimately will pale dismally in comparison. She, that human reporter in that other room, is the one. It wasn't Mariah; although you felt guilty for her death, she wasn't the one for you."

To be quite honest Jacques didn't look any happier about that little announcement than Bas felt. He was simply stating what he believed to be true. So what Bas was about to say could only be construed in the same manner.

"She's a reporter with a job in D.C. that she's going to return to in the morning. I am the Mountain Zone Faction Leader. My life is here in Sedona. Case closed."

Bas decided he would make the exit since Jacques

apparently wanted to appear glued to the spot where he stood. He was just about through the threshold that would lead him to the guest bedroom and bathroom on the other side of his suite, when Jacques spoke again.

"She doesn't have a job anymore. The editor from the *Post* fired her because she never replied to his e-mails about her expected return date. Almost as if she had no intention of returning to D.C., or she had no intention of ever writing the story about the shifters."

In the next seconds Bas heard the faint whishing sound of the door opening and closing. With a deep sigh, he entered the guest bedroom, refusing to think about Priya Drake anymore, knowing that effort would be futile.

At nine twenty the next morning the sky above Perryville resorts looked like it had been snatched from a picture book. The perfect shade of blue, the biggest, puffiest white clouds, and the sun, a golden beacon of a force much stronger than the twenty-two armed shadow guards that lined the walkway of the east side atrium. This small area consisted of three red clay buildings, one at the center, two at the sides. One of the buildings was used as a holistic center, the scent of herbs and incense drifting through the open windows to permeate the air. Another was an antiques shop where an elderly Native American woman and her daughter sold artifacts of their culture. The center building was available as rental space and was usually booked for small weddings or receptions. Between the buildings was the atrium, an open space with a cement sidewalk and huge clay pots stuffed with green shrubbery.

Bas walked the length of the area one more time. He checked and rechecked the podium that had been set up, the chairs sitting behind it where the mayor, police chief, and Rome and Kalina would sit. He went to each building, speaking quietly with the staff, letting them know what was going on and that it would all be over soon. Good relations with his staff had always been his strong point and a signature of Perryville Resorts, so they knew and accepted his presence and his guarantees. He headed back to the main building and checked each of its closets, side doors, exits, entrances.

Finally, as he stood in that doorway he checked his weapons—the gun at his back beneath the lightweight coffee-bean-colored suit jacket he wore. His white shirt was crisp, and the yellow-and-white-checked Ermenegildo Zegna silk tie provided the perfect amount of color to his otherwise dark ensemble. He backed out of the doorway to lean down and check the weapon at his left ankle. Standing again he adjusted the com link in his ear, confirmed that his cell phone was in his right pants pocket.

"This is going to work, Bas. She's going to do her job and this will all be over." X had come into the dwelling as quietly as only a cat could.

Bas nodded in response to the very thing he'd just been trying to convince himself of. "Right. It's going to work and then this will all be over."

"Not all." X shook his head. "Something's still going on over at Comastaz, something big. And this rogue drug and weapons bullshit is just a smoke screen. Somebody wants us to keep running around behind the rogues instead of focusing on what's really going on."

Now, even more thoughtful, Bas asked, "Which is?"

X shrugged. "Don't know yet. But we're damned sure gonna find out."

To that Bas nodded, the cause, his tribe, the life he'd had a week ago, coming back to the forefront. And everything else in between, well, he'd decided in the early morning hours to let all that go with the breeze. He had no other choice really.

The next ten minutes went by in a blur of activity. Reporters had already begun to arrive when Bas first came out at nine, their equipment spread out over every open space. Three rows of ten chairs had been set up behind the podium, reserved for high-ranking law officials and the town government. Directly behind the third row three of Bas's men stood dressed in slacks, dress shirts, and ties, ready to keep watch on the front of the area. The remaining guards mixed in among the reporters and around the buildings.

At exactly nine thirty, the mayor was escorted by the chief of police from a side walkway to the stage. They both took their seats behind the podium. From the other side X and Nick walked in front of Rome. Kalina stood by her *companheiro*'s side. Ezra and Jax filed in closely behind them.

Bas would take the stage in a moment and Priya would follow. Only Bas hadn't seen her yet. Dressing early, he'd left the suite without waking her. A call to Jewel had assured him that Priya would be up and dressed in time. Now, he'd wanted to act like he wasn't looking for her, like worry wasn't beading a tight rope around his spine, but figured he was failing dismally as he searched the area for her once again.

"Good morning."

Bas spun around at the sound of her voice then watched as Jacques walked beside her, coming in from the back entrance of the rental building.

"Good morning," he replied, his chest settling from its previous constriction with every inhale he took. It was the sight of her in a straight white dress, wide yellow belt at her waist, and high-heeled yellow sandals on her feet—as if they'd conferred on color-coding their outfits—that held him still.

"We're ready when you are," he heard Syfon say through the com link.

With a nod Bas looked at Priya once more as she came closer to where he stood. She wore light makeup, her eyes wide and expressive with only a hint of color on her lids, her lips pert and lightly glossed. At her ears were stud earrings, not diamonds, but he loved seeing that bit of sparkle there, around her neck a thin gold chain.

"Jacques will stay with you the entire time," he told her, as a reminder to Jacques not to let her out of his sight.

The Lead Enforcer responded with a curt nod.

Just as he turned to leave, Priya reached out and touched a hand to Bas's arm. He turned slowly, heat searing through the material of his jacket and shirt where her hand rested.

"This is going to work," she told him. "I know what to say to make it work."

Then she smiled and Bas's vision blurred. Everything except her went out of focus and all he could see clearly was her face, and that smile. What he sensed without any doubt was her amazing strength and the new scent—the "sweet" one as she'd called it—that now hovered around her like a full-body halo. Clearing his throat abruptly, Bas nodded then turned away. He had to or he feared he'd never be able to move from that spot.

Twenty steps would take Bas from the entrance of the rental building to the stage. He'd counted earlier and now did the same to keep his mind focused. At eighteen his cell phone vibrated in his pocket but Bas kept walking, wanting to get this all over with as quickly as possible. He stepped up onto the stage amidst flashing lights, clicking and whirling cameras, and a low hum of whispered and expectant voices.

Approaching the microphone, he began immediately.

"Good morning, and welcome to Perryville Resorts."
Bas spoke in a clear and confident tone. He continued
with a brief history of the resort and the statistics of his
guests. He ended with his contributions to the town and
how important all of their safety was to him.

When Bas looked to his left he saw Jacques escorting
Priya onto the stage. He stepped to the side as she moved
to stand behind the microphone. She was shorter so he
reached forward to adjust the mic for her. She nodded and
smiled a thank you, then she spoke.

"Good morning, my name is Priya Drake, public relations for Perryville Resorts."

She sounded confident, intelligent, determined. The title she'd given herself sounded right and made sense given
what she was about to say. He tuned in once more when
she was saying, "We assure you that last night's incident
was an isolated event. There has never been and never will
be in the future any type of animal attacks or threats at the
resort or in the surrounding area. With the dedicated assistance of the local authorities and the added force of our
skilled staff, we will continue to work toward ensuring the
safety of all our guests and the people of this great town."

Loving her words almost as much as the sound of her
voice, Bas was transfixed, caught in the sweet-smelling
and all-consuming web Priya had woven over the entire
crowd. Reporters were still but for their pencils moving
over notepads, cameras had ceased clicking, lights paused
flashing, no one wanted to miss a word she said.

Then his cell phone vibrated again and Bas wanted to
curse. Instead he reached inside his pocket to turn the
damned thing off, annoyed at the constant interruption.
Cupping the phone in his hand and holding it down at his
side so that no one would see him, he read the illuminated
screen.

You took mine. Now I'll take yours.

As he read the last word Bas lifted his head up slowly. His gaze caught Jacques's cool, questioning stare about two seconds before Priya's words were abruptly cut off. She stumbled back, his name falling in a choked whisper from her lips, "Bas?"

He moved quickly to her side just in time to see the red stain on the white dress she wore, a growing circle that solicited immediate screams from the crowd.

All hell broke loose at that moment. Bas caught Priya in his arms as she collapsed on the stage.

"She's been shot!" he heard somebody yell.

"Get a medic!"

"Someone's shooting!"

"Oh my god! Oh my god!"

The voices grew louder and louder in his head. The air around him lifting as the stench of panic and blood seared the air. Bas looked down into Priya's eyes—eyes that had been bright and inquisitive. Eyes that were brown, not blue, courageous and not afraid. A tear fell from those eyes and Bas felt a clenching in his chest that threatened his breathing. She'd cried last night after he'd killed Palermo, broken little sobs that had felt like pinpricks against his skin. This one lone tear was like a hot blade straight to his heart, the bloodstain still growing on her chest, yanking his breath from him in ragged gasps. He blinked once, twice, then again, gritting his teeth all the while. She was still warm in his arms, still alive, still looking at him, wondering if he would save her this time.

"Take her," he said to somebody, anybody, then looked up to see Rome. "Take her, please!"

Rome nodded, replacing his arms where Bas's had been. Kalina was right beside him, holding onto Priya's hand, whispering something to her as the crowd continued to go crazy around them.

Bas removed his arms from beneath Priya. He looked into her eyes one more time just as she blinked and more tears fell. He thought she called to him, asked him to stay with her or something like that. But he couldn't, he wouldn't, not this time. Bas turned away then, standing up to look straight ahead. Then he was off and running, only he knew where, his cat leading. His cat was in hunting mode, ready to break free and find the bastard that had done this, the one that had hidden in wait and struck when he thought the moment was right. The one that had been cocky and foolish enough to send Bas a warning that he was going to take what was his.

# Chapter 29

Bas ran straight to the gate that marked the boundary he expected his guests not to cross. It was an eight-foot-high metal gate that remained mostly hidden by the surrounding trees. Without a second thought he leapt over the barrier, crashing through trees as he landed on the ground on the other side. The minute his feet touched soil Bas shifted, the seams of his six-hundred dollar suit ripping as his bones cracked, bent, reformed.

His cat didn't roar loudly to announce its pursuit of the shooter, but rather bared its lethal teeth and chuffed. Lifting its sensitive nose to the air it picked up the scent quickly enough. Rogue. And took off in that direction. Experienced with this terrain, the cat ripped through the forest, its paws pressing with the full brunt of its two-hundred-plus pounds into the branch-filled soil until the trees parted, opening up to a small clearing where all around it, red rock formations reached skyward. It inhaled again and ran to the left, up then down the face of the beautiful rocks.

Bas knew exactly where they were headed. Ten feet beyond the rise of rocks there was another copse of trees. It stretched for at least forty miles wide and probably half of that in length. This was the private field where Bas allowed his cat and the other members of his teams to run free. It was also where they were trained by Syfon and Jacques.

Once inside the trees the cat moved slower, acutely aware of all that was going on around it and in full predatory mode. This was nothing like the Gungi—the ground wasn't spongy with moss, the sounds of monkeys and toucans didn't speak to the cats about intruders, and the trees weren't so tall and so overgrown that a canopy of shade had been produced, keeping the lower floor of the forest moist and oftentimes humid.

No, this was Sedona, all the air around them was dry and thick, the sun blazed for hours on end, pressing dominantly through trees to burn into the ground. If there were any other animals, such as coyotes nearby, they would take shelter after having scented the rage from the bigger cats. Later, the jackals would come out to claim any carcasses as if they were the spoils of their own personal victory.

A familiar sound, one that was made in challenge, alerted Bas to the fact that he'd found exactly what he'd been looking for. From the trees to his left came another cat, one only slightly smaller than Bas with dark rosettes against its likewise dark coat. Its eyes weren't golden but dull and filled with hunger as it stalked out into the open, coming to a stop only about ten feet away from Bas.

It lifted its broad head in an effort to introduce itself, but there had been no introduction necessary. Bas knew exactly who this was.

Kazmere Rutherford was a twenty-nine-year-old shifter. As a man he stood five feet eleven inches and weighed somewhere around one eighty or one ninety-five. He'd been like Paolo's shadow ever since he arrived at the resort just about a year ago. All the while Bas and Jacques had thought Paolo was the one to be concerned about, it had been this one, the quiet follower. Bas should have known.

Instead of dwelling on the past, Bas made his move

first, taking slow, steady steps toward the other cat. Kaz didn't move. When Bas was maybe three feet away from him the others arrived. Coming from all directions, including behind, Bas could hear and scent more rogues entering the clearing, most likely with death in their eyes, just like Kaz. Well, Bas always aimed to please his guests. So without another thought he lunged for Kaz, catching the cat off guard since he probably believed Bas would hesitate to act now that he was surrounded. His teeth sank into the cat's neck with ferocious accuracy and Kaz yelled out.

Not a second later there was movement as Nick, X, and Syfon arrived in cat form. Bas didn't see them but knew his fellow shadows would appear to back him up without his having to give the command. That's just the way they rolled. With the others there to handle the rogues, Bas focused solely on Kaz, the shifter he'd known had fired that shot. Last night the rogue Palermo had said those exact words: that Bas had taken what was his and so in return he would take what belonged to Bas. With Palermo dead but Kaz obviously working for him, it made sense that he'd feel the same way, that Bas had taken their stash so they should take what belonged to Bas.

Only Priya didn't belong to him.

It didn't matter, Bas thought, coming down on his back legs as Kaz wriggled from his grasp. Right now the specifics didn't matter, the only thing Bas was concerned with was that this particular rogue belonged to him. Kaz moved back, surveying the situation, assessing his opponent, just as he'd been taught. Bas rose on his hind legs and lunged, attacking just as Kaz rose to the same position. It wasn't as he'd taught Kaz. The younger shifter was expecting Bas to circle, assess, then attack. Kaz caught deliberate pounding in his flanks for not being ready for anything. He pushed Bas back, his cat heaving, obviously in some distress already. Bas went in again, biting the other side of his neck. Kaz came back with strokes to Bas's flanks that almost seemed like a two-year-old pounding against a locked door. Bas had years of training on this cat, he worked out in human form almost daily, and he was smarter than Kaz, there was no doubt. So they weren't equally matched, not by a long shot. Kaz knew this, hence the amount of reinforcements he'd brought with him. But the cat was still a youngling, he'd been seduced by the rogues, made to believe he was superior to all other humans and shifters, and he'd been wrong. When Kaz lost his footing and tumbled back a step Bas went in for the kill. He leapt forward, mouth open wide, and clamped down on the top of the other cat's head, piercing straight through to the skull until seconds later Kaz's chuffing, roaring, twitching, and flailing ceased.

Then, and only then, did Bas release the other cat. He took a couple of steps back and looked down at the bleeding carcass, his own flanks heaving with exertion. In the last two days he'd killed four shifters. In the last fifteen years he had killed none. That night in the forest as he watched them attack Mariah, he should have killed them all.

Turning away, Bas surveyed the complete devastation that usually followed a Shadow Shifter fight. Every last rogue was dead. From across the clearing the other three shadows stared at him and Bas looked back at them. They'd gotten the job done, once again.

So why didn't Bas feel victorious?

Syfon and Paolo were on round-the-clock guard duty outside Priya's hospital room. Bas had given strict instructions that no one was to go in or out unless he said so. That equated to her visitors being limited to Jewel and Kalina, himself, and reluctantly he'd agreed to Rome. Assembly Leader or not, Priya was Bas's responsibility.

And he'd failed her. He'd failed a human female once again.

She wasn't dead, Bas reminded himself as he stood at the end of her bed, arms crossed over his chest, brow tight with the frustration he'd been feeling since that shot sounded this morning. He'd been standing three feet away from her. On her other side was his second in command, a man he trusted with his life. Behind her were two more shifters with the capabilities to kill first and take names later. This should not have happened, she should not be lying in this bed hooked up to machines, enshrined in so much white material she looked pale enough to actually be dead.

The press conference had been a bad idea. He'd tried to tell her not to do it, not to get involved with this situation the shifters were in, but she hadn't listened. Just as Rome and Jacques had tried to tell him to get rid of her. She didn't belong in this hospital, let alone in Perryville being captured by rogues, guns held to her head, then a bullet in her shoulder. She should be in her tiny little apartment in Washington, D.C., going to work every day, having the life that she'd planned for herself. In one night, seduced by the darkness, the candlelight, the allure of the swimming pool, and the thought of her naked body submerged in the cool water, he'd sealed her fate.

Making love to her that first time had been a mistake. Each time after that only adding nails to the coffin. He should have sent her away the moment he realized she was there, should have put her on a plane to Timbuktu or something. Anything.

He just shouldn't have touched her, ever.

"At first I thought you were a statue," she said, her voice a soft whisper amidst the endless beeping of the machine she was attached to. "Then you blinked and I knew you were real."

She chuckled softly, then winced with the effort.

"Don't," he warned, albeit late. "I didn't want to disturb you. The doctor said you need to rest."

"Is that why they gave me that tranquilizer?" she asked, this time with a grimace.

"I told them to keep you as comfortable as possible." Because he hadn't been able to do the same, Bas thought.

"Who shot me?" she asked after a few seconds of silence.

Bas did not want to discuss this, but at the same time recognized her need for answers. For Priya it was as if nobody had ever given her what she needed as a child, not the love and attention of a parent or the support of a sibling, from what she'd told him of her past. She was thirsty for knowledge and from the start Bas had a problem depriving her of what she so desperately needed.

"His name was Kazmere Rutherford. He used to work for me," he replied.

She blinked a couple of times then slowly dragged her tongue over her lips. "Did you kill him?"

The question seemed loud in the otherwise semi-quiet room. It also seemed accusatory as if in the instance that his answer was yes, she might not approve.

"I did," he told her anyway.

She sighed heavily. "I should say thank you because I've been feeling pretty pissed off during my bouts with consciousness. But I don't know how I feel about knowing you can kill so easily."

"Killing is a part of our genetic makeup and most oftentimes is warranted, living in the forest among other wildlife. But as a half human living in a human world, it's also a choice." Bas took a deep breath when she did not respond right away. "Kazmere betrayed my trust. He worked with me only to feed information to my enemy.

But I would not have killed him for that alone. Aiming at you, hurting you is what sealed his fate."

He'd released his arms, using his hands to grab hold of the edge of her bed, gripping the metal so tightly his knuckles whitened.

"Thank you," she said quietly.

Bas nodded in reply.

"Can you come closer?"

Bas froze. He had been very still in the first place but now he didn't even blink. Her lids were partially closed but she looked at him expectantly. The words replayed in his mind and he felt a gentle stirring from his cat, a nudge that was intended to move him forward, to do what she'd asked of him. But Bas refused to make the same mistake twice. He could never live with himself if he did.

"I'll come back later to check on you," he told her before turning away.

"Bas," she called to him as he reached for the door handle. "This wasn't how I meant for this trip to turn out, you weren't who I thought you would be. This entire time I've been working toward getting this story and saving my brother. I wanted to be their hero, yet again. I guess that sort of made me feel important, like I had a purpose in this life. You don't have to worry, however, I'll never write that story about your people, your family. I've been researching Rome and the people around him for weeks, uncovering nothing but his loyalty and dedication to those closest to him. Coming here, I had the chance to see up close how committed you and the other shadows are to each other and to your cause."

She paused then, coughing a little, causing Bas to hold his breath in the hopes that she wasn't suffering any side effects from the surgery that removed the bullet from her upper shoulder.

"You can walk away now," she continued. "You can turn away from me and run back to your private suite where you can retreat even further into yourself for the rest of your life. I'll be okay. I'll go home and I'll live my life." She hesitated a second that seemed like a millennia. "I'll live my life without you."

There was something to be said for a woman who could take a bullet only six hours ago then lie in a hospital bed and speak words that made him feel as small and inconsequential as a piece of lint. And that something was phenomenal. Bas knew that without any doubt, just as he knew she'd been absolutely right, she would be okay without him. He knew she would go home and continue on with her life without a moment's hesitation. He'd never thought differently.

In a perfect world he would turn around, walk over to her, and tell her . . . tell her . . . that he was all wrong for her, that her life would never be the same with him in it. Then he'd tell her what he realized the sweet scent that only permeated the air when they were together meant and the constriction he'd identified in his chest signified. He loved her.

Straight from one of those sappy romance novels he'd seen Jewel reading, Bas felt like a botched-up hero. He hadn't protected Priya, but he sure had avenged her, and he hadn't given her enough candlelight and roses, but he had made love to her with an abandon that he'd never felt with another female. He'd told her what he truly was, but he hadn't told her he loved her or what had kept him from loving all these years. And he wouldn't, he thought as he pulled the door open and quietly stepped through to the other side.

He wouldn't doom her to a life full of secrecy and danger; love, for all its frilly and exciting tendrils, was not that perfect.

* * *

He hadn't come back, Priya thought two days later when she was still confined to the hospital bed. Jewel had brought her bag, purse, and laptop from Bas's suite, a sign that he was truly finished with her. A sign that she'd swallowed without so much as a sigh. This was what she did, what she'd had to do all her life—she took the good with the bad and was blessed to live another day regardless.

She'd spoken to Lolo, who wanted to board a plane and head out west to see that she was all right. Smiling into the phone as he'd spoken with such compassion and concern for her safety and welfare, Priya had wondered why she couldn't fall in love with this guy. Why was she so adamant about choosing the wrong one? Her e-mail box had been almost full with messages from Agent Wilson and Maury, who somewhere within those many messages had fired and then rehired her.

After about forty minutes dedicated to sipping on the bland apple juice the nurse had brought to her and cleaning out her e-mail box, there was a knock at the door. She didn't have to give permission to come inside, the two guards Bas had stationed in the hallway would do that for her. The only reason she knew they were out there was because Paolo had come inside to talk to her, to apologize for not protecting her the morning of the press conference. She liked Paolo, thought he was an honest guy, except for his Shadow Shifter secret. Syfon was a little more reserved, but he too had come inside to check on her periodically. It seemed strange, but Priya knew she was going to miss these guys when she went back to D.C. Especially Jacques, who only came when he thought she was asleep, talking quietly to the doctors, giving orders to the nurses, and otherwise making sure she had everything she needed.

The only male shifter she hadn't seen was Bas.

"Hi, honey," a soft voice whispered and Priya had to

blink twice to make sure she was seeing who she thought she was seeing.

"Mama?" Priya whispered as she watched Karen Drake enter her hospital room. "What are you doing here?"

That question died without an answer as following behind Karen came Malik. He was five foot eleven, his slim frame garbed in jeans and an oversized plaid shirt, sleeves rolled up to his elbows.

"Hey, peanut," he said in his raspy voice.

Priya sat up in the bed, closing her laptop and pushing it down beside her. "Malik," she whispered about two seconds before her older brother had crossed the floor, grabbing her in a hug that caused pain to shoot through her shoulder and down to her fingers. She didn't care, she wasn't letting him go and dared him to release her.

"I'm so happy to see you, so happy you're okay," she was saying into his ear.

"I'm glad you sent someone to get me. You're always looking out for me," he said when she finally released her hold on him and he drew back to look into her eyes.

Priya stared up at him, feeling all kinds of uncomfortable to see the sheen of tears glistening in his eyes.

"I'd be dead by now if it wasn't for you," he told her. "All those rehabs and bail outs from jail and now this." Malik shook his head. "I'm gonna do better, peanut. I promise you I'm gonna do better this time."

Priya cupped his cheek where his beard had begun to grow in. The hair made him look older, more mature. The slight slump in his shoulders and the way he reached up a hand to tweak the end of her nose, made her believe his words like she never had before.

"Thank you, baby," her mother said, leaning in to hug Priya when Malik had moved out of the way. "You promised to bring him home and you did."

Priya hugged her mother but didn't really know what

to say. She had promised her that she would bring Malik home safely, but she hadn't really believed herself then. In fact, it wouldn't be possible now if it weren't for . . .

"How did you get here? How did you know where I was?" she asked them.

"Those people that came to get me, they took me to the hospital and waited while I got fixed up," Malik told her. "Then they took me back to Mama's house and told me a nurse would come by to check on me and give me more pain pills if I needed them. You know the hospital wouldn't give me a prescription."

Priya nodded her agreement with the hospital's decision. The last thing Malik needed was to become addicted to another drug.

"Then last night that nice girl came back with these plane tickets. She said you'd been hurt and that we should come and see you, to make you feel better," Karen finished.

Priya's hands shook as she listened to them, nodding. "That was very nice of them," she said. "Very nice indeed."

"The guy, I think his name is Eli, he said he might have a job for me at one of his barbershops. You know, as soon as I get myself cleaned up."

Priya didn't know who Eli was, but she presumed he was a shadow and that he too, was acting on Bas's command. A part of her wanted to pick up the phone and call him to thank him once more. There was also the hope that the call would lead to a visit from Bas, and maybe, just maybe . . . No, it was foolish and she wouldn't put herself through that again. This was the way Bas wanted things and she had to respect that, no matter how much it hurt.

"That would be great, Malik," she told her brother.

"He'll get cleaned up," Karen began, reaching out a hand to take Malik's in hers, then threading her fingers through Priya's. "He's going to get that job and you're going to get better and come home and we'll be just like we were before."

Malik smiled, bending down to kiss his mother's weathered cheek. Priya smiled also, reveling in the joy of having her family here and safe. Her life would be as it was before, only improved because Malik would be better and Karen would be happier. As for Priya, she would be just fine, she would have her job and her friend Lolo, just as she'd had before she'd met Bas. Before she'd known about Shadow Shifters and their secret society.

"So, what, are you like her personal Santa Claus now?" Rome asked from behind.

Bas stood at the hospital room door, looking through the narrow window at the reunion between Priya and her family. He'd called Nivea the day he left Priya in the hospital and asked her to check on Karen and Malik Drake. Sending the airline tickets was an afterthought, a consolation to Priya for all the unnecessary pain he'd caused her.

And none of it had soothed his guilt. Not until she hugged her brother and closed her eyes to the emotion of having him safe in her arms. Then Bas had felt satisfied, and almost happy himself.

"She deserves it after all she's been through," he said without turning to face his longtime friend.

"Eli told me about her brother and where they found him."

Bas nodded. Eli had called him the morning after he and Nivea had found Malik Drake and given him more news he didn't want to hear. "I was going to call a meeting before you left to go back home."

"I can understand that things have been a little unsteady out here," Rome said. "But I have to admit I'm trying like hell not to be bent out of shape with all your secrecy. Why didn't you just tell me why she was hunting down the story? I could've helped sooner."

At that Bas did turn. He walked past Rome to the waiting room down the hall from Priya's room, stopping in front of a row of empty chairs.

"The moment she came here she became my problem. I needed to deal with her on my own," he told Rome, who was already shaking his head in disagreement.

"To be quite honest, she's been your problem since day one at that hotel," Rome told him. "You've been protecting her ever since."

Bas didn't argue with that fact. "I knew she wasn't going to stop until she got hurt. I couldn't let that happen," he said then pinched the bridge of his nose. "Rather, I didn't want to let that happen. I guess in the end I couldn't really stop it."

"You couldn't stop falling in love with her or claiming her as your *companheiro*?"

No, Bas thought. He was not going there, especially not with Rome, not here and definitely not now.

"Eli told you about the rogues and the owner of the house where he found Malik?" he asked, changing the subject.

Rome gave a slight smile, then nodded as if agreeing not to push Bas any further than he wanted to go. "Yeah, he told me. Bianca Adani is listed as the property owner."

Bas nodded. "Which begs the question of why rogues were forcing Priya to expose us. All they had to do was shift in public and the task would be done."

"That wouldn't prove I was a shifter or that more existed and were trying to form a democracy here. Whoever was behind this wanted Priya to expose everything about the tribes, not just one side. And they definitely wanted me and my reputation to come crashing down with the story."

"So this is all about you?" Bas asked. "And they call me the conceited one."

Rome chuckled then, soliciting a grin from Bas.

"It's about all of us and everything we stand for. Somebody doesn't like it and doesn't want us to succeed," Rome told Bas.

After a few moments of silence Bas looked to Rome again. "He's dead, Rome," he said slowly.

Rome slipped his hands into his front pants pockets, shrugging as he said, "We have no proof of that."

And they didn't, which meant there was a good chance the rumor wasn't true. And if that was the case, the situation with the shadows and the humans had just gotten ten times worse.

# Chapter 30

The latest shipment of guns had been late, but the savior drug was pulling in massive amounts of money each week. Enough so that Darel not only had a house in S.E. that they used for their headquarters, but he'd also purchased his own personal condo for times when he needed to get away from the day job. A month ago he'd been at full staff, in two locations. Now, he was only working one, not sure he should trust anyone to start again on the West Coast.

He'd sent one of his best fighters out there with Palermo and both of them had ended up dead. In fact, the entire crew out there had been wiped out, no doubt by those meddling shadows. But that was okay, Darel planned to keep right on building up his clientele on the East Coast. When it was time to venture out he would know, but for now, it was time to simply enjoy his money and the power he was gaining on the streets by keeping his workers armed sufficiently.

Darel paused the moment he walked through the door of his condo. Something wasn't right. All of his furniture was where it should be, the entertainment center covering one wall in the living room with the couch and love seat facing that way, and the desk that ran along a side wall with the picture of Mount Rushmore hanging above it. Darel didn't give a damn about the national monument, it was for humans, not him. But the picture was large enough to cover the hole in the wall that afforded him an unfettered view into his bedroom on the other side. The bedroom where he could hear someone.

Only three people knew about this place and one of them Darel didn't trust as far as he could spit. Bianca had come into his life months ago with a haze of suspicion hovering around her. Seducing Sabar had been a part of a bigger plan for her, Darel had sensed that the moment he saw her. And he'd tried to warn Sabar, who, unfortunately, was too damned arrogant to heed the advice. That was when Darel decided to take matters into his own hands and now, as he came to a stop in the doorway of his bedroom, he would deal with the repercussions of that decision.

"What the hell do you think you're doing?"

Bianca turned quickly, almost falling out of the swiveling desk chair where she'd been sitting.

"You're back," she said, bringing a fluttering hand to her neck. "I was just waiting for you."

Darel wasn't buying that for one hot minute. "You always wait for me fully dressed, at my computer, doing what?" He looked around her because she'd regained her balance in the chair and had eased over so her body would cover the computer screen.

"Sending an e-mail?" he questioned but didn't really expect an honest answer from her. So instead he grabbed her by the shoulders, moving her and the chair to the side so that he now had an unfettered view.

Then he chuckled, turning slowly to see Bianca twirling the edges of her dark hair. Even guilty as hell she was fucking gorgeous. The most perfect and delectable female shifter Darel had ever laid eyes on. Five feet eight inches tall, legs longer than the best orgasm, breasts high, perky, and 100 percent real, a willing and skilled mouth always painted with the most exceptionally shaded gloss, and ice-blue eyes that could pierce through a man's soul if he let them.

In a flash Darel had his hands around her neck, pulling her from the chair and tossing her onto the bed. She gasped for breath as he climbed on top of her, shaking her head as his fingers tightened, cutting off her air supply.

"You're not as smart as you think you are, Bianca." He spoke in a deceptively calm voice. "I knew somebody had to be tipping them off. I knew it was no mistake that they kept hitting my drops."

She grabbed his wrists, smacking at them futilely as her beautiful blue eyes bulged. In moments she would shift into a sleek and gorgeous white Bengal tiger.

"You've been a bad, bad, girl, Bianca."

She tried to talk, tried to explain, he figured, but Darel simply tightened his grip. "What else did you tell those shadows?"

Her head moved from side to side, the tips of her earlobes turning red. She kicked wildly, her knees slapping him in the back and Darel's dick hardened. A nuisance distraction, this arousal that came whenever he got physical with Bianca, even if that physicality was going to result in her death.

"What did you tell them, you little slut!" he yelled, his composure slipping as surely as his focus. "What did you tell them?"

In the next instant Darel was airborne, flying through the air to bounce off his bedroom wall and slide to the floor. Inside his cat roared as he rolled over and attempted to stand, only to be kicked in the face and subsequently knocked back against the wall. Blood filled his mouth as his eyes rolled back in his head. He was just opening his eyes, attempting to take a deep breath when his dick was grabbed in a grip so tight it brought tears to his eyes. They were open now, wide and focused—even if the focus was growing a bit blurry. And he stared into a face he'd hoped to never see again, not in this lifetime or any other lifetime, to be exact.

"Boden," he whispered hoarsely.

There was nothing here, Dorian Wilson thought grimly. He'd searched Priya Drake's apartment from top to bottom and there was nothing. Not one shred of information about her trip to Sedona or what she may have found there.

It was over a month ago that Ms. Drake had e-mailed him asking for his help finding her brother. He'd immediately remembered Malik Drake as one of the addicts he'd tried desperately to flip in one of their major drug investigations. That was the first thing about the e-mail that had caught his attention. The second, and by far the most important, was her reference to "cat people" and Roman Reynolds. For over a year now Reynolds had been on Dorian's radar. The failed attempt at catching the criminal masked as a litigation attorney had been thwarted by one of their own, Kalina Harper, falling for the man. But Dorian was sure there was something going on with Reynolds and his friends, something illegal that he wanted to bring down desperately. So he'd replied to Priya Drake more than a dozen times, only to be ignored.

It hadn't taken much investigating on his part to find that Ms. Drake, although she lived here in D.C., had been staying in Sedona for a while. He recalled seeing a picture of Reynolds and his friends from the president's fund-raiser in the paper and Dorian immediately linked Sebastian Perry of Perryville Resorts in Sedona, Arizona, to the missing reporter.

Days after Priya's departure, Reynolds and his two sidekicks headed out west as well. The next thing Dorian knew the media was in a frenzy over an incident with reported animal involvement. Everyone was up in arms, from the animal rights groups to the land conservationists and straight back here to the president, who immediately returned the funds contributed to his campaign by Reynolds and Delgado, LLC.

Then Priya had been injured and returned to D.C. with her family only a day before Reynolds and his wife returned. As far as news went, since then it had been quiet in Sedona, as well as here in D.C., a fact which concerned Dorian even more. That concern was what brought Dorian to Priya Drake's home today and had him breaking the very law he'd sworn to uphold as he illegally entered her apartment and searched for information he wasn't totally convinced existed.

But there had to be something, he thought, standing in the middle of her living room looking around. She had to know something.

The sunlight from the only window in the room caught something on the top shelf of a bookcase and Dorian moved in to see what it was. He frowned when he realized it was just two key chains bound together. One was from Perryville Resorts and the other from a spa. "The Alma spa," he said, reading the key chain that boasted a very relaxing-looking pool and the name in bold orange letters. The thought of a vacation flitted through his mind quickly, leaving the same way as something else caught his eye.

It was out the window and was just a movement. He shouldn't have been concerned but, hell, he was an FBI agent, so everything concerned him. Dorian walked to the window, still holding the key chains and expecting to see nothing but someone getting out of a car, maybe to come into this building or another one on this street. He hadn't really expected to see her, not again.

Female, coffee-brown complexion, shoulder-length black hair, and athletic build. Today she wore sunglasses, to cover her eyes he suspected, from him. A few months ago he'd seen her sitting outside his apartment, or rather he'd seen her eyes. Freaked the living daylights out of him. The second time he'd seen her had been after work one evening. He'd come out and walked to the parking lot as he usually did, knowing that she was waiting in her car across the street from the office to follow him. He'd driven for hours until finally deciding to book a room at the Hilton Alexandria in Old Town. The next morning she'd been gone and he'd returned to work to run the tags from her car. They'd belonged to a rental agency and their records indicated the car had been rented by a Mrs. Marjorie Jane, a woman who'd died more than ten years ago. He hadn't seen her again until today.

With disappointment a bitter tinge in the back of his throat, Dorian stuffed the key chains into his pocket and hurried out of the apartment. He was going to find out who this woman was and what she wanted with him once and for all.

Dorian took the steps two at a time and pushed through the double doors on the first floor. Running down the front steps he stopped only when he saw a long black limousine pull up. Just as the limo arrived, the blue compact car his snooping little female was driving pulled out. Cursing, he ran a hand down the back of his head and wondered again about taking that vacation. Turning down the street he walked toward the corner where he'd parked his gray, nondescript, department-issued vehicle. He never looked behind him to see who stepped out of that limousine or which apartment building that person went into.

\* \* \*

Priya was still stunned.

"I'd like to offer you a job," Roman Reynolds had said to her as she sat across from him in his office. To his right, Kalina stood draping an arm over the back of his chair. She looked as flawless as ever with her chin-length bob, an orange and bronze color that fit her buttery complexion perfectly. Her dress was simple, long-sleeved gray cashmere that hugged her tightly, but not vulgarly. Black leather boots that reached her knees gave her an edgy appearance and that bling-tastic rock on her left ring finger gave Priya an instant migraine.

"Are you serious?" she'd asked when the words had settled over her mind for a second or so.

Rome nodded. "I am deadly serious."

And since that little sentence was spoken in a matching tone to be followed up by that chilling stare that she'd only seen on one other man in her entire life, Priya was inclined to believe him.

"What kind of job would you offer me?" Another question which reminded her of someone who'd told her she had an insatiable need to know everything. With a deep inhale she quashed that thought, he'd been banished from her daily thinking, or at least during the daylight hours he had. At night, she was a victim of the broken-heart syndrome. She ached for Bas, for his serious looks and hesitation to laugh, his scorching kisses and overprotective gestures that foolishly made her feel like a princess.

"We'd like you to be the public relations liaison for the Stateside Assembly. You would supervise and administer all of our official statements, maintaining a working dialogue between us and the humans," Kalina told her.

Priya swallowed then looked at the woman whom she'd spent quite a bit of time with over the last few weeks. After she'd returned from Sedona and when she thought she'd never see or hear from any of the ones she now knew as Shadow Shifters again, Kalina had called two days later and invited her to lunch. From that little outing there'd come an invitation to dinner where Kalina had brought along Ary and Caprise. After that the foursome enjoyed a couple of happy hours, at Priya's suggestion and Caprise's overjoyed reaction. Still, a job offer had been the furthest thing from Priya's mind.

"But I didn't write the story. I didn't tell anyone who you really are," she insisted.

"We know you didn't and we'll be forever grateful to you for making that decision," Rome stated. "But since we've been back there's been one story after another, all speculation of course, but the questions are mounting. I've been having my secretary take messages from local reporters and international tabloids. The same goes for Nick and X. We want to say something, to issue a blanket statement that will cover us completely, but none of us are experts in that area."

Kalina spoke up next. "You are, Priya. You can write press releases and you can deliver statements. You know who we are and what we stand for, you can defend us as the unknown to the people you know so well."

Priya shook her head. "Let me get this straight, you want me to come and work for you? But I'm not a Shadow Shifter. In fact, I'm one of the very species you don't want to reveal yourselves to."

"You're one of us," Kalina continued. "You're Bas's ma—" she started, only to be cut off by Rome clearing his throat loudly.

"We trust you, Priya," he finished. "We trust you as a professional and a friend. Because you know our secret and you could have told the second you found out. But you didn't, instead you offered to help us. You did help us and took a bullet for your troubles. Come work for us and I promise we'll take very good care of you."

"By that you mean a lucrative salary, health, dental, and vision benefits. Fully vested 401(k) and maybe a company car," she added because she believed they were just jerking her chain anyway, so why not play along?

"All of that and then some," Kalina replied. "You even get a new apartment closer to the new Assembly Head-quarters Rome is setting up in Maryland."

"Moving? Me? Wait a minute, this cannot be happening," she said, continuing to shake her head. In a minute she was going to have a crick in her neck from all the back-and-forth motion.

"I bet you thought that when Bas told you what we really were, and yet here we are," Kalina offered in that kind, makes-perfect-sense way of hers.

She'd left the office with the promise to think the offer over thoroughly before giving them an answer. Now, as she stepped out of the cab and walked toward the front steps of her apartment building she was thinking that maybe it would be nice to have a car of her own and an apartment where the security door really worked and the buzzers to allow people to call up to her apartment weren't a bundle of open wires just waiting to singe somebody's fingers off. Then again, there was much to contemplate about working for, not just another employer, but another species entirely.

As she took the steps she remembered the first time she'd seen those eyes in that alley. She'd been intrigued. The next time she'd felt vindicated that her suspicions had been confirmed. And when she'd seen Bas's cat up close and personal an array of emotions had volleyed for attention, the most prominent one still stalking her to this day. With a frown she pulled out her key and walked down the hall toward her apartment. Her mind was still whirling around the Shadow Shifters, Rome's job offer, and the full circle she'd come with that man and his family, and . . .

wait a minute. Priya paused right in front of her door, the door with the shiny new gold knob and dead bolt. She stepped back and looked up to the apartment number that had been crooked since the day she'd moved in. This was her apartment but her locks hadn't looked like this when she left. Just to assure herself that she wasn't totally losing her mind, Priya reached out and tried to insert the key in her hand into the lock on the door. It didn't work, which did not surprise her in the least. What did give her more than a little start was when the door was wrenched open and a man stood on the other side. She backed up in disbelief and stumbled. He reached out an arm, catching her around the waist, pulling her up to his chest.

And her mind went back to over a month ago when she'd worn a red dress and crept through the halls of the Willard InterContinental Hotel. A man had grabbed her to him this way then, stopping her from breaking into a suite. He was a man she'd never forget.

Bas pulled her into her apartment before she could manage to wrap her lips around any coherent words. He closed the door with a resounding thump, then pushed her up against it.

"Every night you've invaded my dreams until finally I realized what will make a person travel thousands of miles without a second thought. It's this, right here, right now, this between you and me."

His last words were a bare whisper over Priya's lips before he took her. His mouth pressing hard against hers, his tongue not obediently requesting entrance, but pushing its way inside, almost daring her to pull away, which of course hadn't quite occurred to her yet. Instead her tongue readily reunited with his, her head tilted, and she took, damn she took what she too had been dreaming of for weeks that seemed more like years.

His fingers raked through the short strands of her hair,

scraping her scalp as he held her head in place, his mouth ravishing hers all the while. Her back pressed against the door as his front—the delectable hardness of his sculpted abs, toned pectorals, and oh yes, the enticing bulge of his erection—pushed deliciously into hers. She was on fire immediately, her center pulsating with need, her hips jutting forward instinctively.

At that little action Bas purred. She felt the sound as it emanated deep in his chest then ripped free and in response she moaned her own pleasure. With reckless abandon that she figured would lead to a lot of forehead slapping and scolding of herself later, Priya wrapped her arms around his shoulders, grasping the material of the long-sleeved shirt he wore between hurried fingers. She pulled at the shirt until it gave, ripping free of its hold within his pants. Yanking upward she attempted to rid him of it, but for that they needed to tear their mouths apart. Bas made the move, pulling back enough so that she could get that shirt over his head and her busy little fingers on his bare skin. She rubbed along the back of his shoulders where she knew his tattoo began. He buried his head in the crook of her neck, licking and biting her skin there. His hands moved downward until he was lifting one of her legs, pulling it up past his thighs to wrap around his waist.

She'd worn pants to her meeting with Rome, a dove-gray linen pantsuit to be exact, and was now cursing herself for not having the convenience of a skirt to hurry this passionate process along. Still, even the barrier of clothes did not stem the heat building fiercely between them. It did not stall the pressure of his arousal pressing forcefully against hers. In that moment her thighs shook as moisture coated the thick walls of her center. Priya shivered and heard the tearing of her blouse as Bas ripped the buttons free. He kissed along her collarbone and she helped him by pulling her arms free of the jacket and blouse. His teeth scraped over the rise of her breasts seconds before he cupped both mounds, squeezing tightly with his hands. Her head fell back, rapping against the door as she gasped for air. Bas used his teeth once again to tear the bra from her chest, stroking his tongue over the now freed nipples. His hands went to her waist where he popped the button of her pants free then proceeded to push the pants and her underwear down her legs. Priya hurriedly stepped out of her shoes, then her pants and underwear. And then she was naked and Bas was not.

With an impatient moan she reached for his belt buckle and repeated the popping, pushing motions he'd just performed on her. The second they were both naked her legs were wrapped around his waist again. He entered her with one swift thrust, sending her head back against the door once more, her nails driving into the skin of his shoulders, his name tearing from her lips.

"Don't leave me again," he whispered into her ear as he continued to thrust inside of her.

Priya rode the continuous waves of desire as Bas filled her, completing some part of her she hated to relinquish. His strong hands gripped her buttocks, spreading her cheeks as wide as her legs, touching her in that forbidden place he loved to explore. Until Bas, Priya had never been touched there, never thought to allow such penetration, but now, she craved it, biting down on her lower lip as his finger pressed slowly inside. Deeper and deeper he went, all the while his length was stroking her coated walls appreciatively, sensually. Something about the contrasting sensations rippling through her at the simultaneous penetration pushed her right over the edge and she screamed with her release.

Bas walked slowly then, carrying her away from the door. His erection was still hard and deep inside of her, his hands now holding her securely around her waist. He stopped at her couch, pulling out of her gently, letting her feet slowly touch the floor. His hands went to her cheeks once more as he cupped her face and held her stare.

"I came back for you," he told her. "I needed to."

Priya nodded slightly, licking her lips before replying, "I hoped you would."

He kissed her again, an open-mouthed duel between their tongues, a merging of moans and purrs until their sounds filled the room. In the next instant he tore his mouth away from hers, turning her so that her back was now to his front. He held her right there, one arm around her waist, the other hand snaking between her legs. On his silent command Priya lifted her leg, settling her foot on the couch and granted him complete access.

Her head dropped back to his shoulders as Bas worked the tightened nub of her center. She jerked her hips back and forth, loving the rough stroking followed by soft pressure. Her arousal was so clear it could be heard with every motion of his fingers inside her, the smacking sound making her hungry for more. His fingers slid back and forth, granting attention to her clit to the point where she shook with pleasure, then reaching back to dip inside her center, making her buck with desire. When he touched her back entrance again, this time Priya screamed out his name, louder and longer than she ever imagined she could.

"Please," she whispered. "Now."

It wasn't a request but a demand. As strange as it may sound to need something she'd never had so desperately, she needed him there like she needed her next breath.

Bas had never been one to deny a woman any sexual request. With a hand to the small of her back he pushed Priya gently so that she was now bent over the couch, one leg still propped up. He had an unfettered view of her now, from the slope of her rounded ass to the glistening arousal that coated her center and dripped down to her inner thighs and back to her now slick anus.

Inside his cat roared and Bas not only let it, his lips peeled back baring sharp teeth as he growled in dominance as well. A deep inhale filled him with their *companheiro calor*. It fed him, fueled the hunger deep inside, and guided his dick to the puckered rim where he pressed ever so slowly at first.

She gasped and thrust her hips backward. "Please. Now!"

"Shh, baby. I got you," he told her, reaching forward to slip a finger between her drenched folds.

Bas worked her slowly with his finger while gingerly pressing his length into her. She bucked again, sucked in a breath, then relaxed as he inserted another inch. It was like a hungry little mouth grabbing hold of him, sucking him so tightly inside he felt tingles up and down his spine.

"Sebastian!" she screamed when he'd inserted the last of his length so that he was now totally inside of her.

Bas moved slowly, eyes closed, head rolling back on his shoulders. He pulled out then pressed in, gritted his teeth, then decided to hell with it all and growled in response. The sound seemed to spur her on and Priya began to rock against him faster and faster. Every muscle in his body tensed as his release built like a churning volcano until he couldn't withstand it a moment longer and he exploded inside of her.

For her part, Priya shivered and shook as her release ripped free, her center sucking deep on his finger, her essence pouring out of her like a waterfall.

It was moments that seemed more like eons later that they both collapsed onto the couch, naked, sated, completely depleted.

"You broke into my apartment and changed my locks,"

she stated as she lay on her back, her eyes closed, breath still coming in heavy pants.

Bas lay at the opposite side of the couch, in a similar position to hers, only he'd cracked his eyes open to see her. Naked and still open he felt his body hardening again with need for her. Swallowing back that need he thought about his reply.

"I came to see you and your door was ajar. I knew someone had been here besides you. I was about to call every shadow in the vicinity to go out and search for you, but my first call gave your location."

She sat up then. "Gave my location? What did you do, attach a GPS to me when I was in Sedona?"

Recognizing the shift in this conversation by the flash of her eyes, Bas sat up. "I called X. On my command he's had a guard watching you since your return."

Priya shook her head as if trying to digest everything he'd just said. Bas figured he might as well put it all out there at one time and let the chips fall where they may. He reached out to her, taking her hands in his and thanking the heavens that she hadn't pulled away. Taking that as a good sign he slid a little closer to her.

"Look, I was an ass. I'm man enough to admit that. I messed up with you and that's not normal for me. I don't mess up with females. At least I only did one other time." Bas took a deep breath and recited the events in the Gungi all those years ago, saying it aloud for the first time in his life.

"It was right after my parents' divorce when I was already feeling like they'd both let me down in not fighting for their love, for the joining they'd had. I had been dating this girl named Mariah, but broke up with her right after my parents announced their separation. Not wanting to be around anyone I knew, anyone I thought I'd known for that matter, I went to the Gungi for a few days. I had no idea Mariah had followed me down there until I saw her one night in the forest."

He dragged both hands down his face, not believing he was telling this story and yet knowing it was absolutely necessary at the same time.

"Palermo Greer and a couple of his flunkies were assaulting her," Bas reported through clenched teeth. "I wanted to go to her, to help her but I thought about the exposure first. I thought about those stupid rules and I hesitated. Then they shifted and killed her and I was still standing there, frozen in shock. She died right in front of me and I couldn't, I didn't stop it. I felt like I'd let her down at that point, like I was no better than my parents. As stupid and self-destructive as I can now say that was, I refused to let anybody in, refused to ever have someone close enough to me that I could let them down again. And it worked for years, until you came along."

Priya didn't speak, just watched him. It was an intense stare that a lesser man may have fallen beneath. But Bas had come here with a purpose, he'd set his course, made his plan, and there was nothing that he was going to let stop him from at least putting that plan forth to her. What she did with his words, his feelings afterward was completely up to her.

"You were double trouble because I felt something for you the moment I saw you at the hotel. That connection only solidified when you were outside of Rome's office. I wanted you too badly to really think about the consequences of being with you. And then it was just too late, consequences were out the window and you were in my arms. And then he shot you and I was in the Gungi all over again."

He sighed, wishing she would say something, do something, but maybe understanding why she didn't. She needed this from him. Hell, he needed it for himself, so he took a deep breath and finally said what he thought he'd never say to a female, let alone a human, in his life.

"Life with me will not be easy. In fact, everything you've ever known will change. And that's big, Priya. You're a human and I'm a Shadow Shifter. We're not the same and yet I cannot deny the feeling that we are one. Can you?"

She couldn't.

Oh, how she wanted to. The moment he said the woman's name she'd wanted to smack him, to yell at him that he should have never been comparing her to another woman. A dead woman at that! But she couldn't because she knew why the comparison was made, why the guilt had eaten at him and kept him quiet all these years. She knew and she ached for him because of it. She ached for him because for so long she'd allowed herself to be trapped by caring for her family that she hadn't taken the time to do things solely for herself, to make her own life better, just for her.

So no, Priya could not deny that she and Bas were one. It was absolutely asinine for her to even try. And if she were extremely honest with herself, as she accepted that Bas was being with her now, she would acknowledge that she'd felt the connection from the very beginning. She didn't think she had to be a Shadow Shifter to admit that.

"You make things too hard, Sebastian Perry. Sometimes you just have to go with what you know," was her reply. "I wish you would have told me all this sooner but I get that you were doing that brooding male sort of thing. I guess that's universal and doesn't discriminate between species." She'd tried to keep things light, as the emotion in her almost clogged her throat and Bas looked as if he might actually stop breathing if this conversation wasn't over soon.

He smiled then, the genuine smile she'd wanted to see since first meeting him. It was the same one that had reached inside her chest and tugged on something there.

"If I could stand on that balcony and watch you shift from a cat to a man, you should have known you could trust me with all your baggage and your fears. Because we all have them, Bas. Hell, I've been looking for validation all my life and I had to go thousands of miles across the country to figure out I only needed to please and impress myself."

"You know what I also knew the moment I grabbed you in that hotel hallway?" he asked.

Priya shook her head. "No. What's that?"

He released one of her hands and lifted a finger to trace along the line of her jaw. "I knew that you were the other half of me. It was like looking in the mirror at a reflection that was just like me on so many levels, and yet as different as night and day."

Priya was the one to smile this time, her heart nearly about to burst at his words. "I love you, too," was her quick reply.

Later that night as Priya lay in Bas's arms, in the comfort of the Willard InterContinental where it all began for them, she thought of his earlier words about her life never being the same and everything she ever knew changing. It had already begun to happen.

When she'd questioned Bas about being at her apartment, it was then that he informed her of the break-in. After a meticulous search she realized the only things missing were the key chains she'd saved as keepsakes from her trip to Perryville. Bas had assured her that she could have all the key chains she wanted from now on, but both of them knew what that meant. Priya wasn't the only one that suspected something was going on, something unexplainable.

He'd offered to either move her out of the apartment or to let her stay there with an armed guard at her side twenty-four/seven. She'd opted to move.

Two days later he'd taken her to dinner with Rome and Kalina at their home in Virginia called Havenway. There they'd discussed in detail what Priya's job with the State-side Assembly would be and how she could work from Sedona, traveling to Maryland or wherever else they needed her when necessary. The females, Kalina and Ary, also talked about a joining ceremony since she and Bas were officially mated. Priya wasn't 100 percent positive but she assumed in their tribe this was the equivalent of marriage, a place she didn't feel like she was ready to venture just yet. She'd spent years believing—thanks to her mother's past performance and her father's cowardly escape—that relationships didn't work, so moving in with Bas was a big enough step. Surprisingly, Caprise took her side, telling the other females to leave her be and let her and Bas find their own way.

This was a new world for the Shadow Shifters, Rome had said that often at dinner. It was also a new world for Priya, one she decided she was willing to venture into, despite what Bas thought might be a big price for her to pay. She believed in him and in the Shadow Shifters, what she wasn't so sure of was how the world would react when they found out about them, because eventually—and Priya sensed they all knew this—their secret would be revealed.

# Chapter 31

On an otherwise serene night, Nick and Ary lay in bed asleep, only to be awakened by the high-pitched wails of their only child.

Ary was out of bed first, moving quickly to the cradle that stayed at the foot of their bed. It had been their original plan to find their own house and move out of Havenway, but after Shya's birth and because of Ary's job as *curandero* to the Stateside Shifters, they'd remained at the compound with Rome, Kalina, and at least fifty other Shadow Shifters.

Shya was now four months old and for the last six weeks had been having crying spells and running light fevers. If Ary was worried then Nick was beside himself with anxiety over what might be plaguing their child. As she lifted the clearly agitated baby into her arms, cooing and whispering comforting words, Ary thought of Dr. Papplin's advice.

"She may simply have what the humans call colic," he'd explained. "It is normal and usually lasts until they are a year old."

Ary had been taking classes in human medicine so

that she could better assist the tribe in this environment, so she'd had no problem looking up the ailment and coming to the conclusion that Dr. Papplin may in fact be correct. But the fever was a different symptom and as she rested her forehead on Shya's, Ary thought glumly, it was rising.

Nick sat on the side of the bed with his usual worried glower.

"Here, Daddy, see if you can quiet her down. She likes when you rock her," she told him, placing Shya gently into his arms.

In a thousand years she would have never thought Nick Delgado would be rocking a baby, kissing the child on her forehead, and staring down at her with nothing but genuine love in his eyes. They'd come a long way, she thought as she moved to the table where she kept all Shya's supplies to retrieve the thermometer. These last couple of months she'd been trying valiantly to keep a positive outlook, to keep Nick calm. It was taking its toll as Ary too had begun to worry more. When the apparatus beeped, signaling it had completed taking the temperature, Ary looked at the screen and frowned.

"I'm going to call Dr. Papplin," she told Nick.

Dropping the thermometer onto the bed she crawled over it and reached for the phone on the nightstand.

"What's wrong?" Nick asked.

"Her temperature's too high," Ary told him, panic clear in her voice. "Dr. Papplin? Are you still at the compound? Okay, good. Can you come now? Yes, it's Shya."

"He's coming," she said to Nick as she moved across the bed once more to sit beside him.

"It's not colic, is it?" Nick asked.

Ary shook her head. "I don't think so."

He frowned, continuing to rock and attempting to soothe Shya who was now red faced, her tiny fists balled up as she screamed with every ounce of oxygen in her little body.

"This is bull! We're taking her to the hospital," Nick announced, standing from the bed.

"She's not human, Nick," Ary replied. She was wringing her hands, trying desperately to keep it together, but the sound of her child in such obvious distress was killing her. "They'll find out."

Nick only shook his head. "I went to the doctor when I was young. Caprise and I had regular checkups just like other kids. Our blood is red and bleeds into a vial just like humans. We go to dentists just like the rest of them," he argued.

"But we don't get colds. We don't contract sexually transmitted diseases. We don't take as long to heal. Despite trying to fit in, we are different, Nick." Of all the shifters in the world, Nick was the one Ary knew she could say this to.

"I know that," he countered. He'd been the one to always point out their differences, to question the blending in of the shifters and the humans, to them hiding what they truly were. But now he wasn't thinking clearly, Ary was convinced. He was thinking like a concerned parent and so was she.

A knock at the door tore her attention away and she hastily went to answer it, believing it was Dr. Papplin. It was Rome and Kalina instead.

"Is everything all right?" Kalina asked, concern marring her features in what Ary figured might be a mirror of her own.

"She won't stop crying and her fever is 103," she recited, her voice cracking slightly toward the end.

Kalina immediately stepped inside, putting an arm around Ary's shoulders. "Have you called Papplin?" she asked.

Ary nodded. "He's on his way."

Rome moved into the room and closed the door. He looked like he wanted to say something but didn't know what.

"I think we should get her to a hospital," Nick said again to Ary's chagrin.

"And you don't want to?" Rome asked Ary.

That sounded like an awful accusation to Ary and she wanted to scream with frustration. "I want to do what's safe for her, that's all."

"We understand, honey," Kalina insisted. "We'll just wait to ask Papplin his thoughts."

"He's been giving us his thoughts for the past couple of weeks and it's gotten us nowhere! He has no clue what's going on!" Nick yelled, which only made Shya scream more, the sound vibrating off the walls and piercing their eardrums.

"That's not true," Papplin said once he'd entered the room. "I know exactly what the problem is."

"Really?" Ary asked, moving so that she stood right in front of the doctor. "Tell us."

Papplin was a gangly man who looked as if the weight of the world rested squarely on his shoulders. Ary remembered the first time she'd met him at George Washington Hospital, he'd seemed a whole lot different then.

"Shya doesn't have colic," Papplin told them.

"Then what does she have and how can we fix it?" Rome asked. "I agree with Nick that this has been going on for far too long. If she's sick tell us so we can get her healed."

Papplin visibly startled at Rome's cold tone. He removed his glasses, rubbed viciously at both his eyes, then put his glasses back on again.

"Do you remember when you were held captive by Sabar?" he began, speaking directly to Ary.

She nodded. "Yes."

"Do you remember when you realized that he'd drugged you? That he'd sampled the damiana mixture on you to test your reaction?"

A chill ran down Ary's spine.

"I remember."

Papplin cleared his throat, the sound a low rumble compared to Shya's crying. "I tested Shya's blood when she was born. I knew something was wrong then."

"What? You knew something was wrong four months ago and you're just telling us now?" Nick roared.

Shya all but jumped out of his arms with the sound of his voice and Kalina moved quickly to take the baby from him.

"What are you saying, Dr. Papplin? What did you notice when Shya was born?"

"It's customary to take a newborn's blood," he began, wiping a hand over his forehead that was now prickled with sweat. "But when I looked at the vial I realized there was no coagulation. I figured I may be tired, becoming alarmed by nothing, but then I got the results back. There were traces of something different in her blood, compounds that should not be there. I ran more tests and linked some of the compounds to traces of damiana that she must have contracted from you." He looked pointedly at Ary.

"She's reacting to the drug, and that's why her crying is so extreme," he finished.

"No," Ary whispered. "No. That's not possible. The damiana should have been long out of my system before I became pregnant with her and I've never taken it again. There must be some mistake."

Papplin shook his head. "I even sent her blood to another lab to be tested. It's like her body is re-creating the drug so that it stays continually in her system. I've taken samples every two weeks since her birth and each time it's present to the same degree. It's not dissipating."

"So she's getting worse," Rome added. "She's going to get worse as long as the drug is in her system and you don't know how to get it out. Is that what you're saying?" he asked, raising his voice for what may have been the first time Ary ever heard.

Papplin looked from Rome to Ary apologetically. "That is what I am saying."

## Comastaz Laboratories
## Sedona, Arizona

"There's a problem with the sequence, a gap that I can't quite figure out," Dr. Mario DiLaurent told Captain Crowe as Lilah, the lab assistant Crowe had hired for him, stood on the other side of the lab table.

"Maybe it's a genetic gap that goes with a particular family," she offered. "It looks like a mini-strand is missing."

"It is. I've been over this a million times. This is the blood taken from that . . ." he hesitated, "that thing you pulled out of the field and this is how the DNA breaks down. No human lives with a broken DNA strand."

"They're not human," Crowe pointed out.

DiLaurent's brow was prickled with sweat, the man was more than nervous. So much was riding on this project and Crowe was anxious to share this discovery with the whole world. The thought of creating a super-soldier based on the genetics of a real-life half animal, half human would be a phenomenal discovery. It would also be a very lucrative one, especially for the three creators in this room. They had to fix the genetic sequence and they had to do it soon.

"We need another one of its kind, preferably one from its direct bloodline," DiLaurent stated.

Crowe frowned. "Then I guess it's a good thing those assholes lost the blood samples we were going to send for final testing. It held the incomplete DNA so it probably wouldn't have created the super-soldier I've got in mind."

DiLaurent hurriedly shook his head. "No, we do not know what that DNA would produce. I think our best bet is to duplicate what it seems like nature has given that one. Keep everything as close to matching him as possible so there'll be less chance of fallout."

"Great, now we need all new blood samples. Ones that match that creature's exactly. Where the hell are we going to get that?" Crowe asked, cursing this turn of events.

Lilah sighed. "Go back to where you found this one and look for another one. There's bound to be a female somewhere because there's no way a man like this was traipsing around out there all alone."

DiLaurent resisted the urge to roll his eyes at the simpleminded assistant. "It has to be a direct match, a sibling or a child." He paused then ran to his cell phone, pressing buttons wildly. "Wait a minute, wait a minute."

"What is it?" Lilah asked.

"I don't know why I didn't think of this before. A few weeks ago my cousin sent me a blood sample, or rather the DNA strand from a blood sample. He works in the lab at George Washington Hospital in D.C. He said this was left on a microscope and he read it. He thought it was unreal and so he sent it to me to get my advice. I've been so busy working with our tight timeline I didn't pay it much attention. But now that I'm thinking about it, now that we're talking about it . . ." He paused, still looking at his phone. "I got it! I got it right here!"

Moving quickly he thrust his arm forward so Lilah could see his cell phone. She looked at it once, and then looked back at the sequence showing on the screen of DiLaurent's laptop. For good measure she looked back once more. "You need to get both of these sequences loaded and run them together, make sure they're a match," she told him excitedly.

"Does it look like a match?" Crowe asked.

Lilah was already nodding her head. "It does. It looks like a match."

"Then your one and only job for the foreseeable future is to find me the one that blood sample belongs to. I want that one here on this table within the week. Do we understand each other?" Crowe commanded.

Lilah looked at DiLaurent and they both replied, "Yes, sir."

It looked like Lilah would be heading to Washington, D.C., to find out whose blood sample that was in the George Washington Hospital and to bring that someone or something back to Comastaz. There was a lot riding on this, surely this "person" wouldn't mind donating some more of its blood for a good cause, even if that cause put an end to its kind for good.

Read on for an excerpt from

HUNGER'S MATE
by A.C. Arthur

Coming soon from St. Martin's Press

His skin was glossed with a light sheen of sweat, marred by one tattoo over his right bicep. Pure strength rippled along the thick pronounced veins in his arms as he lifted the bar holding at least two-hundred-and-fifty-pound weights on either side. From his position on the bench Jewel had a great view of thighs cut to perfection with muscle, narrow hips, and a bulge in his shorts that made her mouth water and her temples throb slightly at the thought that this was his relaxed—and not aroused—state.

From where she stood across the floor of Perryville Resort's fitness center, peeking around the wall that she used for cover, Jewel had a magnificent view. A delicious view that had awakened feelings inside her she'd thought long dead. She swallowed deeply, figured her lips were just as dry as her throat, and then licked them before releasing a deep breath. How many times had she come down here to work out? How many hours had she spent in this very room, absorbed in her own routine, focused only on the burn of tired and thoroughly worked muscles? Yet for the last ten minutes, she'd been glued to this spot, watching this man lift those weights, wanting him like she'd never wanted anything else in her life.

"Why don't you join me?"

She startled and stepped back at the sound of the male voice. After a second or two she leaned forward once more, easing her head around the wall and feeling absolutely foolish for doing so, until she saw that he'd sat up on the bench and was staring directly at her.

"I said, why don't you join me?" he asked again, the cleft in his chin holding her attention as he talked.

It was easier to find a focal point than to look directly into his eyes. They were smoldering; she knew because she'd just peeked and felt waves of heat pouring over her. It was ridiculous, she knew. He was just a man and she was just a woman, and even considering the distance between them, there should not have been any type of connection.

But there was.

Jewel cleared her throat. "I'm leaving," she announced but failed to move.

"No, you're not," he said in a slow, casual tone that made her feel just as uncomfortable as if he'd demanded she stay instead. "You're still standing there watching me. You'd get a better view if you came closer."

The arrogant jerk, she thought, but didn't fire those words at him exactly.

"I think I've seen enough," she replied instead.

He gave her a curt nod and a shrug of those perfectly cut shoulders. "Suit yourself."

Before she could reply, he lay back on the bench. His feet planted firmly against the floor, his thighs flexing, preparing to hold him steady as he lifted hundreds of pounds. The rippled planes of his abs uncurled, like a feast being uncovered for consumption. As his arms rose, his fingers wrapped around the metal pole, closing, opening, closing again before he boosted it off the rack. Glossy dark biceps flexed, muscles bulged. Jewel's nipples hardened, intense spikes of pleasure traveling from the heavy mounds to rest with a persistent throb between her legs.

He'd just completed his fifth repetition when the heat clawing at her had Jewel's knees about to buckle. Instead of falling to the floor, panting after a man she didn't know, and in desperate need of sexual release that she hadn't required in years, Jewel decided retreat was best. The first step was the hardest—as was probably the norm—but she did finally manage to move one foot and then another, all while still trying to watch every pull and release of muscle on his body, including, but definitely not limited to, the bulge between his legs that she was almost certain had increased in size as she stared. Her mouth watered as her back slammed into another wall, jarring just a semblance of sense into her. Shaking her head, she finally pulled her gaze away from him, turned, and ran like she was being chased by police all the way back to her room.

Truth be told, Jewel always felt like she was being chased, like at any moment her secret would be revealed and everything she'd risked her life and her father's life for had been for nothing. There was no way Ezra Preston, the stranger who had come to Perryville weeks ago behind a lot of hushed conversations and worried looks on behalf of Jacques and Mr. Perry, could know anything about what she'd done before she came here. Absolutely no possibility he could be here to unveil the secrets she guarded so closely. Still, as she closed the door to her room and leaned back against it, common sense said it was best she steer clear of him totally.

Five hundred pounds of steel were nothing in comparison to the heaviness Ezra felt throbbing between his legs.

He'd scented her the moment she'd stepped into the gym:
the fresh, intense scent of arousal that had permeated his
senses, filtering through his body like a fast-acting drug.
The high was instant and powerful, almost causing him
to lose his grip on the bar holding the weights. That's
what made him stop and sit up. He wanted, no, more like
needed, to see her up close.

So he'd called to her and she'd stepped out from behind the wall to address him. But she hadn't come further
as he'd requested. She hadn't come to him the way he'd
craved. Instead she'd continued to watch.

And he'd been content to let her.

Lying back and giving her an unfettered view of his
growing erection and whatever else she'd been entranced
by so long she'd only been able to leave when she wasn't
sure she'd be able to continue resisting.

Ezra heard the beat of her heart, he sensed the thrum-
ming of hot blood in her veins, the dampening of the tender folds between her legs. Everything about her had been
embedded in his mind since the first day he'd seen her
having lunch with Priya. Only twice since that day more
than a month ago had he seen Jewel Jenner at the resort.
She worked closely with Bas's Lead Enforcer, Jacques,
performing administrative tasks. Originally Bas had
thought there might be a romantic link between the two
but Jacques didn't have the *companheiro calor*, the mating scent of the Shadow Shifters.

One morning Ezra had timed his appearance in the administrative offices of Perryville Resorts to coincide with
the arrival of most of the staff. Jewel always arrived first.
She unlocked the front glass doors that were marked in
bold block letters and switched on the lights, her computer, and the Kuerig machine that sat on a stand leading
down a small hallway. That hallway led to Jacques's office and the sales directors' office. Jewel sat up front in a

partially enclosed space, while just on the other side of her the receptionist sat to greet anyone coming in with questions.

Instead of startling her by going in right behind her, a few minutes passed and the receptionist went inside.

"Is Mr. Germain in?" Ezra had inquired once he'd finally decided to go into the offices himself.

"No. He isn't," the receptionist, who looked more like a college student than a professional office worker, informed him. "May I leave him a message that you were here?"

The request was stilted, as if she'd rehearsed it enough to memorize it but not enough to say it with any type of sincerity.

He'd smiled at her efforts, remembering a time when he was young and carefree, or at least young.

"Just tell him Ezra stopped by," he'd replied.

And just like a few minutes ago in the gym, Jewel had peeked around the wall to look at him. When he caught her gaze that time, she'd cleared her throat and stepped completely into the outer area coming to stand right beside the receptionist. She didn't reek of fear, but there was definitely a stand-offish quality to her, as if she'd rather remain out of sight and possibly out of mind.

"He's meeting with Mr. Perry this morning. When he returns I will tell him that you were here," she told him, looking just over his shoulder as she spoke.

"Thanks," he'd said, keeping his gaze steady on hers. After all, she was the one he'd come to see. "I'll stop by later to see if he's in."

"That's fine," Jewel stated in a clipped tone.

Ezra nodded. "Will you tell him that I will be back?" He was speaking slowly, watching, waiting for her to look at him.

He wanted the seal to their connection, the lock of gazes, the first step in the dance Ezra knew they would partake in. When it finally came, it took his breath away. Her eyes were green, a softer shade than his that for some reason didn't strike him as natural, and they were secretive. Ezra was instantly intrigued. Later that day when he'd returned, Jacques was indeed in the office and so was Jewel. She'd been at the receptionist's desk, and instead of having to go back to Jacques's office, the shifter had come out to meet him. As if he'd known what Ezra's plan was all along.

As Jacques stood near Jewel, Ezra noted nothing between them. No simmering arousal, no *calor* signifying that they'd been intimate. That had solicited an immediate smile.

The next time he'd seen her had been at night when she was coming back into the resort. He had no idea where she'd been all day as he'd been looking around for her. She appeared rested and peaceful upon her return, so much so he'd considered that her day had been spent in her lover's bed, legs spread, body open in surrender to another man. A deep rumble in his chest, the barely restrained growl of his cat, signaled just how much Ezra disliked that thought. She hadn't noticed him at all that night as she moved through the entrance, down past the restaurants to the elevators. He thought of following her to her room but didn't think he'd be able to control his arousal or the rage that someone else might have been touching her. The smart option—which Ezra liked to think he took at all times—was to keep his distance. And he had, until now.

# Read more e-novellas in
# The Shadow Shifters: Damaged Hearts series

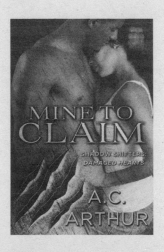